STRAIGHT TO THE HEAD

STRAIGHT TO THE HEAD

FRASER NIXON

ARSENAL PULP PRESS
VANCOUVER

STRAIGHT TO THE HEAD
Copyright © 2016 by Fraser Nixon

ARSENAL PULP PRESS
Suite 202 – 211 East Georgia St.
Vancouver, BC V6A 1Z6
Canada
arsenalpulp.com

The publisher gratefully acknowledges the support of the Canada Council for the Arts and the British Columbia Arts Council for its publishing program, and the Government of Canada (through the Canada Book Fund) and the Government of British Columbia (through the Book Publishing Tax Credit Program) for its publishing activities.

Cover and text design by Oliver McPartlin
Edited by Susan Safyan

Printed and bound in Canada

Library and Archives Canada Cataloguing in Publication:

Nixon, Fraser, 1976-, author
    Straight to the head / Fraser Nixon.

Issued in print and electronic formats.
ISBN 978-1-55152-638-6 (paperback).--ISBN 978-1-55152-637-9 (html)

    I. Title.

PS8627.I963S77 2016   C813'.6   C2015-908286-2
                                               C2015-908287-0

The most beautiful clothes that can dress a woman are the arms of the man she loves.
—Yves Saint Laurent

PORNO PIZZA

1.

. . . .

From the kitchen window, Dorothy Kwan saw a crow picking at the carcass of a seagull in the lane. The backyard was overgrown with dandelions and alien-looking pigweed covered in strange blisters. If you let the pigweed's milky sap touch your skin, it would burn and irritate you, Dorothy knew. She sipped yesterday's gunpowder tea and ate an aged English muffin with Malkin's blackberry jam. From the breakfast nook, Dorothy let her gaze wander over the untended garden. Tomatoes spoiled on the vine. A sagging garage slept in the heat. From the boughs of a crippled hawthorn hung torn red paper lanterns from a long-ago party. She said aloud to no one, "Labour Day. They should call it 'Entropy Day' instead."

Dorothy put down her teacup carefully, turning the handle the way she'd been taught.

The kitchen was nice and cool in the old house, her home. Hers now, hers alone. Upstairs were three bedrooms, one chock-a-block with sewing machines, fabrics, and accoutrements. Dorothy slept there on a hide-a-bed; as a child she'd thought they were Indian—"Haida beds"—and pictured taking the couch's cushions off and pulling out a Native man in a robe and cedar mask. She couldn't bear the idea of sleeping in her parents' bedroom. Last month, in the interests of economy, she'd placed an ad in the *Georgia Straight* and rented out her childhood room to a female foreign-exchange student enrolled at the university for the fall semester.

Dorothy didn't need the money but remained too strongly her mother's daughter. She'd thought that a little undeclarable cash income would be worth the inconvenience of sharing the large house, but becoming a landlady had created unforeseen, irritating problems. Her boarder was late with the rent. It appeared Dorothy had committed an error. The signs were not encouraging, and Dorothy hadn't seen the girl around the house for days.

"*Hai ah*," she muttered.

Her half-cup of tea had cooled, and the crow was gone from its meal. A cuckoo clock in the living room came to life and cried out nine times.

This house, she thought, *this haunted house*. She knew it inside and out, too well, and for the thousandth time wondered what to do. Should she keep it as it was? Renting out a room had been her first small act of change; perhaps it would have been better to auction everything off and start fresh somewhere else. Travel, explore. But that chance had passed her by, it seemed, and now she feared being trapped here forever, caretaker of a museum to her parents' memory and her own living past. Dorothy wasn't strong enough to scatter the carefully laid coloured sand of the mandala into the sea. Not yet.

She climbed upstairs and looked into her tenant's room. A Duran Duran poster had been taped to the wall above an unmade bed. Dorothy peered in to see clothes on the floor and one of those Russian nesting dolls on the vanity. What were they called? She shook her head at the mess and pursed her lips, then went to her room, the sewing room, to prepare for the day ahead.

First Dorothy put on a dove-grey conservative skirt suit and white silk blouse, a strand of imitation pearls, beige nylons, and black Mary Janes. In front of a mirror, she twisted her long jet hair up into a tidy knot with an ivory clip and strung the chain of a pair of her mother's half spectacles around her neck. Their lenses were nothing more than clear glass. Using a bristle brush, Dorothy carefully streaked her hair, starting at the temples, with white shoe polish. Next, she accentuated the faint wrinkles at the corners of her eyes and mouth with an eyebrow pencil. Finished, she examined herself critically in the mirror, and allowed herself a rare, close-lipped smile. Dorothy was now twenty-six going on sixty-five, give or take a decade. Standing up, she allowed her shoulders to slouch, then straightened again. For a moment or two she debated adding a cane to the ensemble, but decided against it.

"Too much. Just a little too much," she said aloud to the empty house.

Dorothy now had everything she needed. She picked up a black plastic purse and left the house, carefully securing the door behind her and tripping down the stairs almost gaily. The heat of the day already burned fiercely. A sickly pink rose trailed onto the concrete of the patio, and an untended clematis wound around a trellis. The house was on an odd bluff shielded from the street by thick cedar hedges. Dorothy descended another set of switchback stairs to the sidewalk. The next block over, a small Portuguese grocery did an excellent trade in buns and coffee, and Jimmy's, an Italian mom-and-pop two blocks west, was great for cheese and sliced meat. Dorothy went north instead, humming "Heart of Glass."

Most of Dorothy's life had been spent here in Strathcona, an old neighbourhood just east of Vancouver's Chinatown, first settled by a mix of Chinese and Italian immigrants from the early railroad days of the city. She walked past elders practicing Tai Chi on the field at MacLean Park. Two small Italian boys, enjoying their last day of freedom before starting grade one, ran by screaming, "*Acqua fresca! Vino puro! Fica stretta! Cazzo duro!*"

At the corner of Hastings and Hawks, in front of the Astoria, Dorothy caught the trolley bus downtown. She gave way for two tiny ladies carrying baskets. They could have been sisters, both draped in shapeless black widow's weeds, though one was a swamp Hakka from Weihaiwei, while the other hailed from the hills near Monte Cimone in Emilia-Romagna. Dorothy paid her fare with dimes and found a seat on the shady side with a window that opened fully, allowing in fresh air. The bus was nearly empty on this holiday morning, and for that small mercy Dorothy was grateful.

East Hastings was a jungle of low-rent hotels, beer parlours, greasy spoons, pawnshops, and newsstands all the way to Victory Square.

There were loggers in Mac jackets, railroad tramps, knots of old drunks loitering on the corners without a single permanent mailing address between them, panhandling Indians, and even a hooker or two this early in the morning. The electric bus carried her through the mire and eventually turned south on Granville and went up a pedestrian mall. As Dorothy passed the James Inglis Reid butcher shop, she whispered aloud its slogan, her private ritual, "We hae meat that ye can eat!"

At Georgia Street, Dorothy got off after the two tiny ladies, her own shoulders now stooped again, her steps hesitant and shuffling. The block between Georgia and Robson was almost entirely taken up by the Eaton's department store, a huge, six-storey blank behemoth, its exterior completely clad in some kind of blank white stone. From her purse Dorothy unfolded a strong paper bag with rope handles from Eaton's eternal competitor, kitty-corner across Georgia: the Hudson's Bay Company. It was now slightly after eleven o'clock. Dorothy entered the air-conditioned, Muzak-filled store. She made her way haltingly to the third floor, ladies' fashion.

A perennial feature of the Eaton's chain was its chronic understaffing, holiday or not. Already items hung haphazardly from racks, and a line-up had formed at the only cashier. Dorothy moved slowly through the field of clothing, stroking Taiwanese polyester blends and checking price tags reflexively. She spied convex security mirrors in the far corners and marked bulky grey fixed closed-circuit cameras. A harried employee rushed by with an armful of dress slacks. Dorothy breathed.

On Saturday she'd done a reconnaissance and was now satisfied that all remained as it had been. The quality of the inventory at Eaton's was generally a good step above the Bay and one below Holt's. Amongst the usual mass-market dross of mid-range brands were a few half-decent lines: Liz Claiborne, Anne Klein, Nygård. Sometimes, though, gold could be picked from the racks. Givenchy. Chanel. Whether it was by accident or oversight, Dorothy didn't know. She moved to a corner where two items waited hidden amongst twin sets. There they were: a pair of beautiful

Christian Dior dresses hanging lonely together by an emergency exit. One navy, one black. Each her size, a European 28, each individually priced at $1,500, enough to overdraw a splurging wife's chequing account. That didn't matter to Dorothy, not one tiny bit.

"So far, so good," she mouthed silently.

For all the world and the security cameras, Dorothy was a quintessential senior citizen, bent over by osteoporosis. She came here once or twice a month and varied her disguise each time. This identity was her favourite. Westerners had an odd blind spot for Orientals, especially little old Chinese ladies. Gliding along the rack and making a final survey of her line of sight, Dorothy opened her purse. Now it was important not to meet anyone's gaze. She felt that the eye sought out the eye. It was necessary to calmly will herself into transparent obscurity. With practiced ease she let her fingers slip up and down the seams of the dresses, finding at the hem what she sought. From out of her purse she took a small pair of strong metal clippers. With a quick snip, off came the electronic tags. Dorothy felt her pulse speed up, a well-remembered arpeggio of excitement and fear. *Good*, she thought. *Stay fluid, dance the steps to the music.* The Muzak overhead played a weak version of "The Girl from Ipanema."

Dorothy palmed one of the tags and with a sweeping movement had the garments in the Bay bag, leaving the naked hangers behind. It's always foolish to go to the changing rooms, the most likely spot in a department store for covert theft. There are cameras just outside the entrance, and horny store detectives usually watch the closed-circuit screens hoping for an accidental free peek. No. Far better to move quickly and without indecision. Keep your confidence. Keep cool.

A harsh squawking from the loudspeaker overhead almost scared Dorothy out of her nylons.

"Attention shoppers. Would the owner of an eight-year-old boy, answering to the name of Michael Bublé, please claim him at the service desk of the toy department? Thank you."

The bag she carried was now heavyish. Dorothy walked to the escalator. Never take the elevator; too easy to be cornered in a box. How many times had she done this? Once or twice every other week in selected stores, cycling randomly and irregularly. Dorothy calmed herself, breathed, slowed her heartbeat, and rode the stairs smoothly down.

Ground floor. She moved a little more leisurely now, making a circuit around the shoe department, doubling back for followers, scanning for store detectives in sports blazers or any heavyset *gweilos*. Dorothy lingered a moment at the sunglasses, using the spinning racks with mirrors to check for stray furtive glances in her direction. A housewife had just finished having boots rung up at a till and headed to an exit. Dorothy bumped into her. The woman blurted, "Oh, I'm so sorry. Pardon me, ma'am."

Typical Canadian, thought Dorothy. *Apologizing when it's someone else's fault.* The housewife went to the northwest exit as Dorothy headed to the Robson Street side. Now there came the moment when Dorothy's nerves sang every time, a wicked, thrilling moment of pure will. Fear and bravado mingled with a touch of controlled panic, and a fatal consignment of her fate to the gods above and below. *Luck, give me luck*, she thought. At the Robson side, the electronic detectors were oddly placed and left a gap on the right. This exit also provided the best outside escape routes. If pursued she could run across the street through an alley to a parking garage and cut back through another alley and freedom. If she was fast enough. And Dorothy knew she was.

In the unlikely case of an overlooked tag, Dorothy swung the bag just outside the sensor column, let go, and caught it deftly on the other side. Nothing. As she pushed outside, she heard an alarm screech in another part of the store. The tag Dorothy had put in the polite housewife's bag went off. Her poor dupe. Dorothy stepped out into the hot air. At that moment the noon horn atop the BC Electric Building went off, the first four notes of "O Canada" rebounding throughout downtown Vancouver.

Dorothy walked along the courthouse side of Eaton's and crossed to the Hotel Georgia. She went into the ladies' room, unpinned her hair, and ran a wet comb through it to remove the shoe polish that had disguised her age, then wiped her face clean with cold cream. At the valet's desk, she stapled shut the Bay bag of stolen Dior dresses and checked it in with a note that read, "To be claimed by Mary Worthington."

The cocktail lounge was pleasantly dark and cool. Dorothy had a nice long Singapore Sling and beat off the advances of a good-looking American lawyer on his way back to the States. He'd just finished a salmon-fishing expedition up at Hakai Pass, near the Queen Charlottes.

"You should've seen how big it was," he said.

"What?" asked Dorothy, almost amused.

The lawyer held his hands about a foot apart and, with a twinkle in his eye said, "The one that got away."

Dorothy laughed. She let the American pay for her drink, accepted his business card, and had the valet hail her a cab.

"Strathcona," she commanded the driver.

In the backseat Dorothy held up her hand. Not a single tremor. The taxi sped east over the Georgia Viaduct onto Prior. She saw a green and red Puck painted on a wall, shilling for Money's Mushrooms, who said, "What food these morsels be!"

Two blocks from Union Street, Dorothy paid off the cab and walked home. She climbed the shielded concrete switchback steps to the patio, looked up, and froze. Two men stood on the front step watching her, one of them wearing a police uniform.

2.

· ·

Trouble came calling halfway through the graveyard shift. Ted witnessed the two policemen appear at the glass doors of the hotel lobby. It was just past three in the morning, the most brutal hour. The AM radio had finished reporting the early news for Labour Day, 1983. Ted buzzed the pair in and waited patiently behind a scarred mahogany front desk.

The Victoria Hotel at the corner of Homer and Pender was no stranger to cops, day or night. It was an old brick rooming house built not long after Queen Victoria's Diamond Jubilee. Since then it had seen its share and more. Nowadays, the hotel was home mostly to dead-enders—pensioners, junkies, and drunks, or some combination of all three. For the most part, they were a quiet lot, burned-out old-timers grinding away the winter years of life in $200 a month bed-sitters (sink and hotplate usually included), a shared bathroom down the hall. Police entered the hotel occasionally to remove troublemakers in handcuffs; from time to time, ambulances arrived and took out a tenant on a stretcher, or in a bag.

Ted turned off the radio. The lead cop was plainclothes, wearing a brown trilby and fawn London Fog raincoat, his partner a dumb-looking young crewcut in uniform, thumbs hooked into a gunbelt under a gut. They stood on the frayed rug and gave the small lobby a once-over, taking in the mismatched chesterfields, broken wall clock, and general air of indifferent neglect. Ted wondered which renter they were after and was startled when the plainclothes met his eye and spoke his name.

"Mr Edward Windsor?"

"That's right."

"Formerly of 1089 West Eleventh, apartment 905?"

"That's me."

"When was the last time you saw your wife?"

"My what?"

"Your wife. You are married to Mrs Irina Windsor, maiden name Lermontova?"

"We're separated," Ted said.

"And when was the last time you saw her?"

The plainclothesman was middle-aged, with a soft, round, clean-shaven face. He seemed a pleasant enough fellow until you caught his eyes. They were pale, almost yellow, and totally empty. *Be careful*, Ted thought, *this man would break your legs at church, then sing in the choir.*

"May I ask who you are, and what this's about?" asked Ted.

"I'm Detective Johnstone of the Vancouver Police."

"And him?" asked Ted.

"I'm none of your fucking business," said the uniform in a strangely high voice.

"This is a routine inquiry, Mr Windsor. You can answer questions here or down at the station."

"Routine? What's happened?"

"Is she your wife, Mr Windsor?"

"Legally. We've been separated since last August, I mean August last year."

"And when did you see her last?"

"Around then. I've been away, out of town. I just got back two weeks ago."

"Where were you?" squeaked the uniform.

"Japan. But what's this about?"

"And you haven't seen Mrs Windsor since your return?" asked Johnstone.

"Not yet. I was going to contact her through my lawyer to start work on the divorce. But what's going on?"

"Well, Mr Windsor, you're going to find it hard to divorce a missing woman."

Ted's eyes opened wide, and he ran his hand through his hair. Johnstone then informed Ted that Irina had been unaccounted for, for over three weeks. She'd first been reported missing by her colleagues at the art gallery near Gastown where she worked part-time. No trace of her had been found at her apartment or anywhere else. Johnstone would question officials at Canadian Customs and Canadian Pacific Air to confirm Ted's alibi, his arrival time at the Sea Island airport. After that, the investigation would be ongoing until Mrs Windsor was located. Ted felt a current coming from these cops for an instant, a tension, a minuscule, vibrating pulse of fear.

"Contact me if you hear from Irina," said Johnstone, "and don't leave the city."

Fat chance, thought Ted.

"What's that?" piped the crewcut.

Ted started.

"Nothing, constable."

Ted didn't have the money for a ticket to the annual PNE Fair, never mind skipping town. It was why he worked nights at the hotel and stayed in a room upstairs.

"One more thing, Mr Windsor," said Johnstone.

"Yes?"

"Did you know your wife was arrested in March at the Hummingbird Cabaret for soliciting an undercover agent for the purposes of prostitution?"

With a faint smile on his pale face, Detective Johnstone tipped his hat and turned to leave. The uniform hitched his belt and snorted. Ted walked to the door and watched the pair get into a maroon Chrysler sedan. He exhaled and looked at the broken clock on the wall.

There were plenty of questions he needed to ask himself but couldn't just now. How had the police found him? The hotel register was a tattered blue book filled with illegible carbon copies, and Ted had paid cash up front. No one knew he was on the coast other than the border officials, his new boss at the hotel, and an indifferent bartender or two. No one knew he worked this shift at this particular hotel. Ted received no mail and made no telephone calls. Before he allowed himself to consider the intricacies of the police tracking network, the most important questions took the shape of a woman.

Where the hell *was* Irina? And what's more, why had she started tricking again?

Mr Lee, a diminutive Cantonese of indeterminate age, relieved Ted at five minutes before seven. Ted yawned and went upstairs to Room 34 on the top floor. Its only virtue was the view, north over the inlet and the mountains beyond. Heat shimmered with the broken dawn. Ted turned on the radio to hear the news and weather. Labour Day would be a scorcher of a last day for the Pacific National Exhibition and the running of the BC Derby Plate at Hastings Park racetrack this afternoon. Ted yawned again as a non-stop drive-time block of today's best hits started off with "My Girl (Gone, Gone, Gone)" by Chilliwack. He snapped off the radio, cracked the window, and leaned out. A long horn sounded in the harbour, the little walk-on commuter ferry crossing to North Vancouver. Despite the brutal summer a few scraps of snow still clung to the very tops of the peaks. Ted imagined how fresh and cool it'd be up there, high above the swelter and smog, looking back down on the city and its million tiny lives. He leaned back in and caught his reflection in the mirror. Not bad for thirty and broke, he thought.

Ted was careful about how he looked, right on the verge of vanity. He wore his hair cut neatly and combed back, a salmon-pink tie and linen shirt. From the mirror Ted's grey eyes looked back, pink around the iris, with bruises of exhaustion under them. Irina had always compared him to a Polish actor from the sixties, Zbigniew Cybulski, Poland's James Dean. She herself looked a little like Claudia Cardinale, dark and dangerous. *Where the hell was she now?*

Ted lay back on the bed and ran through the old story in his head but soon gave up and tried to sleep. Nothing happened. That was one of the problems with the graveyard shift. Seven in the morning was a regular person's five in the evening, or quitting time, but no one working nine-to-five got off work and headed straight to bed. You had dinner and a couple of beers, watched a movie or game on TV, and then went down at eleven or so for the count. Ted could do none of these things at the start of the day. Everyone else was fresh from a night of sleep and heading out to begin another earning cycle. No civilized place served a drink before eleven. Worse, it was impossible to sleep with the light and racket out on the street. These past few weeks, working as the new night-shift man had turned Ted inside out, and to top it off, now the police had his latitude and longitude.

Ted was grateful, however. If not for a lucky combination of events, he wouldn't have had a job at all. His return from Japan was after eighteen hours of travel: Narita to Honolulu, Honolulu to Vancouver. At the airport Ted had managed to change his last 1,000 yen and emergency twenty Yankee greenbacks for taxi fare and let the cabbie choose the cheapest hotel downtown, The Victoria. Exhausted, Ted had slept through the previous night man's crack-up. Pink elephants carried off the screaming clerk; Mr Lee, the morning man, relieved a gibbering mess of a lunatic drunk who was waving a butter knife at the massive owner, Mr Samuel Olaffson.

A few hours after the hullabaloo had ended without injury (the night man was now under observation in a mental hospital), a severely jet-lagged Ted Windsor shambled downstairs for some toothpaste. With one look at Ted's wrinkled Hugo Boss coat, crocodile leather shoes, and command of English, Samuel Olaffson hired him on the spot. Ted agreed to the terms, shook hands with the burly Norwegian, crawled upstairs, and slept for another ten hours straight. He began his duties the following evening after an informative fifteen-minute training session. Ted would be paid cash for his labour: fifty cents an hour below minimum wage, with half-off the rent of Room 34. All in all, it was better than could be hoped, having hit the ground close to skint and dead on his feet.

Now, Ted had additional trouble on his plate. He looked into his bags and pulled out a ring of keys, saved through his travels, from a previous life. Two were to the apartment Irina and he had shared at the Stardust on West 11th. One of the things Johnstone mentioned was that Irina still lived there. That was something for Ted to go on. He splashed water on his face, slapped on a little *eau de cologne*, and went downstairs to the street.

For a quick pick-me-up Ted had an endless cup of awful coffee and decent toast with margarine and plastic jam at the Smile Oriental & Occidental restaurant around the corner, sitting at the counter in front of a giant red Million Dollar Bill. Hell money, which Chinese burned for hungry ghosts. Ted took a trolley south on Granville, away from the downtown core and over the bridge. He got out at Broadway and Granville. Above the busy intersection swayed a complicated cat's cradle of electric wires. From in front of the Aristocratic diner, it was possible to catch any number of other buses, expresses to Garden City, Ocean Road, the Tsawwassen ferry terminal, and the far-off Gulf Islands. *I can get a long, long way from all of this shit*, thought Ted.

Heavy holiday traffic halted as a police cruiser wailed west on Broadway, followed by a cute girl in a convertible Corvette blasting "Gloria" by Laura Brannigan. Ted walked a few blocks as the music dopplered away. He stopped and used a payphone below the Normandy's red and blue neon sign to call the apartment. The phone rang and rang. Ted hung up and kept his quarter.

Ted checked his stern for a police tail at the corner of 11th, slipped around into the alley, and opened the back entrance to the Stardust apartments, a blue breezeblock built in the mid-1960s. He climbed to the second floor, then summoned the elevator to take him all the way up to nine. Their old place was at the rear, a penthouse suite.

Soliciting an undercover cop at the Hummingbird Cabaret? Ted thought.

There was neither yellow police tape nor any other impedimenta at 905, so Ted slowly unlocked and opened the door. Within all was quiet and still. It was nearly bare of furniture. In the living room sat an efficient Danish Modern table with chairs, a sofa, and another stopped wall clock, this one an excellent Pequegnat that Ted had bought for Irina at a junk shop, cheap. Ted went and opened the sliding door to the outside deck for a cleansing breeze. He could tell the apartment had already been searched; Irina, for all her faults, was fanatically neat. Ted checked the refrigerator, empty but for a half-bottle of retsina. He took a swig of the tart wine to relieve his thirst and set to work, searching every cupboard, drawer, and hiding place. A powerful wave of painful nostalgia and bitterness washed over him as he went through Irina's clothes, putting his hand in each small pocket. He could smell her.

Ted searched her small library of Penguin paperbacks for any scrap, then her cosmetics and toiletries, plus any other place he could think of. All the photographs were gone. Had she burned them? Kept them? In a Bayer tin in the medicine cabinet Ted found a small bag of pot, which he pocketed. There was nothing else, nothing unusual, nothing that revealed where she was or what had happened to her.

Ted sat down with the bottle and the silence in the bright white morning light. It was the silence that helped him to remember a story Irina had told him, about a little girl who tricked the Sandman. It was a folk tale from her country, she'd said. The little girl didn't want to go to bed and caught the Sandman creeping in. He promised not to visit her any more to put sand in her eyes. The first night, the little girl was happy to be up, but could find no one to play with, not even her kitten. Everyone else was asleep. After a week of this, the little girl was completely knackered and the Sandman nowhere to be seen. Finally, at the end of her rope, the little girl wandered the house, weeping and praying, until she came to the hall with its grandfather clock.

Ted woke up at the table and said, "Tick tock, behind the clock, said the clock."

It was where the Sandman had hidden his bag of sand. The little girl found it and went to sleep again. Ted went to the clock and opened the panel for the winding key. It was gone. He reached around and touched a piece of wood, pulling it free. Ted held up to the light a small painted doll, what the Russians called a *matryoshka*, that he'd never seen before. He finished the bottle of tart wine and took the elevator to the lobby. There he knocked on the manager's door. Ted couldn't remember the woman's name. An elderly lady in thick glasses and with a long thin menthol hanging from her lip wheezed, "Yesss?"

"I'm here about apartment 905."

"It's rented."

"No, I know that. What I'm here about is the rent."

"It's paid."

"Irina Windsor paid it?"

"No."

"Who did, then?"

"Her husband."

The old lady flicked a Bic and put it to her lit cigarette.

"Excuse me?" Ted asked.

"He paid the other day."

"How?"

"Who are you?" the old lady croaked. She squinted through her glasses and tried to focus through menthol smoke at Ted.

"I'm a friend of hers. I was supposed to give you a cheque for this month, but if it's paid already, I guess I don't have to. How did her husband pay?"

"In cash."

"Did you give a receipt?"

"I always do."

"What did he look like?"

"I don't remember. There's a lot of tenants here. And I don't have to tell you. In fact, I think I'll call 905's husband."

Ash dribbled onto her housecoat.

"The one who paid?" asked Ted.

"Because now I remember him; he's a police officer."

3.

. . . .

The hunter crossed the border at Blaine, Washington, on the north-bound Amtrak from Seattle. He sat reading a Labor Day edition of the *Post-Intelligencer*, listening to *Madman Across the Water* on his Sony Walkman. The train stopped, and he smoked a pipe while waiting for the Canadian border official to finish examining his false American passport. Customs had already looked through the hunter's bag. With official scrutiny of the northbound passengers complete, the Cascade started up again and pulled along the Northern Pacific line through the beachside community of White Rock and then through Surrey, a flat, brown land of highways and farms they called the Lower Mainland. The train crossed over a river on a high bridge and snaked along a narrow cut through the suburbs. Around ten o'clock in the morning, it entered the yards near the Canadian National Station. The hunter noticed shacks and hobo jungles amongst the tangled blackberry bushes alongside the tracks. He turned down the music's volume to hear the conductor walking down the aisle saying, "Next stop. End of the line. Vancouver, British Columbia. Next stop, end of the line. Terminal City."

The hunter turned the music back up, finished his pipe, folded his newspaper, stood, and withdrew his hand luggage from the overhead compartment. He went to the end of the car and waited until the train slowed at the platform, stepping down just before the Amtrak jolted to a stop. The hunter walked into the station and its hum of travellers.

Canadian National did duty as a depot for Via Rail, Pacific Coast Lines, and Amtrak. It was filled with people either coming from or heading somewhere else, to the north, east, or south. Every type moved through the echoing hall: old ladies carrying packages wrapped up with newspaper and string; bell-bottomed, acoustic guitar-toting hippie chicks; grey men in frayed suits and ties, hick kids in jean jackets; toughs; touts; pickpockets;

and the odd vagrant shuffling along. The hunter noted a bored security guard, hands in pockets, surreptitiously scratching his left nut. The assorted riff-raff of a terminus. Carving his way through the crowds and over the terrazzo floor, he clicked off his tape player outside and hailed a taxi.

"Where to, sir?" asked a splendidly bearded and turbaned Sikh.

"Bayshore Inn," said the hunter in his crispest voice.

The taxi left the station and went up Main. The first thing he noticed was the pink-stuccoed Venus Theatre showing *Debbie Does Darth Vader*. A pizza pie sat on display by the ticket wicket, probably the exact same pie as the last time he'd been here. The hunter couldn't imagine anyone stupid or hungry enough to eat it. But then, remembering the annihilation of the past, he was filled with a sudden, dubious nostalgia.

"*Où sont les pizza porno d'antans?*" he muttered.

It was hot in the city; the hunter rolled down the window and smelled Chinatown. He was amused to see an embattled Italian grocery holding its ground amidst the Oriental onslaught: Tosi's, selling oil, olives, and mizithra cheese. At the corner of Hastings, the hunter witnessed a pair of junkies in front of the Carnegie Library scrapping and scrabbling over something as a group of bums joked and hollered. This was the city's Tenderloin, full of beer parlours and clip joints, where a little applied cruelty could go a very long way.

"What's that music?" he asked the driver over the loud radio.

"Indian music, sir. Raga music."

"Turn that *up*."

"Yes, sir."

He leaned back, re-lit his pipe, and watched as the taxi made a left on Powell, which became Water Street through Gastown. Yuppies were beginning to spruce up the old brick pioneer section of the city with boutiques and trendy furniture stores, yielding mild successes and total failures. The cab followed a course nearest the inlet, passing the old CNR terminus before entering a dull preserve of bank headquarters, insurance towers, and dead skyscrapers. The streets here were empty on Labour Day, a holiday also for capital. By and by the cab pulled up at a white hotel in Coal Harbour, opposite Dead Man's Island and Stanley Park. The hunter paid the cabbie off in American currency. Glass doors to the lobby opened automatically. In a corner sat a white-haired, pinstriped businessman with an attaché case, reading the *Seattle Times*. At the front desk a very cute girl in a neat teal uniform smiled.

"Welcome to the Bayshore Inn, sir. How may I help you?"

"I have a reservation."

"Yes, sir," said the cutie.

The hunter read the name on her tag: Tiffany.

"What name was the reservation made in, sir?" asked Tiffany.

For a moment he was at a loss. Which name was he here under? Same as the passport he travelled on? Yes, and a MasterCard to match.

"Thomas Renard," the hunter said.

Tiffany pecked at her computer keyboard and brightened even more.

"Yes, sir, Mr Renard, a suite facing the water, as requested."

"Good."

Formalities were completed. Tiffany made an impression of his credit card, Renard forged an improvised signature, a key was issued, and local directions provided. She smiled sweetly as he nodded to her. Renard carried his own bag to the elevator bank and went up to the thirteenth floor, called fourteen by the hotel. It was the room directly below the penthouse. Here he found an expansive suite, decorated in cool, even tones. A balcony overlooked this cul-de-sac end of Burrard Inlet. Renard slid open the door and went out to watch lazy yellow floatplanes land and take off. Boats worked the harbour. He saw the Yacht and Rowing Club and some sort of fenced military installation opposite his balcony. Renard retired from the heat and picked up the telephone, dialling 0.

"Front desk, how may I help you?" chirped Tiffany.

"I'd like someone to send up a bottle of bourbon and a bucket of ice please."

"What kind, sir?"

"What kind of ice? The cold kind."

"No, I'm sorry, what kind of bourbon?"

"Wild Turkey."

In the bathroom Renard sluiced his hands and face with cold water, looking into the mirror. The hunter saw a man of average height and weight, with thick brown hair combed back and a neatly clipped brown beard. He wore an excellent light-tan summer suit and thin tie. The only distinguishing feature he possessed was how indistinguishable he was. It was simple for Renard to pass as nearly any type of Mediterranean or Levantine, or combination thereof. When in Cuba he'd looked Cuban, in Turkey a Turk. And in America he was nearly anyone he wanted to be. What had been a problem in his earlier life now worked to Renard's advantage. He was a man difficult to remember clearly. He was hard to testify against.

There was a knock at the door. Renard straightened. From his breast pocket he pulled out a large pen and unscrewed its top. A thin stiletto blade slid out into his hand. He went to the door and peered through the peephole. It revealed the white-haired, pinstriped businessman from the lobby below.

"Mr Renard?" came a voice through the door.

"Yes."

"A delivery from Mr Peters."

Renard opened the door and let the man in, remaining well within a swift striking distance. The businessman held the attaché case.

"Fine room," he said.

"It'll do for now," said Renard.

"Mr Peters was happy to hear you arrived safely. He sends his compliments and a gift."

"Slowly. Open it over there, on the bed."

"With pleasure, Mr Renard."

The businessman was about to unlock the case when another knock sounded at the door.

"Relax, Mr Renard," said the well-dressed man. "It is your room service."

The professional tension paused as a gangling young waiter holding a bottle-topped tray entered, carrying with him a bucket of ice. He mutely placed the bourbon on the desk by the TV and presented a chit for Renard to sign. Renard tipped him two American dollars.

"Thanks, mister," gulped the teen.

The waiter gone, Renard and the pinstriped man resumed their business.

"Exactly as requested," the businessman said.

He unlatched the case. It held a Beretta, three clips of ammunition, a short-barrelled .38 special with taped grip, and accompanying box of shells.

"Not easy to find up here in Canada," remarked the gentleman.

"Over there," Renard gestured.

The businessman complied and moved away from the bed to the corner. In a moment Renard stood by the case, his stiletto palmed, the Beretta in his hand as he racked the slide.

"What else?" Renard asked.

"It seems as though your ice is melting."

"Drink?"

"No, Mallory," said the pinstriped man.

"Drink," repeated Renard, and Mallory started. *He must be slightly deaf.*

"Fix me one as well," said the hunter, pointing at the cart. "Rocks."

While Mallory poured bourbon, Renard quickly checked both guns and the ammunition in the light. Satisfied, he accepted a tumbler.

"Cheers," said Mallory.

"*Salut.*"

They drank.

"What else?" repeated Renard.

"This."

Mallory carefully reached into an inside pinstriped pocket, his watery blue gaze never leaving Renard's. The businessman pulled out a folded envelope. He took a final long pull of bourbon, set down his glass, and opened the unsealed flap.

"First, a week's worth of expense money," he said.

Mallory took out a colourful wad of Canadian currency and threw it on the bed.

"This is in addition to any other expenses you may incur. Please don't hesitate to contact us."

"How?"

"I'll leave a number."

"If it's urgent?" asked Renard.

"The number is to a portable radio phone. It will be answered at any time."

"Good."

"There is also your fee. I have here a copy of the draft deposit to the bank you requested, for half the sum. The other half upon completion, naturally."

"Naturally."

"And now, to business."

"Ah."

The Beretta loose in his hand, Renard tasted Wild Turkey. Mallory took out two photographs.

"Detective Ron Johnstone and Constable Bill Hickey of the Vancouver Police."

"How much did they lose?"

"Three hundred thousand dollars. And that much again in so-called *product.*"

"American?"

"No, Canadian dollars. Still, quite a considerable sum on either side of the forty-ninth parallel, wouldn't you agree?"

"What happened?"

"The delivery was made to the detective and his dogsbody. Before the formalities were complete, it appears another member of their party made off with everything. It is something of a tangle, and we wish you to untie the knot, so to speak. With scissors, if you need them."

"I'm even handy with a knife. What happened on their side?"

"It appears the detective and his partner were the victims of a fraud."

"Who by?"

"That's what we need you to find out, Mr Renard."

"Anything else?"

"We believe they had a woman with them. It was she who was handed the product and chose that time to make off with it and the money, as well. A party girl."

"Any leads? Names?"

"None. But we expect the detective or his constable will tell you."

"They will," Renard said, coldly.

"Wonderful. Find the money and the shipment. Mr Peters will sleep most soundly knowing that you are enquiring into these matters."

"Provide him my assurance," said Renard.

"I will. Here is the draft, the photographs, and a card with my number to call in case of need. Mr Peters is hoping for a speedy resolution."

"That's what I'm here for."

"Splendid. Thank you for the drink."

Renard and Mallory nodded at one another. Mallory left. Renard bolted and chained the door. He poured another bourbon, picked up the papers, and went back out on the balcony. Black ink on clean white paper showed that $5,000 had been placed in his secret account. Renard put the photos of the cops in his breast pocket and struck a match. With it he burned the bank draft and lit his freshly stuffed pipe. A gull flashed by and cried in the late summer heat. The black ashes of the paper wafted up and away on a hot gust of summer air.

"Three hundred thousand clams," said the hunter to the sea.

Before leaving the Stardust, Ted checked for mail. He assumed that the same cop who'd posed as Irina's husband and paid September's rent had also searched the suite. Ted's money was on the fat constable. Hers was evidently more than a simple disappearance. Irina had mixed herself up in something bad. *How very, very much like her*, thought Ted. *The woman's a black fucking cloud.* In the lobby he unlocked 905's mailbox and found it stuffed with bills and envelopes, and before anyone could see him Ted took the bundle out through the back door. Outside he looked at the spot where he had once parked his used *arktisblau* 1976 BMW 2002. Ted efficiently mourned the vehicle's loss. To his right he saw the building's swimming pool, its heavily chlorinated water glittering like Windex in the heat. The pool was another cruel temptation, and where the end had started. Ted circled past the diving board and slipped through a gap in the hedge, then walked back over to Granville. At the Normandy, he was given a Naugahyde booth in the air-conditioned rear.

"Coffee and a plate of those silver dollar pancakes, please," he said.

While waiting, he sifted wheat from chaff, colourful local circulars from flyers, junk mail from coupon booklets. Amongst the junk mail were three bills, one each from BC Hydro, BC Tel, and Woodward's department store downtown. BC Hydro wanted twenty-three dollars. Irina hadn't made any revealing long-distance calls via BC Tel. Ted opened the last, for Woodward's. The store had an extensive food floor in its basement; it was the only source in town for many rare and exotic delicacies. The bill was dated from the end of the month and detailed account charges were listed up until August twenty-second. Ted worked backwards. Irina had been reported missing by someone at the gallery where she worked on Monday, the fifteenth of August. This bill was proof that she was still alive at least a week later. He knew it was Irina by the items on the bill: pickled mushrooms, black lumpfish caviar, sour cream, and Winnipeg rye bread. There was something else at the bottom, a five-dollar delivery charge.

"Delivery to where?" he asked aloud.

"Sorry, sir, we serve dine-in only," said the waitress, appearing with his breakfast.

Ted poured imitation syrup over the tiny pancakes and ate. At no point did he consider contacting Johnstone of the Vancouver Police. Details troubled him. He didn't like the idea of some cop paying the rent, or Johnstone's goading of him with Irina's prostitution arrest, or that a plainclothes detective and a uniformed constable were riding around together at three in the morning in a maroon Chrysler. What all these things added up to Ted didn't know, but in finding the small painted doll and this bill Ted felt he'd been dealt a couple of decent hole cards. Now it was a matter of carefully playing them. He put the bill in his coat pocket, tossed the rest of the mail, paid for breakfast, and left.

Despite the refilled coffees, Ted felt weary, a result of his night behind the desk, the broiling heat, and the soporific retsina. In order to fully exhaust himself, he walked north on Granville, past Pacific Press head-quarters, home of the *Province* and *Vancouver Sun*. Before the building stood a mystifying family statue grouping cast in bronze. The fully clothed mother held a baby, father beside her, and in front of the parents strode their naked prepubescent son. Every once in a while someone chiselled off and stole the kid's penis.

Ted strode the busy, ugly bridge over False Creek. Back downtown again the street turned sleazy, made worse in the pitiless glare of a noon-time sun. He passed a peeler bar in the Cecil Hotel, porno stores open twenty-four hours a day, head shops, and punk rock outfitters. At one corner an enterprising long-haired drug dealer propositioned him.

"Needa lid? Pills? Luuuudes?"

On another corner, a burned-out, skinny rent boy played coy and thrust a hip. As he passed the scummy Hotel California, Ted thought about having an early-morning beer, but remembered that stupid song's lyrics. Enough trouble waited for him at the Victoria. Ted wondered if he'd finally done what the Eagles threatened and checked in somewhere he could never leave. He kept walking all the way to Smithe, stopped, turned, and went into the Movieland Arcade. It was a dim, loud room, cooled by three huge industrial fans, no one under nineteen permitted on the premises because of the rows of plywood booths in the back. There you popped in a quarter and peered through a clear cellophane strip at a tiny square where silent 8mm porno loops screened. Sketchy types hung around in the back. The Movieland had pinball and video games, but what Ted came for was to blow off steam. He always chose the machines in the shooting gallery, picking off ducks, four-point blacktailed bucks, and bank robbers one by one until he was out of loose change.

Ted was out on the street again just as the noon horn sounded and echoed around downtown. He counted off eleven hours until the start of his next shift, feeling that he should hit the sack by three to reset the clock, his biorhythms being all fucked up. There was a book he'd read about CIA mind-control experiments and the MKUltra program. Sleep deprivation was the royal road to psychosis. Ted yawned and kept moving. It was no use. He'd keel over if he didn't hit the hay now. With an effort he staggered back to the Victoria and up its wooden steps to the front door. Mr Lee let him in. Ted was about to climb to the top floor on his hands and knees when he heard a booming voice.

"Mr Theodore Windsor."

Around the corner came the massive form of the owner, Mr Samuel Olaffson. Dark eyes glittered deep in his huge, depraved, baby's face, and a faint smile could be made out somewhere within an enormous greying beard. Olaffson crooked a finger at Ted and beckoned him into the back office. Ted attempted a feeble protest.

"Mr Olaffson, please," he said.

"Come, Mr Windsor."

There was no choice. Ted followed leadenly. Olaffson sat behind a cluttered desk in his wheelhouse. The room was stuffed to the gills with the souvenirs of a life lived at sea. From every wall hung framed lithographs of sailing ships, clean white smiling shark jaws, rusty harpoons, orange life preservers, netting, and flags. On an overcrowded bookcase rested a stuffed penguin and puffin and a series of shrunken heads. A photograph on a wall showed a younger version of Olaffson in yellow rain slicker fighting the wheel of an open-deck boat. Below it hung a very fine brass barometer. Olaffson reached over with a long arm, tapped at the mercury with a massive, horny finger, then gestured and commanded, "Sit, please."

Ted collapsed in a chair. From a refrigerator Olaffson pulled out a cold bottle of clear liquid. He filled two glasses to their brims and handed one to Ted.

"Drink."

"I don't know," Ted said.

"Drink."

Ted obeyed, pouring icy fluid into his mouth. Swallowing, it burned clean like vodka and left behind an odd herbal taste.

"Akvavit," Olaffson said. "The water of life."

The owner tipped back his head and drained the liquor in one pour, then refilled both glasses. He leaned back in his chair.

"Now—talk, young man."

"What about?"

Olaffson boomed baritone laughter.

"Mr Windsor, I am a man who has lived. At fourteen, I have left Norway to sail off to sea. All over the world, all of my life. I know the sea when she is calm and when she is trouble, like a woman. I also know men, what they are like when they sailing clear, and when they headed into a storm. You are headed into a storm, Mr Windsor."

"Who told you that?"

"No one. Listen. This is a private hotel, a quiet hotel. For ten years I have owned her. Here there are madmen, but also poets. Always, however, always, there is privacy. Mr Lee has worked for me seven years. I do not even know his name! He is Mr Lee to me, only. Privacy, you see? This is my hotel. Sometimes there is trouble, yes, but mostly quiet. Sometimes there are police."

Here we go, thought Ted.

"You are a young man, younger than others here. Different. This I see, Mr Windsor. It makes me wonder, a man like you, living here, working here."

"Because I need a job and a place to stay," said Ted.

"For the time being, but maybe more. Maybe you are hiding."

"Not from the police. They weren't here for me."

"Then who?"

"My wife."

"See! You work for me, we drink together, and I do not know that you are married."

"I'm not. We're separated. She's disappeared, and the police are looking for *her*."

"Ah."

Olaffson looked at Ted over the rim of his glass. He sipped Akvavit.

"Mr Windsor, do you know of a place called the Fiddler's Green?"

"No," said Ted.

"It is a story an English sailor told me. When a man goes to sea for a long time, he thinks only of the land, of trees and flowers and a grave in the earth. All sailors fear death at sea. Most cannot swim, so if they fall overboard, they will die quickly. When a man cannot sail any more, he leaves his ship and takes with him an oar. He carries this oar and walks away from the sea, into the country. He walks perhaps many days, and when he comes to a place where the people do not know what an oar is, that is where he stops. He finds a woman, he builds her a house, and over the door he hangs the oar. This is the Fiddler's Green."

"Okay."

"You are at sea, Mr Windsor. You should take the oar with you and walk away."

"To Fiddler's Green? I'll think about it. Right now I can't. I'm seriously beat. Sorry, Mr Olaffson, but I need some sleep if you expect me to work tonight."

"Very well. But first, we drink one more."

"All right. Then before I go, let me ask *you* something, Mr Olaffson."

"Please do. And call me Samuel, Mr Windsor."

"Did you ever see a mermaid?"

Olaffson's eyes blazed brightly as he emptied into himself another glass of the spirit.

"No, Mr Windsor, I did not see a mermaid. I married one."

5.

She didn't like the appearance of either one of them. The fat, ugly policeman in uniform stared at her and licked his bottom lip with a coated white tongue. Dorothy repressed a shudder. Even worse than the patrolman was the other one in his hat and overcoat, looking like an FBI agent from an old TV show. It was the way he stood unmoving, hands in pockets, watching her with pale yellow eyes.

"Miss Kwan, is it?" he asked.

"Yes."

"We're with the police."

"I see."

"Would it be all right if we asked you a few questions?"

Dew ne lo moa, thought Dorothy. *After all these years, I've been caught on Labour Day.* She remained perfectly still, feeling ridiculous at how suddenly frightened she was.

"If you must, you must," she said.

"Inside, please."

"I'm sorry, I cannot."

"What's that?" piped up the policeman in uniform.

"Wouldn't you prefer we were inside, Miss Kwan? Away from your neighbours?"

"Do you have a warrant?"

Dorothy couldn't believe she'd spoken the words out loud. Her mother would kill her if she'd heard that. Never antagonize the police, ever. Keep your mouth shut.

"A warrant. Did you hear that?" asked the one in the hat.

"Like we need a fucking warrant," squeaked the patrolman.

"We want to ask her a few questions, and she wants to see a warrant. Interesting. Why do you think we're here, Miss Kwan?" asked yellow eyes.

"I don't know."

"All right then, I'll tell you. We're here about your tenant."

"Who?"

"Don't play stupid. I can see you're a smart young woman. We're here about Irina Lermontova."

"I don't know who you mean."

"You're confused. She probably used another name. Did you rent out a room to a foreign woman, dark hair, dark eyes, speaks with an accent?"

"What's going on?"

The nasty one in uniform unhooked his thumbs from his belt and balled his fists.

"Let me ask her. Stop this dicking around."

"Easy, boy. Miss Kwan wants to cooperate. Don't you, *gai?*"

What did he just call me? A whore? That chilled Dorothy. *What can I do to get them away from here? I mustn't let them inside.*

"I don't know what you're talking about," she said.

"Oh no? Maybe this'll help," said the one in the hat.

He smiled and took a microcassette recorder out of his pocket. He pressed play. Dorothy heard a voice say: "Stop looking for me. You will never find me. Stay away or I'll—"

The cop's heavy thumb clicked the tape off. Dorothy did, in fact, recognize the voice as that of her tenant, who'd called herself Anna Pechorin. She knew it'd been a mistake renting out that damned room, letting a stranger in the house. Look what it got her. More *gweilos*, this time police. Yellow eyes watched her, unblinking, and said, "That call came from *your* telephone number. Now, are you going to invite us in or not?"

"No," Dorothy said.

The policemen looked at each other. Yellow eyes nodded at the fat ugly one, who came toward her. At the house next door, the neighbour lady, Mrs Amorelli, came outside with a wheeled shopping cart, which went *clunk-clunk-clunk* down her front steps. The policemen stopped moving and turned their heads.

"Dorothy?" asked Mrs Amorelli. "Who are these men?"

"Police, ma'am," said the one in the hat.

"Police? Police? What are you a-doing here?"

"We're here to ask a few questions."

"Questions? *Madon.* Dorothy, you don't say a word to these men. Not without a lawyer."

"That's not necessary, ma'am. It's purely routine."

"Ha! *Stronzo!* Police asking routine questions. Two big men asking a little girl. Go on, go away. Dorothy, come here and help me with this."

Dorothy saw the one in the hat narrow his dead eyes. He shook his head and smiled. She walked around the roses bordering the patio and over to Mrs Amorelli.

"Well, then. Come on, Hickey. The ladies don't want to talk to us. Maybe another time. Because you see, Miss Kwan, we'll be back. Oh yes, we'll be back. Next time we might even have that warrant you wanted so badly."

He tipped his hat at her. The fat policeman, Hickey, scowled and horked at a flowerpot. Both policemen went down the stairs to the sidewalk.

"*Testa di cazzo,*" hissed Mrs Amorelli.

"Here, let me help," Dorothy said, reaching for the cart's handle.

"No, *picceri,*" laughed Mrs Amorelli. "I did my shopping yesterday."

"Then what?"

"You think I let the police give you trouble? Those are bad men. You're a good girl. Your mother, God bless her, was a good woman."

Dorothy's eyes suddenly smarted with tears. Mrs Amorelli stroked her head.

"Such a beautiful girl. Now go. Go inside, and lock the door. You call me if there's any trouble. I get my grandsons to come and help."

"*Grazie,* Signora Amorelli," said Dorothy.

"Such a beautiful girl, and such a good daughter," said Mrs Amorelli.

Dorothy sat at the kitchen table in the breakfast nook shivering. She rubbed her arms and rocked gently back and forth. Why was she so scared? *Stop it,* she thought. *Stop it.* She stood up and started to methodically check the lock on every door and window. *If they'd got in and started searching,* she thought and shuddered again. She went upstairs into the tenant's room. Nothing had been moved since the morning. Dorothy would search Anna's effects later. *No, not Anna, Irina something. Why did the police want her?* She thought about the foreign-exchange student. A pretty woman who dressed like a tart, in cheap clothes. They'd hardly spoken the whole time she was here. Dorothy was naturally reserved, almost shy, and her boarder usually left the house early every day and returned late at night, if she returned at all. It had been five days since Dorothy last saw her, the first of the month. Anna, no, Irina, had promised to return with the rent money.

All that time Anna was hiding from the police, hiding her true self in another self, like that Russian nesting doll on the vanity. Dorothy turned to the mirror. The reflection showed her own masquerade, the dove-grey conservative skirt and costume pearls.

"A disguise," she said. "Like mine."

She went to her room and quickly changed into more practical clothing: jeans, T-shirt, and runners, then continued to check the locks and fasteners. In her parents' room, Dorothy opened her mother's walk-in closet. She wasn't concerned about the police searching it. What would they find? *Prêt-à-porter,* ready-to-wear. Dorothy ran her hands along swaying fabrics, touching nothing but the best. Yves Saint Laurent, Lacroix, Givenchy. On a shelf sat a long, neat row of Gucci purses. Another tiered rack held exquisite shoes for every occasion. Every stitch in the closet had been shoplifted, often with Dorothy's assistance.

Dorothy reached up and took a silver-framed photograph out of a hatbox. It was a bright Kodachrome colour picture of her mother as a young woman, pushing a child in a perambulator, taken by a street photographer on Granville in the late 1950s. Her mother wore a light fur stole and beautifully cut mauve Lanvin, effortlessly elegant. Dorothy looked at the child in the stroller, at herself, at her own solemn face. She put the picture back with the rest of the photos that she'd taken down and put away six months ago. All the family pictures were in a box along with the obituary clipping from *Da Han Gong Bao, The Chinese Times*. She touched the last postcard her father had sent home, a view of the Peak looming over Hong Kong harbour. The card had been torn so his message read only, "Dearest Dorothy, Having a Wonderful Time, Wish You Were ..."

Downstairs, Dorothy needed to make a last survey of the house's security, this time in the basement. Below stairs was her father's domain, an area she rarely visited during his life. She unlocked the door and went down the wooden steps. The furnace rested silently, unused through the long, hot summer. It was cool and still in the cellar and smelled deeply masculine: oil, metal, wood. Her father's work bench was filled with various tools and metal dies, mostly press parts. In one corner there was a small ancestor shrine, a young man holding a sword to frighten evil spirits. Ends of burnt joss sticks were still redolent with perfumed incense. Another corner had empty paint cans and a rusty sink. Dorothy went and pried away a rough loose board from the wall. She sighed.

"Thank Christ."

Still there. It was what she'd feared the police finding in a search of the house, what she'd feared more than anything else. Why Dorothy hadn't destroyed it she couldn't say. From a hidden recess the dutiful daughter took out several objects.

The first was a chamois bag that held half of a Hong Kong and Shanghai banknote dated 1951, the year her father emigrated to Canada from Kowloon. In a crumpled envelope were two passports in two different names, neither of them any variation of Harold Kwan. Both had fairly recent, identical photographs of her father. One was British blue, issued in London, the other Communist red, issued in Peking. That was extremely troubling. She knew he also had a Canadian passport, but it was gone, probably the one he'd used in Hong Kong. Lastly, she removed a metal box and flipped open the clasp. Inside it sat a shape swaddled in oilcloth. Dorothy undid the wrapping and picked up the revolver within.

5.

The next morning Renard passed judgment on the hotel's complimentary continental breakfast. On what continent did people eat Froot Loops, yogurt, and croissants at eight in the morning? Asia? Australia? Antarctica? He'd spent the better part of yesterday making provisional escape arrangements, booking open-ended tickets in three directions, and easing into the city. It'd been a long four days of travel, and he'd taken a sleeping pill to go under for twelve hours. Now, alert and keen, his edge re-sharpened, Renard felt in need of a blue-rare steak and cold glass of beer.

The .38 was taped near his ankle, hidden by a grey snakeskin cowboy boot. Stepping outside he went from air-conditioned splendour to the sticky city heat. Sweat bloomed on his forehead and down the small of his back where he kept the Beretta. Renard wore a tailored cotton shirt and striped tie, blue synthetic sports coat, and grey slacks. He carried the minimum of ID and money in a disposable leather wallet. Renard's left outside coat pocket was for his pipe and its paraphernalia, the right held a Swiss Army knife. The key to his room remained at the front desk. In the sunshine, Renard looked as close to a plainclothes cop as you could without carrying a shield. It was a strategy he'd found useful in other cities and other climes. He hailed a taxi.

"BowMac on Broadway," Renard said.

The Black Top pulled away and drove over to Denman and then Beach Avenue along the water. Renard watched a blonde girl in day-glo spandex jog along. Shirtless youths rode skateboards. Runty palm trees swayed in a light breeze. White boat sails could be seen unfurling in the bay. *Like California*, he thought.

The taxi went over the Burrard Bridge and up to Broadway. Another fifteen minutes brought Renard to the car dealership.

A gigantic, four-sided, red, white, and blue sign proclaimed: BowMac. Like a vulgar sundial, it cast a colossal black shadow over the wasteland. According to a guidebook, this was the biggest neon sign of its kind north of Reno, Nevada. On a hot strip of tarmac leading to some flea-bitten casino or the Cadillac Ranch it'd be a painful eyesore. Here, in the baking hellscape of West Broadway's concrete desert, the sign was monstrous. *Dealerships are a helluva lot like whorehouses*, reflected Renard. You made a choice on how to spend your money depending on the year, make, and model of the ride you wanted.

Renard looked over several acres of GM vehicles, from Acadians to Buicks. Rainbow streamers fluttered weakly in the heat while hot dogs and onions grilled on a barbecue. Broadway spread six lanes wide, cutting through Vancouver east to west. Renard could taste car exhaust on his tongue as he lit his pipe. Salesmen stood together in a knot, bullshitting and practicing sincere handshakes. A tall redheaded guy in a short-sleeved shirt spotted him and hustled over.

"Well, friend, the name's Kevin. How can I help you today?" he grinned, holding out a hand.

"I want something cheap and fast," said Renard, hands in pockets as he blew smoke in the man's face.

The salesman's grin never wavered as he put his hand away.

"Well, we've got some real beauties here. Were you looking for new or used?"

"Used."

"I've got just what you're looking for."

They walked to a line of older cars near the back of the lot. The salesman stopped by one.

"Here she is. You're looking at a 1971 Pontiac LeMans, hardtop. She's a base four-barrel 455 cubic inch V8 with 335 horsepower. This baby's lean, mean, and clean. Runs on leaded and I'll get you where you wanna go before you leave the door. The best part?" The salesman crossed his arms and looked at Renard, who finally bit.

"What?"

"You ever see *The French Connection?*"

"Sure."

"This's the car Gene Hackman drives."

That was enough. To spare himself any more spiel, Renard knocked his pipe out on a palm and said, "Fine, drop 200."

Here the salesman started getting sly. "Two hundred, you say? Gee, I don't know. Might have to run it by the sales manager."

Renard asked, in his cold voice, "What happens here to the low man on the totem pole at the end of the month?"

The salesman blanched and blinked hard. He swallowed. "They can him," he said.

"And where were you last month?"

"Next to last."

"Make the sale," Renard said. "Do it now, and I'll pay cash."

"You bet, mister."

In an office Renard signed various legal papers and laid out $750 all-in. He bought a week's worth of coverage from the Insurance Corporation of British Columbia in order to drive straight off the lot. A dumpy lady clerk handed him a piece of paper to tape up on the inside rear window.

"What's this?" he asked.

"Your temporary insurance and registration."

"No plates?"

"No, sir. Not unless you insure for a calendar year."

Renard gritted his teeth. He didn't like this. It made the car too conspicuous. For a moment he considered getting tough with the woman, but with another look at her he knew nothing would shift her short of a bullet to the head. She was one of those unmovable types you found petrified behind the wicket at the post office or DMV. He took his keys and crossed the lot, Kevin the salesman nowhere to be seen.

The Pontiac's AM radio belted out Jay and The Americans'"Cara Mia." At a Shell station, Renard stopped to pick up a city street map and a Pepsi. From there he drove east and turned left on Main, through a bayou of more car dealerships. A forty-foot-high neon sign blared, JIM PATTISON ON MAIN. A competitor's responded, JACK CHINK'S FORD. Across from the Canadian National Station, an elevated concrete track ran back toward the white-domed amphitheatre of newly built BC Place. Some sort of futuristic tourist train ran along it. Renard was reminded of Seattle and its monorail line from the Space Needle, a one-stop, three-minute ride, a hangover from the World's Fair in '62. The one that Elvis made a movie at. Renard drove under a proclamation and read aloud, "'Ride the ALRT to Expo 86.' What the fuck's that?"

He steered the Pontiac straight through Chinatown and crossed Hastings on a green light. On his right Renard saw the police station and courthouse. He turned, parked, plugged the meter, and walked back to the entrance.

From every angle the cop shop was a brutal concrete bunker. Renard sauntered past, crossed the street, and lingered, watching the comings and goings of prowl cars and patrolmen on the off chance his two quarries might emerge. It was a longshot, he knew, but stranger things could happen. Never discount luck, especially bad luck, not in this job. Renard surreptitiously flipped a coin in the air, closed his eyes and said, "Heads."

One time he'd been getting a haircut at a barber's in Mexico City when his target sat down in the chair next to him for a shave. A hell of a coincidence in a city of 15 million people. No telling what might happen in a penny-ante town like Vancouver. Renard opened his eyes and looked at the coin. It was the head of some animal with horns, an elk maybe. He turned the coin over and saw another head: the Queen of England. Shit, you couldn't lose here. Always *something's* head.

There was no point waiting on the sidewalk like a chump. Two blocks down, Renard went into Trader Vic's restaurant. He bought a newspaper and ordered coffee at the long counter. There were phone booths in the back. Renard looked up a number, dropped a couple of dimes, and called the non-emergency line.

"Vancouver Police Department, how may I direct your call?" asked a voice.

"Detective Ron Johnstone."

"One moment."

He heard a click, Muzak, then a wet cough.

"Narcotics, Detective McPherson here."

"Detective Johnstone, please."

"It's his day off. How can I help you?"

Renard hung up.

Narcotics. Very informative. Renard began to feel a tingle of anticipation. It was always a pleasure taking a cop down a peg or two. Even better was taking a cop right down to the ground. And a dirty cop was twice as much fun and could be significantly more lucrative. Arrangements were often made with the victim before the contract was completed to the client's satisfaction. There's always money in a skin.

He re-dialled the same switchboard number, and using a pinched, nasal voice, asked to be connected to Constable Hickey. A dispatcher informed Renard that Hickey was unavailable. Renard hung up again, and started to leaf through the white pages. He found three possible matches for R. Johnstone, noting down the numbers and addresses. A call allowed him the elimination of an old woman named Rebecca Johnstone; the other numbers never answered. There was only one W. Hickey. No one picked up there, either.

At the counter Renard opened his map and plotted his three addresses. The remaining two Johnstones were on the west side, one on Marguerite, the other on Yukon. He'd try phoning again later. Hickey's place was closest, on Wall street, the east side of the city. Renard paid for his coffee and returned to find a parking ticket under his Pontiac's windshield wiper. He tore it up and peeled out.

Renard cruised by Hickey's house. It was half of a duplex Vancouver Special on Wall Street near a cliff overlooking the port. No one was home. It didn't matter. The hunter had nothing planned for daylight. Hickey'd be back, and Renard would be waiting. Other tasks awaited him first, tasks best accomplished by night. Back downtown Renard parked the Pontiac in a garage and caught a double feature at the Coronet of *Metalstorm: The Destruction of Jared Syn* in 3-D followed by *Yor: The Hunter from the Future*.

When he came back out it was dusk, the Granville Mall lit up with neon. Sketchy characters loitered on benches. Renard returned to the parking garage and took an elevator to the highest level, the sixth. Here he was alone among a dozen cars. Crouching down and moving with stealthy assurance, he began to work. With the Swiss Army knife's screwdriver he stripped licence plates off one car and traded them with another, then traded those plates for a third down on the fifth level. This set he put under his coat and took down to the LeMans. He left the lot, drove back to the area near his hotel, and parked on a quiet side street. Here he removed the temporary insurance papers and put the stolen plates on the Pontiac. Satisfied, Renard walked back to the Bayshore. At Trader Vic's, he ate a salad with Javanese dressing followed by chopped sirloin Malagasy, washing the meal down with iced tea. He decided to wait to reward himself with a good steak only after talking to Hickey and Johnstone on his way to hunting down the party girl who'd made off with $300,000.

At the bar a fat lush bored the drink slinger.

"This is one helluva hotel you got here. Remember when old Howard Hughes rented out the top floor and covered all the windows up with tinfoil? That reporter from the paper got a hang glider and tried to get some fly-by photos. Know what happened to him?"

The bartender shook his head.

"Poor bastard flew straight into the wall. Ended up breaking his damn fool back."

The lush's laughter turned to a hacking smoker's cough. His face went red. As he made his way past Renard's chair, the hunter gave him a hand, smacking the fatso so hard on the back his bridgework popped out onto the floor.

After the decent supper and a digestive stroll along the water, Renard returned to his car and drove back out to Wall Street, prepared to wait all night. A block from Hickey's house he stopped, transferred his Beretta to the glove compartment, and cracked a window. With empty patience he watched the new-fangled orange streetlights come on, one by one. The hunter disliked sodium-vapor lighting. The lights made him feel uneasy, insecure, and the colours they created weren't true.

Mr Lee entered the Victoria Hotel at five to seven, carrying a plastic lunch bag and silver thermos of sweet green tea. Ted relinquished his post at the front desk with due ceremony, handing over the cash box, master key, and reservation book. He'd spent the night buzzing in drunks. They'd started shambling in soon after one o'clock, when the bars closed. Junkies had a different schedule and came in and went out again all night long. Their movements prevented Ted from stealing any but the briefest snatches of sleep. This morning he felt jagged and edgy, simultaneously bone weary and hotwired on bad instant coffee. Mr Lee sat down on a high padded stool, opened a copy of the *Chinese Voice*, and began the day-long process of hawking and clearing his throat.

Ted hoped a quick shower might lend him some false energy and took one in the cleanest bathroom on the third floor. He changed into a fresh Pierre Cardin shirt, slacks, and seersucker jacket, and left by a rusty fire escape into the back parking lot, just in case the police had the hotel under surveillance. It was another hot one. From the alley he walked to Hamilton and Pender, keeping an eye out for maroon Chryslers or any obvious ghost cars. Ted cut through Victory Square to an air-conditioned café in the Dominion Building's basement. He needed to mark a little time until Woodward's opened, and lingered over a decent breakfast and Tuesday's *Province*. The tabloid was notorious for being written at about a fourth-grade reading level and concerning itself mostly with grizzly bear attacks and the fortunes of the Vancouver Canucks. The rag managed to eventually yield one nugget of interesting news, about the so-called Squamish Five. They were a radical group of domestic terrorists on trial for some good felonies: bombing a hydroelectric station and a factory making guided missile parts, and torching some Red Hot Video porn stores. The Mounties ending up grabbing five of the gang on the Sea-to-Sky Highway near Squamish, hence the name. The group called itself Direct Action. No one could ever accuse Ted Windsor of being a political animal, but he had the true gentleman's admiration for underdog scrappers, for anyone who took a stand, showed a bit of spunk, and kicked against the pricks.

At eight in the morning, Ted walked to the end of a long line waiting to enter the department store. A black woman in a wide-brimmed straw hat and red polka-dot dress proclaimed the Gospel in a strong Southern accent. The reason for the queue was revealed to Ted when a small girl sang out the Woodward's radio jingle in her clear, sweet voice: "Dollar forty-nine day, Tuesday. Dollar forty-nine day, Tuesday."

"Hush," said the child's mother.

When the doors opened it started a rush. Ted held back until the worst passed. Inside he rode the elevator down to the food floor. A crowd holding pink tickets assembled around the extensive glassed-in delicatessen display, each awaiting their numbered turn. Every red leather stool at the chrome-and-Formica dining counter was filled by a hungry shopper. The delicious aroma of lemon soap, freshly baked bread, frying onions, and ground coffee beans mingled together. Ted stalked through displays of boxed chocolates, stacked pyramids of pâté tins, English tea biscuits, and pickled onions. He found the manager's door and knocked.

"Come in!" barked a rough voice.

Ted did so. A portly man with a walrus moustache, wearing an argyle sweater-vest stained with ash, smoked furiously and was calculating one-handed on an adding machine while growling at a supplier over the phone. Ted barely had time to register an impression of slovenly chaos and a *Playboy* calendar on the wall before the man slammed down the receiver.

"Well, whaddaya want?"

"I'm here about a bill," said Ted.

"Take it to the credit department. Upstairs, fifth floor."

"No, it's about some items charged here."

"Again, you gotta talk to the muckymucks upstairs. I'm busy. Eight-ten and already I'm putting out fires. Seafood truck in a pileup on the Trans-Canada. Jesus, this job's killing me."

The manager donkey-assed a fresh cigarette and grabbed the phone.

"Wait," Ted said, putting up one hand and pulling out Irina's bill with the other.

The manager paused.

"Listen," said Ted, "I've got a bill here from my wife."

"So what?"

"I need your help. She charged some items."

"Yeah? That's between you and the missus."

"She charged for a bunch of things and now she's gone."

"You can't pay, they kick it to a collection agency. They can't find you, it goes to a skip tracer. Sorry, buddy."

"Wait. She's gone and, shit."

"What?"

Ted looked at the wall calendar and had an inspiration. *This guy's a pig. Give him some slop to slobber over.*

"Listen, she ran off," Ted said, sheepishly.

"Tough break."

"She ran off with another *woman*."

The manager stopped dialling. Lechery changed his expression to something even worse. He picked at a nostril with a thumb, sensuously, then took a long haul on his Rothman's, licking his lips and breathing out.

"Jesus. Two broads? Really?"

"Really," said Ted. "Now I've got to find them."

"I'll say. Take some pictures."

Ted ignored that. "I've got to find them so I can get a divorce. She ordered stuff from you and had it delivered somewhere. I need you to check the delivery address for me." He waited. The manager took another heavy drag, shook his head, and set the phone back in its cradle.

"Okay, buddy. Normally I wouldn't do this, but you look in pretty rough shape. Give me the name and I'll see what I can do."

Ted handed over the bill and waited while the manager rooted in a filing cabinet. For once he was grateful that the graveyard shift left him feeling like a whipped dog every morning. It made the falsehood that much more convincing. As the manager grunted and rifled through his desk Ted gazed longingly at the centrefold: 1980's Playmate of the Year, a beautiful local girl from Coquitlam, Dorothy Stratten. Poor girl. Her murder was such a waste. A drawer slammed shut.

"Here you go. Irina Windsor, August twenty-two. Items delivered to 723 Union."

"723 Union, got it. Thanks a lot."

"Forget about it. Take my advice, pal."

"What's that?" asked Ted.

"Lawyer up, hit her fast, hit her hard, and don't ever let her back up off the floor."

The phone squealed and the manager snapped at it. Ted got out of there, disgusted with the manager, himself, and the entire human race.

He took an elevator up to the sixth-floor credit department where he showed Irina's bill to an old sourpuss sitting in a cage behind glass. The crone demanded that Ted produce his driver's licence to confirm that he was, in fact, the customer's husband, Mr Edward Windsor of 1089 West Eleventh. Then she told him that no new charges had been made since the twenty-second. Ted closed the account and promised old man Woodward a cheque in the mail. As he left he remembered the day he'd co-signed the application form with Irina. It was her first credit card. No American Express in the USSR. No new charges in two weeks. That could be interpreted in a couple of ways. He took the elevator down.

Back on the main floor, now in the store's book department, Ted looked up Union Street in a map book. It was in Strathcona, walking distance from Woodward's. He decided to skip the gauntlet of punks, hustlers, and bums along Hastings Street and head through Chinatown. There he wandered, wondering at bins on the sidewalk full of mysterious dried creatures for sale. He ran his hand through a heap of petrified little seahorses. Passing another shop, where a loud radio played Oriental music, Ted stopped short. In front sat a display of flayed lizards crucified on bamboo skewers, looking like demented hand fans for keeping cool at the Peking Opera. He asked the white-smocked Chinese clerk what the lizards were for and was met by incomprehension. Ted pointed and gestured.

"You eat?" he asked.

"Yes, yes," the man nodded.

"How? Soup?"

"Yes, yes."

He couldn't imagine them as cuisine. The lizards had to be medicinal somehow. Ted tried again.

"Good to eat? Healthy?"

"Yes, yes," the clerk smiled widely, with a mouth full of silver. Then he made a fist with one hand and with the other grabbed his forearm, miming a hard cock.

"Strong," said the Chinese man, his smile spreading.

Ted laughed. "How much?"

"Special for you. Cash, no tax."

Ted smiled back, shrugged his shoulders, and pulled out an empty pants pocket. The shopman laughed and shouted something in Chinese to his buddy in the back.

"That's right, round-eye no money, round-eye no hard dick," said Ted, *sotto voce*, walking away.

Both the hard dick and no money part were true. The problems were related. Cash was running short. Payday came on Friday, and Ted had tomorrow and Thursday off. Thin times 'til then. It might be the hour to contact a friend or two, he thought, but not his family, not quite yet. Who could he borrow money from? Ted rode this train of thought as he continued past butcher shops on Gore where pig's heads and barbecue ducks swayed from vicious stainless steel hooks.

He passed from the bustle of commerce into a quieter area of wooden gingerbread houses. Despite having grown up in the city, Ted didn't know the east side well. His world was far from any working-class district; he hailed from a different planet of certain privilege. Two telephone poles on this street were being replaced; they stood splinted to squat jurymasts, their replacements lying along the sidewalk like totems waiting to be carved by Mungo Martin. A wrinkled old Chinese man in a dirty grey wifebeater watered a mean little garden's tomato plants, his wife's cheap underclothes hanging on a line. Along came a mangy dog panting down an alleyway. On Union Street, Ted started to count addresses, growing thirstier every block.

At first pass he thought there'd been a mistake, but he finally noticed the number plate for 723 set high in a concrete wall, with stairs leading up to a large house hidden behind tall hedges. He kept walking around the corner and looked at the property from the rear alley. It was an old two-storey place with a decrepit garage out back, the house and surrounding overgrown garden showing no signs of life. Ted suddenly felt nervous. She lived there. She might be inside the house right now.

What should he do? Did he owe Irina anything after what had happened between them? A sudden ache near his heart wracked Ted's chest. Damn her. Here he was, over a year later, and Irina still the cause of his troubles. He'd put a continent and an entire ocean between himself and the shipwreck of their disastrous marriage, but now all the hurt and humiliation had come washing back to shore. Ted doubled around to a small park at Union and Hawks and collapsed on a bench. Despite the heat his skin was cold and prickling, a fever chill. The recess bell rang at a nearby elementary school, and the neighbourhood suddenly filled with the screaming and laughter of freed children.

This is what I'll do, he thought. *She's in trouble with the cops. I go up, knock on the door, warn her. That's my duty, the smallest courtesy I can afford. I'll tell Irina to stay in touch through my lawyer and that we need to get the divorce underway as soon as possible. Nothing else is my concern. After that I'm getting smashed. Hell of a fucking plan*, Ted said to himself, laughing at the absurd scenario.

So. Ted took a couple of deep breaths and put on a mask of resolution. With a heart that suddenly hammered he climbed up to the old house. In the forecourt shivered the silver paper coins of the flowering plant most people around here called "Chinese money," but what Ted knew of as "annual honesty." He rang the bell. And waited. Ted rang again, waited some more, then knocked. He stepped off the stoop and looked up just in time to see a curtain sway in an upstairs window.

"Hello?" he called out, putting a hand up to shade his eyes from the sun. "Is anyone home?"

3.

. . . .

"Is anyone home?"

The doorbell chimed again in the downstairs foyer. Earlier, at nine o'clock, Dorothy had been startled by the mail slot rattling and a *Pennysaver* falling onto the mat. After the two policemen had frightened her the day before, Dorothy had telephoned a locksmith. She was forced to agree to steep terms, rates doubled because it was Labour Day, but it was urgent, an emergency. New locks and bolts were installed for all the doors. Dorothy's tenant was never, ever getting back in this house. *Let the damned woman knock until her hand breaks*, she thought.

Despite the new security, Dorothy knew deadbolts weren't enough to stop someone really determined to get in, especially the police. A brick through the window is the world's skeleton key. What she counted on, however, was the nosiness of her neighbours. God bless Mrs Amoretti and all Strathcona's sentries. In some ways the neighbourhood was a village unto itself, surrounded by the sprawling city, protected from the outside world by vigilant little old ladies who were incapable of minding their own business. The doorbell chimed again, and a current of electricity ran up Dorothy's forearms.

From the upstairs window it was difficult to see who was down on the step. Through the short night, Dorothy'd waited for the vicious peal of broken glass and splintered wood. Now her nerves hummed taut as fiddle strings, and a fresh knock on the door tightened her sinews further still. She peered from behind a curtain to see a young man on the patio seemingly looking up at her.

"Is anyone home?"

He was dressed in a seersucker jacket and shielded his eyes from the sun. *This one's not a policeman*, she thought, *he's too slender and well-dressed. Good looking too*, she realized, as he walked a few steps back and looked up again. Dorothy retreated farther from her vantage at the window. The man cast his gaze across the front of the house, shook his head, and finally left. Dorothy realized she'd been holding her breath the whole time. Now a slow exhale escaped her before she collapsed on a quilted armchair. For the tiniest moment she closed her eyes.

Afternoon light slanted across the room as Dorothy awoke from tangled dreams. She stretched from finger to toe tip and heard her stomach growl. More than anything her soul lusted for one of her mother's dishes: roast beef with Yorkshire pudding. Dorothy wiped sleep from her eyes and jumped as the upstairs telephone rang. For three rings she debated whether to answer or not until she resolved not to be a prisoner in her own house. She wouldn't let a pair of *gweilo* cops scare her into a corner. Besides, Dorothy suddenly remembered, she knew police of her own. Inspector Brian Kwok of the RCMP, a friend of her father's and fellow Chinese Freemason. He could help. He would help, she was sure. Dorothy picked up the phone and waited for the caller to speak.

"Hello? Hello-o. Anyone home? It's me, Mary."

Dorothy sighed. "Hi, Mary."

"What's the matter? You sound lower than Nancy Reagan's left tit."

Dorothy laughed. "I'm so glad it's just you," she sighed.

"Just me? It's never been *just me* in my life, you stuck-up private school bitch. Just for that you're buying me dinner."

"When?"

"Now. I'll pick you up in five."

"Come by the back alley," Dorothy said.

"Why?"

"Because I said so, you private school slut."

"Meow."

"*Ciao.*"

Dorothy hung up and raced to get ready, with a dab of Chanel on the pulse points at throat and wrists and a touch of gloss to her lips. She quickly decided on trashy chic with her brand-new David Bowie T-shirt from the Serious Moonlight tour, nice and tight under a tailored sienna Italian leather jacket. Jeans and boots would have to do for the rest. Snatching up her wallet and ring of keys, Dorothy raced down and out the kitchen, making sure the new bolts shot home. In the alley Mary's convertible idled, the tape deck blasting "High School Confidential" by Rough Trade.

"Nice," said Mary, eyeing Dorothy over heart-shaped sunglasses.

"Hit it," said Dorothy as she hopped in.

Mary Worthington was a lot of things to Dorothy, but most of all she was fun. Crazy fun, trouble fun. Dorothy's parents had disliked Mary immensely for her reckless good humour, wild beauty, and general irreverence, but couldn't forbid the friendship. Mary Worthington's family was rich, and more importantly in the eyes of Mr and Mrs Kwan, old-money rich. So they'd allowed Dorothy a measure of freedom, and Dorothy luxuriated in Mary's world. Mary was impossible to resist, always up to something, always on the go. Now her fire-engine red Mustang roared through quiet Strathcona, barely slowing at stop signs and causing dogs to howl in its wake. They headed in the general direction of the setting sun.

"We're going to a divine new Japanese place. You ever have 'sushi' before, you know, raw fish?"

"No," Dorothy said.

"You'll love it, it's fucked up."

Mary talked a streak as they burned up Main and then west along Broadway. She was a terrible, furious driver, never signalling or braking, quick with her horn, her mouth, and her middle finger. Near Alma she parked and dragged Dorothy through a line-up of trendsetters waiting to get into The Eatery, air-kissing friends and scorning enemies. An awed waiter hustled them to a waiting corner table by the window.

"Double vodka tonic for me, chop chop," Mary said. "What do you want?"

"I don't know."

"Sake then. It's rice wine. Got that, Bruce Lee?"

The waiter bowed and hurried away.

"So, like I was saying, this place is the new place. Everybody's crazy about sushi. If you don't want it, try the teriyaki. But what am I saying? You'll eat cat—I know you do, don't deny it. But wait, this's for you."

Mary took an envelope out of her bag and pushed it over as the drinks arrived. Dorothy opened it under the table and thumbed $300.

"Your share," said Mary. "Not bad for what, half an hour's work?"

"Beats taking in laundry," said Dorothy.

"Ha!"

It had been a fast turnover for the two stolen Dior dresses. Mary Worthington's wealthy parents had set her up with a small monthly allowance and a boutique on 4th Avenue she'd christened The Day of the Jacket, mostly as a tax write-off, and as something for Mary to do instead of studying at college. Mary had been kicked out of every private school in town, including Little Flower Academy, where Dorothy and she'd first met back in grade ten. When Dorothy had returned from university, Mary bumped into her at a party and the two had fallen back into their old friendship. One drunken night, while her parents were at a Chamber of Commerce dinner, Dorothy had opened her mother's closet and revealed to Mary her secret talent. Right away Mary had spotted the opportunity to make good cash money, and a partnership was born. Dorothy stole couture to order, and Mary fenced the goods through the back of the boutique to her rich friends, while mommy and daddy footed the bill for the running of the shop. In the last six months Dorothy's share had come to nearly seven thousand dollars, all of it tax free.

"Tonight's your treat," said Mary.

"Fine. But you order."

Mary got them something called California rolls and prawn tempura, which Dorothy found delicious. The sake was perfect, both delicate and subtle. Two little bottles later, Dorothy was warm and happy, enjoying the buzz of the restaurant and all the cool people posing and chatting. Mary gossiped like she ate, ravenously. She ordered more food: piping hot gyoza dumplings, chicken teriyaki, and cool salmon sushi on rice. Dorothy tried the chilly raw fish and pulled a face. Mary laughed.

"Brynne puked when she tried it. Speaking of which, look who's here!"

Dorothy turned her head and the happy cloud she'd been floating on burned away. Brynne sat down as her husband held out her chair.

"That slag," Mary said. "Look at her. She dresses like my grandma. Save us from Simpson-Sears. And him. What does he see in her?"

"Old money," Dorothy whispered.

Mary looked at Dorothy. "You poor thing. Well, Kenneth Abernathy's a bastard, and you're better off without the prick. How long has it been now? A year? You've got to move on. Pick up some cutie and go for a ride. Jesus, Dorothy, you're like a nun, I swear. When was the last time you did it?"

"Did what?"

"Don't be obtuse. You know what."

Dorothy emptied her sake with a gulp.

"That long, eh? Well, stick with me, kiddo. Tonight you get lucky."

"No thanks."

"C'mon. There's a party out my way. Come with me, and I'll get you back on the market. Listen, if you don't use it, it'll seal up, like piercings when you stop wearing your earrings."

Dorothy laughed. "Okay, but on one condition," she said.

"Name it."

"You have to let me crash at your place."

"Deal. But, honey, you're not getting any sleep tonight, I promise."

It was a beautiful Art Deco and Moroccan-style house in white stucco that faced north over Locarno Beach. Sailboats played on a faraway sea as the sun set and the lights of freighters and tanker ships winked in the dusk light. Parked along the driveway Dorothy saw Jaguars,

BMWs, and late-model MGs. Music poured over the grounds, David Bowie commanding: "Let's dance!"

Mary echoed Bowie as she spilled out of her Mustang onto the gravel drive. She'd had four double vodka tonics already, and Dorothy hauled her up the steps to the open door. The party was in full swing, with tipsy girls shrieking, college boys chortling, the music bouncing and fragmenting around the plastered rooms. Mary swung away toward a group of friends. Dorothy was more hesitant; these weren't her people. They were mostly rich preppie types, blandly handsome blond twenty-somethings wearing Lacoste and Polo. She moved through the house. In the kitchen a crowd cheered as a tiny woman drank a wine cooler while doing a handstand against the wall, her skirt upside-down and panties showing. Dorothy passed the library and saw another group sitting around someone wearing an antique gas mask hooked up to a large bong. A fat, grinning fraternity boy pushed a drink at her; Dorothy took it just to have something in her hands. From some part of the house she heard a loud crash, then whooping and hollering. She walked quickly away through the dining-room French doors onto the patio. As she looked out over the water, Dorothy sipped her drink and swatted at a mosquito. Hearing giggling to her left, she turned and saw a guy with two topless women fooling around in a Jacuzzi. What was Mary thinking? This was no party for her. She felt instantly depressed. Remembering Kenneth Abernathy at the restaurant further squelched her mood. She wanted to go home. And with a shock of terror, Dorothy recalled the policemen from yesterday. And the man in the seersucker jacket who'd knocked at the door this morning. Who was he? Was it safe to go back?

From upstairs came the unmistakable screech of Mary's laughter, which faded and gave way to police sirens.

"*Hai ah*," Dorothy said.

The last thing she wanted was to get scooped up in a raid. Dorothy walked away from the house down the sloping lawn into the garden. A heady perfume of evening flowers washed over her as she hopped a low fence into the next yard, slipping noiselessly through the property, around a garage, and onto the street. Following the slope of the road led her downhill to Marine Drive and the ocean. It was perfectly lovely. Fires burned in barbecue pits, and Dorothy smelled the tang of salty driftwood smoke, suntan lotion, and frying hotdogs. She walked beside the sea on an old promenade to Jericho Beach, where she sat down on a log and removed her boots and socks. The soft sand felt warm to her touch. A small man with very dark hair tenderly played flamenco guitar in the firelight. Dorothy crossed to the water and saw the whole city lit up in the distance, light crowding out the stars, spotlights from the PNE fair circling in the far northeast. Rolling up her jeans, she waded into the gentle, shallow surf as it lapped around her feet. The tide glowed an alien blue and green with bioluminescence. She was between sea, earth, and sky, completely alone in the immensity of this world.

Wednesday broke with the sky clouded over, and a leaden humidity turning the city sluggish and irritable. Renard felt in sync with the weather, crabbed and annoyed. Constable Hickey hadn't returned to the house on Wall Street all night. Renard made to leave his post when a patrol car pulled up to the driveway. Hickey was inside, in full uniform. He lunged out of the vehicle, and even from a distance Renard observed a thick sheen of sweat on the man's red face. The cop opened a bottle of mouthwash and leaned back to gargle, straining the buttons on his shirt. He spat green fluid on the road. Renard prepared to follow the patrolman inside. He moved the Beretta into his hand as the door to the house opened. A frowsy woman and small girl with pigtails, probably Hickey's wife and daughter, greeted the cop at the stoop. Renard grunted. He wasn't going to lean on an entire family. No, he wanted the pig alone. His vigil had been nearly a total waste. All Renard learned was that Hickey worked the night shift. It'd make him easier to isolate but perhaps more difficult to tail. He checked his watch. It was just after seven o'clock. That meant Hickey would probably sleep most of the day and start up again at eleven. *Get back here at ten*, Renard thought, *and see what's what*. He noted down the patrol car's number, started up his LeMans, and drove away.

At a gas station beside the Princeton Hotel on Powell Street, Renard bought coffee and made another call to the station. Detective Johnstone was on assignment and could not be reached. The coffee wasn't enough, so Renard swallowed a booster pill. He decided to case the two addresses for Johnstone and also get a better sense of the city. For a few minutes, he consulted the map on the passenger seat and laid out a route. The drive took him across town to an area called Shaughnessy. The street grid here was broken; this was a neighbourhood of tall London plane trees shading curved, wide avenues. Enormous old homes stood in haughty isolation, surrounded by rhododendrons. It was a far cry from working-class Wall Street. The only vehicles parked on the street were contractor's trucks and vans. No one walked the sidewalks. For Renard this presented a problem. He couldn't loiter around these rich houses. Some nosy parker would call security. Besides, it didn't factor, a cop living in a mansion. The Pontiac circled The Crescent around a park and spat out on Tecumseh to 16th, then north on Yukon. There he found the second address and stopped.

Surveillance was the worst part of the game. It ruined your digestion and imposed a poor diet of junk food and greasy take-out. Hours spent sitting on your ass, with hemorrhoids the usual price. Bad coffee and amphetamines did Renard no favours, but at least they cancelled out his need to use a toilet. He rolled down his window in a vain attempt to offset the sticky heat and studied the map again. It was eight o'clock. Taxpayers headed out to start the working day. Renard listened to the news on the radio and smoked his pipe. Highs of thirty were expected; Renard tried to convert the temperature to Fahrenheit. He yawned and farted, scratched and fidgeted. Give it an hour, then he'd go back to the hotel.

At five to nine, a maroon Chrysler pulled up and Renard ducked down just in time to avoid identification. The driver had cop written all over him, from the hat down. The Chrysler turned into the alley behind a house. Renard checked the photograph again. No question, it was Detective Johnstone of the Vancouver Police. This was good. Renard wrote down the make and licence number and smiled. He had them both at home now. With this one he would wait. The narcotics detective was obviously the brains of the duo. It was better for Renard to start with the constable, a simpler man to pressure. Now it was a matter of learning the pair's patterns, where they travelled, who they spoke to. First though, food and rest. He started the LeMans and drove back into the city and the Bayshore Inn.

"A message for you, Mr Renard."

Tiffany at the front desk handed him an envelope. He tore it open and read, "Mallory, 619-9846."

Renard went to a phone booth and dialled. The other end picked up. "Mallory," Renard said.

"Ah, Mr Renard, how very nice to hear from you. How are things?"

"Progress. Have their houses and cars. Tail tonight."

"Wonderful. Please keep us informed."

"You bet."

The line clicked off. Renard shook his head. He didn't like employers looking over his shoulder. Whoever this Mr Peters was, he'd contacted an organization man in San Francisco, where Renard had been based lately. Peters had no profile with the syndicate, which was strange. Renard was between assignments and knew Vancouver a little, so when the call had come he'd been given orders. Now here he was, in good old Canada, far from the real action down south. The difference between the big leagues and the bush league. Still, though, it was good to get out of the grind, away from it all, from time to time. A working vacation, *s'il vous veux*.

When he was in-country, Renard preferred to work alone. This business of checking in with Mallory was irritating. Every job was different in its own way, and yet somehow they were usually the same: the fucking customer was always right. It irked Renard. He decided to take the edge off and recharge with a swim. In the bright glare of noon, the outdoor pool swarmed with tourists. As a rule, the hunter chose to stay aloof from unruliness and disarray.

Alternate refreshment was found in the spa. Renard finished fifteen freestyle laps in the company of a woman slowly swimming a lazy breast-stroke. She glanced over as Renard hauled himself out of the pool, so he let her get a good look at what was in his Speedos. Her eyes met Renard's as he walked over to the sauna, entered, and cranked up the heat. As he sweated he waited, listening to the metal stove ticking faster, watching the thermometer rise.

She came in when it was good and sizzling, a woman in her early forties, well-to-do, her dark hairdo a little old-fashioned and uptight. Renard was amused to see that she wore nothing but a clean white towel over a proud bust. The woman was deeply tanned with no lines, and no ring. Sitting primly on a bench she arched an eyebrow. The hunter sprawled nonchalantly in the upper corner. Let her fill her boots and feast her eyes, if that's what she wanted. Do nothing, and wait. Sit here and sweat.

"You are a very powerful swimmer," she said at last.

His ears picked up the formal phrasing and her slight accent. It was German, or Scandinavian. European, definitely.

"Thanks," he said.

"It is good to keep fit."

"Well, you know, a healthy mind in a healthy body."

"Yes, I know this expression. I agree with it."

"Problem is, I don't have a healthy mind."

Her eyes widened a little, and then she gave a lazy cat's smile. "You are joking with me, I think."

"Maybe."

"You are here on business?"

"Mostly. And pleasure."

"Ah, pleasure. Yes, this is also important."

"And you?"

"My husband, *he* is here for business. But yes, myself, I am also here for pleasure, perhaps."

The woman's gaze strayed down Renard's body and back up again. So that was it. The second look. A bored wife. Well. It was just as likely as anything else. He was in no hurry right now, but neither was Renard entirely convinced by her advance. A honey trap was a honey trap the world over. If this was one, the approach was unique. She wasn't your standard bubblehead at the bar, but a seasoned woman with a *soupçon* of class.

"Where are you from?" he asked.

"Salt Lake City, in the state of Utah."

"Mormons," he said.

"Good lord, yes. And nowhere to have a drink."

"The bar here makes a mean martini."

"It may be so. I prefer to drink in my room."

"Sounds lonely."

"The word, I think, is *intimate*," she said, with an emphasis Renard registered.

She rose and adjusted her towel so that Renard caught a flash of her wet nakedness beneath. He looked at her and she briefly met his eyes.

"Room 803 is where I am drinking," she said while leaving, letting in the cool clean smell of chlorine.

Renard stroked his beard and smiled. It was something to think about. What were the odds of it being a set-up? Very long. He wasn't in service, had no information anyone could want. The two cops were small-timers in the grand scheme of things. In the hunter's line of work, it was almost impossible to see things plain. What he had here could very well be the rarest thing: simply what it appeared. *Well, I'll think about it.* The European would definitely be more satisfying than renting a call girl for the afternoon. Married women knew what they wanted. Well-off European wives both knew what they wanted and got what they wanted. At the very least it made a good opening for a letter to the Advisor.

"Dear *Penthouse*, I never believed it would happen to me," said Renard, aloud.

In the spa shower he considered her, and again during the elevator ride up to his room. As Renard mixed bourbon and ice, he started to feel the itch, remembering the glimpse of her tawny breasts and smooth, tanned belly. *I wouldn't mind getting laid right now*, he thought, *not at all*.

"*Bah oui*," he said aloud and swallowed his drink.

Renard was too much the professional to take anything for granted. He lit his pipe and called room service.

"Send up a bottle of chilled white wine, the smoked salmon platter, and a bowl of fruit."

Next he put on a white linen *guayabera* shirt and loose black beach shorts. When the food came, Renard kept the cart, placed the Beretta under a napkin, and wheeled it back to the elevator, which he rode down to the eighth floor. At 803 the hunter knocked and said, "Room service."

A voice came from behind the door. "What? There is some mistake. I have ordered nothing."

The door opened and the woman's mouth made a red circle. "Oh," she said.

She wore a terrycloth robe, and he could see a light dusting of talcum powder on her exposed skin.

"It is you," she said.

"That's right. You said you'd like a drink. I brought some wine."

"How thoughtful. But I am having schnapps."

"Wine won't hurt you."

But I might, thought Renard.

She was suddenly a little hesitant and absently motioned for Renard to push the cart into her room. He did, chained the door, and made a swift circuit, checking the bathroom and closets.

"You are looking for something?"

"Your husband," he said.

"He is with his clients. They are golfing, which means they are getting drunk in the clubhouse."

"And you?" he asked.

"I am drinking alone."

"Not any more."

Renard uncorked the wine and poured two glasses.

"Bottoms up," he said.

"An excellent idea."

She undid her robe, letting it slip to the floor.

10.

From the roof of the hotel he watched the giant W of the Woodward's building spill hot red neon into the darkness. The letter was perched atop a poor replica of the Eiffel tower and turned slowly on its axis. Beyond it, far off across the inlet, North Vancouver shimmered in hazy heat below the dry mountains. An answering letter, a huge turning Q at the Lonsdale Quay, responded. *They riddle each other*, Ted thought. Question: Who, What, Where, When? Most important of all, though, was: Why? Why had Irina left the apartment, why was she on the run? All the other questions would unravel themselves if Ted managed to pull at that one thread of why.

He took a deep breath. Two hours until seven, and the start of two days off. He shimmied down the fire escape and through a window. He went to his room for something to read back at the desk. All he had was a translation of *The Life of an Amorous Man* by Saikaku Ihara. Starting on the third floor, he began to walk his rounds of the Victoria Hotel, down to the second, and to the right through a huge, heavy steel door. This was a wing of former offices that took up the whole corner of Homer and Pender, two levels converted to cheap single-residency rooms. Ted had been inside very few; most of the tenants were suspicious and solitary. An indistinct radio played behind one door. Another leaked tobacco and marijuana smoke, prompting him to remember the small amount of pot he'd taken from the Stardust. How to spend his weekend? He went into a cool stairwell and checked that the fire doors were locked, finally debouching on Pender Street, carefully locking a barred glass door behind him. Ted walked back to the front entrance along the sidewalk and past the few businesses—a military surplus store, a barbershop, a permanently closed café. Ted returned to the hotel's main entrance and climbed up the wooden steps. He paused a moment, watching the light at the corner change from green to yellow, then red, and back again. Nothing stirred. The city was vacant, dead.

Mr Lee prodded Ted with his rolled-up copy of the newspaper. Ted started awake from an anxious half-dream, his mouth forming a guilty smile. Mr Lee appeared as always: ageless, tireless, indifferent. Responsibility for the hotel was passed over, and Ted went upstairs again. He resolved to overset his internal chronometer. There'd be no attempt at sleep. He rolled a thin joint and put it in his wallet. Ted dressed down, preparing for a day's worth of mild slumming. Before leaving the room, he checked where he'd hidden Irina's small painted doll. He'd pushed it into the hollowed centre of a wet cake of soap. There was something about it, something important, and he didn't want anyone to find it if the room was tossed. Housekeeping came only on Saturdays, and Ted reasoned it unwise to carry the doll on his person in case he was stopped and frisked by Detective Johnstone or the other cop. He took a last look out the window as the light of the Woodward's W turned off for the day. Another cooker, sweltering and bright already. Ted's objective this morning was simplicity itself: a cold glass of beer.

Samuel Olaffson had advanced him twenty dollars from petty cash before Friday's payday, an act of Christian charity. Ted again left the hotel by the fire escape into the back parking lot and cut across Homer Street, past Richards to Seymour, where he drifted down against the current. From out of the old red brick Canadian Pacific Railroad station streamed commuters between high white columns. It was pleasant to enter the great space and watch the world hurrying to work. Ted lingered in the churn awhile, savouring his liberty, a cork in a maelstrom. He took an elevator down to the underground parking garage. At the lowest level, Ted walked to a corner where a door opened out the back of the station underneath the bridge gantry that led to the SeaBus ferry stop. Below the span rested a railyard reeking of oil and metal in the bright heat. The Canadian Pacific no longer ran across the country; you had to take Via Rail from the station at Terminal and Main. In anticipation of the 1986 World's Fair, the city was beginning a monorail link from downtown to New Westminster, and a showcase section of the track had already been built from the new BC Place amphitheatre to Canadian National Station. Ted had never taken it. He stood and watched a few freights clang and jerk in the yard, then walked to a solitary line of unused tracks along the station which ended unhallowed in a heap of yellowing grass.

"This is the end of the line," he said.

The terminal point. Look along it all the way east to where it starts, in Halifax, the Atlantic Ocean, the other side of the continent, the skein that binds the Dominion together. All that remains now are grasshoppers creaking over split, slivered, silvery ties and rusted rails. The end of the line is out here in the far west.

"Or the beginning."

Ted stepped onto the tracks and lit the joint, smoking smoothly as he walked along Jack London's iron road. It'd been a long time since he's smoked marijuana; pot was seriously illegal in Japan. The windows of former warehouses and dry goods shops stared down on him blindly. They were the eyes in the backs of the ice cream parlours and fancy shoe stores of Vancouver's historic Gastown district. He ducked through a rent in a chain-link fence and crossed the full width of the freight yard to the water's edge along the inlet. A helicopter's blades filled the air with percussion as it landed in its pad. Ted continued along to a seedy patch of rough weeds where a clutch of Oriental fishermen lay out lines or pulled up traps from a wooden pier. The harbour was busy this morning. A floatplane droned down to skid on the sea. Ted felt the drug working, felt a charge as his vantage point shifted within the kinetic landscape of machines. One pleased angler hauled up a full net glittering with struggling smelts. Not for a pension would Ted eat anything caught in these polluted waters. But that didn't seem to bother the fisherman as he cast out another net. A whistle sounded and echoed between the mountains and the city as another ferry set out across the inlet.

Thirst quickened Ted's pace. He took a footbridge back over the freight yard to Main Street, working his way through the run-down blocks of cheap hotels, wholesale vendors, and shifty international traders. A Chinese produce market spilled everything from dragon fruit and daikon to apples and potatoes out onto the sidewalk where sharp little old ladies picked and squeezed the goods. Next to the store sat a white Anglican church, like a crusader's castle marooned in the Holy Land. It was near time now, so Ted footed it to Hastings—Skid Row.

Unlit neon signs looked cheap and ugly in the morning glare. All Ted wanted was to get out of the noise and stink. He reached his Mecca of the morning, the Empress Hotel, and walked through the Ladies and Escorts entrance just as the beer parlour opened. Inside it was cool and clean, a waft of bleach rising from the freshly mopped tile floor. For a brief moment the bar was empty, and Ted smiled as he took a leatherette stool. After a minute a diminutive Malay glided out to the taps. The bartender nodded, and Ted ordered a fresh pint of Labatt Blue. When it came, he added salt for flavour and swallowed half the mug in a gulp, letting the cold liquid work its way down his gullet. He ordered another, paid, and went past the shabby pool table and jukebox to the rear of the bar as other patrons trickled in. It was nine in the morning.

A framed newspaper clipping hung on the wall. Ted read:

Sally Bids You Welcome

There's no place like it in Vancouver. It's unique here in Canada, and probably the world. Where else will you find judges, prosecutors, defense lawyers, court officers, court clerks, court reporters, and an everflowing number

of off-duty police officers, firemen, newspapermen and
women, news vendors, coroners, businessmen, retired ship
captains, flower children, convicted criminals on parole,
and skid row bums drinking and lunching together?

It was an old article, from the sixties, Ted judged, and Sally must be
long dead. Since the main courthouse had moved to Robson Square,
Ted imagined that the upscale clientele had gone with it. The sight
of his fellow morning-at-the-Empress drinkers bore out the notion.
They were mostly old guys, blue-collar types from the docks or the
yards, many of them just a short, ugly, bloody step from the gutter. A
couple of Indians in denim jackets and straw cowboy hats started to
play eight ball. Rough-looking loggers chortled and compared tattoos.
Pensioners sat with copies of the *Province*. Some lady who might be
a junkie or a whore (or both) giggled and muttered to herself. A sad
group. Ted didn't care. The pot and beer on an empty stomach at the
end of a sleepless night had him turned inside out. He felt happy. He
had seventeen dollars in his pocket. He wasn't thinking about Irina or
the cops or his job or anything. All Ted wanted from this new morning was to chew the fat with someone, so he went back to the bar and
ordered a third Blue.

After his fourth, he struck up a conversation with a raggedy-looking
old gent and bought him a drink. The fellow told this tale:

"Had some bad luck out east. Buddy of mine told me that you could
still pan for gold up in the Cariboo. We went straight for a while and
saved up two cheques' worth to come out this way. Had it all worked out.
Got some pamphlets from the Ministry of Mines. My buddy had panned
some when he was a kid, said it was a good way to keep in kip. Easy as pie.
Hard work, but clean air and good living. By fall we could have enough
to last us out the winter in a hotel, and you never knew. Maybe get lucky.

So we rode the dog all the way from Toronto to Kamloops. Four days, altogether. Beginning of June, as I remember. Everything I had was in one of those bags, you know. We hitched up to Quesnel and bought some gear: pans, shovels, axes, saws, magnets to get black sand out of the flour gold. Some grub as well. Mostly beans, salt pork, corn syrup, tea, flour, and a couple of bottles of cheap rye. I picked up a .22 and a couple hundred rounds. Few sticks of dynamite as well. I grew up hunting. So there we were, with a couple bucks left between us, so we kept hitching, out past Wells, and then we started walking. That was where the big rush was back when, Barkerville and all up around there. After the easy gold dried up, the big operations moved up the Stikine or Omineca. We were after placer tailings, not to get rich, see, but just to keep in beans and whiskey. There were still these old geezers way out in the bush that'd come down with a few nuggets and bags of dust, then head on back out god knows where. We had to keep an eye out for those buzzards or any government types 'cause it was claim-jumping, really. Mostly we just followed a creek as far as we could, looking for old tailings and quartz. One day we came to a spot that looked okay. Old shack and some bust-up sluice boxes. We set up camp and got to work."

The tale-teller drank his beer through his beard, raising the glass with yellow-stained fingers, nails broken, flesh bruised purple as plums underneath.

"Spring came and first we tried the creek to get our hands in. Divvied the jobs: I fixed the shack up 'cause I'd been a carpenter, and I went hunting. My pal started panning, and right away he had some luck. Well, sir, he was a gambler at heart, and that's a fact. Hooked worse'n a trout on a fly. Bit by the gold bug. There was a cherry tree growing in a sunny spot just away from that shack. Figured some lonely prospector'd brought a sapling with him from the south. It was a stunted sort of thing, but it flowered, and soon enough there was fruit on the damned thing. Meanwhile, I brought in a few small deer and once a beaver. It was about to pup, and we ate the whole thing fried up, believe it or not."

"What'd it taste like?" asked Ted.

"Tasted like beaver. Anyway, pretty soon my pal was heading further and further out, up into the hills for days and days while I panned the sluices we'd knocked together and kept the camp going. At the end of July, I went down to Wells for some more grub. Whiskey, mostly. Took me three days to get to that wide spot in the road. We were doing okay, and I felt better'n I had for a long while. Fresh air and hard work and not too much sauce, just enough to keep the sinews good and tight. I traded some dust and got a newspaper. Gold was trading for $150 an ounce then. Well, hell, that was good but no great shakes, and we had maybe three ounces, tops, for three months' work. I was getting the itch again and wanted to be in town. My buddy wouldn't have it. Bit by the bug, like I said. So it was nothing but scrape away, day after day. We ate those bloody cherries, went through the beans and the pork, and soon we were down to flour and syrup. Flapjacks everyday, and no meat."

The old-timer took a long pull of his beer and regarded Ted balefully.

"You seem an educated sort of fellow. Well, there I was with damn all to read and no radio and my buddy going walkabout for a week at a time. He was getting secretive, too, mind. Got that look you see in junkies. I've had it myself. I went into town one more time to lay in another couple weeks worth of food, and when I got back he was nowheres around. So after a few days, I got a pack together and went looking. He'd been cutting marks into trees, and I followed his track, no problem. Looked like he'd been panning here and there but also digging into benches. There were these old claims that he chipped away at, some pretty big works left to rot into the bush. Not just from the rush, but hydraulic works from the Depression. And now I found something else, too. Burned pictures on flat rocks. Weird fish-headed men and odd looking things like octopus. We were deep in Indian country, Carrier country, and these were some of the old signs the Indians'd left behind, I guess. Well, after four or five days, I started getting spooked. Had my gun and enough grub to get back, but the bush was starting to close in on me. Started hearing noises like I was being followed. Then there were wolves at night. I've got good bush sense but don't set myself up as no Daniel Boone. It can swallow you up out there, and it was getting harder to follow my pal's trail. I was getting into the foothills, too. That's where the lost mines were. Crazy stories. Secret places. Forgotten mines with the motherlode. But I didn't care about gold anymore. I just wanted a warm bed and a cheeseburger."

Another pull at his beer. Ted strained to hear his compatriot muttering.

"Until you really get out into it you have no idea how big this Goddamn country is, even one corner of it up there. Makes you wonder how they did it back in the long ago. There was nothing around. Nothing. Couldn't even hear a plane overhead. Finally, I'd had it. Maybe my pal'd taken another route down to the camp, and I'd missed him. So I pushed on one more day and stopped at a stream to fill my canteen when the hairs stood up at the back of my neck."

He stared Ted straight in the eye.

"I looked up, and ahead on a ridge, up against the sky, was a man. Standing dead still. This was broad daylight, but close to dusk, so the light was tricky. Couldn't make out anything for sure, but then the man pointed to his left, up into the hills. Now damn it, I was starting to shit. Chambered a shell and went toward the ridge. It was all rocky, lousy country, and by the time I got up there the man was gone. So I looked the way he pointed, and on a cliff face about half a mile away I saw a rockfall. Went toward it and it was an avalanche, all right, but there was a pick and some rope and some other bits of our stuff, including three big chunks of ore with veins in them, more gold than I'd ever seen before. And the face of that cliff was all new stone, cracked and broken by some blast, like. Well, I guessed what'd happened. My buddy must've found a mine, and it caved in on him. I dug away 'til dark, made camp, and started again in the morning. It was no use, no getting in. If he was in there, and who the hell knows how long he'd been buried, I couldn't get him out myself. If the cave-in hadn't got him, then maybe something else. Didn't like to think about it. But then who the hell was the man on the ridge? That's when I really got spooked. A front started moving in, so I saddled up and cut my way back the way I came, but something went wrong, and I got lost. Had a compass but it wasn't working. Took me two days to figure out that the magnets we used on the black sand were in my pack, flipping everything around. Now I was in big trouble, and I was beat, too. I started leaving caches and cutting markers. First it was my pack, then the big chunks of gold, then my gun, and finally I was down to the last of my grub and a bag of gold dust and my canteen. Could hear the ravens croaking and kept heading west, but it was deep bush now and raining hard so I couldn't start a fire. Was getting close to dying of exposure. I almost gave up the ghost then and there, and d'you know what happened?"

Ted shook his head.

"I come out on the road! Highway 16, near Penny Station, an old logging camp. I'd been headed *east* the whole time. You know how many miles I'd covered? Well, I don't either, but a trucker picked me up and gave me a lift all the way to Prince George. I cashed in my dust and got a ticket south and never said a word to anyone about what happened for fifteen years, not 'til now. My buddy became one of those folks who disappear from the face of Mother Earth, and I almost joined him."

"So, why're you telling me?" asked Ted

"You bought me a drink, and like I said, you look like an educated man, sort of. How'd you feel about a business proposition?"

"What's that, then?"

"For a small finder's fee, I'll draw a map to my buddy's mine, starting from that cherry tree. What you do with it after that's up to you."

11.

Dorothy walked all the way back from the beach. It had taken hours of marching along the shore in boots unsuited for the trek. Well past three in the morning, she returned to the house, sneaking into her own home like a burglar. Though footsore and exhausted, she still couldn't sleep and spent the dark hours before dawn huddled in the locked sewing room, a carving knife from the kitchen beside her on the floor. *I shouldn't have fled the party*, she thought. *I should've slept over at Mary's house*. But when Dorothy had heard police sirens and seen the flashing lights, an irrational part of her brain feared the arrival of the detective with the yellow eyes.

Dorothy imagined Mary at this very moment and snorted. She was probably snoring in bed with a suntanned trust fund hunk and'd wake up with a wicked hangover and herpes. *Good*.

At seven-thirty Dorothy telephoned the RCMP and asked for Inspector Brian Kwok. He wasn't in. Now nearing collapse, Dorothy started awake from a half-dream when the phone rang. It was him. They spoke quickly and arranged to meet at noon, four hours from now.

Relieved, Dorothy managed to sleep for an hour, woke, showered, changed, and made a cup of coffee using her mother's recipe: two table-spoons of Folger's instant crystals added to hot water straight from the tap. On the way to Chinatown, bright light and fatigue left after-images on the insides of her eyelids as she blinked. Telephone poles and stop signs doubled, the red of a mailbox smeared across her vision. She put one foot in front of another, fighting exhaustion, and came to the doorway of the Chee Kung Tong building on Pender Street, headquarters of the Chinese Freemasons.

A querulous old man's voice asked Dorothy her business over the intercom. Brian Kwok's name prompted the glass door to click open. She climbed a flight of stairs lined with framed black-and-white group photographs of sober-looking men in somber suits. At the first floor, she went into the common room. Another old man, or perhaps the same one as on the intercom, shuffled past her wearing nothing but slippers, shorts, and a damp towel around his neck. A group of elders sat around a table smoking and playing cards. Flies boiled in the middle of the room, their flights weaving a complicated arabesque under an unmoving ceiling fan. On a far wall hung a large portrait of Dr Sun Yat-Sen next to a very young Queen Elizabeth II. Brian Kwok sat in the corner near an open window overlooking the street. Dorothy walked to his table and bowed. He smiled at her.

"Sit, please," he said in Cantonese.

"Thank you, Uncle."

Brian Kwok was no relation of Dorothy's by blood. He was her father's lodge brother and had been a constant, reassuring presence all her life, both unofficial godfather and honorary uncle. Dorothy was a rare creature in the Chinese community in that she had no living relatives in Vancouver. The usual vast network of interfering great aunts and shiftless cousins twice removed were all back in mainland China and Hong Kong, or so she'd been told. That meant that Brian Kwok was now, in a sense, her only remaining family. He was himself a childless widower. As a consequence, Uncle Brian had spoiled her outrageously every birthday, Christmas, and Lunar New Year's. Inspector Kwok was still a slim and handsome man at sixty, with a neat military moustache and distinguished touch of grey at his temples. He looked at Dorothy affectionately and poured out jasmine tea.

"You look tired," he said.

"I am. I can't sleep."

"Why?"

"The policemen."

Inspector Kwok folded his hands together, cast a calm gaze in the direction of the card players, and switched to English. He softly asked, "Who?"

Dorothy was relieved, and not only by the show of quiet concern. She understood the Cantonese of her parents well enough but spoke it poorly, save the occasional exclamation, pejorative, or insult.

"Two men from the Vancouver police," she said.

"Tell me everything. Omit nothing."

So she did, starting with renting the room to the young woman called Anna, or Irina, her disappearance, and the arrival of the two policemen at Dorothy's doorstep. She relayed to Uncle Brian the veiled threat in their parting words, then described the pair, especially the one with the smooth round face and yellow eyes.

"Yellow. Are you sure?" asked Kwok.

"Yes. Yellow like an animal's."

"I see."

"Do you know him?"

"I think I do."

"What should I do?"

Inspector Brian Kwok sighed. "It's my fault. I should have helped you more after your parents' death, should have been there for you."

"You were very good to me," Dorothy said. "Always."

"No, I wasn't. It's my job, you see. I've been away."

"Where?"

"Hong Kong."

Dorothy picked up her teacup and held it to her lips. Kwok studied her, tapping his fingers on the tabletop. She had the most curious sensation, a combination of *deja vu* and premonition. *He's going to tell me something important*, she felt. Kwok turned his head to the open window.

"Look there," he said.

Dorothy followed his gaze. In front of a bakery paced a fat man in a boiler suit, sweating in the heat, handing out flyers. With him was a skinny, spectacled creature holding a megaphone and hectoring pedestrians in Mandarin-accented Cantonese, screeching, "The revolution is not a dinner party!"

"Communists," said Kwok. "Still fighting the war. It never ends. Three thousand years we've been killing each other. Ch'in against Han, White Lotus against Mongol, Taiping against Manchu. We're supposed to obey heaven and follow the way, and all we do is cut each other up and swim in blood. How many millions? Kuomintang against Communist, 14K triad against, oh, some poor boy with acid thrown in his face. I'm tired of it. I'm sorry, Dorothy."

She put down her teacup. Kwok shook his head.

"I'm like you," he said. "I was born here. We should have left it all behind when we came to Canada, all the killing, all the lying. I thought I could stop it by joining the police. For a time I truly believed that I was helping to make a difference. Do you remember back then, coming to the barracks with me when you were a little girl?"

Dorothy did. The RCMP barracks were housed in a grand mock-Tudor pile that resembled a hunting lodge, way away at 33rd Avenue and Cambie. Kwok had shown her the stables, where beautiful service horses were kept, the forensic laboratory (like Madame Tussauds, with its eerie wax models of criminal faces), and most thrillingly, the firing range. Sworn to complete secrecy, never to tell her parents, Inspector Kwok had let Dorothy fire his revolver at a melon bought for the occasion. She'd drilled it through and through.

"My little Annie Oakley," he'd said, smiling at her.

When amused, Brian Kwok's eyes would disappear in meshes of mirth, laugh lines etched on his face like a fisherman's net, his bright smile flashing gold inlays. But right now Uncle Brian looked like he hadn't laughed in a long time, she thought. *He's getting old*, Dorothy realized with a sudden sadness. Kwok poured out more tea.

"This business with the two policemen, I'll look into it," he said. "But there is something else I want to talk to you about."

Here Dorothy allowed her premonition to speak. "Is it about my parents?"

"Yes," said Kwok.

Now he became uncharacteristically uneasy, fiddling and straightening his tie, avoiding her eyes.

"There are some things that I can tell you, and some I cannot, for your safety. But perhaps you'd better know, because I need to know some things that only *you* can tell me. Does that seem fair, niece?"

"It does," said Dorothy.

"Well then, you know about your father's business."

"The print shop, yes."

"That was not his only business. A man in his position is well placed to learn a great many things. A printer can be very useful to many people."

"What kind of people?"

"Honest people. Also, dishonest ones."

"Was he dishonest?"

"No," Kwok said. "Your father was a good man. But sometimes he had to do dishonest things."

"For you?" asked Dorothy.

"Yes, when I asked him to. In the name of the law. It's my job, you see."

"What kind of things?"

"Suppose a man comes who wishes to copy documents or certificates or government papers—he would go to your father. Your father would do the work and receive his fee, and also help me."

"The police."

"Yes."

"He was an informer," Dorothy said flatly.

An informer in any culture was worse than a dog. Judas Iscariot.

"No, not exactly," said Inspector Kwok.

He leaned closer. "Dorothy, your father loved you and your mother very much. He wanted to protect you. He may have *died* protecting you."

"But it was an accident," she said, shocked.

"Perhaps," said Inspector Kwok.

She was now alert, all tiredness gone. Dorothy heard the snap of playing cards as the old men continued their endless game, the cheap, ugly cawing of crows quarrelling and snatching spoiled fruit from beneath produce stalls down on the street, the irritating patter of the nasty loudhailer spouting the murderous wisdom of Chairman Mao.

"Perhaps not," Kwok said.

She felt cold again and rubbed her arms.

"I don't know for certain," he continued. "After they died or even before then, did you find anything unusual in their effects?"

Her mind flashed to the British and Chinese passports and the heavy revolver hidden in the basement. Should she tell him?

"I haven't looked at everything yet," she said, stalling. "There's so much. So much."

She felt tears prick at her eyes, looking at her uncle's kind, concerned face. He reached across and touched her hand. She shivered again and he got up, came across the table, and took her in his arms. She heard the card players stop their muttering and their game but didn't care if they were looking. Let them. For too long she'd been alone, an orphan in an empty house with no help from anyone. Dorothy allowed herself some pity and softly wept as Brian Kwok held her.

"It's all right," he said. "Come with me. Here, take this."

He handed her his monogrammed handkerchief, and Dorothy wiped her face with it, then burst into fresh tears. The handkerchief smelled of bay rum, of her father, of a lost past.

"I'm embarrassed," she said.

"Don't be. You're tired. I'll take you home."

Kwok's car was parked in the alley beside the society building, an RCMP card on the dashboard. Dorothy composed herself in the passenger seat with an act of will, drying her eyes, breathing calmly as they drove. In a few minutes they were back at her house. Kwok turned off the ignition.

"Go up and get some rest. I'll wait outside for some time and see if anyone comes to bother you. Before I leave I'll ring the bell three times to let you know. Keep the doors locked and stay close to the phone. I'll find out what these men want and come back to see you later, perhaps tonight, probably tomorrow."

"Thank you, Uncle Brian."

"Don't thank me, Dorothy. You're a very strong young woman. And you must do me a favour. Please try to remember if your father left you or sent you anything, anything at all. No matter how trivial. And remember our golden rule. Do you?"

"Yes," she said.

"What is it?" he asked.

"Never tell anything to anybody about anything."

"Good."

Kwok squeezed her hand as she left his car. She waved to him from the top of the steps and unlocked the door. Inside nothing had changed. Upstairs Dorothy took off most of her clothes, crawled into her makeshift bed, and allowed her mind to float away. She slept fast through the day, through Kwok's three rings on the doorbell. It was only when she awoke at quarter to midnight that Dorothy remembered the postcard. The one with a torn corner that her father had sent her from Hong Kong.

12.

. . . .

The hunter fucked her twice before the ice chilling the white wine melted to water. She'd cried out to the Teutonic god while climaxing. Now the woman lay sleeping on the unmade bed, her tanned skin caramel on the clean white sheets. Renard went to the room service cart, picked up his pistol, and drank neat schnapps. He turned for the toilet as the phone rang. The German opened her eyes and picked it up, then nodded and murmured something into the mouthpiece.

"You must leave now," she said to Renard. "My husband is coming."

"Thought you said he was getting drunk at a golf course."

"He is waiting for you to leave."

"*What?*" Renard stopped moving.

"Yes. He wants me while your scent is strong."

"What the fuck are you talking about?"

"The smell of another man upon me drives him wild. It is a game we play."

She smiled at him insolently. Renard felt disgusted. It explained her willingness and greed. He began to reach for the pistol in the waistband of his shorts. No. The hussy deserved a lesson, but not that. He had an idea and stared at her until she went rigid. She suddenly got up, and in her glorious nudity went past him into the bathroom. When she came back she said, "What are you doing?"

"He likes my smell? Then he'll love this."

Renard took out his cock and began to piss all over the bed. When he was done hosing down the quilt and sheets he turned to her and said, "Enjoy. You're next."

"*Schwein!*" yelled the *salope*. She slammed the bathroom door.

For good measure, Renard took the bottle of wine and flipped over the room service cart, then left the suite. Upstairs in his own room, the hunter washed and changed into a suit. He packed his valise and went downstairs to check out of the Bayshore Inn. From a payphone he called his employer's liaison.

"Renard here. I'm moving."

"Trouble?" purred Mallory.

"Precaution," he said.

"Do contact us when you're situated."

He hung up. It was a wise move no matter how you looked at it. Renard resolved to be more wary of womankind, her wiles, her husbands. He'd planned to move tomorrow anyway. The hotel was in the wrong part of town for his needs, too far from the house of Hickey, the patrolman. Renard walked to where he'd last left the Pontiac in a marina parking lot. There he exchanged licence plates again with a random vehicle. He drove away and turned left on Georgia, slicing east through the city's nucleus. Now the hunter was oriented again, motivated, angry.

While driving, Renard forbade himself from relishing the stolen afternoon of carnality. It was all tainted now. The radio pulsed Pat Benatar. Reflecting on similar episodes from the past, Renard added the German wife to his list of dangerous exotics. There had been a plump Lao in Vientiane who stole his wallet and false French passport, the Brazilian travel agent who had nearly scratched his eyes out with a potted cactus, the holidaying Frenchwoman on an island in the Aegean whom he'd stopped from diving off a balcony while high on LSD.

Closer to his heart were two Renard had had, wanted to keep, and lost. Samantha, his cool blonde from Terre Haute, a walk-off home-run he'd met at a New York warehouse party. And his southern firecracker, the horse trainer in Lexington, Kentucky. She'd been ridden hard and put away wet, as they said down in bluegrass country. The Kentucky girl had been a real problem. Where Renard was from, they'd have called her *bonne à rien*.

All of Renard's women had been lost because of the fundamental nature of his work and what it did to him as a man. Man conceals his basic nature from the fair sex as a matter of course; the added layers of secrecy and deception Renard employed to disguise himself aggravated relationships with women beyond what was sustainable. Hell, in most cases he was under a work name and false papers from the get-go. Never himself, whoever that was. Was he still the wide-eyed Louisiana shitkicker sent to the swamps of Indochine? Or the man with a stiletto waiting in a darkened room of Istanbul's Pera Palace Hotel? Neither, and both. Renard was a man who could not trust anyone. Nothing could grow from that poisoned seed, no friendship or true equality between man and woman. As he checked the reflection in the rear-view mirror, Renard saw only the lines of age and stress etched on his face, an invisible scar hidden beneath the first trace of grey in his beard. It was all hollow, when it came down to it. *Because of what I do to get by, I might just die alone.* The loneliness of the long-distance killer.

"*Le Juif errant,*" he said.

Hitting the viaduct, Renard accelerated to sixty m.p.h. but soon controlled his empty anger. He kept to the speed limit from then until he stopped near the foot of Victoria at Powell. Across the street, Renard checked into the Princeton. Here there was no cute young thing at the front desk but an egg-shaped *pédéraste* wearing a clip-on bowtie. It was a working man's hotel, not too squalid, catering to sailors and railwaymen sweating around the harbour. At the Princeton, cash stopped tongues from flapping. Renard booked the week ahead and paid an extra ten dollars for a room away from the street.

"Other side's over the tracks," said the clerk.

"How often do they run?"

"Not often. Only two or three times an hour."

Renard shook his head but didn't belabour the point. He was here for work, not comfort. Up on the third floor, he watched the trains awhile and smoked his pipe. The hunter set his alarm, lay on the hard bed, and thought of the German woman. He could still smell the chlorine in her damp hair, mixed with smoked salmon and schnapps, now the acrid scent of betrayal.

At quarter to ten, Renard dressed for the night. He brushed his teeth with bourbon, checked his weapons, took a Gideon's Bible from the bedside table, and left the hotel. Next door at the gas station, he washed down a Benzedrine tablet with a shitty cup of coffee, then lay in supplies for surveillance: a litre of Pepsi, a bag of beef jerky, a dubious ham and cheese sandwich. He took a spare paper cup to piss in. In front of Hickey's house on Wall Street, the police car he'd seen that morning was still parked. Renard stationed himself and checked his notes to confirm it was the same vehicle. He'd barely settled in before the front door opened and a uniformed Hickey shambled out, hitching the gunbelt under his belly.

The slow night began with Renard tailing the patrolman discreetly to the police headquarters on Main Street. At eleven-thirty, Hickey was back out with his marching orders. First stop was a grocery store. Renard received the impression that Hickey leaned on the proprietor because the cop came out of the door counting money with a wetted thumb. Hickey's patrol took him on a halting line east on Hastings for the next hour. The prowler stopped, and Hickey cautioned a drunk outside the Savoy at twelve-thirty. At one he radioed in. At one-thirty Renard was amazed to see the cop write a teen-aged longhair a ticket for jaywalking across the empty street. *What a prick.*

Nearing two the cop pulled over and appeared to nap. Three o'clock saw Hickey in a booth at Tom & Jerry's at Hastings and Renfrew where he kibitzed and chowed with a tall Mountie until three. Renard waited, ate his sandwich, checked his map. The diner was near Vancouver's border with Burnaby, and Renard assumed the meeting was nothing more than friendly fraternization with an opposite number. This presumption was confirmed when Constable Hickey continued to patrol north along Boundary Road, the eastern limit of his round. With traffic nonexistent, Renard stayed well back, and from time to time ghosted along, headlights off. Cops consider themselves the highest predator on the food chain, but Renard had already formed a very low opinion of Hickey. *This cop is a side of meat, mine when and where I want him*, he thought. *I'm hunting again, relaxing into the rhythm, following my prey, learning its squalid patterns and dirty secrets.*

Soon something was revealed. Hickey began to cruise the waterfront near the grain elevators beside the Second Narrows Bridge, making an unhurried progress back toward the city. Occasionally the patrolman would flash a spotlight from the passenger-side window into dark spaces between containers and piers. The exposed, empty road between freight tracks and harbour didn't provide enough cover for Renard to tail discreetly, so he drove parallel to the cop along Wall Street, unhappy to lose his quarry. According to the map, the two roads met up again. He gunned it west to Clark, crossed the tracks, and turned right on Commissioner to come at Hickey from the opposite direction. The Pontiac passed alongside shipyards and empty wharves before Renard sighted the patrol car. It was empty, engine running, idling next to a cold-storage building on a jetty. Hickey wasn't around. Renard parked in a shabby lot in the lee of a pickup truck. He slid out of the LeMans and crouched behind a row of oil drums. Reason told him that Hickey's only value was connected to this waterfront. This police beat. It fit with what Renard knew of the usual organization and his employer's interests. This was the job at hand. Find the product and the money.

Quietly, Renard stalked around a chain-link fence to the warehouse. He waited and moved, waited and moved, working himself to where he supposed the cop might be. An open service door let light fall out into the warm night. Voices echoed from within.

"A few more days, that's all," said one, high-pitched. Hickey, had to be.

With his Beretta now drawn, Renard carefully peered through the gap, meeting a gust of refrigerated air. Hickey was inside talking to a massive long-haired man. Renard typed him as Samoan. He had the same huge build, oversize arms, and superior indifference of the Polynesians that Renard had met in the service. The Samoan rumbled something indistinctly, a plume of cooled breath pouring from him in the dimly lit warehouse.

"A few days, that's all," repeated an angry Hickey.

The cop seemed to boil as he thought of something insulting to wing out. Renard watched the big man's reaction. Hickey opened his mouth and was about to speak again, but apparently took note of the Samoan's heavy displeasure. Renard smiled. Hickey closed his mouth, shrugged his shoulders, grimaced and turned toward the door. "You got no choice," he said, walking away.

Renard took cover around the corner while Hickey returned to his cruiser. The service door growled on its rollers as it was closed from within. He made a note of the building and went back to the LeMans. Hickey had already driven off but posed no problem to follow. Renard resumed his tail, headlights off. The patrol car stalled near a phone booth while Hickey made a call. *He doesn't use his radio*, thought Renard. *That's significant. That's a very telling goddamn gesture. And he's arguing with the man on the other end of the phone. Johnstone, no question of it.*

"He's the man I want to know," Renard said out loud to himself. "He's next."

The rest of the night passed deadly slow. Hickey berated a few vagrants sharing a bottle on a bus-stop bench. With the first stirrings of morning, the cop stopped again, this time for a Styrofoam cup of coffee at a greasy spoon on an industrial block across the street from a warehouse full of live chickens. As the heat of the day rose, Renard smelled hot fowl and ammoniate chicken shit. He rolled up the windows, lit his pipe, and cranked the AC. The diner had a board advertising cheap fried-egg sandwiches.

White-smocked employees from the chicken house crossed the street for an early breakfast. Renard's stomach turned. He washed down another pill with the last of his Pepsi. Hickey's shift would end soon.

Before full daylight, Renard was dismayed to see the cop pick up a sketchy hooker working the early-morning roughneck crowd. There followed a five-minute blowjob in an alley (Renard timed it). The hunter was now thoroughly disgusted by the cop. *A wife and kid at home, and the fucker was getting skull off some junkie.*

Out of the corner of his eye and a block to the right, Renard spied the Princeton. He checked his watch. Six-thirty. He decided to skip Hickey's return to the police station. *What I'll do is hit the hotel for a quick piss and spritz, then finish the stake-out at Hickey's house. Need to take a breath. After watching this pig work, it's going to be a pleasure to make him squeal.*

Renard waited as Hickey returned home. The patrolman was still in uniform, now driving a Chrysler sedan. His wife came out with the little pigtailed girl in tow, both dressed for the day. She kissed Hickey as he lifted the child and tossed her around. The tender family display did nothing for Renard's mood. Jagged edges of caffeine, bennies, and irritation scraped away behind his eye sockets. He found himself ready for violence.

When the wife took the car keys and buckled the moppet in the backseat, Renard knew it was near time. Hickey stood on the doorstep and waved at the little girl as the missus drove away. *This is what I'm paid for,* the hunter thought. *Initiative. Not elegant rococo stratagems. Direct simplicity.* He checked the magazine of the Beretta and straightened his necktie. The neighbourhood in early morning rested peacefully. A milk truck drove by. A nice-looking woman with big breasts pushed a stroller. Someone started up a lawnmower. Renard put on gloves, picked up the Gideon Bible, locked the Pontiac, and walked to Hickey's front door. He rang the doorbell insistently, really leaning into it, holding the Bible in front of his chest with his left hand, the gun beneath it in his right. Behind the door he heard Hickey bitching, "All right, all right, Jesus fucking Christ."

Close enough, thought Renard. The door opened, revealing Hickey barefoot in undershirt and uniform pants, a sulky look on his face. Renard smiled in return. Hickey squeaked out, "Well, what the fuck do you want?"

"Sinner, have you heard the Good News?"

13.

Ted woke from a dream of ironing the carpet on his hands and knees. He was in a sorry state. Sometime yesterday he'd smoked a cigar. A cheap one, by the taste in his mouth. With extreme unwillingness Ted gradually opened his eyes and began a tender examination of his body. No clothes were torn or bones broken. He found the reeking remains of a Cherry PomPom Opera crushed in his shirt pocket. The revolting smell spurred him to rise and throw wide the drapes of Room 34. For a moment, Ted was at a loss. What time was it? Then he noticed the fall of shadows. It was close to sunset.

"Vampire," he said.

Ted opened the window and tossed the butt. A pigeon dropped down to peck at the charred tobacco. Heat radiated from the tarred roof of the hotel. Rusty barbed wire tangled around a fire escape ladder. A police siren reverberated along Pender Street. Ted breathed what fresh air he could summon and began to assess the damage.

He conducted an inventory. Seven dollars and fifty cents in change remained in his pockets, along with the key to the room, a pencil stub, a few paper salt packets. That's what'd killed him. Salt in your beer provides an effervescence and touch of savour to the usual flat swill pulled from the taps. It also helps sterilize whatever they poured in the low pubs down on Hastings Street. In tandem with alcohol, salt also crenellates your brain cells faster, gets you drunker quicker, and provides a worse kind of hangover. From the sink faucet Ted sucked up warm water, swallowed a Japanese aspirin, and tried to remember.

He hadn't lasted long. Five pints of Blue at the Empress's beer parlour had set Ted reeling through Skid Row. After that he had an indistinct memory of stopping at an even worse dive: The West. There he'd knocked back a couple more with Howard Hughes. The god who watched over drunks and fools seemed to have protected Ted the rest of the way back to the hotel, where he'd passed out and slept until now.

"I'm not a pheasant plucker, I'm a pheasant plucker's son, and I'll sit here plucking pheasants 'til the pleasant fucking's done. Shit."

Ted removed his wrinkled clothing and went for a long lukewarm shower. While dressing the telephone rang, rattling him. Who could it be? His mind conjured possibilities, few welcome. The police? His mother? Irina? *Who knows I'm here? No one. It's probably Olaffson downstairs. Needs me to work tonight. He'll keep calling if I don't answer. Pick up the receiver.*

"Ted?"

A woman's voice. His heartbeat quickened. "That's right."

"You don't know who this is, do you?"

"Let me guess."

"Bet you can't." The caller chuckled throatily. That did it. Ted knew.

"Pauline," he said.

"Bingo bango bongo, baby's going to the Congo."

"How are you? How'd you find me?"

"Wowzer. You don't remember a thing, do you? Where were you yesterday?"

He put a hand to his head. What had happened between the beer parlour and the hotel?

Pauline carried on. "They said you stopped by the gallery. Said you were high as a kite. You left me a message and this number. Boy-o-boy, you sure know how to proposition a lady."

The gallery. The fucking art gallery. His intestines squirmed. The gallery Irina worked at, the one in Gastown. He must have blundered in and made a scene. Pauline laughed in his ear.

"No one sees you for a year and you come thundering back like Marlon Brando. You beast. They hate you now."

"They always did. What's going on? Where are you?" he asked.

"I'm at home. But I hear you're looking for Irina. The girl at the gallery say she's gone, hasn't shown up for work in couple of weeks, and they called the police. Is that true?"

"Looks like it. I haven't seen her."

"When'd you get back?"

"A few days ago. I think I'm still jetlagged."

"And hungover, I'll bet. Well, you can tell me all about it later."

"Tonight?"

"You're coming with me to an opening," said Pauline.

"An opening? Pass."

"Attendance is not optional."

"Well then, if you say so, I reckon I am, then."

"Darn tootin.' What's this place you're staying at?"

"Hotel downtown."

"Never mind all that. Meet me at the Bodega, eightish. We'll have a bite and catch up."

"You say jump, I ask how high."

"To the moon, you beast. 'Bye."

Cradling the phone, Ted felt a strange relief. Pauline Campbell, that rarest of creatures, a female friend. Ted had mailed her postcards from Hiroshima and Nagasaki but hadn't seen her since before his own personal nuclear disaster. He allowed himself to think. *How long do I plan to stay hidden here at the Victoria Hotel? At some point I'll have to return to something resembling my former way of life. Seeing Pauline would melt a little of the ice around my heart.*

Ted put on his seersucker jacket, tied his shoelaces, and went back out into the world.

The Bodega was a red-and-white checkered tablecloth kind of hangout for artists and musicians, or those who pretend to be. Sitting at the bar, Ted heard loud laughter rising to the main room from the basement. He'd gone down there to peer through a blue haze of affected imported cigarette smoke and had recognized a clutch of conceptualists recontextualizing a serviette dispenser, and some New Wavers sword fighting with breadsticks. Members of the band UJERK5 (the 5 was silent) split a pitcher and a large Hawaiian while arguing the merits of "Echo Beach" by Martha and the Muffins. Downstairs the Bodega's menu specialized in cheap pizza, beer, and sangria for the indigent art crowd. Ted classified himself in that category, but planned to play a different part tonight. In the afternoon, he'd made the pleasant discovery that his savings account at the Bank of Montreal held more than he remembered, nearly $200. He'd withdrawn a pink fifty dollar bill. *Tonight I'll splurge*, he thought. *Death or glory.*

At twenty past the hour, the door opened and Pauline wheeled in. She scanned the room and gave a yelp on seeing Ted. He walked over. She pulled him down for a strong kiss.

"You animal," she said. "Let me eat you up."

"Dinner first. I'm famished."

"Not nearly as much as I."

She wouldn't let him push her to the table and swatted away an officious waiter.

"Food and strong drink," she commanded. "That Spanish wine, what's it called—Rioja. And meat. I'm carnivorous. Give me rabbit's hearts. I want to feast on their essence."

"And for *signor?*" asked the waiter.

"Just the wine, for now. And I'll have the *criadillas.*"

Pauline grinned wickedly. "How masculine and potent," she said. "Homoerotic. Eating balls. Did the fabled Orient change you that much?"

"Just a little, when I'm not writing haikus or contemplating the moon. What about you? Still terrorizing the Vancouver art scene?"

"On my better days. But I've been away a lot. I was a month down in L.A."

"Painting?"

"Among other diversions. You know, typical Hollywood decadence. Steamy threesomes with Warren Beatty and Jack Nicholson in the swimming pool."

"Not the hot tub?"

"It was being serviced."

When the wine came, the pair toasted and drank fully, in a single toss. Ted refilled Pauline's glass and admired her looks. She had her thick, tawny hair done up in a ponytail. Mysteriously, amid the gold of her hair was a streak of sable-white that ran up and away from Pauline's left temple. Earrings, bracelet, and necklace were silver and turquoise Navajo jewellery that matched her eyes. She wore a black suit jacket and dark jeans, no makeup. Pauline's wheelchair seemed customized, like something designed by Philippe Starck, very chic, very *soigné*. She'd been the inevitable statistic of her high school senior class, the girl who got in a sports car with a drunk jock on grad night. He'd suffered death-by-windshield (with a tree an accessory after the fact), and she'd ended up paraplegic. Afterward, Pauline claimed that the healthy insurance settlement had saved her from a baleful fate: motherhood in the suburbs, voting membership at the country club, PTA bake sales, and a Valium addiction. Destiny led Pauline to art school instead. Ted remembered their first meeting, at a throwaway bohemian party, and their immediate kinship. Some people were just like that, they added to you. Irina was not one of them. She took.

"I want everything," said Pauline. "Tell me all."

Over their meal he revealed what he'd felt about Japan, his return, the hotel, the cops, and a few words about Irina. Pauline snorted.

"Still muddying pools and poisoning wells. I wonder what trouble she's in."

"It's anyone's guess. It seemed like more than a simple missing person case. She'd been picked up before."

"For what? Plotting treason?"

"Prostitution."

Pauline pursed her lips a moment, squeezed her eyes shut, lost the battle, and exploded with a bark of laughter that turned heads. Ted joined in.

"Priceless," she gasped. "Her true *métier*."

"I know, right? I should have listened to you."

"You should have married *me*, you beautiful fool."

They finished supper and had a civilized Calvados after. Pauline refused to let him pay. "My invitation, my shout," she said. "Besides, the night's not over yet, not by a long chalk."

They drove to the opening in Pauline's black El Camino, specially converted with hand controls. She steered them over the Granville Bridge, east alongside the Fairview Slopes into an unfashionable low-rise district of dull buildings between Cambie and Main. On 5th Ted noticed wholesale electronics vendors, plumbing supply depots, something called the Human Garment Company, industrial drycleaners, emptiness. Block after block sat dark in the summer night. He saw the gallery ahead. It had commandeered an anonymous storefront and was the only knot of light and noise around.

"What is this?" he asked.

"A group show. Are you really looking for her?"

"Kind of. Why? Is she here?"

"I doubt it. But someone else is."

"Who?"

Pauline said nothing as she concentrated on parallel-parking and wouldn't be drawn as he pushed her across the street. The show was already packed with various trendy types holding plastic wineglasses, smoking Gitanes, flirting, posing. Pauline's wheelchair cleaved a way through the crowd. The wide space was painted flat-white from floor to ceiling. In a corner a hi-fi played creepy selections from Bauhaus. Another corner had a busy bar next to a table selling drink tickets. Ted took in a few installations. There was a paint-spattered mannequin with a television for a head, the screen tuned to static. On a wall hung a red, white, and blue lithograph of Ronald Reagan as Herman Munster. Heaped in a corner smashed plates and crockery mixed with ripped packets of Kraft Dinner, bright orange synthetic cheese powder spilled throughout. Ted groaned.

"All that's missing is a shopping cart full of doll parts," he said.

"Or something painted with a tampon in menstrual blood."

"Why're we here?" asked Ted.

"Go get a catalogue and meet me at the bar."

She wheeled herself away. Ted found a Xeroxed copy, listing the artists and their mission statements. The show was called *The Anatomization of Heterogeneous Registers*. He met Pauline and read her part of the curator's manifesto:

"The idea of representing (or not representing) a kind of external manifestation of an interior experience is the crux of the artistic trialogue. Representation of this symbolic conclusion both in time and with time is an attempt to connect the possibility of real time into relationship with form, and this form into relationship with historical formats and memory formations. Fucking hell. The interstices between memory and fucking loss."

"Really makes you think," said Pauline said. "Here, drink this." She gave him a rough cheap red to swallow, and he bought tickets for three more. Ted started to get pissed off.

"The same old shit," he said. "How do you stand it?"

"I don't," laughed Pauline, gesturing at her chair.

"What a clusterfuck. Everyone looking over each other's shoulder, looking for someone better to be seen with."

A supercilious dandy with a striped cane and candy-coloured suit bumped into Ted. Ted bumped back, hard. Pauline grinned. "Watching you's better than anything hanging on a wall," she said. "How badly do you want to find her?"

"Not very. I might be able contact her through her father. Last I heard he had a fellowship in South Carolina, Texas, one of those redneck colleges down there. I wouldn't know where to start."

"Look at the cast of characters in the catalogue," suggested Pauline.

He flipped through it. Each artist had a short biography and list of relevant works. Near the end he saw a name and froze solid.

"Nordhaal Velkdor," he hissed.

"Just over there," pointed Pauline.

This was one of the men Irina had ended up with after leaving him. Maybe the last one. Did this bastard know where she was and why the cops were after her? Suddenly, Ted didn't give a shit. He looked at Velkdor in the middle of his huddle of admirers. The fucker always managed to draw flunkies, despite being the living definition of a pretentious bore. For years Ted had wondered at this bizarre power. *Weak minds allow themselves to become enthralled to confident authority*, he thought. It explained a lot, but not what Irina had seen in the cunt. Velkdor wore an old-fashioned three-piece suit and bowler hat, looking like a cross between a travelling knife grinder and cut-rate rabbi. Ted saw his pale skin, his long face, his flat hands making cheap, antic gestures.

"You knew he'd be here?" he asked Pauline.

"I thought that if you're looking for her, start with him," she said.

Ted went to the bar and traded tickets for two more wines. Pauline wheeled over and extended her hand for a drink. Ted slugged one back, then another, and handed her the empty plastic cups.

"Gee, thanks a lot," she said.

He wiped his mouth with the back of his hand and marched over to the group. They listened raptly as Velkdor spouted words, pointing at his work. It was a mosaic of animal bones overlaid on red-tinted photos from Nazi rallies. Ted stood at the fringe of the clique and heard:

"What I'm trying to do is to juxtapose the eternal and the horrible. To rationalize the irrationality of this century's dichotomy. What I'm doing is—"

"What you're doing is a crock of shit," said Ted.

The face of Nordhaal Velkdor rotated Ted's direction. *My blood's absolutely boiling*, Ted thought. A pretty, stylish girl looked his way with contempt. An elegant vampiress curled her lip. Two pairs of matching, fluttery queens in bright Qiana shirts stiffened and put on pre-fabricated sneers.

"Well, well," smiled Velkdor. "Looking for your wife?"

"She's right there."

Ted pointed over Velkdor's shoulder.

Velkdor turned around. With a good wind up, Ted kicked the motherfucker good and hard right up the ass with the toe of his boot.

14.

"Why'd you take off like that? I thought you were going to stay at my place."

"You know how it is. I wasn't having any fun. And I don't like police."

Mary Worthington blew a raspberry. She sat in the sunshine wearing sunglasses, drinking her third piña colada. Dorothy had a Shirley Temple, a childish indulgence.

"Oscar Meyer baloney," said Mary. "I know you. Goody two shoes. You missed out."

"On what? The cops arresting a bunch of drunk rich boys?"

"Better. They caught Phoebe Redden in the conservatory getting gonged by the Ramsey twins."

"Gross. Sounds like the worst game of Clue ever."

Mary screeched. Dorothy waited for her friend to catch her breath. They were at an outdoor table facing west toward the Granville Bridge, overlooking bare-masted sailboats tied up to a half-finished wharf. Dorothy drank in the warm sunlight and felt her batteries charging. A light wind gusted over False Creek and snapped a colourful regiment of flags to life. It was refreshing to sit in the breeze, picking at a Caesar salad, listening to Mary's gossip and barbs. Dorothy felt fully human again.

"What about you?" she asked Mary. "Who'd you go home with?"

"Barry Munro. It was horrible."

"Why?"

"He had the littlest whiskey dick in all of BC. I'd almost feel sorry for him if he wasn't such a jerk. He actually wanted me to make him breakfast in bed."

"Did you?"

"I threw him a Pop Tart and told him to piss off."

"Ah, the elegant life of the idle rich," said Dorothy.

"We're a classy bunch of fuckers," said Mary.

"So now what?" asked Dorothy.

"Well, first, we've got to find you a man. How about him?"

Mary pointed to a pipe-smoking, white-haired gent in a crested blue blazer who walked a dog along the seawall promenade.

"Too old?" asked Mary. "Okay then, check out the young hunk."

This time she gestured at a baby in a perambulator. Dorothy laughed.

"Oh, I get it," said Mary. "Geez, you're pretty picky for a spinster."

"What about him?" asked Dorothy.

Mary looked over to a punk rocker with a mohawk haircut playing with a yo-yo.

"That one's mine. I want his baby," said Mary.

"I'll be the godmother. I'll get a safety-pin through my lip."

They both laughed some more. Mary finished her drink and signalled for the bill.

"But seriously, what're you looking for?" she asked.

"I'm not looking at all."

"Right. You change your mind, and I'll call up the Ramsey twins for you. You can be the smooth-flowing caramel inside the Caramilk bar."

They drove over the Cambie Bridge in Mary's ruby Mustang, its top down. Dorothy felt a delectable sensation, as though they were playing hooky from school. Confidence had returned with Brian Kwok's assurances; knowing the RCMP inspector was protecting her allowed Dorothy to breathe again. Today, even the city looked inviting. Once a logging boomtown with a railyard dressed in humble brick, it was a rough gem, set within a beautifully carved band of sea and mountains. When Vancouver appeared this way, without pretension, without attempting to ape San Francisco, Hong Kong, or Sydney, she enjoyed it for what it was. They headed for the city's apogee: the Hotel Vancouver, a heavy bastion of granite respectability, topped by a green-coppered chalet roof. Mary pulled up to the revolving door, tossed her keys at a valet, and soon the two friends were at loose downtown.

First stop was the Holt-Renfrew in the Pacific Centre Mall. Mary had a shopping list of requests.

"Mrs Blenkinsop saw a red size-four Christian Lacroix here last week."

"Four?"

"So she says. Better go with a six. I'll replace the tag in the shop. Unless you could do both?"

"One at a time is the rule," said Dorothy.

"Your mother's or yours?"

"Both. Think of it like poaching game. A deer here, a pheasant there. If I come in and start emptying the place out they'll tighten security too much."

"You're the boss."

"Call me *tai-pan*."

"Yes, honourable one." Mary bowed, hands together like Confucius.

They found the dress and Dorothy smoothly examined it. As always, she was astonished by the prices couture labels charged for ready-to-wear.

"It's all perception," she said to Mary. "The name on the label. Most of the time you can get the same tailoring, or even better, for far less."

"I know," said Mary. "Sometimes I wonder if we should just find some slavey with a sewing machine and start running up our own knock-offs."

With a slow eye Dorothy surveyed the store's layout. She'd been through Holt's a few months back and little had changed. That didn't mean she could afford to get complacent. *There's always chance*, she thought. *Be quiet, be quick, be careful.*

"I'll be back tomorrow for it," she told Mary. "Now what?"

"The next order's a challenge."

They left the store and walked down Howe to Edward Chapman for Women.

"How about it?" asked Mary.

"No," said Dorothy. "It's too small. At best it'd take two people to do it, and you'd be burned forever. Not worth it."

"Thought so. Okay, next batter," said Mary.

As they entered the Marks and Spencer on Granville Street Dorothy laughed. "Why?" she asked. "What's the point? They might as well pay full price. There's nothing in here worth stealing."

"I know. But you have to understand the psychology of these rich old bitches. First of all, a lot of them only have an allowance from their husbands, so they have to cheat when they can. Secondly, rich folks are as a rule cheaper than Scotch Chink Jews. That's how they got rich in the first place."

"And third?"

"I forget. Come and take a look."

The store was a monument to Britain, transplanted wholesale to the Empire's western coast. For the most part its clientele consisted of retirees in broadcloth. Kippers and shortbread were in stock alongside jars of Marmite and weeks-old copies of the *News of the World*. Dorothy was amused to hear a middle-aged East Indian couple speaking to one another in clear Oxbridge accents as they selected marmalade and biscuits. It reminded her suddenly of her mother, a woman who'd wholeheartedly adopted English ways at an Anglican boarding school in Hong Kong. Dorothy wondered at the mindset. In the house on Union Street no chinoiserie was permitted, no ancestor scrolls or portraits, neither black lacquer dragons nor jade carvings. All was proper, severe, ruthlessly Occidental. Except for her father's shrine in the basement. He'd held on to the past and buried it away from his wife's judgment. For the 888th time Dorothy wondered who her father truly was. Three passports, a broken coin, a gun, and a torn postcard from Hong Kong. She'd give Uncle Brian the card when he came over. That and a Rogers' chocolate.

"Well?" asked Mary.

She gestured at a herringbone Harris tweed skirt and jacket. Dorothy examined it critically. "Really?"

"I love corrupting my betters," said Mary. "It's worth a hundred to us, and'll be good advertising. The buyer'll flaunt it to her chums at the Hycroft Women's Club and soon I'll be turning them away. You'll have to hire an assistant."

"I'll do it right now. Wait for me across the street."

"You're the best, gorgeous," said Mary. She made kissy lips and went out to the sidewalk.

The theft was simplicity itself. For the bonus round, Dorothy pocketed the chocolate and picked up the suit. She lingered a moment near the door. A small, wrinkled, pixie-ish duffer struggled with his two-wheeled shopping cart.

"Please allow me to help you," said Dorothy.

"Would you, sweetheart?" asked the little man.

Dorothy folded the suit over her forearm and backed the cart out the door, keeping her eye on the harried tellers. Her pulse never changed. The cart wheeled smoothly onto the pavement, and she returned it to the gnome.

"Why thank you, dearie," he said, winking at her.

He then gave Dorothy a surprisingly deft pinch on the bum. Dorothy was too astonished to move. The little man grinned, followed the pinch with a wolf whistle, and shuffled away. She caught Mary's eye in a group waiting for a bus and motioned up the street. Mary nodded her head, smiling. They met at the corner and walked to Georgia. Mary put the stolen clothes in a bag.

"That saucy imp," she said. "Old enough to be your grandfather. And you—amazing. Nerves of stainless steel."

"Too easy," said Dorothy. "It's lunchtime. The guards spell off and leave the store to the tellers, but the place is full of people on their break from the offices around here. Too much for them to deal with. It's simply a matter of timing."

"And picking your unwitting accomplice. Well, he managed to get a piece of the action. A piece of your ass."

They continued to walk. Mary asked Dorothy, "Do you ever think of branching out? Jewellery? Or money?"

"No, I specialize. It's safer."

"And here I was calling you a goody two shoes. You're a bad girl. If I was lez I'd be all over you."

"You can dream," said Dorothy.

Dorothy declined a drink in the Timber Club of the Hotel Vancouver as well as a ride home. Mary kissed her on both cheeks and held her hands before they parted.

"You may not believe it, but you're trouble, Dorothy Kwan."

"And you would know."

As she drove away, Mary threw Dorothy another kiss. Dorothy crossed the street to the square behind the old courthouse, soon to open again as the new city art gallery. Mary was right. She needed someone in her life, a certain type of trouble and strife to match her own. The impression of the kiss on Dorothy's cheek burned lightly. Simple human contact had become an odd thrill. Touch, the smell of lipstick, the warmth of skin. Dorothy sat by the fountain. From the water rose a jagged piece of rock, a sword carved into its face. *Excalibur*, Dorothy thought. The male principle guarded by the Lady of the Lake. She felt a stirring of warmth combined with a delicious chill. From the Georgia Medical Dental Building the statues of the three nurses looked down. Vancouverites called them the Rhea sisters: Gona, Dia, and Pyo. A lovely old woman in a floppy hat came into view. She pushed a modified shopping cart carrying a goose perched on a piece of green turf. The goose wore a knitted blue sweater and a smaller version of the same floppy straw hat.

"Would you like to have your fortune read, young miss?" asked the lady. Dorothy smiled.

"Then you must make a donation to Charley."

Looking more closely, Dorothy saw a tobacco tin set into the turf and a double ring of printed cards around the goose.

"Charley is an angel sent from heaven here to assist all the lords and ladies of the earth. He came to me first in a dream and told me to help mankind. Your donation will go to a lottery for poor people who wait in line at soup kitchens."

The woman spoke in a bright, cheerful, young voice. Dorothy noted her costume jewellery, her brightly patterned skirt, the smeared rouge on her cheeks and glittering, slightly manic eyes.

"I have been blessed and given a gift. Charley is an angel sent from heaven and is the only goose in the world who can cry real tears. Are you lonely, young lady?"

The question caught Dorothy. Involuntarily, she nodded. The woman reached out her heavily beringed hands.

"I was also given a gift. My childhood was a lonely, painful one. Take my hands."

Dorothy reached out. The woman's hands were soft and strong.

"Look into my eyes."

Dorothy did and felt an electric charge run through her. The woman smiled.

"You poor thing. So much sadness. But don't worry. You're not alone. Do you see it?"

For a fleeting moment Dorothy had a vision, white wings circling over a blue sea. A warmth spread through her.

"Yes," she said.

"When I was young, God came down and spoke to me. It was the most wonderful thing, like being wrapped in a towel warmed by the fire. Do you feel it?"

"Yes," Dorothy said, surprised.

"Good. Now don't you worry any more."

The woman squeezed her hands again and let go. Dorothy now heard the water playing in the fountain and cars honking, and smelled sweet marijuana smoke wafting from a group of teenagers on the courthouse steps. She looked at the goose lady again.

"There you are. How do you feel, Dorothy?"

"Much better, thank you." Dorothy reached into her purse and took five dollars from her wallet. She put the bill in the tobacco tin.

"Choose a fortune, Charley," said the woman, as she clapped her hands.

"Honk!" Charley said.

The goose waddled a semi-circle and picked at a square of paper. The lady plucked it from his orange beak and handed it over to Dorothy, then smiled again.

"Close your eyes, hold it in both your hands, and count to thirty-one. Charley has blessed you. Thank you and praise be."

Dorothy did as instructed. When she opened her eyes, the woman was gone from the square. Seagulls dove and squabbled over fries in a McDonald's bag. Suddenly Dorothy felt a strange awe.

"She knew my name was Dorothy."

She stood up and looked around for the lady and the goose. Vanished. *That's pretty spooky*, she thought. *How did she know my name? And that feeling when I held her hands. A goose sent from heaven, wearing a blue sweater. It's too, too weird.* Dorothy shook her head and opened the fortune. She read, written in green ink:

It's all up to you.

15.

. . . .

"Buzz off. I don't need any god-botherers this morning," said Hickey.

"But I bring good news. I have the key."

"What key?"

The hunter looked quickly over his shoulder, saw that the street was empty, and pulled the Beretta from behind the Bible.

"The key to eternal life, you piece of shit."

"Whoa, hey," said Hickey, raising his hands, his high voice rising an octave. "What the fuck're you doing?"

"Back up nice and slow."

"I'm a cop."

"Back up."

"Okay, take it easy."

Hickey stepped backwards.

"Slow," said Renard.

"You got the wrong guy. You hear me? I'm a cop."

Renard stepped into the house and kicked the door closed. He dropped the Bible.

"You're making a mistake," said Hickey.

"We'll see."

"Jesus, you're crazy."

They stood in the living room on a shag carpet. The television showed a kid's program, a man with a flute talking to a purple giraffe and a rooster in a bag. Renard saw Hickey's gunbelt hanging over a chair. Hickey wasn't frightened yet. That'd change.

"Stand still. Make a move and I'll blow your balls off."

Hickey went white.

"Okay, okay. Take it easy."

Renard moved to the chair holding the gunbelt. He unclipped the handcuffs and threw them to Hickey, who caught them reflexively.

"Sit down."

Hickey obeyed, his eyes darting at the gunbelt, looking for some opening. Renard smiled and unholstered Hickey's service revolver. He pointed both weapons and said, "You've got a choice. I shoot you now for your wife and daughter to find. Or I wait and kill them in front of you when they get back."

Hickey gulped. Renard had him trembling now. *Good.*

"Cuff your right wrist. Put it behind you and cuff the left through the chair slats."

Shakily, his hands heavy and clumsy, Hickey complied.

Renard circled to check the job. He put the revolver on the dining room table and yanked the chain, then tightened the cuffs.

"Nice try," he said to Hickey.

"What do you want?"

"We'll get to that. When do they get back?"

"Who?"

"Your wife and kid."

"They're gone for the day."

"You better hope so."

Renard made a circuit of the house. He turned off the television, closed the Venetian blinds, locked the front door. The two bedrooms were empty, same as the kitchen. It was a small house, furnished straight out of Sears-Roebuck. Renard saw no evidence of affluence. If Hickey had any money it didn't show. He returned to the living room.

"Listen," said Hickey, "I don't know what you want, but whatever it is, you can have it."

Renard picked up the revolver again and emptied the cylinder. Hickey babbled.

"Anything. Anything you want. Money. Drugs."

"I want $300,000 and a shipment of cocaine."

"Oh, shit."

It took a little while. Renard sat down and waited. Hickey clamped his mouth shut. He shook his head and squeezed his eyes closed, fighting himself. At last he squeaked, "I can't."

"You can. You will."

Renard watched the cop sweat. It was always instructive to see a man against a wall. There were ones who cried and pleaded, others who summoned an inner nobility. Renard wondered how he himself might fare. During his youthful training he'd undergone several serious mock interrogations, but the inner knowledge that it was all just an exercise had prevented any ultimate break. Here, out in the real world, the mean game was played for keeps. Renard had never been caught and so didn't know, *yet*. Still, it was interesting to think about, but maybe at another time.

"Tell me," he said to Hickey.

The cop opened his eyes. "I don't think you'll do it. I'm a cop. If you kill me, the heat'll come down so hard you'll get nothing."

"Because of your partner? He's next, Hickey. I'm giving you a chance right fucking now."

"No."

Renard was almost impressed. Hickey straightened in his chair and raised his chin. Renard sighed. He rose, shook his head in disappointment, and went into the kitchen. There he rooted through the cupboards and found what he was looking for in the fridge.

"I've always wanted to try this," he said.

The hunter walked toward Hickey and the patrolman winced, preparing for a blow. Renard hooked the toe of his cowboy boot under the chair and sent Hickey backwards. The cop screamed as his full weight crushed his handcuffed wrists. Renard stood back while Hickey moaned and cried.

"That's a start," Renard said. "Now, look at this."

Hickey opened his eyes. Renard held a bottle of Tabasco sauce. He quickly dropped and put the weight of one knee on the cop's chest.

"Tell me what happened," he said.

"I can't," said Hickey.

"See this stuff? The pride of Louisiana," said Renard, shaking the small red bottle. He slammed his palm onto Hickey's sweating forehead. With his finger and thumb he pried apart a closed eyelid.

"Watch the birdie," he told Hickey.

The cop tried to buck and squirm but Renard put the full dead weight of his body on Hickey's chest. He tilted the bottle of sauce. "This might sting *un petit peu.*"

A drop of Tabasco hit Hickey's eyeball. His whole body bucked. Renard hopped up.

"Tell me," he shouted.

Nope. Not yet. Hickey held out. It took splashes of hot sauce on both open eyes, up both nostrils, and in one ear before the cop cracked. Renard had to give the fucker some credit. Tears and mucus streamed from the pig's face. Hickey's eyelids were swollen shut, face a lobster red, his breathing fierce and laboured. In the kitchen Renard filled a plastic jug with water. He emptied it on Hickey's head. The cop slobbered and moaned. Renard sat down and pieced together the story.

It was the woman, the party girl Mallory had told Renard about.

"She double-crossed us," said Hickey.

"How? Begin the beguine."

Back in the spring Detective Johnstone of the narcotics detail began working the Hummingbird Cabaret, a storied strip club downtown, long notorious for vice. The woman had been tricking there, offering neck massages at the table and penis massages in the back.

"Name?"

"She was calling herself Tasha then. Real name's Irina something. She also goes by Anna. We found out later she's married to some civilian."

"Is he in the picture?"

"Don't think so. He was out of the country until a little while back. Works at a flophouse downtown."

Renard studied Hickey. The man was a mess and looked as though he'd been stung by a nest of wasps. *I wonder what would happen if I made him drink the whole bottle?* thought Renard. *Would the shock of the Tabasco kill him, burn him up from the inside out? Might answer my own question if Hickey stops co-operating. So far, he's doing nicely.* Renard put the bottle on the table next to the service revolver.

"Go on," he said.

Hickey searched his memory and continued his tale. Johnstone had discovered that most of the wholesale cocaine sold in Vancouver was being pushed through the strip club. He'd suborned the woman on a solicitation charge and made her an informer. Hickey'd been brought in when Johnstone made a connection between the club and the docks.

"Why you?"

"We go back, and I wanted the dough. Look at this shithole. My kid needs braces."

"And Johnstone? What does he want?"

"He wants control."

Vancouver's heroin came via the Orientals, Chinese running it from Burma. Pills, dust, and speed were brought up by Americans who also trucked in marijuana from Mexico. Hippies made acid, grew lousy local pot, and sold mushrooms. Cocaine was monopolized by the Hummingbird Cabaret, an Italian club, a tiny West Coast cell of bent guys.

"Mafia?"

"No. We're too far away, small-time. These guys are bit players. That's why Johnstone thought we could take them. We were going to become like the main event."

"Until you blew it. What happened?"

"The girl. Johnstone started throwing it into her. He got her out of the club. She was smart. She put together the system, how the coke was coming in. When it was time for the wops to get a shipment, Johnstone and me busted them up good."

"Then what?"

"Then we offered our service. We promised security and distribution. We made the connect to the money man here. It was fine, the first couple of times. Until she fucked us over."

"How do I find her?"

"Jesus. If I knew that I wouldn't be here."

Renard yawned. He stuffed and lit a pipe, discarding the match in an empty 7Up can.

"What're you going to do to me?" asked Hickey.

"Give me everything I want, and I'll let you live."

For the next ten minutes, Renard wrote down in his notebook a list of names, telephone numbers, and addresses. He got Irina Lermontova's aliases, apartment number, and last known whereabouts, a house on Union Street. He hauled Hickey upright.

The cop slumped over, exhausted by the torture and confession, a sponge wrung dry. Renard pulled out his Beretta. Hickey perked up instantly.

"You said you wouldn't kill me," he shrilled.

"I might not. You're going to make a few calls."

Renard explained that Hickey was to contact Johnstone, his wife, and the police department, in that order. He'd first warn the narc detective about Renard.

"Why?"

"The man needs an extra incentive to find this woman. A little fire."

From the hallway Renard brought in the telephone on a long extension cord attached to the wall jack. He dialled Johnstone's number and pointed the gun at Hickey's head as the patrolman recited his litany. When Renard heard Johnstone's voice rise in objection he ended the call. Hickey looked up at him with the soft, pleading eyes of a whipped dog trying to please his master. Renard smiled.

"Now call your wife. Tell her to come home right away."

"Why? What's going to happen?"

"You're going on vacation. Starting today."

"Where?"

"Wherever pigs go. Stay gone at least a week. Better make it two."

Renard phoned Hickey's in-laws and let the cop convince his wife to return home directly. She agreed, after a whining argument. The last call was a courtesy to the police department. Hickey pleaded a family emergency necessitating immediate travel.

"I'm doing you a favour," said Renard. "Take off and keep your head down. If I see you around again, I'll kill you *and* your family. Do you understand?"

Hickey nodded. He'd sweated through a shirt stained with red splashes of Tabasco. Renard sliced the telephone cord and placed the handcuff keys on a coffee table. He loaded and took Hickey's revolver.

"When your wife gets back she'll unlock you. If your wrists are broken find a vet. Pack a couple of bags and get lost. I'll be somewhere outside. Be gone by noon."

Renard picked up the Gideon Bible and tossed it on Hickey's lap.

"Read that, sinner, and count your fucking blessings."

16.

. . . .

A soft, warm breeze stirred white linen curtains in a bright room. Her apartment was up on the tenth floor, facing west. At ten in the morning, the clock radio clicked on, humming out smooth music. Ted opened his eyes to the bare walls, the strum of a guitar, the urgency of a full bladder. Very gently he slipped from the bed and took care of his needs. The bathroom connected to a hallway. Buck-naked Ted entered the living room. Floor-to-ceiling windows and a sliding door opened on to a balcony that overlooked English Bay and the sea. The room had a bubble window in one corner, with spider plants hanging in macramé holders. Bookshelves were stacked haphazardly with heavy art tomes. Above the bar hung a framed reproduction by Tamara de Lempicka of a woman in a green dress, fighting against the wind. A person's furnishings reveal so much about them. On the coffee table Ted saw half a bottle of tequila, chewed lime wedges, a couple of blackened roaches, a lacy bra. It had started on the couch. She'd licked his hand with her warm pink tongue and applied the salt.

Ted made coffee with a French press and scrounged up cups, milk, sugar, and a jar of Nutella. He carried them on a cocktail tray back to the bedroom. As he entered Joni Mitchell sang "Help Me." White sheets tangled around a nude body. Despite the open window the room had a spicy, musky smell. *The lair of a wild animal,* Ted thought. *A fox, a vixen.* Her scent. He gently put down the tray. Lazily, sleepily, she opened her eyes.

"Ain't you a dreamboat," she purred.

"Room service," said Ted. "How do you like it?"

"Sweet and creamy," she said. "Just like you."

Pauline reached up and pulled him in for a kiss. The taste was sour but clean. She nipped Ted's lower lip, pushed him away, and propped herself up on the pillows. Her thick hair spread loose and tangled, an owl in an ivy bush. The turquoise necklace nestled between her breasts. Ted stirred sugar and milk into the coffee and handed her a cup. Pauline swallowed a mouthful.

"How do you feel?" he asked.

"I need to pee."

"Let me help."

"No. Relax."

He watched as Pauline swung herself out of the bed and away with the aid of crutches, her upper body thin and strong. The radio kept playing and a wind moved the curtains. A gull wheeled straight up past the window. He felt as though they were floating above the city, ensconced on a cliff face. Ted closed his eyes for a moment.

Now the light had changed. Her hand rested on his chest. The radio was off. Pauline breathed gently. Ted leaned over and drank cold black coffee. Her hand moved down his body to cup Ted's cock.

"There he is," she said.

Last night had been surprising: wild, fast, drunken, and clumsy. They'd laughed in the living room, undressing in haste. He'd stumbled to the bed with Pauline in his arms. Another surprise was when his mouth had touched a ring of metal pierced through Pauline's clitoris.

"It helps me feel," she'd said. "Like that. Mm."

"Mm," mouthed Ted, as he'd licked the soft pink flesh and hard steel.

That was last night. This morning they took it more slowly. Ted stroked Pauline's hair with one hand as her willing tongue slid into his mouth. His other hand cupped her breast. She turned and gripped his prick with a strong, nimble hand. He felt her body flush and her breathing thicken. Ted rolled her over and moved his mouth to her neck. Pauline put her arms around him. Their bodies tautened. Ted ran his hand down to her belly.

"That's good," she said.

She shifted her weight. With her right hand she moved her legs apart. He felt her thighs, so warm and smooth, the muscles toneless. Only the faintest hint of cold metal. She'd explained the ring to him the night before. Some feeling remained to her below the waist. Pauline could still come. The clitoral piercing helped augment sensation. That and his touch. Ted took another sip from the cup. Last night had been amusing. But then his return to Vancouver was surprising. Had he really lived in Tokyo with a Japanese woman for nearly a whole year? All gone, and Irina still missing. Thoughts of the past aside, he moved his hand down to a new slickness and warmth. Pauline arched her body. He turned her around so she lay on her side, her small buttocks against his hard cock. With his mouth to her ear Ted whispered, "Tell me."

"Yes," she said. "Yes."

The most wonderful word in the language.

Pauline opened herself up, and Ted entered her from behind, her arm curved back around his neck. They moved together, finding a rhythm, lost in each other, bodies tangling up in the sheets as the radio clicked on again. Pauline gasped, her eyes closed, as she pushed her coffee off the side table where it fell with a clatter, staining the white carpet. Her fingernails dug into Ted's flesh as her head craned back. She opened her eyes and said, "Round and round the mulberry bush."

Ted laughed. He kissed her and ran his hands through her hair. They kept moving.

Seagulls wheeled outside the window as the sun arced over the western sea.

"Help me," she sang.

Pauline ate Nutella straight from the jar, licking the spoon like a greedy, naughty child.

"Can you stay?" she asked.

"I have to work tonight."

"At that dump? Quit. Come and be with me for a while."

"Let me think about it. What about you?"

"I want to paint. That show last night gave me *muchas ideas picantes*."

"I'll say."

Pauline flung down the spoon and shot out, "Seeing that garbage, all that conceptual crap, it always gives me a sort of negative inspiration."

"That's because your work is unfashionable," said Ted. "You're too good."

"Don't I know it."

Pauline's art was out of step with local trends and what they taught at school. She specialized in an abandoned genre: figurative realism. Pauline drew well. She liked to paint in acrylic and finicky oils. She played none of the theory-riddled conceptual head-games of her peers or faculty. Ted admired her resolution, her stubbornness, her fire. Her willingness to be herself and no one else.

"I want to paint *you*," she said.

"What, now?"

"Yes."

Ted eventually agreed, secretly flattered. The apartment's second bedroom held Pauline's studio. Ted flipped through a stack of stretched canvasses. Her work showed some interesting influences: Alex Colville's precision hotwired with David Hockney's, but done in a way all her own. Her paintings were mostly all male nudes, sharply drafted and delineated, framed against bright primaries, a West Coast palette of elastic blues, yellows, reds, and greens. Pauline wheeled herself in, wearing nothing but a man's white dress shirt, sleeves rolled to the elbows. Ted picked up the program from the group show last night. He flipped to the biography of Nordhaal Velkdor. As Pauline prepared her materials he read aloud:

Nordhaal Velkdor is Lord Snicker, known also as Archduke Gristle, a.k.a. Frater Hemogoblin, a.k.a. Moriarty Iscariot, each psychologically dependant. I am a vagabond elf imprisoned in flux. I yearn to live in Jerusalem instead of Vancouver. I hate this town. I am an accumulator of obsessions and a reverse chameleon, and admire a simplicity I shall neither know nor have. I possess a heart broken as a fractal mosaic that shines like a disco ball to dazzle an ink-dark night. I am an emotional charlatan who falls in love recklessly with merest mortals. I persist in delusions and the voices which urge me onward, exhausting myself in search of the Eden-dream. I am built like a whippet, an ectomorph, an ivory mantis. I am a collector of animal bones, medical instruments, volumes of Hebrew spellcraft, and eldritch phantoms. I am careful to avoid danger and remain standoffish, but now aim to become the centre of attention. I may appear pretentious and narcissistic as a consequence, but this in fact is not quite true. I believe my soul is an ancient one, though I take pride in my childishness. I think Death is a comedian, and that I will live forever.

Pauline gagged. "You see what I'm up against," she said. "He thinks he's the Messiah."

"Impossible," said Ted. "I am."

"You're circumcised, at least," said Pauline. "It's a start. Stand over there in the corner. Show me the foot that booted that poseur."

"It was you who started it," said Ted.

"I just stoked your fire."

Velkdor had been knocked to the floor by Ted's well-placed kick. He was clumsily helped up by a claque of sympathizers while he clutched his ass and groaned in pain. Pauline preserved the moment and prevented a scene by wheeling up cackling with laughter and singing out a prophecy.

"What did you say?" asked Ted.

"'His own iniquities shall take the wicked himself, and he shall be holden with the cords of his sins.'"

"Where's that from? You looked like an avenging fury."

"*Proverbs*, I think. Stop talking. Lift that left foot and rest it on your knee. Bend down as though you were untangling a blackberry cane you stepped on. Like that. Good."

Her hands flew over the yellowish-brown newsprint page, sketching alternately with soft charcoal and a square of hard black conté. She looked him up and down, nodded, whistled through her teeth, and bent down to her work. Ted strained himself holding the pose. She tore off a sheet, then another. Muscles across Ted's back began to whine. He looked up at a flash. Pauline put down a Polaroid camera.

"Perfect," she said. "The light. You can relax. I've got it."

"Who are your other models?" asked Ted.

"Hustlers off Davie. If you're hard up, you could hit the street yourself."

She looked him up and down, licked her lips, laughed, and smiled. Ted shook his head in mock censure. Pauline continued.

"Everyone makes fun of Michelangelo's David for the size of his *piccolo*. But he had it right. When you're scared, it shrinks, doesn't it?"

"Also when it's cold. When you swim in the ocean. The scrotum-tightening sea, someone called it."

"You don't look cold," teased Pauline.

"Then you should be scared," said Ted, moving in on her.

Hat trick. That afternoon Pauline showed Ted something absolutely new to him. Later, he dozed while the light lengthened. Pauline busied herself in the kitchen. For supper they shared chicken salad sandwiches with rippled Old Dutch sour cream and onion chips. Ted drank tomato juice. Pauline refreshed herself with a tequila screwdriver. The sun turned tangerine orange as it sank. Far-off sailboats became silhouettes as the living room cut into strips of black and orange light. Throughout the evening they listened to Carol King's *Tapestry* from start to finish on

Pauline's turntable, then flipped the platter over and started again from the beginning.

"Where is she?" asked Pauline.

"I don't know," said Ted. "But I have to find her."

"Why?"

"She's in trouble."

"What's it to you?"

"Her trouble has a funny way of becoming my trouble."

"Even after what happened?"

"We're still married. At the very least I need to know where she is so I can divorce her."

"And then what?"

He heard a tone in her voice and looked over.

"I don't know. What about you? What do you want?"

"We'll see," she said.

While Pauline worked in her studio Ted showered and dressed, then stood and watched her. She had an elegant, sure touch. The figure she was drawing was rough but strong. He wondered what Pauline saw, how she felt. At the sound of his step, she stopped and turned. He raised her chin and kissed her.

"Call me," she ordered.

"Yes, ma'am."

As he closed the door Ted took one last look at her in the clear lamplight. Pauline tore at the sketch and threw the paper on the floor. Carefully, precisely, she started over again from nothing.

17.

In the morning Brian Kwok came by the house. He sat in the living room with a cup of tea under a wild Tretchikoff portrait of a musical Negro trio. Dorothy handed over the ripped postcard her father had mailed from Hong Kong.

"This was it? Your father sent nothing else?" asked Kwok.

"So far as I know," said Dorothy.

With some difficulty Inspector Kwok masked his sudden inner excitement. Dorothy had only ever seen him similarly tense when they'd visited Hastings racetrack at Exhibition Park, that thrilling moment when the horses rounded the quarter-mile's final curve. She felt him coiling within, a tautening piano wire. He turned the card over and ran a finger along the jagged corner.

"Yes," he murmured.

"What is it?" she asked.

"Probably nothing. Perhaps something." He looked at her. "Probably nothing at all, but we'll see. Nevertheless, I want to thank you for this."

"Anything you ask, Uncle."

"Your parents were very proud of you, Dorothy. Your father, especially. He trusted you. And loved you. I know he could seem cold, but you must remember what he went through to come to this country. What he gave up."

"I do," said Dorothy.

"No, not everything."

"Can you tell me?"

"Soon, perhaps."

Dorothy nodded and poured more tea.

"Have those policemen who bothered you returned?" asked Kwok.

"No."

"Good. Keep your eyes open and the doors locked. Call me if you see them or anyone like them. I know who they are. Your tenant was mixed up in something, a Vancouver Police matter. They don't share with us so I need to be circumspect. I know it's difficult, but we'll have to wait and see. I'll come back this afternoon if I can."

"Thank you, Uncle."

Brian Kwok surprised her by doing something he'd never done before. He stood up and gestured Dorothy to do the same. Then he took her hands in his and bent to kiss them.

"No, Dorothy, it's you I must thank."

Sunshine fell on the pair as they parted on the stoop. Kwok bowed slightly and went down to the street. Dorothy waited for his car's engine to turn over. Perfume from the fading roses mixed in the warm air. She felt calmer now, happy, and somewhat hungry. But first, to work.

At the dining room table Dorothy began going through stacks of bills and bank statements. Instead of using an adding machine, her fingers flew over an abacus while she noted sums on a sheet of lined paper. Next Dorothy checked receipts from her father's print shop, now run by his minority partner, a close-mouthed toiler named Benson Wong. It was steady, unglamorous income. Since her father's death, she and Wong had come to an implied arrangement. For his extra work Dorothy allowed him a reasonable squeeze from the till. *It's better to close one eye and let him steal a little than have him rob me blind*, she thought. A precedent established was, however, a practice liable to be eventually exploited, and with her calculations now complete, Dorothy noticed that more than the usual amount had vanished from the books. She sighed and put the columns of figures to one side. Her pleasant mood began to evaporate.

"On and on," she muttered.

STRAIGHT TO THE HEAD

She saw an unwanted future stretching ahead, a future of paperwork—Hydro bills, insurance payments, tax assessments. In this future
she scrabbled after nickels and salted money away beneath the floorboards.
Was this her true nature, or had it been nurtured by her mother and father?
They'd worked so hard and saved every penny, instilling a stern ethic of
thrift and frugality in their offspring. She was now the culmination of
those countless generations of peasants and farmers bred to fear disaster,
the calamity that breaks the rice bowl. *When did it go too far? When did
I go too far? When I'd rented the room out,* Dorothy thought. *I don't want
to be a landlady. I want something more than this. I want something to eat.*

Dorothy was no cook. In dire emergencies she could boil an egg
or slice a grapefruit for breakfast, but not much else. These days she
mostly ate out or ordered in. It was lonely dining by herself in the empty
house. Sometimes she'd pick up delicious Bayonne ham sandwiches at the
Portuguese deli or fresh cold pasta from the Italians down the street. At
this very second she didn't want to leave the house, in case Uncle Brian
called. For the first time in an age Dorothy checked the refrigerator for
any edible foodstuff. She opened the door and wrinkled her nose.

On the second shelf sat items left behind by her erstwhile tenant, Anna
Pechorin, or Irina whatever-it-was. It was strange fare, not the supermarket
specials Dorothy associated with *gweilos*. Where were the staples of what
Mrs Amorelli would call *mangiacake* white Canadian cuisine? Where was
the rubbery cheddar cheese, bland Hellman's mayonnaise, the tasteless
iceberg lettuce and egg salad on Stoned Wheat Thins? Anna/Irina enjoyed
more exotic dainties: pickled mushrooms, a dark loaf of unsliced bread
now turning green, heavy sour cream, and a wilted, slimy cucumber. Little
appealed to Dorothy's taste until her eye fell on a jar filled with tiny black
eggs. Caviar. It was lumpfish, sure, but still good.

"Jackie O," said Dorothy.

From beneath the sink she pulled out a burlap bag half-filled with
potatoes. Most had sprouted long white alien tendrils. Dorothy washed

two benign specimens off, stabbed them all over with a fork, swaddled each in aluminum foil, and set them in the oven. *To hell with her and her food*, she thought. *What's-her-name. Irina. I've waited long enough. For my reward I'll eat like Jacqueline Onassis.* A baked potato topped with cream and caviar followed by a glass of sparkling white wine.

Half the bottle had gone inside of her before the food was ready. Dorothy ate and drank while watching *Days of Our Lives*. Her pleasant mood returned with the adulteries and betrayals performed by the citizens of Salem, USA. Mary Worthington always swore by soaps and romance novels. Once, in mixed company, and to Dorothy's intense mortification, Mary had loudly proclaimed, "Who needs men when I've got a Harlequin and my left hand?"

The woman was over-sexed and underbred, for all her family's money. But, in spite of that (and here Dorothy's thoughts channelled her mother's), Mary did happen to have a point. As Ms Kwan sat she sipped her afternoon wine while watching an actress melt into some dumb lunk's arms. They'd hit on a winning formula, those purveyors of gentle smut. Think of all the man hours that went into analyzing the female mind, all the advertising studies and marketing reports employed in the service of weaving the subtle comforter of desire for suburban homemakers. There was money in it, in providing fantasies of escape, of speaking to some hidden self. Could Dorothy create a fiction and change her life, author a string of raunchy potboilers?

"Veronica St. Veronique-Smythe," she said, trying on a pseudonym, and continued, "*The Lighthouse Keeper's Daughter*, by Ethel Featheringhampton. A torrid tale of lusty desire. A lusty tale of torrid fire."

She closed her eyes. The wine was relaxing her nicely. On the television, sand fell through an hourglass, another end to one of our life's days. *If money didn't matter at all, what would I do?* wondered Dorothy. *I could go back to school.* She opened her eyes, repulsed by the notion of florescent-lit classrooms, duotangs full of foolscap, overpriced textbooks crammed with page after page of meaningless facts. No, it wouldn't do. Even in her present state of aimlessness, she knew enough to rule out any further higher education. It was not near the time for that. She had her right to grieve, to try to answer the riddle of her parents' lives, and deaths. Uncle Brian had hinted that there was something more to the accident. All that her parents had left behind on earth was here in their house, their shared creation. And when it came down to it, wasn't she, Dorothy Kwan, both the question she was asking herself and that question's answer? *Who am I?*

Forget about it, and have a drop more wine. In the kitchen Dorothy scraped empty the jar of fish eggs and licked the spoon. Then she threw out the rest of her tenant's food. Tying up the bag, she went outside into the backyard and the rubbish bins by the alley. From there she looked back at the house. A cherry tree's leaves hung limp and yellow in the dry heat. The house itself was losing some lustre, it seemed. Slow changes as the season stretched. Petrified moss clogged the eavestroughs, ragged cobwebs hung in high corners, dandelions turned to white cotton in the heat. All of it the inevitable decay if you don't keep raking and painting and polishing. Would she crumble with it, into an empty spinsterhood? The responsibility threatened to paralyze her. Dorothy almost wished for a disaster, a fire to come and force her to act. It would obliterate the museum, incinerate the sheer physical mass of all the damned stuff it'd be necessary to go through if she even began to start thinking of the remote possibility of making some kind of theoretical future move. To have it taken out of her hands would be a weird relief. She could point to anyone who shook their head and say, "See? An act of God. All gone. The mandala of life."

Dorothy uncoiled the garden hose and sprayed water over the poor cherry tree. She sprayed it on the house, over the coloured glass stucco sparkling in the light, rough gems of brown, green, red. Brown was beer, of course, green for wine bottles, white for pop, but where did the red come from? Rarer still, Dorothy saw points of blue glass, from medicine or sherry bottles, she supposed. All that liquid, gone, drunk down by dead people, the glass smashed and spread over the walls she'd grown up within. Sharp-edged bits, not like the smooth glass pebbles you'd find on the beach. As a little girl she'd sometimes picked shards from the wall by her mother's straggling clematis vine and would bury the little cache of jewels in empty matchboxes, a hidden, forgotten treasure map drawn by a young hand to find them again. All gone now, maps, gems, childhood. From the hose Dorothy shot a jet into the air and stood beneath it as it spattered down, cooling her head, wetting her clothes, a girl dancing through a sprinkler. She then drank gulps of the metallic-tasting water and rinsed out her mouth. No more wine or nostalgia. Back to work.

Inside, Dorothy dusted. She clipped together and filed the bills, swept the floor, and corked the bottle. She washed the dishes and organized the cupboards. While she worked she hummed more Blondie, "Heart of Glass" again. If the house was destroyed at least everything would be in order. No rebuke from her mother's shade on that score. It only remained to finish one more job. She unrolled two large white Glad bags. It had come time for her to empty the boarder's room and set things right. Should Irina/Anna dare show her face again, Dorothy'd tell her to fuck right off to wherever she'd come from. If the woman protested she knew the very thing to say: "Shall we call the police?"

Dorothy smiled. With every trace of the Russian girl gone, the policemen would have no more business considering the house on Union Street. She could disconnect the phone and turn off the water heater, leave a key for Mrs Amorelli to collect the mail. *I'll pack a bag*, thought Dorothy. *Get some American Express traveller's cheques, go to the airport, buy a one-way ticket to a tropical island. Hawaii.* She stopped still and to the empty hallway said, "You'll need a passport."

On Monday Dorothy would have to go to a government office for the proper forms and pick up that item Mary had commissioned from Holt's. Which she should have done today, come to think of it. *Never mind. I'll get my picture taken at one of those little places.* You needed an official person to endorse the photos, a priest or doctor or mayor or someone like that. *Uncle Brian would do it.* An RCMP inspector was as official as it got. She began to mount the stairs, lost in this lovely notion, dreaming of distant lands. The doorbell chimed. *He's back,* she thought. *Funny. Just as I was thinking about him. Synchronicity. Come to tell me more about the Hong Kong postcard and what it meant.* Dorothy pulled the door open without thinking and started with shock. A stranger stood before her. He said, in surprise, "Oh, I beg your pardon, miss. I was looking for Irina Windsor."

18.

• •

A madman had plastered badly mimeographed posters all over the neighbourhood. Renard saw them as he walked to his car. They were on brick walls and telephone poles, slathered over blank windows of disused warehouses. The dire warning, clumsily printed in block letters shouted:

ATTENTION PEOPLE'S

TODAY LOOK-UP TOWARD THE NIGHT SKY, AT 9:30 PM-1AM TO NIGHT.

YOU WILL SEE THE GUARDIAN'S THAT WAS PROPHESIDIN THE BIBLE THEY ARE EXTRATERRESTRIALS!!!

THE STARRS ARE THE SHIPS!!! THEY ARE NOT STARRS. THE LIGHTS WILL CAUSE NO REFRACTION AN SIT MUCH LOWER THAN SATELITES!!!

THIS IS NO JOKE. ALSO

THE ALDEBARAN; A GIANT SUN. THE KEY STAR OF TAURUS CONSTELLATION; LAST TIME SEEN WAS THOU-SANDS OF YEARS AGO.

IT IS BRIGHTER THAN THE MOON.

AS PROPHESIED IN THE BIBLE!!!!!

MAJOR DESTRUCTION!!! THIS IS PART OF THE "SIX SEALS"

Renard always found exhortations such as these vaguely unsettling. He mistrusted insanity and considered it highly contagious. War did that to men like him. In addition, the nature of his occupation often meant that Renard shared company with dubious characters in unsavory locales. Most men who operated in the twilight world of organized crime and secret intelligence were deadly bores, concerned only with information and money, but a surprising percentage turned out to be imaginative cranks. In a low bar outside Saigon, Renard had drunk cobra whiskey with a former Army Ranger who claimed to have been the sniper's spotter on the grassy knoll in Dallas. Renard rubbed shoulders with redneck John Birchers and dumbfuck Klansmen, sleek Cuban Communists, Mossad agents, and PLO plants. CIA men were mostly millennial Mormons. Mafia guys liked predicting a coming race war with the jigs. There were plots to destroy the Dome of the Rock and build the third Temple, whispered assurances about the Soviet moon base. A paranoid Bulgarian dissident in Naples had confidently told him the true reason for the assassination attempt on Pope John Paul II (Karol Wojtyla was a deep cover sleeper KGB double agent who'd gone rogue and been born again into the Holy Roman and Apostolic Church). Renard had seen voodoo killers smeared with chicken blood in Port-au-Prince and a decapitated Chinaman flung from a boat into the Pearl estuary, the corpse covered in Kabbalistic tattoos. In the murky swamp of the nowhere country anything could happen, so Renard had picked his careful way, and kept his antennae tuned for static interruptions. You never knew. The anonymous lunatic who opened the Book of Revelations and saw destruction in the night sky only had to be right one fucking time. As Renard reached the Pontiac he looked up for Aldebaran. A meteor streaked across the heavens just at that moment. *Spook-o-rama.*

"So it begins," he muttered.

He lit his pipe, started the LeMans, and began the midnight shift.

The lights were off at Hickey's house on Wall Street. After leaving the house that morning, Renard had tossed the pig's gun in a sewer grate. Later, he'd watched the entire family drive away, Hickey pushing and pulling his exasperated wife and a whining little girl into a station wagon filled with hastily packed suitcases. No doubt Hickey had warned Detective Johnstone about the enforcer on their trail. Renard counted on this new pressure to yield interesting results. He was lighting a fire under the wasp's nest. Now he shifted into low gear and drove over the freight tracks to the waterfront.

At the same phone booth that Hickey had used the previous night, Renard called his contact's radio telephone for an update. There was no answer at the other end; Renard chalked it up to the late hour. For a moment, standing on the empty portside road in the feeble glow of street-lights, Renard felt himself a target. His scalp prickled as the crosshairs of a riflescope centred for a headshot. An animal instinct to run and frantically burrow into dirt almost overwhelmed him. He mastered the anxious fear, and drove over to park by the cold-storage warehouse where Hickey had met with the Samoan. The same dusty pick-up truck, chain-link fence, rusty drums of oil. Renard reconnoitered the warehouse, satisfying himself that he was alone. A sign on a locked office door read Royal Maui Import / Export. The rolling door was also locked. He'd anticipated this possibility. At the office door Hickey took out his lock-picking rig, painted flat black to swallow stray light. Thirty seconds of fine work had him inside. He felt humidity. Enough light spilled through the steamed-up window for Renard to see the tiny, scruffy office. Against a far wall orchids grew in a terrarium, and potted tropical plants hung from hooks in the ceiling. Renard appreciated a framed poster of a girl in a white dress, paused in the middle of a tennis match to scratch her naked bum. Sweating down to his cowboy boots, Renard rapidly investigated the drawers of the desk and a couple of filing cabinets, finding nothing of interest. The hunter went through another door into the warehouse proper.

The dim blue glow of a television, far off in the corner. Sound of canned laughter. Faint outlines of crates and cardboard boxes. It was cold in here, refreshing. Renard suppressed a reactive shiver and grasped his Beretta, moving slowly to the entertainment's source. As he got closer, it got strangely warmer, and he smelled pungent marijuana, a good strain of strong stuff. His eyes now made out an improvised shipping station with desk and order sheets, a red push-button phone, beer fridge, and a stack of *Screw* magazines. Unlike the office, this area was definitely occupied. In a Barcalounger sat the huge Samoan watching Gilligan getting chased over the island by a big-game hunter. The ultimate sport. Renard watched the large man's belly rumble in time with the canned hilarity. The heap of man wore a huge T-shirt that read Home of the Whopper. At the commercial break, Renard stepped into the Samoan's line of sight and said, "You ever see *The Most Dangerous Game?*"

Stoned eyes turned to Renard, who continued, "It's a good one. Same idea. Big-game hunter on an island starts stalking men. Rod Serling wrote it. The *Twilight Zone* guy."

"*Twilight Zone* doesn't start 'til one. KVOS 12 from Bellingham," said the Samoan.

Renard looked at the regulator clock on the wall. "Well, we've got half an hour then. You like Gilligan? What island you from?"

"Hawaii."

"Aloha," said Renard.

The Hawaiian started to move his arm and Renard shook his head. He admired the big guy's coolness.

"Careful. I want to talk to you. Don't take it that easy."

"Just gonna toke some *pakalolo*."

"Okay, then."

Renard watched the Hawaiian set fire to a massive joint. It was like seeing a white virgin being sacrificed to a volcano. A heavy, sweet fog filled the warehouse, and despite himself Renard felt a little contact high. Pot was usually a roll of the dice, sometimes the nastiest brand of paranoia, other times gentle bliss. This stuff was drifting in a pleasant manner, had Renard feeling nice and calm after two days of blurred speed and caffeine.

"You get that good shit from home?" he asked.

"Direct from the mountains, man. You want a hit?"

"Why not?"

He took the thick joint and inhaled, then passed it back to the big man. With the smoke Renard felt his frequency start to match the Hawaiian's, felt why the man didn't move or freak out when a dude with a gun showed up out of nowhere. At a terrific volume Cal Worthington and his dog Spot hawked used cars on the TV screen. Renard moved a step and turned the sound down. He faced the Hawaiian.

"What's your name?" he asked.

"Charlie."

"Charlie, you're a long way from Honolulu."

"Lots of us here, man."

"Hawaiians in Vancouver."

"Kanakas. Us and the Italians, we run the port. Like, shipping and receiving. I got cousins called Santangelo. We're brothers, man. Nothing gets in or out without us."

"You born here?"

"Yeah. But I grew up back on Lanai."

"Okay. So you got yourself a nice little thing going. I got one more question for you though."

"Go for it," said Charlie.

Charlie kicked back his chair and closed his eyes. Renard just smiled and shook his head. This character was putting on an act. Smarter than he looked.

"What're you doing hanging around with that fucking idiot Hickey?"

Charlie toked. "Listen, man, the fuzz come to me, say, we know about the weed you bring in, but we don't care. Me, I'm just a dumb islander. I nod my head and say, 'Okay, mister policeman.'"

"Right," said Renard. "This was Hickey?"

"No, the other dude. The narc."

"Johnstone?"

"Yeah. He say, go ahead, bring in all the reefer you want, but we got a special job for you. You're gonna hear from us, watch out for when a ship comes in. We tell you. While they wait for Customs to get their dicks out of their hands, you're going to pick up a special package. Like a suitcase, no big deal."

"And did you?"

"Shit, man, they're cops. My uncle's the boss. He hears about this, he says, 'Charlie, I like cops to be my friends, not my fucking foes.'"

"Then what?"

"Then I have to go out on a fucking boat in the middle of the night. It's cold out there, man."

"How many times?"

"Two times. No, three."

Charlie's eyes strayed to the TV, where Gilligan was running around like a retard. Renard snapped it off. The buzz kept him in a groove with the man, but he wasn't going to allow too many distractions.

"Pretty simple set-up," he offered.

"Not any more," said Charlie. "Used to get the stuff, they meet here with another guy. Older dude, business man. He's like the shipper. They pay him off and take the bag. Now it's all different."

"What happened?"

"Something fucked up, man. The cops, they brought this girl with them last time. She was suppose to wait in the car. So the cops come with the money, and the other dude is there to get paid. But I don't know what went down. I go to take a piss, and when I come back they're all running around with these guns out, looking for this girl. She took off with the money and the dope and the car. Smart chick."

"You see her?"

"One time. Nice looking little thing."

"Alright. So when Hickey came here last night, what did he want?"

"He wants me to sit on something, man. Some shit that's coming in."

"How's it coming?"

Charlie's geniality shifted. His eyes lost their smoky opacity and cleared with an accidentally revealed cunning. He began to hoist himself out of the lounger. Renard shook his head again, showed the Beretta in his belt and said, "I want you to stay sitting right there."

"Yeah, but who the fuck are you?"

"I'm your new partner. Tell me more about this stuff you're going to sit on."

"What about these cops? That asshole Hickey?"

"He's taking a long vacation."

"Doing what?"

"Mini-golf tour of the lower forty-eight."

"Good riddance."

"You bet. And Charlie?"

"Yeah?"

"Fire up another one."

Maybe it was the pot. Renard felt a growing fellowship with this huge Hawaiian. The man was unflappable, a monument to mellow inertia, concealing himself and his intelligence in plain sight. Renard respected that, and he began to unbend a little, feel this man-mountain out. He told Charlie his name, and about what he'd done to Hickey. The big man's low laughter was seismic enough to register on the Richter scale.

"Okay, I tell you how it's going to be," said Charlie. "You tell me how it goes, and I'll tell you if it could work."

Charlie explained the new delivery system. Renard was amused.

"Smart play. That must be Johnstone pulling strings. Okay."

An idea developed. All the small things Renard had noticed about this job since crossing the border began to shift into a pattern, and that pattern revealed an opening. Cumulative irritations about his profession were combining to weigh him down. It was the constant travel, the false names and cheap hotel rooms, mute surveillance work and steady grind of hunting. His was a bitter job with no benefits or pension. *Here I am in an open town, and I could set myself up for the future*, he thought. There was a way of creating a vacuum, then filling it.

"You like it here on the coast?" he asked Charlie.

"It's cool."

"You want to do this forever?"

"Shit no. I got investments man. RRSPs. Keep the straight job and earn cash on the side, put it away, soon I got my own place on Molokai. Get me a *wahine* and open a bar. I'm gonna sit on the beach and watch the sun go down."

"How long'll that take?"

"Four, five years."

"Too long for me," said Renard. "Vancouver's an open town, far as I can tell. No real mob or FBI. I'm thinking this place needs a new player to step in."

"Who?"

"Me."

At that Charlie looked him up and down. He nodded and said, "Better than those fucking cops."

Renard turned the TV back on and they watched *The Twilight Zone* together, the one with William Shatner in the roadside diner trying to learn his fate from a fortune-telling machine. By the time it was over,

Renard had kicked around his rudimentary plan. He'd go over it again in the morning with a clear head, but for now the Hawaiian sat in his chair, nodding in agreement, and inhaling the last of a roach. Charlie roused himself to stand, and stoned out of his coconut but with a placid look of understanding, he shook Renard's hand island-style.

"You crazy, man, but it could work."

Renard smiled. "It's a cinch. All you have to do is play dumb."

"My specialty. You my brother now, we gonna do this thing."

"We'll do it right."

He got Charlie's home number and a fat joint for later, then left the warehouse, *Twilight Zone* music following him out into the night. Far above, beyond the lights of the port and the city, all the stars in the night sky had swung around Polaris. Hanging low on the western horizon, ripe, red, and brighter than the moon, Renard swore he saw Aldebaran returning after thousands of years, come to destroy us all.

19.

· ·

Two o'clock in the morning on the far western coast of North America. The whole continent had had its fill of fun already and in most places was long in bed. Never did Ted feel more remote from the whole of human civilization than he did watching *Hockey Night in Canada* during the regular season. After the inevitable Toronto Maple Leafs opener, the CBC would usually broadcast a western game, starting around seven p.m. Pacific Standard. If that match went into extra periods (and it could), sometimes it wouldn't finish until eleven, or two in the morning New York time. Then there'd be studio commentary, a player interview, a recap of league highlights, and other videotaped errata. Nearing midnight the show would end with a reel of footage that emptied Ted completely. To the musical accompaniment of a spare, slowed-down version of the famous theme song, the CBC ran footage shot from the window of a car driving at night through the empty streets of Edmonton or Winnipeg or Vancouver. For Ted it somehow perfectly evoked existence on the absolute periphery of this northern country. He pictured empty buses reaching windswept terminal depots, swaying traffic lights at vacant intersections cycling though their endless, thoughtless, automated changes of red, yellow, green, and back again, eternally. The pure void, followed by the national anthem and a test pattern. Then you were alone, the last person on earth with the lights on, staring blindly west across a benighted ocean with a busted lip. Ted touched the aching spot gently with his tongue.

The day was already well begun in Asia. Sixteen hours ahead, it was lunchtime in Tokyo. Ted listened to the inaccurate clock in the lobby of the Victoria Hotel, measuring out portions of oblivion. He was taken far away, back to the minuscule apartment in Japan and the woman he'd left there, Minako. She played the piano but couldn't fit one into her tiny efficiency unit, so she'd practice on a scroll painted with all eighty-eight keys, humming Chopin as her fingers struck imaginary notes. Minako's only accompaniment was the metronome, a Seth Thomas pyramid that Ted had picked up at the Oedo antique fair, a flea market in Ginza. Minako was good to him, balm to his wounded soul after the scorching from Irina. She was one of those rare, tender Japanese with a gentle sense of humour. They'd met after an Australian girl had broken a date with Ted, leaving him holding two tickets to a recital. At the school where he was an unofficial substitute teacher, Ted had placed a notice on the corkboard for someone to come along. Minako had shyly responded. After the recital they bonded over a shared love of Glenn Gould. Her English was far better than Ted's Japanese. She taught him a tongue twisting phrase he spoke aloud.

"*Niwa niwa niwa no niwa-tori ga iru,*" he said.

For no one at all Ted translated: "There are two chickens in the garden."

One day Ted took French leave of Minako. What a cad. He'd cracked, quit tutoring a bored salaryman prepping for the Cambridge exam, emptied his bank account at the post office, packed a bag, and bought a ticket home. CP Air on a Boeing 737. Ted ended up drinking most of his yen away even before leaving the ground, downing whiskies at a dingy bar near the airport. What had prompted it? *I did the math,* he thought. *Womankind owed me one. Poor Minako, the leftover part of the equation, the remainder. It wasn't to say I needed revenge; by and large, I've had a better-than-decent batting average with women. Well, by-and-large.* Still, it was startling to discover that he'd been the wrongee far oftener than the wronger.

For many men this kind of experience soured them on the sex, turned them chauvinists, but in Ted's case it was the opposite. He'd felt himself getting tangled up again, that his heart was too open, and he hadn't wanted to get trapped in Japan. There were too many maladjusted Western men who connected with Japanese women for the wrong reasons. It was something lacking in their psychology. So he'd split, run back home, and now he sat alone at the front desk of the hotel, hearing Minako's fingers tapping out a nocturne as the clock's pendulum swung back and forth. Like he had, west across the Pacific and back again—to what? A missing wife, an old friend made lover, and now someone else, someone unexpected. A new pain. A busted lip and the flavour of salt from blood. Ted could feel it starting to happen again, the same dangerous frisson. Earlier today he'd met a new woman, one who now crowded out all the rest, past, present, and future. He'd met Dorothy Kwan.

Ted's heart hammered as he pressed the doorbell to the old house on Union Street, Irina's last address. Even a day later, Ted was still feeling flush and easy from the unexpected (and kinky) lovemaking session that Pauline and he had enjoyed. *And now I'll find Irina, or some trace of her whereabouts*, he thought. In his pocket he carried the copy of her Woodward's food bill and the small wooden doll. Caviar, sour cream, Winnipeg rye. She liked to smoke pot and play backgammon before sex, then smoke cigarettes and eat afterward. Dunhill cigarettes, in London, Paris, New York. He remembered the taste of tobacco mixed with the delicacies Irina preferred, pickled mushrooms and cold vodka. Ted's heart slowed, and he pressed the bell again. With a sudden jerk the door was pulled open by a Chinese girl, a pretty one, holding a plastic garbage bag.

"Oh, I beg your pardon, miss. I was looking for Irina Windsor," Ted heard himself say.

"She doesn't live here anymore."

"Oh, I'm sorry. Do you know where she went?"

"She left."

"But where?"

"I don't know, and I don't care. Goodbye."

"Wait!"

Ted pressed his hand against the closing door and made his confession. "I'm her husband. What I mean is, she's my wife, and she's in trouble. Do you have a minute?"

"One," the woman said.

She blocked the entry. Ted clumsily took out the food bill and held it up. "Her name's Irina Lermontova, and my name's Windsor. See, here it is. She ordered food to this address."

"So?"

"And now the police are looking for her. She's in trouble," he repeated.

"What do you care?" asked the woman.

That startled him. "I beg your pardon?"

"I said, what do you care?"

"Well, she's my wife."

"Where's your ring?"

Ted's right hand went to his left ring finger as though it'd been stung by a wasp. He felt himself fluster. It was bad enough that she was unexpectedly pretty, but she was also damned sharp.

"We're separated," he said. "I'm just trying to help her."

"Help yourself. She's no good."

"What do you mean?"

The woman planted her hands on her hips and said, "She came here and used a false name. She left owing me rent. Now I have to clean up her room and deal with you and who knows what. The police again?"

Ted held up his hand and felt a surge. "Hold on. The police were here?"

"Yes."

"Creepy guy with yellow eyes? Asshole with a crew cut?"

"Yes," she said, crossing her arms.

Ted paused. He was no great master of body language, but hearing about the two cops had caused the woman unease. He softened himself and deliberately spoke again, quietly, wearing a gentle smile, meeting hers with a bashful eye.

"I'm sorry. They pushed me around too. That's why I'm worried. I don't know what they're after or what she's done, but it's my duty to help her. We may be split up, but when it comes to cops, I stand with anyone. Did they search your house? Did you let them in?"

"No," said the woman.

"Good."

Ted extended his hand. "Forgive my manners. I'm Ted. Ted Windsor."

The woman stood tensely a moment, then loosened to uncross her arms, putting her hand in his with a certain grace. Her hand was cool and dry and perfectly formed. He held it lightly a moment, and made the ghost of an antique bow.

"Dorothy," she said.

"If I may, I'd like to ask you for something, Dorothy."

"What's that?"

"I'd like to see if she left behind her wedding ring. You see, it was my mother's," he lied.

Irina's room was uncharacteristically disarrayed, Ted noticed. Her standards were slipping. What did that indicate about Irina's state of mind? He saw the light-blue walls, a messy bed, the vanity holding scattered cosmetics. For a moment Ted caught a flicker out of the corner of his eye: Irina in nothing but a silver camisole, tossing clothes on the quilt, deciding what to wear. He'd always taken a lazy erotic pleasure watching her dress for work in the morning; in a way, it was more intimate than disrobing, seeing her turn inward on herself, assessing her own beauty, choosing that day's disguise. Dorothy stood at his elbow as his eyes moved from a Duran Duran poster to an unbuckled suitcase.

"How much does she owe you?" he asked.

"She left without notice. Rent is 250 a month."

"I'm sorry. Let's see if she left anything. If we find something you think might help compensate, maybe we can work it out."

"Perhaps."

Ted was overly mindful of another woman's presence as he moved into the room. His first, savage inclination was to tear the place apart, flip over the mattress, rip up baseboards, slit seams in cocktail dresses. Instead he exhaled comically, playing that sympathetic character, the weary husband.

He moved carefully and tried to think, sensitive to Dorothy's scrutiny. Even when they hated one other, womankind remained a sisterhood, and he needed to show Irina's possessions the proper respect. So he opened a drawer and found loose stockings, unzipped a suitcase pocket, thumbed a few dresses in the closet. He was looking for a clue, a note, a code, a secret cipher. Ted hoped that Irina's mind would reveal itself, that a stray comment from a half-forgotten stoned conversation would trigger inspiration. But his wife's mind was too tricky, too foreign. She'd lived too many lives and spoken too many languages: Russian, English, Greek, Communist, Capitalist, Art, Adultery.

She was smarter than Ted, well schooled in deception, a creature of the Soviet. Again he felt himself a perfect amateur in her vicious world. The soft western bourgeois boy facing a woman who knew the pitiless KGB and the gulag. Irina's cynicism had often frightened him. Ted was too English and sentimental, lacking the ruthlessness of this age. And yet, he remembered Irina tearing up watching that treacly Coca-Cola commercial, the one where some kid tries to teach the world to sing. North American advertising sometimes proved too sophisticated for her makeup. *We're the ones who've been exposed to the true brainwashing*, thought Ted. Madison Avenue's a million times more subtle than the Ministry of Information. So it'd be something sentimental, something she'd treasure. A keepsake or souvenir. *Kitsch*. It was a word Irina had taught him, a word from her alien mindset and vocabulary, like *nomenklatura* or *weltschmerz*. *Kitsch*. Ted put his hand in his pocket as his eye met the nesting dolls resting on a dresser. He turned to Dorothy and gave her a tight smile.

"She's a complicated woman, but sometimes the only one who understands her is her man," he joked.

He held up the tiny wooden doll that normally lived in the centre of the *matryoshka*. It was the same one he'd found hidden behind the Pequegnat clock in their apartment at the Stardust. Ted put it down beside the painted wooden *babushka* and as Dorothy watched, took doll after smaller doll out and ranged them on the flat surface. At the second-to-last doll he looked in the mirror, at himself in his seersucker jacket from Brooks Brothers, at his dirty blond hair and foolish Canadian face. And then he looked at the woman in the doorway, now standing at attention, holding her breath. He filled his lungs.

"Here we go," he said.

In the centre of the second-smallest doll was a key. Ted laughed. "Round and round the mulberry bush. Do you happen to have anything to drink?"

They shared the remnants of a bottle of white wine. Dorothy poured out a generous tot for each. Ted felt full and empty, and completely absurd.

"It's just like her, you know. When we were together, she'd hide things. We joked that if anything mysterious happened to either of us (and it was her we were talking about, always), we'd place an ad in the personals of *The Globe and Mail*. I always knew one day I'd come home and she'd be gone, and I'd be left wondering."

"What happened?" asked Dorothy.

She held the wineglass by its stem and took a good sip. Ted took her in, her neat appearance, her poise and control. *What must she think of me?* he wondered. It was no time for raillery or tricks. Honest speech, clearly delivered. The young lady's level gaze and intelligence demanded nothing less.

"She ran away with a man. Then another. Then I ran away to forget."

"Where?"

"Japan."

"Oh?"

Ted smiled. "It seemed like a good idea at the time. Have you ever been?"

"Not to Japan."

"You're Chinese, yes?"

"Yes."

"But you were born here."

"I was."

"Well, she wasn't. She was the most exotic, dangerous, beautiful creature I'd ever met. You know what it's like in Vancouver. Stores closed on Sunday and no such thing as a cocktail lounge. I didn't want to lose her, so I married her. For all the good it did."

"It happens."

"And what about you? Is this your house?"

"Yes."

"What on earth compelled you to rent her a room?"

"She seemed level-headed."

Ted choked on the wine he swallowed, laughing out loud. "Oh, that's great," he said, wiping away a tear. He mopped up the spilled white so it didn't stain the table, took a breath, and asked, "The better question is, where's she got to now? What did the police want?"

"Her whereabouts."

"Whereabouts. Well, if I know her at all, and I don't, less and less every day, she could be anywhere between here and St. John's, Newfoundland."

"Why?" went Dorothy.

"She doesn't have a passport yet. Half the reason I married her. So she's certainly in the country. And she probably wants that."

Ted pointed at the key on the table. "What we have to do is find out what it opens," he said.

"We do?" asked Dorothy.

"Well, if you want the rent she owes you."

Dorothy stood up and went to the window, turning her back on Ted.

"I didn't mean to presume," he said. "But aren't you curious?"

"Not really. Your wife was more trouble than she was worth."

"Did the cops say they'd come back?"

"Maybe."

"Well, we'll get ahead of them."

Ted spoke quickly. He didn't know precisely what his plan was, but he didn't want to lose this charming, enigmatic woman. Christ, his weakness. He loved complicated females. He told Dorothy where he worked and his phone number and how they should maybe stick together to figure it all out.

"Why?" asked Dorothy, turning around.

"To keep them from coming back. Are you doing anything else?"

She cocked her head and thought a moment. Then, and for the first time, Ted saw amusement. She smiled, showing her even white teeth, so fetching in her tawny face.

"You know, I really am not," said Dorothy.

They agreed to meet the next day for a coffee. Ted would keep the key. She accompanied him to the door. Without thinking about it, Dorothy unlocked the latch and turned the handle. Ted was about to say something as they went from of the darkness of the foyer out into the bright glare outside, but there was an interruption.

"Well, look at that," said Detective Johnstone. "Here, have a big smooch, loverboy."

The cop took out a sap and laid a neat, clean, hard blow on Ted's mouth.

20.

· ·

The shock of the bright light after the cool dark house was enough; when Ted got hit in the face and knocked to the ground by the cop Dorothy didn't know quite what to do.

"Want another, loverboy?" asked the policeman.

Detective Johnstone of the yellow eyes raised his hand as if he meant to hit Ted once more with the black licorice sap. The policeman checked his swing and shouted, "Where is she?"

"I don't know," said Ted thickly.

"Then why're you here?"

Ted coughed and spat out blood, then put his hand to his mouth. Dorothy had gone rigid. She'd never witnessed this type of violence before. Ted spoke carefully. "Because I was trying to find her. She's still my wife. But it's a dead end. She's gone from here."

"How can you tell?" asked Johnstone, his sap hand still upraised for another stroke to the face.

Ted smiled and looked up with his cold blue eyes. He touched his split lip again, and his hand came away all bloody. Dorothy felt terribly ill. Ted looked at his red hand and laughed resignedly.

"Have you ever been married before, Detective Johnstone?"

"No."

"A husband knows, even a dummy like me. She's gone. I'm just the fool that went looking for her."

"Why?"

"What?"

"Why're you looking for her for?" asked the cop.

"To divorce her."

"I can make you talk," said Johnstone. "It won't be fun, not for you."

"With a witness present? Police brutality's bad press, even in Vancouver."

"Who, her?"

Johnstone jerked at Dorothy with his chin. She almost flinched just from the look in the policeman's animal eyes and the snarling curl of his lip.

"She won't breathe a word about me, I can promise you that, Mr Windsor. Not after I'm done."

"I wasn't thinking of her," said Ted.

"Who then?"

Ted pointed his bloody finger past Johnstone's shoulder. The cop lowered his sap and turned. Dorothy followed his gaze and felt a flush of fierce warmth.

"Her," said Ted.

Mrs Amorelli to the rescue again, thought Dorothy. Her neighbour stood along the fence, holding her shopping in two string bags. The look on her face was awesome, pure wrath and black fury.

"Go!" she barked at Johnstone.

Johnstone shrugged his shoulders with an attempt at contempt. One hand held the sap and with the other he reached into a jacket pocket for his badge or gun. He started talking. "Listen, lady, you're interfering with an official police inquiry."

Mrs Amorelli swung the bag at the end of her right arm with a wicked twist and clouted Johnstone hard on the ear, knocking off his hat and dropping him to a knee. Both sap and badge fell out of his hand.

"Fuck!" he said.

"Go ahead, *cabrón*," said Mrs Amorelli. "I got more. *Voglio rompere il culo a tua sorella.*"

The cop was furious, impotent. He grudgingly left of his own dissatisfied accord, unable to pin a charge on any of them. He muttered strangely to himself all the way back down to his ghost car. Dorothy nursed Ted on the front steps. Ted chuckled and seemed not to mind anything at all. Dorothy nodded to Mrs Amorelli and silently mouthed, "*Grazie.*"

Her neighbour nodded back, and they understood one another com-pletely. Kneeling down beside Ted, Dorothy put her hand on his face. She heard Mrs Amorelli walk away, leaving them to do what was next. Ted chuckled again. A powerful flood of fear and gratitude welled up inside of Dorothy. Then a crow in the red cedar let out a raucous, mocking laugh. Dorothy snapped and asked Ted, "What's so damn funny?"

"What?"

"Why'd you lie?"

"Because," he said, smiling with blood on his teeth.

"Because why?" she echoed, suddenly shy to look at him.

"You've never been married, either. Lies are the first truth. See?"

Ted opened one hand to show Dorothy the little wooden doll. "He doesn't want her or us. He wants this."

Ted carefully worked his tongue around in his mouth and from between his red lips pushed out the silver key into his other hand. "Everything gets better, Dorothy Kwan."

"How could it get worse?" she asked.

Look at his foolish, handsome, bloody, white-toothed, clear-skinned, dirty-blond, blue-eyed, white boy, gweilo face.

"*Hai ah*," sighed Dorothy Kwan almost inaudibly. *Go to the devil. What's he to me? Nothing. Less than. What's that he's trying to say to me?* she wondered as he winced.

They sat in the kitchen. Dorothy applied alcohol to Ted's cut lip. Afterward, he pressed a paper towel to staunch the flow of blood.

"I'm sorry this happened," he said. "I didn't come looking for trouble. You okay?"

"I think so."

Dorothy sat down and watched him awhile. "I hardly knew her," she said.

"Who?"

"Your wife. What's-her-name."

"Irina."

"She never called herself that. I barely even saw her around here. But I should have known she was difficult, I guess."

"Well, don't feel too bad. She had that effect on people. When you met her she had a way of casting a kind of spell. Only afterward would you wake up with a headache and an empty wallet. Have you ever been in love, Dorothy Kwan?"

Some question, she thought, looking at the silver key sitting on a lace paper doily. Despite that, she was amazed to hear herself say, "Yes."

"Can you tell me? And may I have some ice in a towel to keep the swelling down?"

Dorothy got up, rummaged in the freezer and found a full tray and her former tenant's forgotten bottle of cold vodka. *Good, I need it*, she thought. From the cupboard she took out two clean glasses, then broke the tray open and turned the cubes over into a bowl.

"Wow," said Ted.

"What?"

"In my whole life I've never cracked open an ice tray without getting cubes all over the floor. You're amazing."

Dorothy let herself laugh. Their eyes met a moment, then she put fresh water in the freezer for more ice. She placed the whole chemistry set on the table . As she poured the vodka, Ted made himself a cold pack. Before him Dorothy placed the tumblers on the table. He took one look at the bottle, then at her, and cocked an eyebrow as he gave her an impish smile.

"Yes. Let's finish her bottle," he said. "Ladies first."

Now I know why she married him. I would. He's beautiful, she thought.

They raised glasses.

"*Gombui*," she said.

"*Nazdarovya*," said he.

With the first flush of warmth Dorothy now heard herself telling a stranger the story of her life.

"I was brought up very strictly. My parents put me in a Catholic girls' school across town because of its scholarly reputation, and I was expected to get straight As. I did. They also enrolled me in ballet classes from the minute I could walk, and I trained as a dancer. One day I was supposed to somehow become first ballerina at the Bolshoi *and* dance *Swan Lake* in New York. If I failed, eternal shame upon my ancestors. I tried my very best. Good grades for my father and dancing all day for my mother. She would sit front and centre at recitals in her pink Jackie O. Chanel suit surrounded by all the rich old *gweilo* ladies dripping with diamonds, and she'd watch my every *sissonne* and *sous-sus*. I was the only Chinese girl in the class, so I had to be better than all of the others put together.

"Every afternoon after school, I'd take the bus home all the way across town from the Little Flower, studying the whole time, before ballet practice at the Goh Academy. The one on Main Street. Do you know it?"

"I think so."

"The only boys I ever saw were little neighbourhood boys with their mothers going to the corner store." Dorothy took a sip and her memory left the kitchen. She could see him now.

"The first boy I ever loved played the cello for this theatre piece our academy was part of. It was Shakespeare, *A Midsummer's Night's Dream*. We performed in a tent on a field by Jericho Beach, the year I was sixteen. The student string section from a music school played accompaniment, and we dancers dressed up as nymphs or fairies, I guess, in some of the dream parts."

Here Dorothy took a breath, poured another vodka, sipped, and looked at Ted with her jet-black eyes.

"He was there. Playing, I don't know, a pastiche of Debussy and Saint-Saëns. I danced to his music with my troupe, but I never had eyes for the actors on stage pretending to be gods and donkeys or for the audience watching us, but only for him. And he had eyes only for me, it seemed.

"We went all the way through rehearsals, and it wasn't until the end of the run before we finally had a chance to talk to one another. Closing night. The solstice. There was a party after, with the director and the actors and the musicians and the dancers and everyone else. My mom didn't come to pick me up because she thought the show was still on, so I went. Everyone was drinking wine and beer and punch and people were still in costume and I hadn't even changed out of my dress and all of a sudden there he was and I remember like yesterday the first thing he said to me."

"Are you thirsty?" asked Ted.

Holy fuck. It was exactly what *he'd* said. The small hairs stood up on the back of Dorothy's neck.

"Yes."

Ted spilled out more vodka. He saluted her and then winced as he drank his, but his mouth had stopped bleeding, she noticed. She let the cold essence slip inside her.

"He had a little cooler next to his cello case, and it was filled with ice and a bottle of champagne. Veuve Clicquot Ponsardin. I remember it exactly. And he had those little plastic wine cups they use at weddings where they don't want guests to break any glasses. I'd hardly ever had anything to drink in my life before he popped the cork. It was perfect. The party kept going, but even though we were there it was like we weren't, you know? It was all part of the dream, like the play had kept going after the curtain went down. And he and I were alone in the champagne bottle with all the bubbles."

Dorothy sipped again.

"What we talked about I don't know, but it was like we spoke a language of our own, one that no one else could understand. He wore a tuxedo with a clip-on bowtie, I remember, but most of all I remember his eyes and his smile and the feeling of meeting someone who understood me. Someone who I understood. Without even saying anything we left the noise and all the drama in the tent and walked away across the field. I could smell the beach and the sea, and the driftwood fires. The grass was long and yellow; there was a moon, too, like a mandarin orange. He had the bottle of champagne, and we laughed and babbled together. Remember, I'd never hardly even talked to a boy before, and here we were alone together in the warm night and we found a glade among the trees and—"

Suddenly a tear filled Dorothy's eye, and she was back in the kitchen with Ted. He looked at her.

"I understand," he said. "What happened?"

"That fall he went to school in Montreal. We wrote back and forth. He sent me letters at my friend's house so my parents wouldn't find out. He was supposed to come back here for Christmas break and we'd see each other again."

She felt cold. Ted sat silently, watching her.

"I didn't find out until after New Year's. Back in Montreal, he'd been carrying his cello on a hilly sidewalk and slipped on the ice. He bit his tongue off and bled to death before the ambulance even got to him."

Silence. Then, quietly, Ted asked, "How old was he?"

"Nineteen."

"And what about you?"

"I kept living, unfortunately."

Later, when they felt better, Ted indicated the oddly shaped key.

"Look close," he said.

Dorothy picked it up and turned it around, holding it near her face. It was neither a house nor a car key. She thought she recognized it. *Yes! Safety deposit box.*

"Hold it at an angle to the light," suggested Ted.

Doing so, Dorothy squinted, and catching a stray glance of reflected sunlight saw small scratches on the metal surface, regular little lines, like runes or Chinese characters.

"Roman numerals," said Ted.

"Really?" asked Dorothy.

"One of Irina's little tricks. She had a lousy memory for numbers. I remember her showing me how she'd scratched her locker combination in Roman numerals."

"What does it say?"

"LV. Then: MMCDXXVI. Then: VIII."

"And what's it supposed to mean?" asked Dorothy.

Ted smiled and made a quizzical face, then shook his head and laughed. "Stick with me, and we'll try to find out. If for no other reason than to spite that cop. Sure you're with me?'

Again, Dorothy was astonished to hear her own voice.

"You know, I guess I really am," she said.

21.

In a curved, Corinthian-leather booth against the north wall of the Hummingbird Cabaret, Renard stuffed his pipe, watching a poor peeler indifferently dance around to her second song, "Glamour Boy." Her first had been the Guess Who's "No Sugar Tonight." It was all right by him. As she lazily turned around the stage, apathetically removing her panties to show some bush for the paying punters, an asshole on Gynecology Row shouted out from between cupped hands, megaphone style:

"Turn up the smell!"

Renard looked at his glass of ginger ale and Canadian Club on melting rocks. They were out of Wild Turkey. Fantastica the stripper mockingly gyrated through her routine. Didn't matter what she did. The hunter was waiting.

He lit the bowl of his pipe and drew in rich tobacco as she slid into her third and final song. Learn a stripper's psychology through her music choices. Fantastica's closer turned out to be "Undun." Evidently she was a Burton Cummings fan. The dancer slowed down the pace and seemed to get into it. Man, could she move. Truly a beautiful dancer. Here and now. She started to work on him.

"*Hélas!*" muttered Renard.

He bit the plastic pipe stem, gesturing for another drink. One more killer's cocktail before the arrival of the pig, of Detective Johnstone of the VPD.

Renard had already reconnoitered the men's room. The last time he'd been in Vancouver he'd stopped at George Paley's joint, a bar in the style of the bootlegging twenties, where the brick wall from the St. Valentine's Day massacre (chipped by machine-gun fire) was preserved behind Plexiglass. The Hummingbird had no such relic. In crude felt-tip pen, for-a-good-time phone numbers and turgid cocks were scrawled over the urinals. After emptying his bladder Renard had passed through the saloon bar and noted all three ground-floor exits. The owner and operator of the joint had the unlikely name of Croccifixio Delbianco, known to all and sundry as "Cooch". Upstairs, he enjoyed a private suite and offices, where he kept his safe. Down in the cellar was the shit-pit, delivery doors, and who knows what. Buried deeper, deep under the basement, were the bodies, claimed the word on the Vancouver street. Renard had never met Cooch Delbianco but knew him by second-hand reputation as some sort of mildly legendary West Coast guinea, semi-demi-hemi connected. *Never forget the vowel at the end of a greaser's name. Especially an eyetie with a fucking taxi stand.*

And speak of the devil. Joe Delbianco came down the steps, smiling, slapping backs, and glad-handing. Light glistened off his brilliantined hair. He snapped a finger at a waitress and ordered a round for a table, shook hands with a wizened gent in a booth, and scanned the room, probably calculating the take. A great big friendly guy who'd buy a drink for his assassin was Don Giuseppe Delbianco. Pictures on the wall showed him chumming around at various times with Louis Armstrong, Sammy Davis Jr., Gary Cooper, and the Duke. For a moment Delbianco's eyes rested on Renard and seemed to recognize him. A bartender distracted the boss and commanded his attention. Without changing speed, Delbianco took off his coat, unclipped his cufflinks, rolled up his sleeves, and started to mess with some kind of machinery behind the bar.

The hunter's mind cast itself upon the payphone on the back wall by the emergency exits. The LeMans was across the street, keys under the driver's side footwell floor mat, with windows cracked wide. His car was being watched by a bunch of pretty decent, with-it, high-class hooker ladies he'd smoothed to keep an eye out for him, *pretty please, and here's a twenty.* Pretty sharp ladies, in fact. He respected strollers as fellow independent professionals at the top of their game. *We ride a vibe of* pourquoi pas? he thought. *Money. Business is as business does.*

Then it occurred to the hunter that he hadn't called his employer lately, Mr Peters.

Mr Peters? wondered Renard. *Is that right? Too many employers with too many fake fucking names. Peters, Peterson, Petersmith? Christ. Get off the cross, we could use the fucking wood. What's my fucking name in Vancouver? Vancouver. Wait. Vientiane, Vienna, Vladivostok. Three out of four ain't bad. Thomas Renard. In Vientiane, I sometimes went as Stevens. Vienna's just a blur, Wien in German. 'Vostock's off-limits. No one in or out but Soviet Navy or KGB.*

"Russkies, Cubans, Commies, Red Chinese, Koreans, Vietcong, the Pathet Lao," said Renard aloud. His knife was beneath the driver's seat of his wheels across the street.

His next call to Peters could wait until Renard had harder information. *Like, for example, where the girl was, whatsername, the one who made off with the money and the other stuff. The cop'll know. Be careful with this trou de cul, though,* thought Renard. *Clever bastard, smarter than his dumbass partner.*

Renard sat clean, per the usual Company regs when meeting with heat, keeping a left eye out. He carried neither piece nor knife nor garrote upon his person because a cop (times two for a bent cop) is faster than a motherfucker to frisk you, just to hang a concealing or possession jacket, or to feel out a wire. With good reason in this case. Renard'd been through the routine plenty and now knew better. Combined age, wisdom, and experience. *Let's see what this narc does.*

He breathed in his pipe and exhaled the luxury blend through his nostrils, trickling smoke over moustache and beard. Renard's thoughts continued, his mind composed and active, body rested, ready for anything. Prior to ordering his first highball, the hunter had salted his .38 behind the yellow pages underneath the payphone next to the gents. His escape hatch out, if needed.

Music hiccupped while the wonderful dancer turned onstage. Fantastica stumbled and coughed. Renard's heart skipped a quarter-beat.

The stripteaser recovered her dance, and now she'd become real, real as anything. Not a hologram or replicant. Better than your standard pleasure unit.

"Damn," whispered Renard through smoke.

The greasy MC boomed: "Ladies and gennelmen, put your hands together for the dramatic stylings of Fantastica! Great, great set. Any of you gennelmen wanna meet Fantastica, she'll be waitin' over there at the bar inaminnit. S'drink's a Shanghai Sunset, ain't that right, sweetheart?"

Fantastica blew the scumbag a poison kiss as she picked up her panties and paraphernalia from the floor. Renard finished swallowing his drink while the waitress brought his next. When in Roma.

"*Grazie,*" he said, slipping her a twenty, then hollered in her ear, "Next drink I order is for my guest. Put it on this. Should more'n cover both. But hey, watch out, he's a cop. Keep the rest. Thanks for everything. You're wonderful."

"Aye-aye, skipper!" said the young darling.

She was all curls and chipper dimples, flashing him a lovely amateur salute and toothpaste-ad smile, disappearing in a white flash of bum. Only then did Renard register her sailor get-up. Navy-blue crossed anchors over both cheeks. Same kind of uniform as a whore he'd had a long time ago in a port far, far away. *Where was that?* he mused.

The MC laid on a new platter and oozed, "Ladies and gennelmen, please put your hands together for the dramatic stylings of the lovely and talented Anastasia!"

"San Diego," said Renard under his breath as Anastasia began her dance with a strut. The fleet was in.

Overhead, over-amped speakers busted out "Pearl Necklace" by ZZ Top at maximum volume, causing Renard to become suddenly alert.

And there was Detective fucking Johnstone of the Vancouver pig farm at the top of the red Hummingbird stairs, slightly overweight, wearing his Calloway fedora and London Fog overcoat, rocking on built-up Cuban heels, surveying the scene below at the booths and tables before glancing at Renard with his evil yellow eyes, irises visible even in the burgundy light.

Renard stroked his beard and continued to smoke his pipe.

Anastasia's second song came on as she discarded her bra. She twirled and Renard wondered if maybe he'd chosen the wrong profession. Good song, though. What would he pick to get naked to?

He looked up into the face of the cop.

"So?" went the cop.

"Yeah," said Renard, as he watched Anastasia pirouette.

"No need for formalities," said the cop as he sat down. "What do you want?"

The waitress dropped off Johnstone's drink, and without breaking his eye contact with Renard, the cop absently fondled her sailor's bum. The song ended.

"Anastasia is now fielding requests!" boomed the MC. "Any takers, gennelmen?"

Renard held up a ten, the Canadian banknote a deeper purple in the light.

"Cocaine!" he shouted into the silence. The spotlight zoomed to Anastasia who shot a quick glance at Renard, then at the hidden MC in his booth. She nodded. Renard let the bill hit the table. The little sailor girl took the opportunity to free herself from Johnstone's caress and snapped up the money for her colleague. Clapton started his slide.

"Cute," said Johnstone, smiling and breaking his gaze to pick up the free drink. He sniffed it.

"Schweppes?" he asked.

"Canada Dry," said Renard, smiling. "The champagne of fucking ginger ales."

He drew on his pipe, pointed its stem at Johnstone, and said, "Now I want your side of the story."

Johnstone was cop to the bone, and gave it like a report.

"There's a World's Fair coming up in eighty-six. Know what that means? A million tourists, and a ton'll want blow. Right now the Italians at the docks control the trade, real small-time. I got bigger ideas and know some folks who share them. You know how much a cop makes? Me, I have a widowed mother to keep, and a goddamned boat that keeps leaking. In three years, I want a clean trade up and running. No dealers on the corner pushing to ma and pa from Iowa. A nice, orderly, profitable business. So I sold my services to your boys down in the States to start laying the groundwork."

"What happened?" asked Renard.

"This semi-hooker I picked up here knew a little bit about it, and she had a head for the bigger picture. Long story short, I trusted a woman, and now she's in the wind. Need I say more?"

"Not really. Now what've you got?"

"Well, thanks to you, I lost my helper."

"He wasn't helping you."

"Granted. So now it looks like I got you."

"You bet your ass."

They came to an agreement, ignoring everything else that carried on in the cabaret. At one point the cute sailor waitress came back and started to massage Johnstone's neck. Another set of strippers started their canned routines, and Renard broke a rule to have another drink with the fuzz. The cop was trying to get a bead on him, figure out what the hunter was, trying different word combinations to raise a reaction.

"Seeing how you're buying, *ese*," said the bent cop with a crooked smile.

It was like this: the cop would give up the missing girl's name and jacket, plus any developed or developing leads. There was an estranged husband, probably a non-factor, but maybe a line on her whereabouts. And a young chink chick, landlady at her last known address. Other than that, Renard got the girl's statistics. She'd made off with all the product, and more importantly, all the money.

"Five-foot-two. Brown and brown. Foreign national, Russian, here with the aforementioned dipshit husband, Landed Immigrant card. Educated, beautiful, sneaky. Goes under any name and can be Russian, Romanian, Bulgarian, spic, wetback, kike, greaser, whatever. Speaks a couple of those languages and English with an accent. Half-decent in the sack. Likes money, men, and fast cars. I'm looking for her to hide in a high-class hooker joint or with some rich sugar daddy. Still think the husband and the chink landlady are good to follow, because I've seen them together. Shake the pagoda tree and down come the dollars, you know?"

"What's her real name?" asked Renard.

"Irina Lermontova, maybe," said Detective Johnstone. "For all I know, she's the last Empress of all the Russias or the Pope's love child."

Renard made a note in his book. "Better way to reach you?"

"I got one of these." Johnstone took a beeper from his overcoat pocket. "Seeing as how we're in business together, maybe a *quid pro quo?*" asked the cop.

"You and me are together for now. But I work for certain parties that aren't that pleased with you. Remember that."

"Whatever you say, *comanche.*" Johnstone smiled levelly over his drink and said, "Leave a little more for expenses. You want to know the secret for living to a hundred? Drink a glass of rye whiskey every night for twelve hundred months."

Renard peeled off another twenty and got up. As he slipped out of the booth, Johnstone grabbed his sleeve and pulled the hunter down to shout harshly over the music, "You remember, *paisan*, that I'm still a cop in this town and you're just a fucking *tourist.*"

Renard paused, looked over at the new dancer a moment, and kneeled down to return, "Last time I got called a tourist was when I worked for the Phoenix Program. For a souvenir I took the dink's ears. I'll be in touch, *cabrón.* "

He left by the emergency doors while Golden Earring played "Twilight Zone," picking up his .38 en route. Outside by the LeMans, the girls kept up their stroll.

"Good time, daddy?" asked one.

"The best," said Renard.

He got behind the wheel. He had names now.

Irina Lermontova, Edward Windsor, esquire, and Dorothy Kwan.

When the bullet hits bone.

"Wanna date?" asked a decent blonde with long legs.

Why not? He drove her to a parking garage and up the ramp to its open roof. In an obscure corner Renard negotiated the price a little, handed over a twenty and a five, and leaned back in the car seat. He put on his Walkman headphones and started the tape. Elton John sang "Indian Sunset" while Renard gazed out at the hot spill of neon light streaming up from Granville Street. The hunter smoked his pipe as the hooker smoked his pole. Atop the Vogue Theatre, a winged, Art Deco Diana was poised to leap off into the void.

•180•

22.

· ·

The front desk switchboard rang in the middle of the night. Ted looked at the blinking red light with distaste. It meant work when all he wanted was rest. Ted picked up the receiver. He heard, "Mr William Linden here, Room 202."

Mr William Linden was the second-longest-serving tenant of the Victoria Rooms' distaff wing; the longest was the senior renter in 101. Few had seen 101 in the flesh. Once, while doing his rounds in the wee small hours of the morning, Ted had heard the mournful sounds of a harmonium from behind 101's door, and an old man's quavering voice singing, "Halleluiah! Halleluiah!" over and over again.

Mr William Linden in 202 was another character completely. Ted heard his brisk, reedy, senile voice start a report: "Smoke detector going off on the second floor."

The particulars of Mr Linden's senility proved nettlesome to a hotel night manager. He was a small, elderly bachelor with white hair and a crisp white moustache living in a tiny room. Ted had seen Mr Linden in the hallways; the fossil looked like Field Marshal Montgomery left out in the desert for a hundred years, now in badly reduced circumstances. He wore an eye patch under spectacles and moved about with the aid of a cane. Mr Linden smelled of stale tobacco and witch hazel and perpetually wandered the hallways of the Victoria noting burned-out lightbulbs, leaky faucets, and other bits of ephemera. Sometimes Mr Linden would call the front desk, but mostly he'd leave strategic, miniature, misspelled notes written in shaky schoolboy's copperplate, always opening with, *Mr William Linden, tenant, Rm. 202.*

He reminded Ted of the saddest comic ever printed in the paper. It was by Len Norris, from the Vancouver *Sun*'s Christmas Eve edition. Norris was the greatest editorial cartoonist in Canadian newspaper history, and the cartoon had run back in 1959; Ted saw it in one of his yearly yellow annuals. Len Norris was a superb draughtsman and artist who'd been inspired by his contemporary, the famous Giles of the *Daily Express*; they both wrote and drew comedy from character. Norris was, in fact, the better of the two, in Ted's amateur opinion.

In the cartoon, a lonely pensioner in a single-occupancy room sits on his iron bedstead at a small table. The plaster on the walls is cracked, a lonely Charlie Brown Christmas tree sheds needles. There's a loaf of bread under a "Merry Christmas" banner suspended over a hotplate and teapot. You can see a photo of a younger married couple on the wall, framed by a small garland of fir. The pensioner is hunched alone in a sweater vest, a forgotten widower, his left hand gnarled around a cup of tea. The other hand holds one end of a Christmas cracker.

Ted shuddered to think what Mr Linden's Christmases were like. But he had to deal with the man now.

"What room?" Ted asked the receiver.

"Room 202."

"What?"

The owner, Samuel Olaffson, had fortunately disconnected the old-fashioned fire alarm sprinkler system in the bedsit rooms on that side of the hotel. Mr Linden was pretty much the only renter with a working phone that reached the front desk. If Olaffson had left the ceiling sprinklers and phones operating, the building would probably be drenched every night by junkies burning popcorn, or crisscrossed by drug dealers calling from beer parlours and street corners. There were too many transient or resident madmen, down-and-out Indians, coffin cases, and broken souls. As a sop to the fire inspector, in each room a plastic stick-on smoke detector was installed. Craning his ear at the front desk Ted could hear one of them going off right now.

Linden's room. Jesus Christ.

Ted rushed up the stairs and went through the connecting vault door where he was immediately assailed with smoke pouring from 202. Mr Linden stood in the hallway.

"What happened?" he asked the old man.

"Don't know."

Ted pushed the door open to be instantly struck by its size. It was tiny, a shoebox, but more than that, the room was filled with locked steamer trunks and cardboard boxes stacked almost to the ceiling. Black burning smoke choked the space. Ted quickly appraised the narrow camp bed, the sheer insanity of an old man. A frying pan filled with eggs incinerated on a hotplate as the smoke detector shrilled. Ted saw that the small window was hidden behind a curtain. First thing he did was to step up on a trunk, pop open the detector, and take out the battery. Now he could think. Ted grabbed the skillet and looked for the sink. No. It was filthy as only an old man could make it, with moustache shavings, crusted toothpaste, shaving cream, and grease. Ted lunged at the curtain, wrenched it aside, tore open the window one-handed, and chucked the frying pan with the burning eggs outside, shouting, "Heads up!"

Behind him in the doorway, pipe in mouth and cane in hand, eyepatch on but spectacles missing, Mr Linden muttered through clenched teeth, "Don't know what caused it."

"Air," said Ted, controlling the situation. "Fresh air."

"Never happened before."

"You need fresh air," said Ted, in a louder voice.

"Never happened since I been here."

Ted turned off the burner, aired out the room, checked to see if any of the neighbouring hotel lunatics had been disturbed by the clamor, and got out of there before he caught Mr Linden's particular brand of madness. Ted had enough on his own hotplate already. And with luck, the switchboard would not ring again that night before Mr Lee took over the Victoria at seven.

There he was, the same industrious, indestructible Oriental, with his flask of tea and copy of *Qiao Sheng Ri Bao*. Ted was relieved to hand over the keys to an intact hotel. He went upstairs and watched another hot day unfold. Strange notions plied his head, the result of the long wakeful night and backwards life. With cold water he washed his face and in the mirror examined his busted lip. Ted needed a haircut, preferably before a bath and change of clothes. Nothing on earth was worse than the little hairs a barber left dancing around a man's collar. He checked the time, grabbed coat and wallet, then went out through the Pender Street exit.

A block or two to the west there huddled Macleod's Books in an old brick building. Ted walked there, and tried to peer through the cluttered shop's windows. Displayed were a panoply of used volumes: *Under the Volcano, How It All Began, Son of Socred*. Inside, he glimpsed paperbacks balanced in precarious piles and shelves groaning with hardbacks. Thankfully Macleod's was closed, or else he'd feel compelled to buy something. Ted hadn't even got halfway through *The Life of an Amorous Man*.

In the same building Ted went down steps underground leading to the Continental Barbershop. Its proprietor was already up bright and early, turning to Ted as the bell jangled on the door. First customer. One chair. The barber was a small man in his sixties, discreet, professional.

"Good morning, sir," said Ted.

He removed his jacket and placed it on a hook.

The barber motioned at the chair and Ted climbed in. A clean white cloth was thrown around his neck. Seniors were cut for three dollars; five for adults, a shave, two extra. The barber met Ted's gaze in the reflection and appraised him with a glance. Before starting he asked, in German-inflected English, "What would you like, sir?"

"A good healthy trim. Head's too hot. Something for the ladies."

"What style?"

Ted took in the homely ambiance: blue fluid-filled jars of Barbasol, a pin-up calendar on the wall. He was between mirrors: *spiegel im spiegel.* A radio played light airs, Offenbach.

"I put my head in your hands. Kind of a cross between Bobby Kennedy and the Hitler Youth."

Too late Ted's eye caught a sign over the door leading to the gents, *Otto Werner, Barber Since 1934.*

Quietly, Herr Werner went to work.

Ted had good hair and was definitely getting his money's worth. Because he had nothing to read and wanted to avoid staring at an infinite decaying series of his own face with a busted lip, he ventured small chit-chat with the barber. First the weather, then the Canucks, the government (rising from city to provincial then federal), and lastly Ted ventured, "1934, eh? Did you start cutting hair in Germany?"

"Yes, sir, I did," said Otto Werner, snipping with his scissors and examining the effect critically.

"Were you in the war?"

"I was."

"As a barber?"

"Ya."

Holy shit, thought Ted. *An actual Nazi barber.* And it showed: the man was damn good. Ted liked what he saw so far. The SS always had the best haircuts and uniforms, after all. Hugo Boss. Sinister style was excellent for morale. The scissors kept snipping.

"How is that, sir?" asked Otto Werner.

In the mirror Ted looked better, cleaner, and now his head would be cooler too. It was the type of haircut that could take over the world. "Good," he said and grinned at the barber.

Werner took a straight razor and gently brushed foam into the back of Ted's neck. Dexterously, he shaved a pure line and cleaned the blade on another cloth. Then he picked up a bottle from the counter and poured it into his hands.

"What's that?" asked Ted.

"Bay rum."

The barber applied it, and Ted smelled its aroma at the same time as he felt its mild analgesic sting. The barber whisked hairs off Ted's shoulders with a brush and held a hand mirror to the mirror so his patron could examine the back of his head. The infinity of his self opened up again, reflected in the looking glasses, deteriorating at about the eighteenth iteration (Ted counted).

Mimicking Gregory Peck in *The Guns of Navarone*, Ted said, "Better than good. *Perfekt.*"

Otto Werner made a professional bow and Ted got up.

"Thank you," said Ted, moving to his coat and wallet.

He handed over a five and two ones. Otto Werner took the money and shook Ted's offered hand. Ted made a small bow of his own, threw on his coat, and left to the tinkle of the bell.

He climbed the stairs and made a right. It was now a little after eight. Vancouver was back in business, its sidewalks beginning to fill. The next building over wore a sedate granite front. Ted felt much better, without any of the usual torturous bedeviling hairs after a cut. *Take a small walk,* he thought, *then back to the room for a shower, sleep, and a fresh start with a clean shirt.*

With a private smile, Ted turned to an open stairway leading up to a floor containing an antique fair. This was a sort of permanent flea market where a hundred thousand types of good junk were sold in a warm warren of little shops and stalls. Ted entered, to be immediately overwhelmed.

Here was the entire history of the world in ancient postcards, stereographs, piles of the *London Illustrated News*. Straight razors, bowling trophies, flint arrowheads, die-cast Dinky Toys of Lockheed Shooting Stars, cigarette tins, antediluvian cakes of Ivory soap still packaged in yellowing paper, capped green-glass Coca-Cola bottles filled with pop and original carbonation. It was all here, too much to process. Ted wandered awhile, looking at beautiful old things, survivors, the antiques much like their collectors, odd people gathered to sell their wares. He stopped at a small cubicle where an elderly, severely dressed Continental woman displayed an incredible collection of knick-knacks. He admired a wee statue of Puck and she asked, "Are you interested?"

"Only in you," leered Ted, chivalrously.

He'd planned on buying nothing, but a compliment to an older lady was always free to give, and usually had the pleasant effect of making her entire day. That's how he felt just at the moment, with a fresh haircut and a busted lip.

"*Charmant,*" she said, smiling, her wicked brown eyes pure distilled mischief in a slightly creased face. Her expression changed, however, as she sniffed, "What are you wearing?"

"Bay rum," said Ted, leaning over and offering her his neck.

She took a long, appreciative inhale, looked at him, and breathed out, "You smell *vunderbar.*"

23.

The needle lowered to the record's groove and "Modern Love" played out. The music poured from her parents' enormous walnut hi-fi set in the living room, probably the first time the machine had ever heard Davie Bowie. Dorothy usually listened to her LPs on a small turntable in her room with headphones on, so as not to disturb her mother and father. Nothing could do that now; they were in Hong Kong forever, their graves to be visited by Inspector Brian Kwok of the RCMP.

He'd telephoned in the morning from Vancouver airport, en route to the Orient. Uncle Brian thanked her again, speaking hurriedly in Cantonese. He apologized for not having been able to see Dorothy before flying out, and promised to honour her parents' memories at the cemetery in Happy Valley. Everything would be explained when he returned to Vancouver. Dorothy hadn't been to their grave markers. In fact, she'd barely left the house for the month following the news of their deaths. Now she was actually impatient while talking about her parents, lest Uncle Brian tie up the line if Ted Windsor was trying to get through.

Ted Windsor. He bore more thinking about. Sitting with him yesterday at the kitchen table she'd felt a tiny pull, two magnets clicking together. And when he left the house, the same small tug as the energy split apart. Was it an illusion? Did he feel the same way? He was in trouble, that was certain, and married, technically, and was too good-looking not to be a scoundrel. But it didn't matter. She was interested again, and that was more important than anything else. He'd roused her curiosity and appealed to her intelligence. She'd had so few lovers, and those mostly disasters. The last one, that prick, what's-his-name. But Ted needed her help, and Dorothy felt herself strangely willing to give it to him.

So she went to the cabinet and turned up the volume. It was ten o'clock in the morning. David Bowie suggested it, and for the first time in an age,

Dorothy danced. She started with a few half-forgotten formal exercises to limber up, then laughed and did whatever she wanted. Sunlight streamed through the windows as she spun on the living room carpet, not in her red pointe shoes but bare feet. No one was watching her, and she closed her eyes. When the next song started up, the sound of the toy piano, like a gamelan, cut her to the bone. She stopped moving and listened. *My lord,* she thought, *it's coming true.* When the music finished, Dorothy lifted the needle from the record. She felt cold, despite the morning's warmth, then looked out the front window unseeing and said, "China girl."

Upstairs, Dorothy methodically tore her old bedroom apart to rid it of every trace of her tenant's occupation. She ripped down the Duran Duran poster, swept lipsticks and makeup off the bureau into the trash bin, upended dresser drawers, yanked Ted's wife's clothes from hangers, and tossed the lot into Glad bags. A cold fury seized her. It wasn't fair. *At the very moment I feel as though I can fly away, an arrowshaft of doubt pierces through me and brings me back down to the hard ground. The age-less gods or my mother's ghost or four thousand years of history sends the barb deep, to remind me I'm just a girl, a Chinese girl in the saltwater city by the gold mountain in the land of the big-nosed, white-devil barbarians. Everything and nothing belongs to me. I have insurance money that paid out double-indemnity twice over, an inheritance, commercial property, a house in my name, too much past, and no idea what I'm going to do tomorrow.*

Her anger was presently given a tangible outward expression, one that might help restore that lost balance. Dorothy steeled herself, and in a cold fury utterly erased Irina Windsor's presence from her family home. She threw the earthly goods of the *saihausai min* out in the back alley for scavengers and crows to pick apart. Walking across the yard to the back door, her mouth a hard line, eyes furious and black, Dorothy stopped a moment in the sun. She balled her fists as hard as she could, screwed her eyes shut, tightened every nerve and sinew to the breaking point, contracted to a white-hot diamond of inchoate sensation and emotion and thought and fear and doubt and desire, and triggered a total explosion.

"Aieeeeeeeeahhhhhhhh!" she screamed, startling sparrows from branches.

She opened her eyes to the world outside her again, heart pounding, body trembling. A pure blue sky, warm yellow sun, the light breeze stirring small leaves and a tattered paper lantern hanging from the boughs of a cherry tree.

There, said Dorothy to herself. *That's better*.

She went back into the house for a nice salt bath to cleanse her aura. But before that she slapped a Blondie platter on the stereo and turned it up really loud.

"Rip her to shreds," Dorothy growled along, smiling.

The phone rang.

She chose a black velvet jacket, ivory silk blouse, and grey skirt. It was far too fine a day for the bus so Dorothy walked west through Chinatown. At the New Town Bakery, she indulged in what they advertised on a sandwich board for *gweilos* as a Chinese hamburger. *Siapao Bola-Bola*, steamed white bread filled with a salted duck egg, mushrooms, and ham. Delicious. She threw the sticky wrapping paper in the gutter by Shanghai Alley and walked a few more blocks uphill in the shadow of the verdigris, copper-domed Sun Tower. Dorothy paused at the corner and gazed up at the proud breasts of its topless caryatids. A tall man bumped into her. He turned, and Dorothy saw his pleasant, erudite face framed by neatly combed snow-white hair, thick white sideburns, and a dapper polka-dot bowtie.

"Stop the presses, young lady."

With a start Dorothy recognized the man from television. It was the newspaperman Pierre Berton, panelist on *Front Page Challenge*. He smiled roguishly, winked at her, and proceeded to jaywalk in the direction of the Avalon Hotel.

More strangeness, as a lady tramp pushed a baby carriage full of light bulbs to Victory Square. Dorothy came toward the intersection of Pender and Homer, the Victoria Rooms, where Ted lived and worked. She checked her wristwatch. It was nearly twelve, so she quickened her pace past a row of almost Elizabethan townhouses of white stucco and black wood which housed, from east to west, an Anglican bookshop, the office of a Queen's Counsel, the International Order of Foresters, World Wide Ladies Shoes Limited, and The Hole in the Wall. Over on Seymour Dorothy made a left and entered the Hudson's Bay department store. The dim, cool stairwell echoed with voices. Climbing up she saw the whole payphone bank occupied with people talking. It was a day for odd wonders, seemingly.

The elevator took Dorothy to the sixth, which housed large appliances, furniture, and the Seymour Room. The space was so vast that Dorothy was unable to see the far wall. Nary a soul browsed among the chesterfields and bedroom sets. Noises and smells came from her right. She followed the particular pong of Canadian cookery to the grill: boiled potatoes, roast beef with gravy, weak coffee percolating in urns all day. At a table, gazing out the window, waited Ted.

It's kind of like we're on a first date, thought Dorothy. As she got close, he turned her way and lit up, his split lip causing a wince as he smiled. He stood.

"Good," he said. "There you are. Look, I'm sorry to ask you here. I know the food is terrible, but it's comfort food, you know. And only old people come here for lunch, so I thought anyone following us would stand out."

Ted was right, Dorothy noticed. Around them were senior citizens, grumbling over their trays of Jell-O and grilled cheese sandwiches. Planted amid them, Ted was an iris growing from rusty dry ferns, she thought, then wondered, *what about me?* He came around and pulled out her chair, then motioned at the cafeteria.

"I only came for a chocolate malted, anyway. Do you want one, or something else?"

"A chocolate malted would be perfect, actually," she said.

As he went to the counter she looked out the window, past the spire of Holy Rosary Cathedral, northeast all the way to Burnaby mountain. A haze had developed over the harbour. It was another hot, sticky day, and a malted was the perfect antidote. When he came back, she spooned a little of the treat into her mouth and felt better. *It really is like we're on a date*, she thought again, but it wasn't, as well, and her nerves began to settle with the cool chocolate.

"How about you?" asked Ted. "Did it feel like you were followed?"

"No, but I can't say for sure. I was in a hurry so I didn't notice. I bumped into Pierre Berton."

"Really? Cool. Well, we have to be careful. Let's get out of here and walk around. That way no one can listen in. I've got something to tell you."

In the furniture department, Ted waved away a hopeful salesman. Dorothy and Ted wandered alone between the empty recliners and ottomans, eating their malteds. The light was so low it felt like they were in a museum display or archaeological excavation: *Treasures from the Hudson's Bay Company, 1983.*

"I'm pretty sure I found it," said Ted.

"Where?"

"Look."

They sat down on a sofa and he showed her a scrap of paper.

"LV is fifty-five. MMCDXXVI is two thousand, four hundred, and twenty-six. VIII is eight."

"So?"

"There's a post office at 2426 8th Avenue at the corner with Pine. It has a PO Box number 55."

"How do you know?"

"I was there this morning."

"Did you open it?"

Ted balled the scrap, stood up, and turned away from her. "No. You're going to think I'm chicken, but I had a bad feeling. Maybe I'm just being paranoid, but it felt like someone was watching me. I didn't go in, I just kept walking."

"You're just being careful."

He turned to face her. "Listen, this could be really dangerous. Those cops want whatever's in that box. Knowing Irina, it could be a time bomb. Or empty. She's caused you enough trouble already. You shouldn't get mixed up any more."

"And what about you?" asked Dorothy.

He met her eye. "All I want's a divorce. The quicker the better."

When he held out his hand Dorothy took it to raise herself from the couch. They finished their malteds, leaving the empty cups on an $888.88 mahogany dining room table made of wood from the jungles of the Mosquito Coast. *Lucky number*, thought Dorothy.

"We need some kind of plan," said Ted. "They know me and they know you. If they're watching, they'll grab me the minute I open the box. We need another person, maybe."

Dorothy stopped.

"No, we don't."

Ted turned to her. "Why not?"

"Because I have an idea."

She told him her plan. It was lovely how simply it came to her, a gift from the sky. She tested it out on Ted, and together they probed its weaknesses. A few details were refined, but the main scheme was sound.

Ted laughed. "It's brilliant," he said.

"I try," smiled Dorothy.

STRAIGHT TO THE HEAD

"Man, are you a cool drink of water to a thirsty traveller in the desert." His voice became more jocular. "And tricky. Boy oh boy."

"Well," said Dorothy, "we're a crafty people."

"Right, I forgot that."

"Pernicious too," said Dorothy.

"Don't forget inscrutable."

They laughed together.

"Well, it could be worse," said Ted. "You could be Japanese. They still haven't apologized for Pearl Harbor."

"Never. Do you know what we say about the Japanese?" asked Dorothy.

"No."

"That once upon a time, one of the Emperor's daughters was in a garden when she was raped by a monkey and became pregnant. The Emperor was so ashamed that he sent her to some islands off the coast, and that's how the Japanese were started."

"That's pretty bad."

"So was Nanking."

"*Touché.* Do you know how Canada got its name?" asked Ted.

"No."

"When the Portuguese sailors came back and were asked about this land so it could be put on the map, they said, *cá, nada.* Which means: 'nothing here.'"

She laughed. Ted then asked her, "What's Hell money, exactly?"

She paused a moment to consider, then said, "Monopoly money, sort of. No, not really, but, it's strange. Some Chinese people believe that after you die, you are judged by Yan Wang, Lord of the Earthly Court. If you were good, you go to a different realm, but the Chinese are very practical, and even in the afterlife we believe that spirits of the dead need money. As an offering to the ghosts of our ancestors, we burn Hell money on special occasions so they'll have cash in heaven."

By this time they were back at the elevator, where a lone man waited. He looked over blandly as Dorothy laughed, got in before them when the doors opened, and stood by the controls.

"Which floor?" asked the man.

"Main, please," said Ted.

Dorothy's eye caught the stranger's for a moment as he pushed the button. She noticed the faintest ghost of a smile at the corner of his bearded mouth as she heard him say, "Ground floor. Going down."

24.

· ·

They lingered near the perfume counter. It was sweet to see the Chinese girl apply a drop of Chanel to her wrist and hold it up to the Canadian for judgment. Renard had his back to them, watching from a spinning mirror at a sunglass rack. He tried on a pair of shades and was pleased to see how well they went with his tan suit. Pushing them to the top of his head, he followed the couple out of the store's Granville Street exit without paying.

Johnstone wasn't much use to him today; the cop had what he called "real police work" to do. In addition, Renard's targets, the Chinese and white boy, both knew the detective by sight. Christ, the cop was more liability than asset the way he operated. This left Renard solo, but unknown to both. He'd staked out the Victoria Hotel since before dawn, watching the loser husband work the front desk. At noon in the department store, the hunter's curiosity had been roused by the husband's meeting with the girl. There was nothing the hunter could do as they played friendly in the furniture department, so Renard had contented himself by sharing the elevator down with them. He was getting a feeling that this tail was a bust. The husband was nobody and the girl a dead end. They were into each other a little, that's all. Detective Johnstone of the VPD had a wild hair up his ass about the pair, indicating that there was something he wasn't telling Renard. *I'll humour the fuzz for forty-eight hours, twelve of which are now gone, then go for blood.* It was Irina Windsor *née* Lermontova he was after. She was both the problem and the solution. Always, *toujours*, there's a better play. Outside the store, Renard dropped the shoplifted sunglasses over his eyes and shadowed the couple.

When the Chinese got on a trolleybus, Renard had his choice of who to stick to. He chose the husband. The chick might have made him in the elevator. Some nut came walking along, and the husband stopped to talk to the crazy. The nut was wearing a sandwich board, and the sandwich board was printed with a full black-and-white photograph of a tramp from the thirties, himself wearing a sandwich board that read, *The Self-Made Man.* The nut wore a suit and tie and a peaked officer's cap. He had a neat beard much like Renard's own. The nut gave the husband a pamphlet. When he walked past, Renard accepted a pamphlet of his own. Craziness really is catching. Self-made madmen.

Vancouver's a weird kind of town that way, thought the hunter. Renard walked under the neon waterfall of the Niagara Hotel, home of a desperate strip club. Across the street was the competition, the Marble Arch, an even sleazier peeler pit. *It's getting to me, a little, working into my blood.* Renard tried to compare Vancouver to Seattle or Los Angeles, but couldn't quite pull it off. Vancouver lacked that tough Yankee energy, that real money hunger. It had something else going on, a kind of low-key, insidious mellowness. If what the pig Johnstone had said about the World's Fair coming up was true, this might be a town ready to join the future. Under a pitiless florescent light, back in the department store's mirrors, Renard had noticed a little more grey in his beard. It was getting time to think about leaving the game. Where would he end up? You could do worse than this shithole. Better, too.

"The self-made fucking man," he muttered, as the husband went back up the stairs into the shabby rooming house called the Victoria Hotel.

It was obvious the husband was going to crash after working a graveyard shift. Renard felt plenty stretched himself. He went up the block to Dunsmuir and went into the beer parlour of the Alcazar Hotel, better than the World-Famous Marine Club across the street. Inside, he ordered a beer and Mott's tomato juice to build himself a red eye, with ice. As the hunter drank his vitamin C with his vitamin Pilsner he read:

The Self-Made Man asks: Are YOU a "Free Person" or a "Voluntary Slave?"

THE CHALLENGE TO YOU IS THIS:
Can you call yourself a free person if you are working half your life for someone else? Does this not make you a VOLUNTARY SLAVE?

What Can Be Done For You?
Our educational Programs and Consultation will give you the answers to your questions and fill in the blanks regarding most situations that you find yourself in.

We provide you with valuable information that is most often contrary to established belief and the myths that are perpetuated by the news media and our system of education. Most of the information we are used to relying on can be proven to be ignorant or biased or both. In fact, you will know you are on both moral and legal high ground and they are not. How many good causes could you support if you weren't bleeding to death?

The question is very simple:
Are you a "Free Person" or a "Voluntary Slave"?

Don't REACT out of Anger. Be EMPOWERED with Knowledge!

For information about these and other issues please contact:

The Self-Made Man

318 Keary St., New Westminster, across from the Royal
Columbia Hospital

Suggested Donation: $5.00 at the door.

There were plenty of roughs in the dim saloon, shooting pool, bragging,
telling lies. At the bar a happy drunk told the stranger beside him a story:

"I was in this bar and after a couple of drinks had to go to the can.
When I walked in there were these three dudes. The one in the middle
wore a red toque. He was fucking one guy in the ass while the guy behind
him fucked *him* in the ass."

"What'd you do?"

"I got the hell out of there and went back to my drink. I told the
bartender: 'Hey there's three dudes in the can fucking each other up the
ass.' And you know what the bartender asked me?"

"What?"

"He asked me, 'Was the guy in the middle wearing a red toque?', and
I said yeah. And you know what the bartender said next?"

"No."

"'Oh, that's Charlie. He's lucky at bingo too.'"

Enough. Renard finished his redeye and got the hell out of there. Back
at his room in the Princeton, the hunter sat on the bed, watched freight
trains go by, and cleaned his guns.

That afternoon, after a refreshing nap, Renard called his employer from
a payphone at the Chevron station next to the hotel.

"Reporting," he said.

"We are all ears, Mr Renard," came the smooth tones of Mallory, the
go-between for mysterious Mr Peters. In the background, Renard heard
a woman squeal and a splash, probably into a swimming pool.

STRAIGHT TO THE HEAD

"The cop's in pocket. Two leads on the girl. Working both. Will give it two days and then turn the screws," said Renard.

"I must say that we are becoming ever more eager for a resolution," said Mallory.

"You've got three choices on this job right now," said Renard. "Cheap and fast but no good, good and fast but not cheap, or done right. Which one do you want?"

Mallory chuckled urbanely.

"I think our Mr Peters would prefer the latter. Thank you for the update."

Another squeal and splash before the connection clicked off, to be replaced in Renard's ear with a semi downshifting in front of the Chevron, and some bastard laying on the horn at the fuel pumps. Renard could almost taste the gasoline and oil in the air, it was so hot on the brute asphalt. He bought a Pepsi to scour out his mouth and went back to the phone with a mittful of change. Dialling a long-distance number in San Francisco led him to an operator's instructions to feed an ounce of silver into the slot. On the fifth ring, someone picked up and grunted.

"It's O'Brian," said Renard, using an old work name.

"Whaddaya want?" said the voice on the other end of the line.

"A bird's nest."

"Okay. Where?"

"Up north. Vancouver, Canada. One of those new portable jobs. But it's got to be registered somewhere."

"Give."

Renard passed over Mallory's contact number and arranged to phone back in a day or two. *I need to get on the far side of this whole deal,* he thought. *Moves are being made in another corner of the board that could knock me out of the game. The hunter wants to know where Mr Peters eats his fucking breakfast.*

From the same phone, Renard tried three times over the next hour to raise up Charlie the Hawaiian at Royal Maui Import/Export. He wanted to know if there'd been any movement on the docks. More product was coming in. If Renard was going to make it his, he needed hard information from the big man, the Kanaka.

That afternoon Renard didn't bother to page Johnstone. The cop was on duty all day, doing highly important police work staking out some smokehounds with a bale of ditchweed pot. For due diligence, Renard got into his Pontiac LeMans and drove over to Union Street to case the Chinese girl's house. Curtains were drawn and the neighbourhood rested quietly. He could do nothing but draw attention to himself in this summer somnolence, so Renard moved on, ending up at Irina Windsor's second-to-last known address at the Stardust apartments. Her present whereabouts: the wind. Renard couldn't even think of a reason why she'd still be in town, with 300,000 clams and that much in coke. But Johnstone swore she was still here. Two more days.

Renard insinuated himself into the Stardust, rode the elevator up, and carefully broke into the penthouse apartment, number 905. The hunter passed the next hour meticulously searching the suite. He could tell it had been tossed already, by more than one set of hands. Renard's only score was a crumpled photograph of the girl. When Detective Johnstone had snagged Irina what's-her-name at the Hummingbird Cabaret for hooking, the cop had never booked her before, so had no mugshot for Renard. It was tough to find a woman when you had no idea what she looked like. Typical of the *cochon*, sloppy. The whole set-up was too fucking loose. The photograph was in the last place anybody ever looked, squished under the couch cushions.

"Amateurs."

Sitting at the table, the hunter looked closely at the snapshot. She was easy on the eyes, it was true. An exotic cast to her features, brown hair and brown eyes as advertised, pretty enough to be a model. The girl looked a little like a movie star, but for the life of him Renard couldn't say which one. How she'd ended up with her dope of a husband was beyond him. *The same shit all over the world*, he thought, *the undying mystery: why's that beautiful woman with that dipshit?* Usually the explanation was simple—money. But once in a while, you met a real puzzler. Psychology of the female. The hunter actually sighed and reached for his pipe, then thought better of it and got away from the apartment, letting gravity guide him down the stairs for a few floors before catching a descending elevator.

Late lunch at Szasz, where Renard washed down Hungarian sausages and hot mustard with good Czechoslovakian Pilsner Urquell. Afterward, he drove to the Canadian Tire hardware store on Broadway to purchase an awl, two drawer knobs, polyurethane sheeting, a hundred feet of nylon rope, and a hacksaw. At an Army surplus store, he picked up three pairs of handcuffs, an Israeli ventilator mask and, after some bobbing and weaving with the fat-bellied counterman, one mace canister from a back room. At a big music store on Terminal, Renard browsed their entire inventory. He flipped through catalogues of sheet music, from Handel to Supertramp, admired an entire wall hung with gleaming brass saxophones, and listened to an energetic kid trying out a massive drum kit. In the end, all Renard purchased was a length of piano wire.

25.

· ·

At five to seven on Thursday morning Mr Lee came trooping up into the lobby, favouring Ted for the first time with an acknowledgment of his existence. The Chinese wordlessly nodded in Ted's direction, and Ted gravely returned the salutation. *Well, hell*, he thought. *I've arrived. Next thing you know it'll be the summons to Buckingham for a knighthood.* Up in his hot, cramped room, Ted squared everything away and put on his good Pierre Cardin summer suit. If all went well, he'd be seeing Dorothy later today. Ted wanted to look sharp.

They'd spoken once on the phone in the three days since their meeting at the Bay. Ted had picked up what she'd asked him to from the print shop and dropped off an item of his own. During that same time, he'd also tried to reach Pauline at her pleasant artist's garret in the West End, leaving a couple of messages with her WesTel service. He felt like he owed Pauline something; something for their night (and morning and afternoon and evening) of lovemaking, a proper gesture, like a good meal, or a rematch. Ted was enough of a man to admit he could manage summoning respectful affection for two women at the same time. Two were always better than one, and one was infinitely superior to none.

"You're quite the goddamned gentleman," he said to himself in the mirror.

Ted watched his hands knot a striped salmon-coloured tie in a single Windsor.

Payday. Downstairs, Mr Lee handed over an envelope containing six twenties. With fresh life Ted bounded out onto Homer. In front of the medical laboratory across the street sweltered a drunk in a toque and Cowichan Indian sweater, belting out, "Away, away with fife and drum, here we come, full of rum, looking for women to pat on the bum in the North Atlantic Squadron!"

Too conspicuous to be a shadow, thought Ted. Cops don't have that kind of imagination. Over the last few days Ted had become sure someone was following him, either Detective Johnstone or another party. In their brief phone call, Dorothy had said that she felt the same way. She assured him that she could handle anyone who came knocking. Dorothy surprised Ted. First she'd come up with their plan, and then she'd revealed a fascinating hidden talent. *Remarkable, the masks we wear*, he thought. *Mine for today? Put on your bold front for the world. Don't assume your true face. Dust off the one you use for job interviews and blind dates.*

Traffic seemed to be stalled in every direction. Several kinds of sirens sounded tangled screams in the distance.

"What's up?" he asked a driver listening to news on the radio.

"Solidarity march. Fucking pinkos."

Solidarity were a party of public-sector workers and their supporters protesting British Columbia's Social Credit government and its Premier, Bill Bennett. Bennett was the kind of politician who had five o'clock shadow by lunchtime, when he swallowed his first triple martini. Ted passed the tail of strikers' marching on Dunsmuir, where they'd managed to snarl the downtown corridor. Politics didn't interest him right now. He didn't care much about Pierre Trudeau or Ronald Reagan or Maggie Thatcher. Who was the Premier of the Soviet Union? Who cares? Today, Ted's thoughts were music from a chamber piece for four to five parts. All the Solidarity protest did was make it harder for someone to follow him in a car, he reckoned. So Ted sauntered in the burning morning sunlight, following his idle fancy. He passed the main Canada Post Building, a monumental, block-spanning Stalinist cube. Ted peered through a window at a mural in fine socialist-realist style. It detailed the march of progress in mail delivery from pony express to supersonic V-2 rocket. Forward into the future went Ted, complicating any pursuit by traversing one of the city's countless parking lots. It was probably possible to go from one end of the city to the other by crossing only acres of asphalt. Vancouver was thin on the ground.

On Granville, Ted admired a cute girl dressing mannequins in a shop window. A fellow playing Pink Floyd on the violin by the Capitol 6 movie theatre received all his remaining loose change save bus fare. Ted bided his time, catching a trolley bus, standing around and waiting for the number ten in front of a porno place advertising a wide selection of adult movies on both VHS and Beta.

West 8th and Pine was a most undistinguished block, hard off Broadway. How Irina had found the spot Ted couldn't possibly imagine. The post office itself sat on a raised platform stepped up from the sidewalk, a one-story concrete box faced with a glass front, over which sat a molded cement abstract bas-relief frieze. Around it ranged boring buildings: a block-sized, perfectly anonymous stuccoed complex that could house anything from Interpol's Pacific field offices to a vending machine whole-saler, and the scruffy, obscure, revivalist Church of the Good Shepherd. Nobody lived anywhere near this no man's land somewhere between Broadway and the disused train tracks by West 4th. From Ted's vantage in the miserable shade of an alley-side elevated courtyard, he could see a postal employee open the bureau and begin the day.

"I get it," said Ted, a truth revealed by his subconscious mind. *Irina chose this post office because it's familiar to her,* he thought. *It looks positively Soviet. Concrete brutalism in a harsh, nature-free environment. She saw it, and it reminded her of home. I'm sure of it.*

Ted tried to remember what Irina had said about her upbringing behind the Curtain. She was always obscure and crafty when he tried to pin her down for details. There were hints of forced exile; Irina had once alluded to being labelled an "anti-social element." He wasn't even certain where she'd been born. Her family were White Russians, he thought, from Odessa in the Ukraine. Or were they? Every Russian family had been torn apart by war and revolution and famine and deportation and exile and worse, so that there was no way to say for sure where anyone was really from, or if it even mattered. Irina's father had been just as vague as his daughter about their past, especially concerning the details of his defection. *They must have thought me the perfect fool*, thought Ted again. *And yet, she'd loved me. Once, maybe only for a single day, but she'd loved me. I thought that would be enough. Wrong again. Well, we'll see what she's hidden here. This is the last door I go through for my wife.*

"Last but one," he whispered.

Ted's wristwatch said nine-thirty. It was time to go.

Again, Ted felt an invisible watcher tracking him. *Either way, damn soon enough I'll have a better idea of what the hell is going on. Might lead me to more trouble (and knowing Irina, it probably will), or it could be pure anticlimax, a popcorn fart.* Soon. Ted's blood started to pump harder, and he felt a tingling excitement that cooled the sweat along his spine. *Watcher or not, I am opening that box.*

Mr Windsor walked out onto Broadway into the sunshine and six lanes of traffic, as an express bus to UBC full of standing students thundered past in a pall of exhaust.

Make a right on Pine, walk half a block, and climb the steps. Chivalry and good manners compelled Ted to help a tiny, bent crone pull her wheeled shopping cart up the steps to the door, which he opened for her. He blanched when he saw the line-up. Didn't these folks have anything better to do than mail letters? And where the hell were the tellers? Every wicket read *Guichet Fermé*. Ted reminded himself that he wasn't here for commemorative stamps or collectable silver dollars, and the unworthy delight at skipping the queue overwhelmed any remaining anxiety coursing through his nervous system. The door closed, and the air-conditioned post office suddenly turned into a walk-in cooler, with that hushed quiet common to all federal government spaces. A photograph of the Queen and Prince Philip hung just a little bit above the Canadian Coat of Arms.

There was a maple-leaf flag limp on a pole. Next to the monarch he saw a framed copy of the new Charter of Rights and Freedoms and a pictogram of a teller that indicated, English/*Français*.

All along the left-hand wall, visible from the street, there were tiered rows of little silver square doors from floor to eye-level. Ted walked along calmly, now positive that he was being watched and that he'd been followed from the hotel. He took the silver key from his pocket and slid it into a hole. It fit, but it wouldn't move. His stomach turned a little. *Fuck. After all this, I'm at the wrong post office. I read the Roman numerals wrong, or Irina was just screwing with me. Her last little joke, and meanwhile she's in the Yukon right now, drinking Everclear and laughing at me.*

Ted fiddled with the key in frustration and it clicked over. He turned it all the way around and the door swung open.

A folded manila envelope rested within. Ted pulled it out with a now-unsteady hand. He didn't dare look over his shoulder. Next, he slid the envelope into his inside jacket pocket, re-locked the box, and began to leave. When he opened the door to the outside, he registered the change from a climate-controlled chill to baking heat, which instantly dried his sweat to salt powder. *Which way should I go?* He went down the steps. Pine Street sloped northward, and Ted let gravity lead him. He crossed 8th Avenue and went through a gap between parked cars to the east side. Ted stepped off the curb past the alley and two strong hands like clamps grabbed his upper arms from behind while another pair took his hair in a painful grasp.

"Mail call, loverboy," hissed Detective Johnstone. "Cash on delivery."

26.

. . . .

Dorothy watched Ted get grabbed by Detective Johnstone and a bearded man who hustled him into a car. Her throat closed and body weakened. This is what they'd both been afraid of, even having imagined this outcome. Dorothy felt her heart drop. They had him. He'd been caught. While she play-fumbled with forms at a desk by the front window of the post office, Dorothy whispered a tiny, secret prayer to herself. The car pulled away, and she wondered if she'd ever see Ted again. He'd promised her she would.

The next person in line went to the wicket for an airmail package. Dorothy shuffled over to the PO boxes, pulling her shopping cart awkwardly behind her. Her eyes found the two numbers 54 and 55 side by side. She took out the key and opened 55. It was full. There was a single package wrapped in brown paper. Dorothy removed it, careful not to attract attention, and put it in her cart. It felt like espionage or shoplifting. Reverting to training, Dorothy behaved as she did when taking high-end fashions. Her mother's daughter again, a professional thief. A gentleman opened the door for her and helped Dorothy, still in character as an old lady, out of the bureau and down to the sidewalk. Ted had been the one to help her up—a saucy touch, she'd thought.

"Teamwork," he'd whispered.

Nobody else paid her any mind. Heat and pollution hit Dorothy like it was coming from an open charcoal barbecue grill, but she was still cold all over.

Two days ago, Dorothy had rented PO box 54, next to 55, then mailed it a manila envelope. She and Ted were certain that Johnstone had eyes on both of them, and it was Dorothy's idea to use her secret talent to deceive the cop, just in case. If no one was watching, fine, but their precautions had been justified. Ted had acted as the lure, a tethered goat pounced on by a tiger. He was a lure that'd been sacrificed to beasts, she thought.

"What'll they do, kill me in broad daylight?" he'd asked her, back in the furniture department of the Bay.

"They might," she'd said.

His laugh, his careless grin, the way he brushed back a loose curl of hair. The hair Detective Johnstone had grabbed in a rough handful. Mouth bone dry, Dorothy pulled the cart up Pine to Broadway and waited for a bus to take her away. She was not going home, no, not going back there anytime soon. *Maybe next year, 1984, Year of the Rat. If Ted can lie his way out of police custody, I'll see him later today. Give me an auspicious sign. Anything—a penny on the sidewalk, a four-leaf clover growing from a crack, the number eight spray-painted on a wall. My private encyclopedia of superstitions: deaf, blue-eyed cats, red flowers, cracked walnut shells. Universe, please tell me we did the right thing. Take the danger off us.* The bus came along and Dorothy hoisted up her cart, paid the fare, and sat in a front seat reserved for the handicapped and elderly. It was an express bus full of university students, so Dorothy suffered, listening to their inane chatter and second-hand Valley-girl-speak all the way west.

"He was like, I'll call you, but like, he never did," whined a short blonde.

"That's like, totally bogus," said her gum-chewing friend.

"Gag me with a fork," said Dorothy.

The bus continued along Broadway, turned left on Alma, right on Tenth, and climbed uphill. Before it technically left the city and entered the University Endowment Lands, she pulled the cord and clumsily alit at Bianca, the bus driver helping her down. Dorothy was now in Point Grey, a part of Vancouver almost alien to her. It bore passing resemblance to a village and seemed seriously Anglo-Saxon to her eye. There were low, one-storey shops for English butchers, florists, both the Canadian

Imperial and Royal banks, a fish and chip shop. The Union Jack flew over a diner called The Diner. Even from across the road she could smell old grease, sausages, fried eggs, and brown sauce. Still disguised as a grandmother, Dorothy blended right in with the elderly wives of remittance men and retired colonial administrators. There used to be so many Englishmen working the bureaucracy at Vancouver City Hall that local mandarins called it "the Foreign Service."

Careful and slow, Dorothy traversed a busy parking lot and went into the Safeway. Near the bakery she found a restroom for handicapped people, locked the door, and transformed herself.

Gone was the little old lady when Dorothy emerged, the disguise in the garbage, disposable cart folded and abandoned the moment she left the toilet. She wore unassuming street clothes, picked up a red wire basket and started to shop. For the next ten minutes, Dorothy selected various non-perishable items, testing every technique she and her mother employed when stealing *prêt-à-porter*. To pass the time she prepared an imaginary picnic for a possible lover. Bick's dill pickles, SunRype lemonade, a tin of cognac pâté. At last satisfied that no one was tailing her, Dorothy took one more precaution; she abandoned the basket in the dairy cooler, stepped quickly through an employee door in the rear, then strode confidently through a storeroom to a loading bay and out to the alley behind the supermarket.

The change in temperature caused her skin to prickle in pinpoints of perspiration, and she slipped away into a pleasant residential neighbourhood of Arts and Crafts bungalows and shady plane trees. Sprinklers watered green lawns and rose beds; the heat wave didn't touch this upper-middle-class preserve. Still feeling completely foreign in the country of her birth, and ignoring the weight of the unfamiliar package in her purse, Dorothy maintained a steady pace downhill. She tried not to think and doubled back and forth, east and west at random, until she was back in a minor commercial district at 4th Avenue and Alma. A blue BC Tel sign hung over a doorway, and now thirsty, Dorothy entered Jerry's Cove.

First she used the bathroom, this time for real. Graffiti over the toilet paper dispenser read: men=pain. women=trouble. Dorothy made a payphone call, then waited in a non-smoking booth invisible from the front door. She'd never willingly sat alone in a pub before; despite clean Porsches and Mercedes parked outside (belonging to the real estate agents and lawyers eating lunch within), Jerry's Cove was still mostly a working-man's watering hole. Dorothy ordered a glass of ice water. The waitress suggested the drink special.

"It's a Bloody Caesar with Mott's Shimato juice."

"Shimato?"

"Like Clamato, but with shrimp."

"On second thought, I'll have a white wine spritzer instead," said Dorothy.

As she drank, Dorothy organized her thoughts. Blondie's "Rapture" played sinuously from the speakers. Was that the sign she'd been waiting for? Music was luck. Where was Ted now? She didn't allow herself to imagine the worst. Too often her thoughts would leap masochistically (or was it sadistically?) to the most negative outcome. Not this time. *Despair is easy. Distract yourself*, she thought. A television showed horse racing, and it surprised Dorothy to notice the broadcast came from the Happy Valley track in Hong Kong. Uncle Brian must be there now. What was *he* doing?

When her parents had flown off on vacation last year, Dorothy had felt no apprehension at all. For days after receiving the official telegram about their accident, however, she'd become completely inert. It had been unbelievable. At any moment a taxi would pull up, and she'd hear her father cursing as he carried up the luggage, her mother nagging him to hurry along. When the torn postcard arrived in the mail some weeks later, the one which had so excited Uncle Brian, it was as though it'd been mailed from a different world, a forgotten planet trapped in the past. A last message from father to daughter, thrown across the Pacific, from death to life. Why had it been torn? How incredibly long ago it seemed now, something that'd happened to a different human, a different Dorothy Kwan. *I've changed,* she thought. *I'm different.* And while she lost herself in her own past, sipping her wine, Dorothy failed to notice a predator circling.

"How about another drink?" asked a strange man.

Startled, Dorothy looked up at a tanned pick-up artist oozing confidence. Guffaws from the bar led her eye to his buddies, elbowing each other and looking her way.

"Why would she want anything from a limp-dicked little faggot like you?" said a voice behind the sleaze. His eyes went wide and he turned around to reveal Mary Worthington.

"Screw off to your bum boys," said Mary, jerking her thumb at the two jokers.

Then, louder, she said, "There's a sale on Judy Garland records and Vaseline down the street. Better hurry up, girls."

It shut them all up, and the waitress at the bar concealed a smile. The realtor slunk back to his partners. They grumbled at each other, radiating angry vibrations, dogs rapped on the snout with a rolled-up newspaper.

"My god," breathed Dorothy in relief.

"Your goddess, more like it. Now, what're we drinking?"

Dorothy forgot Ted as Mary set sail with gossip and stories of low doings in Vancouver's high society.

It was cool and quiet in their cozy back corner. Dorothy felt pleasantly at ease, not even minding the mysterious package in her purse. They'd open it together, she and Ted, later. And after that? Maybe it was the wine, but Dorothy felt a current running through her, an arousal, an animal sensation. Mary said,

"One more story, and then we'll go."

"Please."

"This one you're sworn to secrecy on."

"Like you were, I bet," said Dorothy.

"Ha! It's the latest, and'll make your day. So, this is a true story, cross my heart and hope to die if I tell a lie. Remember Brynne McKnobbit, married your special slime, Kenneth Abernathy? We saw them at The Eatery the other day."

"I remember."

"Well, it turns out that a while back, back when Kenneth and Brynne were in college and engaged, Kenneth was sharing a house with a couple of his rich school buddies. He was roommates with this guy Carlos, an Argentinian here for business school before he took over his family's horse ranches. Carlos is an *amazing* dancer, by the way."

"Among other talents, I'm sure."

"And *then* some. Well, the last year before they graduated, one morning Kenneth woke up and started looking for Brynne, who wasn't in bed. She wasn't in the bathroom, or the kitchen, or the living room, or out on the patio, so he knocked on Carlos's door and poked his head in. Guess what he saw? Brynne and Carlos in bed together, naked and asleep."

"What happened?" asked Dorothy.

"Well, Kenneth woke them up and asked what the hell was going on. And do you what Brynne said?"

"What?"

Mary paused, smiling, and took a sip of wine. With a twinkle in her eye and mischief on her lips she said, "'I must have come into this room by mistake! I don't remember anything! I must have been sleepwalking again. I used to sleepwalk when I was a little girl, but I haven't sleepwalked in years.'

"So, Kenneth turns to Carlos and asks him what's going on. And Carlos said that he was so drunk last night that he passed out and had no idea Brynne was even in his room until Kenneth came in."

"And Kenneth believed them?"

"What are his options? Like you said, her family's loaded. So, they got married, remember?"

"*Yes, I remember,*" said Dorothy.

"Oh what do you care, you got your new guy, don't you?" Mary sailed on, hitting her hand on the table so hard that the wine glasses jumped. "But, this is the best part!

"Last Christmas, just after Brynne had Sophie, they took the baby to Brynne's family's house for supper. And I don't know *how* it happened, but over turkey Kenneth made some joke to Brynne's mom like: 'I hope Sophie doesn't inherit sleepwalking from her mother.'

"And you know what Brynne's mother said to him?"

Mary's eyes went wide and her mouth opened.

"'Oh no, it wasn't Brynne who was a sleepwalker, it was her younger sister Carol.'"

The wicked loud laughter from Mary and Dorothy caused the waitress, the bartender, and all the regulars of Jerry's Cove to look to the booth at the back of the bar.

27.

· ·

Renard got behind the wheel of his LeMans after Johnstone manhandled the husband into the back seat. In the rear-view mirror, he watched the cop drape an arm around their captive's shoulders and shove a pistol into his ribs.

"What've we got, loverboy?" murmured Johnstone. "Let's take the scenic route."

The engine started, and the cop gave Renard directions. They drove north on Pine, over the tracks to 4th, where Renard waited for a green. He glanced at the husband again and noted his pale face drained of blood. *Scared is good*, he thought. *Scared plays well.* He steered the Pontiac a few more blocks into another interzone of stereo wholesalers and foreign-car dealerships to more abandoned train tracks, which the car paralleled until Johnstone told the hunter to go through a rusty gate in a chain link fence onto a gravel drive. The radio station played Trooper's "Three Dressed Up as a Nine."

"That's perfect," said the cop. "Listen to that tune. You're not gonna waste our time, are you, loverboy? Stop here, this's good."

Renard parked the car in a gravel clearing underneath the Burrard Street Bridge and got out. To their left sat the Molson Brewery. He could smell warm cereal, barley and hops malting. More broken train tracks here, high blackberry bushes and jungly woods on both sides. The vast concrete foundations of the bridge were stained with graffiti. Renard was amused to read *Fuck les Flics* on one. From far above them fell the grey noise of streaming traffic. For all of that, the trio were now all alone in a wasteland of broken bottles, the only life grasshoppers flitting and clicking through the ragged grass.

The cop kicked Ted Windsor out of the car and followed with his pistol still drawn. Renard watched calmly, observing the way Johnstone handled the scene. From his belt the detective took out a pair of handcuffs and snapped one around the husband's wrist and the other to the Pontiac's rear door handle. He then frisked Windsor expertly and from a coat pocket pulled out a folded manila envelope.

"Let's see what we've got," Johnstone said. "Treasure map, maybe?"

Whatever it was, it wasn't money or product, thought Renard, even before the cop tore open the flap with a thumb. Out spilled a sheaf of weird, cheap looking banknotes.

"What the fuck is this?" Johnstone suddenly barked at the husband.

He pushed the package into Windsor's face.

"Hell money for alimony," said Windsor.

Renard picked up a red note for 100,000 dollars with a Chinaman on it. He looked at the husband again. Windsor stood upright, hadn't pissed his pants, and seemed to observe Johnstone from a distance. *Maybe he's not a dipshit*, thought Renard.

"I know it's from the PO box, but what the fuck is it?" spat Johnstone.

For effect the cop kicked Windsor's feet out from under him and the husband landed on his knees with a cry, arm behind his back still cuffed to the door.

"A divorce application," said the husband through gritted teeth.

"Ha!" grunted Renard.

Johnstone turned to him.

"You think this's fucking funny, you fucking fuck? This jagoff fucking with us?"

"He's not fucking with me," said Renard.

"Oh, so that's how you want it. Well, laugh at this. Give me your keys."

"Why?"

The cop turned soberly toward him and said slowly, with a furious burn in his voice, "Are you asking a police officer a question and failing to comply with my request? When I tell you to do something, you snap to it, you fucking tourist."

"You want to shoot him in the trunk?" asked Renard. "No dice. Should've brought your own car for that."

Johnstone took two steps forward and stood chest to chest with Renard, who now felt the pistol barrel pressing against his own kidney. The pig stank of stale sweat and whiskey, with eyes bloodshot in the morning glare. It'd been an agony staking out the post office with him, but this was worse, and the cop's exhale entering Renard's nose almost made him retch. He hadn't realized until right this second how desperate Johnstone was. Renard found it difficult to take amateur criminals seriously. The hunter stood expressionless while the cop growled into his face.

"I said, give me your car keys. This is me asking politely for the last time."

"Here you go."

With keys in one hand and his gun in the other, Johnstone returned to the husband, who was now standing up again. Viciously the cop kicked the rear door closed, dropping Windsor to the ground again. He put the gun barrel to the husband's nose.

"You're going to tell me what she did with my shit, and you're going to tell me now."

"I don't know what you're talking about," said Windsor.

"Cute, little loverboy. You'll tell me, or you'll die. And if you don't, your little chink bitch will."

"Who?"

"Cute cute cute. Let's see how cute you are in a minute."

Johnstone got into the driver's seat of the LeMans, started the engine, and curled his lip at Renard. "Love this car," he shouted over the engine.

With that he ground the gears and punched the gas. Ted Windsor was pulled up almost before he could get to his feet and run. Renard watched the cop do fast doughnuts around the bridge's uprights, kicking up plumes of dust and dragging the husband in a circle until he suddenly braked.

"Where is it?" shouted Detective Johnstone out the window.

The husband lay against the Pontiac's body panting.

"Won't talk?"

The cop hit the gas again, and Renard watched him drag Windsor around some more.

The hunter had been witness to various interrogations in his professional career. He'd employed a number of improvised techniques of his own. Renard remembered splashing Tabasco into Constable Hickey's eyes just last week. So many methods. Meat is frail. Car batteries attached with jumper cables to the scrotum, pliers to yank fingernails, various exotic combinations (needles, lit cigars, chains, insects), in addition to good old-fashioned beatings. Man was most inventive, he thought, when torturing his fellow man. Fuck Leonardo da Vinci and the *Mona Lisa*. The iron maiden or the rack showed a far superior Renaissance artistry. Maybe it was the accumulation of all those memories, or this fucking pig Johnstone he'd had to put up with for this lousy contract, or simply a growing, sneaking sympathy for Ted Windsor, but watching the cop drag the poor bastard around started giving Renard a bad taste.

"Once more around the block, driver!" cried the cop. "And don't spare the whip!"

More dust as the Pontiac did a figure eight, and the husband stumbled along, trying not to have his arm pulled from its socket or his leg run over as Johnstone weaved and turned. The cop suddenly braked hard. He threw open the door. Windsor collapsed, covered in dirt, unable to speak.

"Where is she?" shouted Johnstone. "Where's your whore of a wife? Where's the stuff?"

Renard watched in amazement as the husband weakly held up a hand and slowly beckoned at Johnstone with a crooked finger. As the cop leaned close, Windsor extended his middle finger right in Johnstone's face. Renard smiled to himself and shook his head.

"Hey!" shouted a voice.

Both Renard and Johnstone turned in the direction of the woods west of the bridge.

"Hey! What're you doing?"

Almost hidden amongst the trees Renard saw a tramp, an Indian, peering over at them. The tramp cried out again. "What're you doing to that guy? I'm-a call the cops!"

Renard turned to Johnstone who looked back at him furiously. Whoever the bum was, he was now a witness. The interrogation had suddenly become complicated. The cop motioned at Renard with an out-flung hand, commanding, *go get him*. Renard shook his head and gestured sideways like a waiter ushering diners to a table, as if to say, *after you*. The detective stood tall, hitched his belt, roared, and ran toward Renard, almost body-checking him as he took off after the Indian, who'd disappeared into the bush. Renard watched the cop crash into the tangle. The hunter took pipe and tobacco from his coat pocket, then filled and lit a bowl. He smoked, listening to the diminishing sound of Johnstone blundering through the brambles and bracken, shouting, "Stop! Police!"

It was peaceful beneath the bridge now, with dust settling, a warm dry hum of summer in a forgotten corner of the city. Renard could go up to the husband, offer him a drink or a cigarette like the *commandante* of a firing squad, and then start breaking the poor sucker's fingers. Or he could wait and let the dirty cop do the dirty work. Weighing his options, Renard inclined toward the latter. Ted Windsor now leaned back against the car, still gasping for breath. The husband's coat was torn at the shoulder, trouser knees ripped to shreds, and he watched Renard with exhausted, wary eyes. Finally, in a croaking voice Windsor said, "You were in the elevator."

"Not bad," said Renard.

"Going down," said Ted, weakly.

He almost collapsed. Renard put his hand on Windsor's sweat-soaked chest, propping him back up.

"Your wife has got you in *beaucoup* trouble," ventured Renard.

"Estranged wife," gasped Ted as he closed his eyes.

The man has some grit, thought Renard. *I've been in tight spots like this and probably managed just about as well, and I've been trained. Not bad for a rookie.*

"One time," Renard heard himself say.

Shit, he was talking to the target now. Bad idea. But why not?

"One time, we were waiting on a guy," he continued. "We needed to ask him a couple of questions. So we staked out his apartment. We couldn't go in because of too many neighbours, but we knew he had to come out sometime. We must've been there for a week, three guys in shifts, twenty-four hours a day, itching and sweating and stinking. When we finally got fed up and kicked down his door there was a note on the table waiting for us."

"What did it say?" asked Windsor.

"It said, 'Fuck your mother.'"

"How'd he get away?"

"No idea. We never caught him."

"I don't understand."

"It's like this: we already have you. Keep playing it cute, but we're going to keep asking you questions until we have what we want. You're not getting away."

Just then there came a shout from the bushes. Renard took out his Beretta and walked back toward the woods, pipe smoldering between his teeth. He soft-footed into the lee of a bridge pillar and looked around. Branches trembled and Renard heard a groaning. Johnstone tumbled out, hat missing, his long coat smeared with gluey brown clay.

"Lost him," grunted the pig.

Renard walked to help the cop up. He took an elbow and pulled Johnstone to his feet, then brushed off some filth. The detective pushed Renard away.

"Hands off."

He knotted his tie and looked over Renard's shoulder back in the direction of the Pontiac.

"Son of a bitch," said Johnstone softly.

"What?"

"Loverboy's getting away."

28.

He'd taken the mortal chance and now ran with what strength remained to him. Ted could almost feel the gun barrel pointed at a spot between his shoulder blades as he stumbled under the Burrard Bridge. Breath came in hot, burning gasps, with sweat stinging his eyes. There were less critical pains elsewhere—his wrist wracked and wrenched, handcuff still attached, his knees scraped raw. In furious desperation and agony, Ted had torn the door handle off the car. *Ignore everything else and run. Run faster than a bullet through your back.*

He had a damn quick decision to make. If he ran to the right, it would be into a snarl of blackberries or back down the rutted easement that led into the wasteland. Going that way, the cop and the bearded guy could easily drive him down. Leftward would mean jumping onto the seaside path that ranged along the woods, and Johnstone might cut him off to make an arrest in plain daylight before joggers and bicyclists. *That's if he doesn't immediately shoot me on sight.* That same path went back the other way alongside a marina filled with fishing boats and then in the direction of Granville Island. The problem there was that Johnstone and the beard might circle around to nail Ted anywhere along the exposed promenade. He didn't have the speed or energy to outrace them. There was nowhere to hide. Ted couldn't climb up the gigantic bridge. He was trapped, boxing himself in, a fox bayed by hounds, running out of energy, running out of breath, running out of options. He kept on running anyway.

Breaking out from between the bridge pillars, Ted's feet stumbled over a rusty rail then onto a defunct train track heading north toward False Creek. Without thinking he followed it, not daring to look back, the only sound in his ears his own ragged respiration and blood pounding. He crossed the jogging path, running parallel to the line of the bridge. Ahead of him Ted heard a booming horn, and suddenly he remembered exactly where he was and how he could get away. He ran faster.

"C'mon," he gasped. "C'mon."

This railway track was part of an old interurban and freight system. From the derelict junction point under the bridge, the system once connected to tracks in several directions. A set of rails went back to Granville Island, another hooked up with 4th Avenue and the Arbutus line south out of the city to Sea Island. Most importantly, the junction had once been fed by a train bridge from downtown Vancouver proper. And there it was, the Kitsilano trestle, an old swing bridge. It was supposed to be torn down last year, but like all government initiatives, the destruction was delayed and over budget. Ted hustled. If he could get across it, he had a chance. The bridge was a low, wooden affair, long overdue for destruction, so old that the swing in the middle remained its only working part. It still needed to function. The brace and tracks opened right in the middle of the span, turning on a pivot forty-five degrees to let boats in and out of upper False Creek. The sound Ted had heard was a boat horn.

There, on the right, a line moving along the waterside. As Ted lurched closer he saw a red-hulled tugboat pulling a gravel barge. And now a bell started ringing. He sprinted along the track, struggling over split ties and tufts of Scotch broom, straining to avoid broken television sets and abandoned shopping carts. Ted pushed through overhanging blackberries whose thorns tore at his hands and forearms and suddenly came out into the clear open, onto the trestle itself. It angled ahead of him toward the great CNR yards on the north bank of False Creek. Ted slowed and chanced a quick look back, but the brambles had closed behind him. To his right the tugboat and barge plowed through the water and the warning bell kept ringing. Ted felt a sudden tremor underfoot as ahead of him the swing section pulled away.

He ran. It was difficult on the ties; they weren't spaced for a man's walking stride, never mind his frantic run. Any misstep could put Ted's foot into an empty space and bring him down with a broken ankle or worse. This was the chance he couldn't afford to miss. If Ted failed, he'd have to jump. It wasn't a fatal long drop, but in the water he'd be dangerously exposed again, the cop or his partner easily able to shoot down on him at their leisure. *No time to think. Keep going. Go, goddamn it, run.*

He jumped onto the moving section as it turned. Ted still had thirty yards to cross on the swinging platform to get to the other side or be stranded in the middle, stuck between two stools. He fell. He fell flat on his fucking face and almost gave up, almost began crying with pain and exhaustion and terror, but with a final surge of fear he pushed himself up and staggered the last few feet to jump the gap to the other side just as it opened on a void. Ted dropped to his knees a moment, turned over on his back, and sat up. At the far side, he saw the man with the beard thrash through tangled bush and emerge at the bridgehead. His pursuer was too late. The swing section creaked to a stop, and the tugboat pulled its barge through the breach. Ted was on one side, his seeker the other. Weakly, Ted stood. The man with the beard held a gun. He kept walking forward along the bridge. When the stranger got within shooting distance, Ted raised his hand, handcuff dangling from the wrist, giving him a salute. The man stopped, met his eye, and slowly shook his head. Fox and hunter. He put away his gun. Ted turned and trotted away along the trestle track to the other side, the city, and safety.

"Safety. The tying run, safe at home."

Ted made it out of the maze of freight tracks into Yaletown, a slowly dying section of Vancouver filled with warehouses, machine works, abandoned cooperages, and wooden boardinghouses. Industry faded as the railyards were being shut down for good. The CNR site would play host to the coming World's Fair, and after that, it was zoned for eternal condominium towers of glass and steel.

"You're covered in dirt, your pants and coat are torn, you're bleeding in several places, you're wearing a pair of handcuffs. Safe and fucking sound," Ted said.

For the moment, he was at a loss. He needed to get out of downtown, off the streets, back over to the side of the water from which he'd just run. The bridges were no use. If Detective Johnstone wanted to, the cop could simply choke off the Granville Bridge with prowl cars. Ted wasn't able to summon up the nuts to head straight back on Burrard, directly over the spot where he'd been flung around like a tether ball. The Cambie Bridge was too far away to the east, the wrong direction entirely. Taxis were out, easily traceable, all equipped with radios; buses and trolleys too fucking slow and obvious. Walking around on foot wasn't much good either. Ted had to clean up so as not to attract unwelcome attention from people on the street.

On top of it all, he now panted with thirst. In Yaletown's warren of sun-heated brick buildings he felt himself cooking. Mingling together in the leaden air was the sweet-and-sour foulness of garbage, warm tar, and dog shit. He took off his coat, careful not to strain his twisted muscles or open any clotting wounds, and draped the fabric over the silver handcuff. *Where was Dorothy Kwan right now, and what was she doing? What had she found in the post office box? Lord though, she'd been right all along*, realized Ted. *If not for her, I'd be worse off. Much worse. But how exactly?*

Ted hiked along, mostly down alleyways, avoiding open streets, with the notion to head roughly west and bide some time. Then he stopped a minute, snapped his fingers, and doubled his pace. He headed more or less right back to the Burrard Bridge, reasoning that Johnstone and his bearded partner would figure he'd hightailed in *any* other direction. There was one more way off the downtown peninsula. Ted kicked himself for nearly having forgotten it.

He crossed Pacific and went under the north arch of the bridge, coming out on the seawall. A little to the west Ted entered a large, brown, windowless building by the water, a pyramid with sloping sides, truncated into a trapezoid. The Aquatic Centre. Inside he was assailed by echoing screams and shouts, wet heat, a broken rectangle of artificial blue water, and chlorine so thick in the air he could almost taste it. Ted paid for entry and went no farther than the changing room. He stripped, showered, and sponged his clothes clean with wet paper towels. An inevitable pair of naked elderly men with loose skin and grey crotches stood around, nattering interminably about John Turner's chances of becoming Prime Minister. A few homosexuals cruised Ted charily, clearly intrigued by the handcuffs.

"Rough day, sweetie?" asked one.

"And how."

"I can make it better."

"Got a hacksaw?"

"No, but I do have a foot of pipe."

Ted laughed, dressed, and left his suitors behind. He continued to keep his coat folded over the cuff and walked back down to the seawall and a small dock close to the beach. In a few minutes a small ferryboat resembling a logging sidewinder tied up. Ted paid fifty cents and climbed on. The boat powered off into the water, west into English Bay, threading through incoming sailboats and more working tugs that pulled barges and small logbooms. The day had turned around. Out on the ocean, Ted felt light again, dried by the bright noontime late-September sun, cleansed by rushing sea air.

The little ferry pulled into a pocket marina sheltered by a breakwater off the tip of Vanier Park. Ted was back on the south side again, in Kitsilano, no more than half a mile west of the Burrard Bridge and his near-dismemberment. He walked through the park. In front of him sat a structure that looked like a modern Scandinavian church. It was a wood-and-glass A-frame nautical museum holding the St. Roch, first icebreaker to crack the Northwest Passage. Behind it stood a proud Centennial totem pole, carved by Chief Mungo Martin for Queen Elizabeth II. It represented the ten tribes of the Kwakiutl nation, whose land this once was. Lost tribes in the white man's Babylon.

Away across the field lurched another feature, an immense broken rusted square standing upright, an avant-garde monument to the northwest passage itself, designed by a Chinese artist. Grasshoppers screeched thinly from the yellow grass then suddenly stopped. The earth lay hard and dry beneath Ted's feet, his footfalls sounding as hollow as drumbeats. He walked through the square monument in the spirit of the immortal troubadour Stan Rogers and made a northwest passage of his own.

All the parkland next to the Burrard Bridge was once an Indian village called Snauq. The forgotten patch of bush between bridge and park remained the last scrap of a moth-eaten, uninhabited reserve. Ted felt a heavy loginess, a result of the pain and adrenaline wearing off. Fatigue and thirst welled up again. He needed to stop and sit and rest a bit, so he continued along, his slurring steps leading over a small creek spanned by a tiny Japanese bridge. A rank brown pond lay choked with bulrushes. Somewhere here you could dig up a chest full of gold coins, buried by the last old Indian lady of these parts, he remembered. They'd never been found. Ted checked his pockets and discovered loose silver.

In search of a vending machine and a cold drink, Ted went into the cool, quiet museum and planetarium next to the pond. It was a conical white building built in the shape of a West Coast Indian's cedar hat. Downstairs in the dim atrium, he bought a Coke, draining the bottle in one long refreshing draught. Ted checked a clock. Still time to kill. The elevator door opened on an empty chamber. *Okay*, thought Ted. *Let's go.*

"Please select a floor," said the elevator.

"Hold your horses," Ted said. "I'm-a coming."

He pressed a button. The box lifted him up to the top floor. The door opened and the same metallic female voice said, "Planetarium. Going down."

"Thanks, darling."

Ted stepped out into an empty curved hallway lined with windows looking out over the park and False Creek. It was like the corridor of a space station. Along the far wall rested smooth black leather couches facing the wrong way. Ted drifted along, searching for a quiet corner where he could close his eyes for a moment. There was no way anyone could have followed him here. Then he laughed.

"Looking for a corner in a round building. You're an idiot."

With that he came to a velvet rope in front of a half-closed set of doors. He heard a brass fanfare begin and slipped inside.

This was the planetarium theatre and a show had just begun. Ted sneaked to a seat as the screen filled with the immensity of outer space. A long tracking shot through the inky blackness passed by galaxies and stars, gradually closing in on one system. The camera flew past a comet, then Pluto, Uranus, Neptune, Saturn, Jupiter, and Mars before zooming onto the Earth. A voice with a thick Indian accent said, "In the beginning, Raven was flying through the darkness. On the beach by the sea he saw a clamshell with little creatures in it. Raven was curious, so he landed and discovered that the creatures were men. Raven wanted someone to perform mischief with, but the men were too small and cold. So Raven flew away, and stole fire to give to man."

The screen now showed flint striking sparks on steel, once, twice, thrice, then all of a sudden a blowtorch igniting. Boom! Now everything happened at once: refinery flares burning bursts of orange flame, masked welders, molten metal pouring into molds, the pounding of rivets into girders, skyscrapers rising, foundries smoking, and loggers chainsawing down trees. B-52 bombers dropped clusterbombs, the Zapruder film stuttered, gridlock clogged a massive interstate clover-leaf. Apollo 13 lifted off, followed by an atomic mushroom cloud on the Bikini Atoll as Ursula Andress rose glistening from the water in *Dr. No*, all to Deodato's funky version of *Also Sprach Zarathustra*. The voice of God himself, Lorne

Greene, began booming out something about mankind and civilization, with Spaceship Earth adrift in the cosmos, and the danger of permanent nuclear winter. But by now Ted's eyes had closed and mixed in with the bombastic narration his fading mind heard:

"USSR versus Anglo-Saxondom! Is our Empire doomed? Once again the nations stand at the threshold of disaster—our failure will precipitate the elimination of the freedom we cherish. The Bible alone holds the key to the future of the Anglo-Saxon-Celtic people. The prophecies relating to Judah and the lost tribes of Israel must be understood. The coming conflict between East and West is inevitable. The Lord promised that the line of David would continue to occupy the throne of Israel 'until He come whose right it is, and I will give it to Him.' We can trace her most Gracious Majesty Queen Elizabeth II's descent to Kenneth MacAlpin, the first King of Scotland, to the kings of Ireland, back to Heremon, the husband of Tea Tephi, who was the daughter of King Zedekiah of Judah, and thence back to David, appointed King of Israel in the eleventh century before Christ."

Someone shoved his shoulder, and Ted started awake to an empty theatre. A dry old stick of an usher in waistcoat and bowtie said, "Sonny, there's nothing on your ticket that says that you can sleep here."

"Okay, okay."

Ted went back into the curved hallway, again empty. He read a poster on the wall advertising an exhibit from 1969, *Mansions of the Sun*. The same elevator opened automatically and the same female voice said, "Planetarium. Going down."

Back downstairs Ted went to the men's room for a slash and to splash water on his face. When he stepped back out, he checked the clock again. It was time. Next to the gents' a payphone started to ring. Ted picked up the receiver.

Now all of sudden there was no one else in the room. No Mary, no bartender or indulgently smiling old lady drinking Harvey's Bristol Cream. They'd all disappeared. Ted and she were alone, and Dorothy had the sensation of a wild hummingbird flitting around inside her ribcage.

"I'm fine," she whispered.

Mary broke in. "Your guests, are we? I didn't know you were an Army man."

"I'm not. Air Force cadets, way back when."

The bartender visibly relaxed. As Ted bowed at the old woman he said, "We have time for a quick one. Another sherry for Madame, I think, and a bottle of very cold white wine for us."

"Do you hear that, Arthur?" laughed the lady. "Hop to!"

The bartender threw a white towel over his shoulder and shook his head good-naturedly on his way to fill the order. Ted, Mary, and Dorothy sat down at a corner table. Dorothy heard the pop of a cork, and soon a glass of chilled wine rested in her hand.

"To crime," said Ted.

They clinked and drained their glasses. Ted poured again, and at the same time the two women noticed the handcuff attached to his wrist. Her first flush of excitement over, Dorothy saw his ripped, stained shirt, and how wired and tired Ted was, a wild current of electricity carefully contained, an overbright lightbulb about to flash and crack.

"Kinky," said Mary, motioning at the cuff.

"And how," said Ted.

He turned to Dorothy. "Were you followed?"

"No," she said.

"And?"

Beneath the table Dorothy opened her shoulder bag. Ted reached down and felt the package within. Again, she felt his barely contained enthusiasm and wondered, who is it for? For himself, or for us? She noticed Mary watching them slyly.

"Well, you two conspirators are up to something, but never mind little old me. I'm just the wheelman."

"More than that," said Ted. "What are the odds you two were friends?"

"It's a small town, your majesty."

"What do you mean by that?" asked Dorothy.

"Ask *him*," Mary laughed.

"It's an old story," said Ted. "Later, please. You know what? I think we should go. I'm getting the yips out here in the open. Do you two mind?"

"Whatever you want," said Mary. "I'll be in the car."

She swallowed his wine with a wink and left them. Ted went to pay. When he came back to where Dorothy stood he said, "I'm so glad you're okay."

"Me too. What happened? Are you hurt?"

"Just my pride and my carcass. You were right all along. I was being followed. If not for you, well, I don't know what would have happened. Thank you."

They stood apart for a moment. Then Ted brushed back a loose strand of her dark hair and tucked it behind her ear.

"Not here," she whispered, taking his hand and pulling him behind her, back outdoors.

A great horse laugh whinnied from the old lady in the corner as they left. "Did you hear that, Arthur? To crime!"

On the walkway outside Dorothy stopped. "Can I ask you something?"

"Anything."

"Do you see the glass stucco on the walls here? Well, I've always wondered, where do the cobalt blue bits come from?"

Ted thought a moment, then smiled and said, "It's perfect."

"Perfect?"

"They're from Milk of Magnesia bottles. Vancouver's enough to make anyone sick to their stomach."

The Worthington house in Point Grey hid behind high, sculpted hedges and overlooked the beach. Mary's father had inherited quite a tidy bit upon his mother's death and had made much more on his own as an executive for BC Gas. To Dorothy's eye the place was like somewhere the Kennedys gathered in Hyannis Port. She could picture the Worthingtons playing friendly roughhouse games of touch football or devious croquet or riding horses on any one of the many separate lawns. The whole clan usually dressed in casual polo whites, everyone happy, blond, and tanned.

"Where are your parents?" she asked Mary as they pulled into the garage.

"London, I think. The place is mine 'til Thanksgiving. Make yourselves at home."

They entered the house and passed through a mud room filled with squash racquets and golf clubs to a large white kitchen hung with gleaming copper pots and pans. From there they traversed the main hall and Mary lead them briskly into a sitting room filled with costly things. She made straight for a drinks cabinet, helping herself to club soda on the rocks.

"*Mi casa*, et cetera. Your stuff's upstairs, Dorothea." Mary cocked her head at Dorothy. "How long'll you be here for?"

"It depends," said Ted.

"On what?"

"On what Dorothy has in her bag."

"Ah, the pig in a poke. Well, children, even though I'm dying to know what you're up to, I think it's better if I don't, so I'm going for a dip. Ta-ta."

She was now alone with him. Dorothy suddenly suffered from shyness, sensing Ted felt the same.

"Show me around," he said.

"You've never been here before?"

"No. Why?"

"Because you know Mary. How? Did you ever...?"

"No, never," he said.

He gestured at her to pick up the bag, and they explored the premises. The main floor had a book-filled study, grand dining room, spacious Regency-style living room with cavernous fireplace, and a games room with a billiard table.

"Any secret passages?" asked Ted.

Dorothy swallowed a lump in her throat. "Let's see what's upstairs," she said.

Six bedrooms and three baths. The guest room had a balcony overlooking the swimming pool, north lawn, and the ocean beyond. On the bed rested the suitcase of clothes Dorothy had brought days before. She heard a splash as Mary dove into the pool.

"Shall we?" asked Ted.

Dorothy turned, her face flush, to see him looking at her, then at the bag in her hand. She nodded. *I don't actually want to know what it is*, she thought.

"On second thought, let's wait," he said.

"Yes," Dorothy heard herself say, her voice husky.

She dropped the bag as they came together in the balcony doorway, a waft of wind stirring pale cream curtains around them. He held her, and she pulled him close, looking at his face, searching it with her eyes, feeling him tremble, echoing the shivers coursing up and down her skin. He traced the line of her jaw with a fingertip, and she closed her eyes as his lips touched hers softly. His other hand, the one with the handcuff, pressed against the small of her back, and she felt a warm core of heat building below her belly as he kissed her gently, then harder. *Again and again*, she thought. *More.* He moved his hand to stroke her hair, brushing the nape of her neck, sending icy sparks flying to every part of her body. Her pulse quickened. She opened her mouth to his, and they kissed even more deeply.

He ran his hand along her quivering body as she pushed herself against his chest. Now they unfolded each other. He moved his hand to her breast, and as he began kissing her neck Dorothy sighed aloud. *I want him*, she thought. *So help me, I want him.* All her fear evaporated. She touched him, felt his hard cock against her, felt herself rubbing against his leg, and wanted even more. Dorothy kissed him hard and felt his hands at the buttons of her blouse. She reached down and unbuckled his belt, amazed at her own boldness but now on fire, wanting, truly wanting something for the first time in what felt like forever. *Heat melting ice*, she thought, the delicious chill of a popsicle in summer. She slipped from her blouse and felt the cold metal of the handcuff along her back; in a moment, Ted had unhooked her lacy black bra to free her breasts, her nipples brushing against him as they stepped nearer to the bed.

They didn't make it, instead kneeling together on the carpeted floor as Dorothy slid her hand inside Ted's unzipped pants to free his cock, warm and thick in her hand. His hands moved across her bare body and undid her pants, pulled down her panties, and without another thought, Dorothy and Ted slid free from their clothes. She was entirely sure only of this moment with this lovely man and how much she wanted to be taken by him. To take him. He pushed her back and put his mouth on her neck, then on her breast, and trembling even more, she felt him kissing and licking down her belly to the source of the heat. He kissed her everywhere as she ran her hands through his tousled hair. A bolt of lightning struck Dorothy the moment Ted put his mouth between her legs. She felt her own slippery wetness, his lips, and then his hot, strong tongue. She gasped as he tasted her. *Oh.* And again. *Oh.* She pulled him in closer and clamped her legs around his head, and a dazzling jolt of flashing fire coursed through her in waves as she let herself come. *Oh.*

Downstairs, Mary knew. She'd impishly put on a record and turned up the volume, so while Dorothy and Ted continued to make love, they heard Roxy Music's *Avalon*. After the first crescendo there came more. Ted kissed Dorothy and lifted her to the bed, where he spread her apart to the smooth, decadent romanticism of Bryan Ferry as he slid inside her. Dorothy arched, closed her eyes, and now felt a roaring in her ears. She didn't care what time of the month it was or that she wasn't on the pill; all Dorothy felt was lust. A pure, healthy lust for this man, for his cock inside of her, for his heat and his scent and the pressure of his naked body on hers. Time twisted away. She lost count of the kinds of pleasures her body felt in the softness of the bed; she simply glided along. Some part of her mind noted the light changing, and then a silence downstairs as the record stopped. And soon, after Ted had exhausted her, she began drifting away. Part of her knew that he hadn't come yet, but the greedy, selfish, satisfied part of her didn't give a tuppenny damn.

When she woke Ted was standing naked on the balcony in an amber evening light, his skin glowing, his slim body easy on the eyes. Dorothy felt as sleepy as a cat sated after a fresh kill. When she moved her head on the pillow, he turned around to her, framed against the deep blue bowl of the low-lying sea, a golden Apollo.

"There you are," he said.

"Mm," said Dorothy.

"Have a drink. Mary left it for us outside the door. Such a wonderful hostess."

On the bedside table sat a bottle of champagne in melting ice. Ted came over and put a sealed envelope from Mary into her hand. She clumsily opened it to read Mary's writing.

Bad girl.

He handed Dorothy a shallow crystal goblet. She took a sip of the delicious cold wine, the ticklish bubbles in her nose causing her to close her eyes a moment.

"You'll need it," he said.

"Why?"

"Look."

She opened her eyes to Ted pointing at the dresser and the opened package. Dorothy focused her gaze on a substantial pile of money and clear plastic bags of what had to be drugs.

"Feel like getting away?" asked Ted. "We'll travel the world in style. With the cocaine we might not even need a plane. Do a couple of lines, and fly direct, faster than the Concorde."

"I can't," said Dorothy, feeling sick.

"How come?"

"I don't have a passport."

30.

They cruised the streets for hours trying to track their rabbit, Renard becoming more disgusted with the cop at every block. Detective Johnstone interrupted his self-pitying, indignant monologue to bark brusque directions.

"That goddamned loverboy. My whole life I've been up against jerk-offs like him. Make a left here. Rich kids. Private school motherfuckers. They take sailing lessons. Sailing lessons! Too good for a diesel. You get them in the force. Especially the brass. All the muckymucks rubbing elbows together with their thirty-dollar haircuts and secret handshakes. Make a right. Too clean to get their manicured hands dirty like the rest of us. Turn their noses up at real police work—work that keeps this town fucking humming. Making a bee-line from university to a soft little desk job and two-hour wet lunches at the club. Look at me. I walked a beat on Skid Row for eight years before I clawed my way into plainclothes. And I'll show them. Another right. They think narcotics is just cracking the skulls of chink hopheads or busting hippies for a lid of grass. No vision, no thought of the future. Don't need it; they're lazing on their daddy's porch while I'm out sweating in the field. Go straight. Any wonder I'm out for myself? You try supporting a widowed mother on the kind of chickenfeed they pay an honest cop. No fucking dice, *comanche*. But I'll show them. Pretty soon I'm gonna be the one soaking in a Jacuzzi up in the British Properties, looking down on all the midgets fighting for crumbs. This town needs me. Call me Mr Fucking Vancouver. Stop."

Renard braked the Pontiac in front of the Victoria Rooms on Homer.

"There's no way he'd come back here," the hunter said.

"Could be," said Johnstone. "That doesn't stop us looking around."

Johnstone badged past a Chinaman at the front desk and huffed his way upstairs to the top floor, followed by an unwilling Renard. The cop shouldered open the door to Room 34, startling a noisy crow from its perch on the windowsill. *Weird omen*, thought Renard. He crossed his arms, stood in the doorway, and watched Johnstone tear the room apart. First the cop ripped out the desk drawers and plundered the empty closet, then took out a switchblade and slit open pillows and mattress, filling the enclosed space with down feathers. The detective growled as he rooted around, sweating heavily, his face flushed crimson. *Un cochon sauvage*, thought Renard. When Johnstone took down the mirror and smashed it on the floor the hunter said, "Bad voodoo."

"Fuck you."

For a frightening instant, Renard felt a mammoth presence looming behind him before being body-checked aside. All of a sudden, the tiny room was totally filled with the huge form of a red-bearded Viking.

"No, fuck you!" boomed the giant.

With a massive hand, he picked Johnstone up by the throat and pinned him to the wall. The detective clutched at the ogre's forearm. With a purpling face he managed to squeak out, "I'm a cop."

"You are shit. Where is the warrant, Mr Policeman? Where is habeas corpus? I am the owner here, and what I have is a trespasser."

The hotel owner turned Johnstone's pockets inside out, removing his pistol and wallet and throwing them on the ruined bed. The cop rolled his eyes, pleading at Renard, who was too taken aback to move, and was in no way inclined to put himself in the middle of this. The hunter felt like Jack up the beanstalk and didn't want this giant sniffing around for more blood. The big man pulled Johnstone's badge free and flipped it open.

"Ah, yes. I have been seeing you hanging around here. But where is the right of it? A man's home is his castle. You are a vandal."

He let go of Johnstone and the detective fell to the floor, gasping for breath. The Viking turned to Renard, eyes filled with the kind of smouldering fury that waited for oxygen to spark it into roaring flame.

"And you," he rumbled, "are you another barbarian at the gates?"

"I'm a peace lover," said Renard, holding up his open hands.

This man was not the enemy, and this wasn't the field of battle. Detective Johnstone's luck was way out, and Renard knew better than to throw his lot in with a loser on a bad streak. Enough was enough. All day he'd watched the cop get butt-fucked. *I'm out*, he thought. He made the peace sign and backed off. The Viking rewarded Renard with a grim smile.

He boomed, "No, you are more civilized, I believe. Go with God, and do not come back here, or I will rip your dick off."

That was it. The hunter's association with the police had been officially severed. Renard drove back to his hotel. At the gas station, he tried to reach Mallory and Mr Peters to relay the news. The phone at the other end rang and rang. Frustrated, Renard had a drink in the Princeton's bar and tried to read the local paper. Trains rumbled by the picture windows, rattling the liquor bottles on the shelf. One geezer joked to another, "Why's Jesus such a lousy hockey player? Because he's always getting nailed to the boards."

Renard ducked out to call his birdwatcher down in San Francisco and see if Mallory's portable phone number had been traced. Again, he failed to connect. The hunter felt antsy and restless, so he drove back closer to downtown and ate a bowl of wor won ton at the Pink Pearl.

Ted Windsor had done them both brown. Renard recalled the details of the encounter on the swing bridge, the husband's salute before turning away and jogging off. *This job is getting old*, he thought. *Here I am, dragging myself through another foreign city, mixed up with fuck-ups, all for a couple lousy bucks in the bank. No home, no family, no friends. This is your life, Thomas Renard, if that is your real name. Start thinking about getting out.*

"To do what?" he asked himself. *I have no talent besides manhunting and violence. A resumé that starts with killing Vietnamese. Do I want to open a bar or a hardware store and start paying taxes? Who do I know who retired clean to the square life? Sam's a bum, pissing his golden years away loitering around the racetrack. Fred's history; a full-scale heart attack at fifty-one. Draw up a* census of former trained murderers and all you'd count up are divorces, drunkards, deadbeats, and corpses. It's not a profession with much of a pension scheme. *My retirement plan's been the promise of nuclear war*, thought Renard. *Solve all our fucking problems.*

Renard recalled the close ones: the Berlin airlift, Korea, and Cuba. An air-raid siren over the general store in Renard's Louisiana hometown had wailed and wailed that October day. What about the flight of birds over Sakhalin, or the vodka-soaked Soviet general who almost started the big one because a passenger jet strayed out of Finnish airspace? Christ, Ronald Raygun would press the red button if Billy Graham said that God told him to sort out the quick and the dead.

These were morbid thoughts. Renard went back to his hotel. Waiting for him at the desk was a note from Charlie the Hawaiian, requesting a meet tomorrow night. *Saturday night in the city*, thought Renard. He now had no line on Irina the Russian, her husband, or the Chinese girl. Without further orders from his employers, Renard determined to observe a private Sabbath, clear his head, and start all fresh.

The next day the hunter rested. He went to the Hastings Steam & Sauna, its benefits advertised on a card in the window.

Burns Calories and Controls Weight...

Eases Joint Pain and Stiffness...

Improves the Immune System...

Removes Toxins and Mineral Waste...

Relieves Pain... Reduces Stress and Fatigue...

Increases Blood Circulation...

Purifies Skin Tissues and Cells...

Improves Skin Quality and Tone... Since 1926.

"Sign me up for the lot," Renard said to the counterman.

He got a private room so as not to mix with the queers in the basement and cooked out all his ill humour for ninety minutes. Back outside Renard felt resurrected. The weather seemed to be turning: dry, bright, and windy. One of those Technicolor days. On the other side of the road, a paint store's wares popped in a vivid rainbow spectrum. Some quality in the light was giving Vancouver the intensity of a Kodachrome slide. At moments like these Renard felt fully North American, a twentieth-century man. Here there was no past, just the promise of a new and improved life. He caught himself whistling and smiled at his reflection in a storefront church's window. *Fuck it.*

"*Venez aussi, mon cher ami,* and sit down by me, son, and I will tell you *bon* story of old time long ago. When everything she happy, and all the birds she sing, and I am strong like moose and not afraid nothing," chanted Renard.

As he turned off Hastings onto Campbell, back in the general direction of his car, Renard felt a change. The environment no longer had any American brio. It felt impoverished and cheap. On one side of the road sat square wooden row houses, most splintering to flinders, paint peeling, porches sagging, front lawns full of dandelions and weeds. Opposite them an ugly set of Socialist housing blocks had been callously cemented. And that was it: he had the sensation of being undercover behind the Iron Curtain. Slack wires strung together slumped telephone poles. An indestructible, shapeless old woman with a headscarf grunted by. Renard caught a glimpse of steel teeth in her grim mouth. The Finnish-style steam baths he'd left were a product of the neighbourhood. As if to validate his intuition, Renard walked past a squat brick Russian community hall which sat next to a miniature Orthodox church, its tiny onion domes glinting gold in the sun. As a wind from the east world kicked along, Renard tasted dust and coal smoke and the first faraway promise of the long northern winter to come.

That afternoon Renard treated himself to a nap, and in the evening swallowed a rare steak and a couple of Löwenbräus at the Brave Bull. His variable mood persisted into the night. Charlie the Hawaiian wanted to talk about their scheme; with independence from the cop, Renard felt unhampered, returned to his natural element as predator and solitary hunter. There was no betrayal of an equal partner involved. Johnstone had lost the plot and was no fucking good. Some men attracted trouble the same way that naming fate called it to you. Best to be self-reliant, to walk from shadow to shadow, between the raindrops.

At midnight Renard steered his LeMans over the tracks and to the docks, where he pulled up at the Royal Maui warehouse. The wind blew parched and gritty. From underneath a side door seeped blue light. Renard entered the office. The same portrait of the tennis girl with her bare ass. He went into the cold storage room and its smell of chilling Freon. The hunter moved toward the television glow and sound of John Wayne drawling. Charlie's Barcalounger sat empty. Renard stiffened and he felt an abrupt stab of alert animal fear. He stood in place, craning to hear, swiftly considering his options. Every instinct screamed: get out now.

"Too late," said a voice behind him.

Renard swivelled and heard a hammer cocking.

"Slowly."

He turned to see Johnstone negligently pointing a gun at his belly.

"You got your weapon back," said Renard.

"Throw-down piece. If you make a move, you can bust its cherry for me. Put your hands behind your head and take your medicine."

Behind Johnstone stood two figures. One was Charlie the Hawaiian, who looked embarrassed. The other moved forward. Renard's scrotum tightened and a sick nausea spread from his stomach. Constable Hickey leered at him. The hunter saw beads of sweat where the constable's crewcut met his forehead and an ugly glint in his swinish eyes.

"You measured your own rope," said Johnstone. "First you mistreat Hickey, then you leave me with that ape. No one likes getting humiliated, especially a cop. And now I gotta explain that I lost my badge and gun. You know how much paperwork's involved? How much shit I'm gonna have to eat?"

"Always thought pigs loved eating shit," said Renard.

Johnstone smiled, and his eyes went more yellow. "Oh, so now you're begging for it. Don't worry, you'll be on your knees soon enough. What have you accomplished? You've alienated the local constabulary. And we hear you want to cut in line. Charlie told us about your little play. You really thought you could take us out?"

"It's what I'm paid to do. My boss won't be happy to hear about this."

"That's funny. You know why? Your boss was the one who gave you up. Remember what I called you at the Hummingbird?"

Renard shook his head. He'd played his only card and had been caught bluffing. *This could be it. Should I say my prayers? Christ,* he thought, *I was a fool to feel that iron pyrite confidence. Lost my edge. What's worse is the cosmic injustice of it all. If I've got to go, I want to go with style. Against someone worth it. Not this* cochon.

"I called you a *tourist*," said Johnstone. "So tonight we're going to take you on a circle tour, show you the sights."

Hickey moved around and took Renard's Beretta. The .38 was still in the Pontiac, for all the good it did him. Constable Hickey leaned in, reeking of sweat and halitosis. He whispered scorchingly, "My turn, hot stuff."

Renard had been beaten before, undergone stress positions, had been trained to withstand interrogation. This was a bad one. Hickey showed no refinement. There was nothing fancy about his technique, just a straight pummelling. Renard got kneed in the balls and punched in the stomach. As he writhed on the floor, Hickey kicked him in every soft spot. After a while Hickey lifted Renard to a chair and beat his face. Everything became pain. Soon there was no colour or light, and it took all Renard's effort simply to breathe. Hickey hit him with a hard thing, maybe a billy club, and Renard heard something break. It continued: pain, and more pain, and nothing but pain. After a while the beating stopped, but the pain reigned forever and Renard lost consciousness.

Cold water dousing his head brought him back to what was left of his life. Johnstone lifted him by the hair and pushed his face in close.

"Sucker's nearly done. Nice work, Constable Hickey. You, Charlie, come here."

The big man shambled up, head low between his shoulders. "What's up?"

"See this?" glittered Johnstone.

He stood, belted his gun, put his hand in his pocket to scratch his testicles.

"Yeah?" asked Charlie.

"Take him on your boat and dump the body in the harbour."

"Whatever you say, *ali'i*."

The hunter closed his eyes.

INDIAN TIME

31.

• •

Even though he hadn't had any sleep the night before (and in the meanwhile had enjoyed something of a long day), Ted couldn't lose consciousness. The woman on the bed showed nothing of the same trouble; he heard her soft, rhythmic breathing as she slept. Sometimes she made small movements on the sheets, other times she made smaller, almost feral sounds. He envied her. It was the worst hour for insomnia, three in the morning, with an age of darkness ahead of a dawn that might never come. Somewhere outside the open window hung a warped moon. It didn't matter. The stars might fall from the sky for all Ted cared. *If I heard a comet hit a UFO,* he thought, *I wouldn't turn around.* No celestial body, however spectacular, could possibly compete with close to $300,000 in hundreds and what was probably about two kilograms of cocaine sitting on the dresser. Ted looked from the display to a vanity mirror that reflected his exhausted face.

What had happened? As of today there could remain no question that Ted was directly in the sights of a corrupt policeman and some sort of fixer. They wouldn't ever let up. Worse than that, he'd drawn Dorothy Kwan into their lethal orbit. *I've fucked it all up,* he thought. *Again. Totally responsible for this woman's safety and inadequate for the task, an unworthy man. Can I be blamed if something goes wrong? Yes and no.*

If you walk it back to first causes, it's all Irina's fault, thought Ted. *She's the one who started this whole damn thing. She stole the money and cocaine, she rented the room at Dorothy's house and led the cops to the door. But it's me who pulled Dorothy closer. And it was my fault marrying Irina to begin with. That means that it's really all on me. Instead of going it alone, I let Dorothy become involved. Doesn't matter how willing she is. Before today we were playing an interesting game, following Irina's breadcrumbs to the house in the woods. And it's led us here, to the kind of shit that gets people killed. How can I keep her safe? And when the weight falls down, will I be ready?*

When he finally awoke the house stood still and quiet. The bed was empty. Ted went into the bathroom and had a surprisingly intense shit. It must have been the extreme tension of the day before that had shut down his system. *I'm pushing diamonds,* he thought. The experience left his tender asshole chafed and raw. He found lotion under the sink and made the mistake of applying it without reading the contents. Alpha hydroxy stung him like a cigarette cherry; things got worse as he winced hopping into a freezing jet from the shower. Sweating now, Ted's chilled body trembled in the hot water as he blindly shaved with a ladies' disposable razor; a delicate, left-handed operation with no mirror in the slippery bathtub and a handcuff retarding his right. Somewhat more composed, asshole still stinging, Ted dried off and dressed in his wrecked shirt and the bottom half of the ruined Pierre Cardin suit, then went downstairs to the kitchen. No smell of coffee or frying onions, and no chatter of ladies. Ted swallowed a raw brown egg topped with a shot of Lea & Perrins Worcestershire sauce and took a cold tomato juice on the rocks outside into the bright glare. The sun burned directly overhead. Past a small pool pavilion, Ted located a shed where he hunted around for tools. At the bottom of a box, he found a hacksaw with blades. He set himself up over a block of wood and started to work.

The next uneasy half-hour Ted spent sawing at the metal around his wrist. Any slip would result in a nasty cut, and from certain angles it looked like he was amputating his hand. However, after the first few hesitant attempts he managed to find a groove. Soon skill and confidence increased enough for Ted to stroke the blade to the beat of an old Newfoundland song:

"I's the b'y that builds tha boat, and I's the bye what sails her, and I's the bye that catches tha fish and takes her home to Liza."

There. The metal fell to the ground and Ted rubbed his wrist where the skin had chafed and torn. It was something. He tossed the handcuffs into a shrub and sat in the sun on the grass. He felt its lush, green warmth and allowed himself to put aside the majority of his worries for the immediate moment. The situation wasn't totally desperate yet. *Here I am*, he thought, *backed into a corner, but what a corner. A pile of cash and blow. A new lover. All you could ask for was here at Mary Worthington's house. Hot and cold running champagne, two pretty girls, six bedrooms, a swimming pool, and me. That's pretty good math. So slow it right down. Take your time, look around, and wait. There has to be a way.* Behind him a snake started hissing. Ted jumped up, but it was too late. The automated sprinkler system spat out in all directions and chased him back to the pool, just as Mary and Dorothy came out of the house through the French doors. They took a look at him and burst out laughing. He shrugged, stripped naked before them, and dove to the bottom of the deep end.

Their bodies glowed with pleasure, the charm of newness strong. Ted tasted Dorothy on his lips and felt himself prickle with her touch. New lovers always exuded a power—excitement mixed with a stranger's mystery. Two people become removed from the rest of humanity and enjoy losing themselves in a shared desire. The sensation of secrecy was amplified by the erotic power of danger and seclusion. They were all alone, hunted by bad men, and this dark knowledge caused their skins to burn with warmth in the snarled white sheets of the bed. Dorothy and Ted explored and tested one another, both selfless and selfish, seeking pleasure through movement and pressure. He'd heard her cries when coming, and now she knew him at his peak of pleasure. At last she was on her hands and knees, looking back as he thrust into her and finally released a burst that emptied desire from every fibre of being and corner of mind. Ted collapsed. They embraced before fading away again in the soft afternoon light.

"We'll make Mary jealous," murmured Dorothy, kissing Ted awake.

"Jealousy and competition bring out the best in all of us," he said.

"Is that what happened with your wife?"

"You got me."

"Were you jealous?"

"I could easily have run her over in the street."

"Why didn't you?"

"There're already enough skeletons in my closet to keep a Hallowe'en party going for a month. And if I'd done anything any differently, I'd never have met you."

"Good answer."

"You bring out the best in me," said Ted.

"Tell it to the money and cocaine over there."

"We need to talk about that."

"Later," said Dorothy. "First we have to eat. You're going to need your strength."

"What for?"

"Just you wait and see."

They ordered pizza pies delivered to the house and shared them with Mary out by the pool, seated on orange plastic Hong Kong chairs. Sips of chilled pink champagne alternated between bites of a tangy Italian salami laced with mushrooms and anchovies. Mary had a saucy smile, playing the indulgent chaperone pleased by her two young honey-mooners. She wore a bikini and sarong, her hair in a ponytail, every bit the fresh, freckle-faced California girl. Dorothy had on a white blouse and black shorts borrowed from the house. She was stunning with her supple, astonishing body and decidedly superior mind, thought Ted. He suspected that she might be smarter than he was. It's very often the case. Irina was crafty, gifted with an ear for languages and treachery, and Mary possessed a deeply cunning mind beneath her reckless exterior. *Women are dangerous wonders*, he mused. And so, idly, as they finished a bottle and moved to another, Ted wondered at his chances for the night. He admitted to himself that he was enough of a man for that. One woman was perfectly fine, but two at once a possibility not to be ignored. Here they were in front of him, happy, gorgeous, slightly drunk. But there could be no forcing it on his part. *Any false move would be deadly*, he thought. *Ride the vibe. Let food and drink build blood and bone. Admire these beautiful creatures you have all to yourself.* Dorothy giggles as Mary tells another dirty joke, a wicked flash from Mary of the feline smile. *Be a good boy. You've escaped with a whole skin and full belly. Bad manners to press your luck. And why are they looking at you like that?*

"Well?" asked Mary.

"What?"

"Dorothy asked you a question."

He saw her dark eyes on his, a combined cool, quizzical gaze. Dorothy and Mary shared a look. He'd noticed this type of thing before. Two women against one man equalled instant female solidarity. Now they regarded him with mildly amused contempt. Cats.

"What was it?" he asked.

"Why does she call you the King of England?" asked Dorothy.

"Because he is!" laughed Mary.

That again. His whole life.

"Do you really want to know?" asked Ted.

"Please."

"Then let her tell you," he said, pointing at Mary.

Mary threw up her hands. "I'm only a pauper and a parrot. I've never heard the real story."

"That's all it is, a story," said Ted. "A fairy tale."

"Then tell me," said Dorothy. "I like bedtime stories."

She winked at Ted and he felt himself flush. The setting sun cast a mellow, buttery yellow over the yard and pool. All and all, as lovely a scene as you could wish: the smell of damp grass, so welcome after weeks of dry heat, two fetching women drinking rosé. When Mary lit a joint and passed it around, his satisfaction was nearly complete. He inhaled and felt a shiver as the pot entered his bloodstream.

"I'm waiting," said Dorothy.

"My family's English. You want to know *how* English? My grandfather refused to eat pineapple because the Hawaiians murdered Captain Cook.

"Once upon a time, way back in the twenties, the Prince of Wales made a tour of the Commonwealth and came out here to the Dominion of Canada. He was the bee's knees. The whole country fell all over him, because he was so young and dashing, and the war was finally over. Think *The Great Gatsby*. When the royal party came to town, the Prince stayed at the Hotel Vancouver. Go there sometime and look at the pictures on the wall. There's a portrait of him sitting with a bunch of honourable Reverend fathers, Rotarians, bankers—dullards to a man. He looks so young and bored to tears. In real life, he was a helluva sport and liked to have himself a good time. He set the new tone, dancing and drinking and carrying on.

"There was an official supper somewhere and some suck-up decided to please the Prince by seating him next to a pretty young thing. This was my grandmother. She was chosen because her last name was Windsor, like his. It was a little joke, I guess. Because the Royal family had changed their name during the First World War. So, you can see where this is going. The Prince and my grandmother (who was a virgin of twenty, you can bet) had it off in the rumble seat of a roadster. He went back to England, and she never saw him again. But she became pregnant, and to cover up the scandal there was a marriage to my grandfather, also named Windsor, her second cousin. We're like the Roosevelts, I guess. My grandfather got rich in land with the Guinness corporation. They're the ones who put in the Lions Gate Bridge and opened up the British Properties. My family house is on the water in West Vancouver, in Caulfield. Very English. The highway runs to The Dale and along the way is St. Francis-in-the-Wood.

"Eventually the king died, and the Prince became Edward the Eighth. You probably know all about Wallis Simpson and the abdication. So his brother becomes George VI, last Emperor of India, followed by our Lizzie. It's weirder than just that."

He sipped pink champagne.

"How so?" asked Dorothy.

"When the Second World War started, things didn't look good for the British. We thought we might lose. All of the gold in the Bank of England was shipped over to Montreal, Ottawa, and New York for safety. If the Germans invaded Britain, the plan was for Churchill and whoever else could be saved to retreat to Canada and keep fighting from here. But there were also plans within plans. Kooks came out of the woodwork. The English have all sorts of strange ideas. My grandfather became involved with a group called the British Israelites. They believed the English were one of the lost tribes of Israel, and that the British sovereign was the rightful heir of King David. If George VI and Elizabeth were killed, and Edward was put on the throne by the Nazis, or if the kingdom were destroyed, they wanted to preserve the line. I still don't understand how they could consider the Royal Family to be Jews. Queen Victoria was a German, for Christ's sake."

He looked at Dorothy.

"If worse came to worst and a new king was needed, the British Israelites knew where they could find one, even if he was just a royal bastard."

"Your father," said Dorothy.

"That's right. And when he died, me."

"My God," said Dorothy. "I can't believe I've been sleeping with the rightful King of England."

"How was he?" asked Mary.

32.

● ●

Dorothy woke around dawn with an ache in her belly. The song "Sailing" by Christopher Cross had featured in her troubled dreams. She slid her naked body from the bed and slipped into the bathroom. There, on the toilet, she saw what was happening. Her period had started.

"*Hai ah.*"

That explained the dull pain, tenderness, and a growing headache. Dorothy tasted a drop of her own blood, as her mother had taught her, a method of self-diagnosis. Any potential maladies could be detected by distinctly different flavours, went the theory. She didn't know if either Western or Oriental medicine endorsed the practice; the salty, copper-penny tang seemed normal. *Like Clamato juice*, she thought, sighing. *Shimato juice! Shit. Just as Ted and I were getting really good.*

That might explain it. Their regimen of lovemaking had suddenly flooded Dorothy with various hormones. She was like one of those deserts furiously blooming after a sudden cloudburst of unexpected rain. Well, at the very least the blood meant she wasn't pregnant. That would've been too much. The worst part, Dorothy knew, was that carnal desire would only increase in the next few days as her body flooded. Nature's little joke on womankind; her private irony. What would Ted think? She flushed the toilet and found a Tampax under the sink. Last night had been near-perfect. They'd begun to find their groove in bed, the delicious fulcrum between sweet and nasty, sugar and spice. Now everything would have to wait.

Dorothy showered, towelled dry, inserted the tampon, stepped into her panties, and put on a summery dress. She watched Ted sleep for a moment as the light grew. Her sense of smell had become extremely acute. He seemed to exude an odour of salted tamarind.

"*Sampalok,*" she said.

Sampalok was a sweetmeat from the Philippines that Dorothy loved, a comfort food: lightly sugared and salted tamarind fruit, sometimes dusted with hot chili pepper. Delicious and savoury. Having conjured them in thought she now craved their taste.

"*Sampalok* and Tylenol," she said, out in the hall, beginning her hunt.

Aspirin she found in Mary's bathroom, but for tamarind Dorothy would have to go to Chinatown. And that was an unwise move at the moment. It was too close to home. Dorothy went downstairs to the kitchen. A radio played soft classical music. Mary sat curled into a wicker chair, drinking tea and reading a magazine. She looked up and said, "Good morning, sunshine. How're tricks?"

"For kids. What kind of tea is that?"

"Ceylonese. Help yourself."

Dorothy drank a warm cup with a thin slice of lemon.

"Splosh," said Mary.

"What?"

"That's what the English call a warm cup of tea. Perfect thirst quencher on a hot day. Like today. 'Give me a cup of splosh,' they say. I love it. Just in case himself asks for a cup. Now you know."

"That's nice."

Mary showed Dorothy her magazine. "Look at that!" she said. "Isn't that the most radical stuff you've ever seen?"

Dorothy appraised a spread and was amazed by the fashions. Tattered girls wore T-shirts with images of naked black men, cocks hanging out. Gloves with swastikas. Coats and trousers full of straps and zippers, like straightjackets. A blouse printed with the face of the Queen, a safety pin through her lip. Dorothy had heard of punk before but not encountered much of it up close. Sometimes, as she rode on the bus, she'd see teenagers on East Hastings with coloured mohawks and studded leather jackets. They'd taken over the Smilin' Buddha Cabaret. This stuff was like what they wore, but more direct, very direct and nasty, straight from the source.

Direct from London. It had an edge far from the severely elegant Dior and Chanel that Dorothy usually shoplifted. She liked it.

"Who is it?" she asked.

"Vivienne Westwood. Man, isn't it the coolest? That's her old stuff, now she's doing this."

Together they pored over pages documenting a recent catwalk show in Paris called *Savage*. Very bold colours, with exotic geometric patterns on rough fabrics. Crude seams and weird lines, both Japanese and Aztec at once. The friends bemoaned their lot.

"We're so far from the action it makes me sick," said Mary.

"I know, it's like we're always last to the party."

"In Vancouver the party was cancelled after the invitations were sent out. And they didn't bother to let anyone know."

"So what do we do?" asked Dorothy.

Mary stretched prettily, like a cat, and kicked up her legs. "Sixes and sevens," she said. "We really should start to make our own stuff. Have you thought about it?"

"I've been a little busy," said Dorothy.

"Well, I want to *do* something. With your brains and my money we could shake it up. Forget about knock-offs. We'll make originals of our own. That's what punk's about. Do it yourself, and to hell with everyone else."

"Maybe tomorrow."

"*Mañana, mañana.* How you say that in Chinese, honourable daughter?"

"*Hauh yaht.* But that's more like the day after tomorrow."

"Day after tomorrow. The story of our lives. Well, I don't feel like opening the store today, but you two probably don't want me hanging around here like a dirty shirt."

"It's your house," said Dorothy.

"Doesn't matter. What if you two want to do it out on the lawn?"

"Not today. I've got a visitor."

Mary lightly slapped her own cheek. "You poor thing. So the down-town dining and entertainment district is closed?"

"We're cancelling all reservations," said Dorothy.

"Okay then, what now?"

Dorothy heard Ted's step behind her. The women turned to see him in the doorway, where he held up a thick stack of hundred dollar bills.

"Let's go shopping," he said.

They played dress-up with clothes from the various closets in the house. It was like raiding the tickle trunk. Feeling childishly playful, Dorothy wanted to satirize her youth. She modified her usual technique and put on Mary's old school uniform. Even at twenty-six, it was fairly easy for her to pass as a teenager. An adolescent quality seemed the *leitmotif* of life in the Worthington house, a spirit Dorothy hadn't been allowed to indulge in at school. This was playing hooky as a grownup, for real, and no one could peach to her parents.

She parted her hair severely and clipped a barrette to the soft fall. From the wardrobes of Mary's father and brothers, Ted put on a red nylon windbreaker, white deck pants, and purple Lacoste shirt. He topped the ensemble with a novelty blue holiday eyeshade that read *Here Today, Gone To Maui*. Mary abstained, having finally decided on a strenuous day of sun-tanning beside the pool. She did, however, loan the couple her Mustang with their promise that they buy her good gin, tonic, Angostura bitters, and fresh limes for later on.

First, Dorothy asked Ted to stop at a corner store on the way, a mom-and-pop with an Orange Crush sign above the door and a *Province* push bar on the glass door. Just like every other corner store in the city, it was run by an old Chinese lady. The bell jingled as Dorothy went in, and she saw a woman absolutely nothing like her mother sitting behind the counter. She became a blur in the sudden tears brought on by the mere thought of her mother, but poised again in an instant, Dorothy went down the confectionary aisle until she found what she'd come for. On a dusty back shelf away from abandoned cans of soup and tins of sardines, Dorothy located a glass jar. There was no *sampalok* here, but as a consolation prize she found a mixture of spicy ginger Ting Ting Jahe and White Rabbit milk candy.

Perhaps it was the schoolgirl outfit, or her period playing up, or the woman who looked nothing like her mother, but Dorothy shoplifted a pack of Juicy Fruit right in front of the woman while paying a quarter for her candy. Outside, the Mustang idled, and Ted listened to the radio playing "Eyes of a Stranger" by the Payola$. Dorothy popped a White Rabbit candy into her mouth and tasted the thin rice paper dissolving on her tongue. She sashayed over to the driver's side, unpalmed the gum, and waved it in front of Ted like a Milk-Bone.

"Look what I got for you."

Ted smiled his white smile, and she saw lines of humour around his eyes crinkle otherwise smooth skin. *As the nuns used to say*, anno domini *comes for us all*, thought Dorothy.

"You really shouldn't have," said Ted.

"Here," she replied, tossing the pack to the passenger side.

Ted slid across the white leather, and as he did Dorothy scissored over the door and into the driver's seat. She summoned her father's driving instructions from Sunday afternoons in the empty parking lots of a Safeway supermarket. With one foot, Dorothy pushed down the clutch and shifted into first, with the other she stepped on the gas. "My turn," she said.

They didn't stray too far. Dorothy did a nice legal fifty miles an hour on Chancellor past the gates into the University Endowment Lands, then switched back down to a steady fifty on Marine by the water. The tide was way, way out, and a remarkable number of people sported out on the golden sand. No one in the city had anything else to do today, it

seemed. Indian summer reigned over Vancouver with a seedy authority. Parking lots were crammed full, station wagons idling and waiting
for any open spots. Traffic slowed to ten miles an hour as slouchers
in flip-flops crossed the road, sucking on soft ice-cream cones. Hot,
dusty wind carved around them as Dorothy shifted into second onto
4th Avenue. Here traffic backed up again.

"Let's get out of here," said Ted.

He pointed and Dorothy slammed it, catching the green to make a
left on Alma. She drove them further on and found a spot under a tree
near Hastings Mill Park. Here the land was cooled by an ocean breeze.
They walked hand in hand over parched grass past an old mill store made
into a little city museum, preserved in state by the Native Daughters
of British Columbia. Under an exhausted willow, its boughs limp and
yellow, Ted kissed her so that she stirred again. He tasted her candy lip
gloss and chuckled.

"What is it?" she asked.

"This museum here. You ever been in? They've got all sorts of weird
little things inside, voodoo dolls and streetcar tickets, elephant foot
umbrella stands and Tiffany lamps. And there's this piece of ivory, a sort
of tusk. The label says it's a paperweight."

He smiled.

"Well?" went Dorothy.

"Oh, it's just that I visited an antique shop in Tokyo and saw the same
thing there. Except the Japanese called it a *harigata*."

"What's that?"

"Something the geishas use on themselves, each other. For fun."

"Pepsi-Cola," said Dorothy. "I prefer a Coke."

"What do you mean?"

She pushed him up against the tree and ran her hand quickly down his
front, to feel him tense and harden instantly. Dorothy darted a nip with
her teeth and a lick at his ear, whispering, "You know. The Real Thing."

After a furtive, thrilling grope under the willow, Dorothy and Ted walked together again, alive to each other, their bodies thrilled to be in contact. She found herself touching him whenever possible, trying different handholds, bumping up against him, breaking off, having him chase her, wanting to be caught. It was the simple pleasure of human contact that coursed through Dorothy, tangled with the amusement of teasing and toying and playing the flirt. And then they sat on a bench, looking out at boats on the water, and she asked the necessary question. "Now what?"

"Well," said Ted, "how do you feel about buying one of those boats and sailing away?"

"Where to?"

"You tell me."

She stared out at the ocean. "My father always said that the longest journey he ever took was the Star Ferry from Kowloon to Hong Kong."

"Is it far?" asked Ted.

"About ten minutes from one side to the other. What he meant is that his whole life changed in the crossing. He escaped from the mainland after the revolution. In Hong Kong he met and married my mother, and then they came here."

Ted sat still beside her. Dorothy spoke her thoughts aloud as she hadn't before to anyone. Not Mary, or Uncle Brian, or God.

"Six months ago, they went for a holiday. It was their first trip back to China together. My father would usually go by himself every year for business. I never saw the connection before, but he'd meet my Uncle Brian there. Uncle Brian's with the RCMP."

"And your father?"

"Now I'm almost positive he was a spy. But what I don't know is for who."

"What happened?"

"My father and mother flew over for their anniversary. One night they went out for dinner. The boat people, the Tanka, some of them have little restaurants on their sampans. Quaint and picturesque, but illegal. No regulations. They cook your dinner over charcoal or a kerosene brazier. You go out into the harbour at night, just the two of you on the boat with the cook and his wife, maybe, have a tasty meal, look at the lights of the city. It's very romantic."

"Sounds nice."

"The stove exploded. The boat caught fire and sank. My mother and father were both killed."

"Good Lord."

"My mother always used to say that the water you drown in is always an ocean. That's the strangest part about it all. My mother on a boat. She hated the sea. She was terrified of drowning."

33.

· ·

When he came to he was laying on a chesterfield across from Chief Dan George. The chief smiled at him. He wore a top hat, dressed like he was in *The Outlaw Josey Wales*, and he had a teacup and saucer in his hands. Chief Dan George said, "You look like a fella I once saw who fell off a horse."

"Oh yeah?" croaked Renard.

"You know what he did?"

"He got right back on it."

"Hell no! He sold that horse and bought himself a mule. Never fell off again."

Dan George paused a while, then leaned forward, hands on knees.

"Let me ask you a question. How come you never see cowboys riding a cow? Sometimes they ride bulls, but then they should be called bullboys. But mostly they ride horses, so what should I call them? Horseboys? Or these days they'd be called pickuptruckboys. The only people I know who ride cows are Indians. Yes, Indians ride cows."

"You do?" asked Renard.

"Yes, in India, Indians ride sacred cows."

He chuckled at Renard, who found himself laughing along, then felt a sharp pain at his left shoulder. Chief Dan George motioned and said, "Your collarbone is broken. You have to stay still until it gets better. Here, what hand are you?"

In Chief Dan George's palm was a penny. Ted tried to reach with his left and felt the stab of pain again.

"I knew it. Well, you're a rightie now, so here you go."

He dropped the coin into Renard's hand, which clutched it on its own.

"Now what?" asked Renard.

"Rest," said Chief Dan George. "It's a good day to be alive."

When he next opened his eyes a quiet, grey-headed grandma was vanishing behind a steaming hot cup of greenish tea. The light was that of either dawn or dusk. The hunter lay on a chesterfield with his left arm cinched to his body by a tightly bound white sheet used as bandage, trussed tight as a webbed fly. His whole side hurt. He felt bruises on his face, a cut to his lip, scraped skin beneath his beard. Renard checked himself for flowing blood and open wounds, finding only scratches and fiery fresh scabs that hurt like hell. At least he was clean. There was no hint of the smell of rot. *Here I am, on a couch, in a room, looking out onto a deck through an open sliding door.* A warm wind from the south streamed in. It was nearly time to start asking questions. *Where am I? Who are these people? And where'd Chief Dan George go?* Renard opened his right hand and discovered he held a copper penny from 1899 with the profile of *Victoria Dei Gratia Regina* on one side. Canada. *Wait a minute.*

"Grandmother?" he asked after the old woman.

She appeared in the doorway and cackled from her creased, happy face, then pointed at the cup. Renard complied and drank the slightly bitter, minty mixture of steeped herbs.

The feel of the sea was close in the room as Renard sipped, his body going from hot, then warm, to a nice mellow cool. He rested some more, listening to the insects humming, short waves lapping at a nearby beach. The room was filled with spider plants, philodendrons, and cactus. A square of sunlight outdoors moved across the deck. He felt the tea take effect and placed the taste: marijuana. Renard's body slowed and soothed itself. He closed his eyes again, a rectangle of light flickering on his lids beckoning to a doorway that led within.

Next he heard "How Long (Has This Been Going On)?" from a transistor radio tuned to a fuzzy AM station. Renard opened his eyes and the music snapped off.

Now it was Charlie who sat on the chair previously occupied by Chief Dan George.

"Hey, *kahuna*, how's it hanging?" he asked.

Renard slowly replied, "The angle of the dangle is proportionate to the heat of the meat when the throb of the knob is constant. Who set my collarbone?"

"Don't worry. Was a good guy, man. But hey, you're talking again, so that's a start. You're not dead."

"What happened?"

"Listen, man, I'm sorry. Those cops got to me first. I say what I have to say to them."

"And me?"

"They wanted me to drop you in the chuck, man. But you're gonna be okay."

"How do you know?"

"I got this good feeling inside," said Charlie.

They smoked a joint together. Afterward, Charlie pulled out a gourd filled with kava. He poured the cold liquid into coconut halves and passed one to Renard. Renard let the slippery fluid into his mouth and swallowed. Its taste spread a chill pepperiness. Soon he felt his lips, tongue, and throat become frozen and rubbery. A complete, smooth relaxedness unfolded. Renard's mind rested in its body, tranquilized. This went on. Hours melted away. Renard drank quarts of the stuff, sitting still, feeling the entire earth turn on its axis. Charlie would get up from time to time, returning with potato chips or to smoke another joint. The hunter no longer felt hunger or pain, just a peaceful lassitude. All he could do now was wait and heal.

A few days later, Renard was sitting on a lawn chair next to Charlie in the sun on the deck overlooking the water. He learned he was on Indian Reserve No. 3 on the Dollarton Highway, east of the Second Narrows Bridge in North Vancouver. They had a view over the ass-end of the inlet and an oil refinery on the southern shore. Stacks burned bursts of blackened orange flame. The natives here were some kind of Salish tribe, Renard learned. Charlie told him that when the Hawaiians came as fur traders to Vancouver with the Hudson's Bay Company, some families mixed with locals. There were similarities between the tribes. They were boat people, tough fishermen, warriors, headhunters. Charlie's neighbours worked with him and his family at the port, on the docks, the railyards, and mills on both sides of Burrard Inlet, alongside Italians, Poles, and Chinese. The connection hadn't ended. There was still a back and forth. Vancouver and Honolulu had competing baseball teams in the Pacific Coast League, the Canadians and Islanders. Travel distance between diamonds: nearly 3,000 miles.

"Not exactly a subway series," said Renard.

Charlie's family's house was beside a small cemetery to one side and a greasy beach crowded with plastic pink flamingos and small boats on the other. Renard heard Indians working, laughing, and talking a mixed lingo of English and their own tongue, but couldn't make out the flow of words. Kava ebbed and surged in his bloodstream, unhurried, allowing him to listen and think. He asked Charlie, "Why didn't you drop me in the water?"

"Hey, I'm a lover, brudder."

"They won't like it if they find out."

"That's why I'm thinking, like, maybe you get to those cops first. *A'ole huhu.*"

"What's that?"

"It's like, don't get mad, bro. Get even."

Play the part, become the part, thought Thomas Renard. That identity wasn't much good any more. He'd have to revert to his own, withdraw money from a safe bank, start making some moves. There were handicaps beyond his injuries. The Beretta and knife were gone, along with the .38 and hardware in his car, and for that matter, the car itself.

Charlie sheepishly admitted that Johnstone had ordered the LeMans be towed away and stripped. But Renard began to form a funny little idea on how to improvise a replacement for his lost weapons. By this time, the Princeton Hotel would've long turfed Renard from his room. *That leaves me with nothing*, he realized. *Not even my Sony Walkman. So what's the part I'm supposed to play now? A hunter hunts, a killer kills. Nature red in tooth and fucking claw. In this sorry state I'm in right now I'm barely able to kill time.* Merde.

But he got better. The reserve was in fairly rough shape, but no one seemed to mind that too much. Renard had no clear knowledge of the number of people in the house. The door was always open; Indians came and went, obeying instincts and rhythms of their own. Some would sit down across from him and talk about the weather, others seemed indifferent to his presence. One, a cheerful, portly, middle-aged man with a brush cut (a great uncle, or fifteenth cousin twice removed) was a Mormon, and went on about the Three Nephites.

"Who?" asked Renard.

"Disciples of Christ. He granted them immortality. They walk the earth unknown to the Jew and Gentile, and aid folks in their time of need."

"So they're out there right now?"

"Yessir."

"All three together, or do they split up and go their separate ways?" asked Renard.

"Some people'll meet one, others'll see all three."

"Sounds like Crosby, Stills and Nash. And sometimes Neil Young."

"Who?"

Renard got stoned and slept, ate beef broth, Loco Moco, wind-dried salmon, bannock with butter and jam. He drank cannabis and Labrador tea, dozed and rested, watched television with Charlie's smiling grandma. She loved *The Price Is Right*, especially the Cliff Hangers game with its little yodelling mountaineer. As the puppet climbed, she'd rock in her chair and clap along to the singing, laughing if he fell off the edge. Renard was more of a Plinko man himself. The clothes Renard had worn had been cleaned and stitched up by her competent hands. She'd even polished his cowboy boots. So he relaxed and simply drifted, allowing himself to stop caring, to drop out of the flow. Flies turned endlessly in the centre of the room, describing some weird geometry that he tried to work out, seeking a pattern. There was nothing Renard could do, so he waited, building strength. Soon enough, with mind clearing and body stitching itself together, Renard began to plan his revenge.

Throughout the week he walked around the reserve, increasing his wind. On the Saturday afternoon following his beating, he made it east to a little store on a wide spot up the road. There Renard treated himself to a Dr. Pepper vanilla ice cream float, sitting at a picnic table on a square of Astroturf under a runty palm tree as the occasional car growled along the Dollarton Highway. His arm felt better. The collarbone appeared to have set and continued to knit. A warm breeze washed along, and then a blue 1954 Corvette rammed past. *Car of my childhood*, he thought. Bobby Carmouche's older brother had one up the street back home in Alexandria, Louisiana. Renard allowed himself to remember that time for just a moment. See the USA in your Chevrolet. Next thing you know, you're furiously reading the *Pocket Guide to Vietnam* you're handed before getting deployed. He remembered the appropriate number from the *Nine Rules for Personnel of the U.S. Military Assistance Command* that applied to his present situation:

"Remember, we are special guests here. Join with the people, understand their life, use phrases from their language, and honour their customs and laws. Always give the Vietnamese the right of way."

And then Renard was jerked back to the present, to the bench he sat on. Here he was in another foreign country, hunter without quarry, behind enemy lines. In the reflection of a window he saw a dark, bearded man, now pale and weak. Himself. *Soon*, he thought. *Soon*. A large shadow fell over the picnic table, and Charlie sat down. The Hawaiian still worked nights at the Royal Maui warehouse, slept during the day, and usually wasn't up before five in the evening. Right now Charlie had bags under his eyes and looked worried.

"Those cops come by last night and talk to me," he said.

"What'd they ask?"

"What I did with you. They're waiting for a body to pop up."

"Really?"

"Parts come washing up all the time, man. They get cut off at a sawmill somewhere, or on a log boom, then they go on a journey. Mostly legs, feet."

"Legs?

"Shoes have rubber. They float better."

"You want to cut off my foot and give it to the cops?"

"No, but maybe you could cut off their heads."

Charlie got up, went into the store and returned with a Fudgsicle.

"How much time have I got here?" asked Renard.

"Couple more days."

"Okay. I'll need a ride into town."

"What you gonna do?"

"What I do best. Hurt people."

At supper the next night, Renard sat down with Charlie, his grandma, and pair of plump identical young girl cousins who were in grade four. Together they ate a mountain of macaroni and cheese larded with Spam, *poi*, and fried chicken with biscuits and gravy. The kids drank milk, the grown-ups rum and Coke. The chicken was almost as good as what he'd eaten in Kentucky that time a million years ago with the cute redhead, but not as good as the fried chicken at Joe's Stone Crabs in Miami. Renard had to leave the next day and abstained from liquor. He'd need a good night's sleep. What little conversation there was at the table came only between intense bursts of feeding. For the most part it was polite, inconsequential talk. One thing Renard admired about Charlie's people was that they didn't mind cultivating silence, didn't feel the need to fill the air around the dinner table with meaningless chitchat. During the Jell-O dessert he finally spoke, breaking the spell.

"When I first came here, I met Chief Dan George, the actor. Is he around?"

Renard looked up from the clean bones on his plate. This new silence had a different quality. Charlie, his grandmother, and the young cousins had all stopped eating. Eight dark eyes now looked keenly at Renard. He felt himself taken aback, slightly ashamed, obliquely embarrassed, sensing he'd made a social error, trespassing on taboo ground.

"I'm sorry. Have I made a mistake?"

It was Charlie who spoke. "The Chief is from this reserve."

Renard exhaled and said, "I never knew that. He was kind to me. Could I thank him?"

Charlie looked at his grandmother. "Maybe," he said.

"Where is he?"

"Well," said Charlie. "You could say he's next door."

"Which side?"

"The west."

Renard frowned.

"But that's the cemetery."

Charlie nodded.

Next day near sunset Renard walked amid gravestones swallowed by parched golden grass. The piercing calls of crickets and grasshoppers shrilled through the heat. Renard flexed his left hand. The arm felt both weak and heavy, finally released from the bandage. With his fingertips he touched the healing cuts and bruises on his face and body, smelled the dry earth and the sea and the promise of cool dusk. Whatever else there was, it was good this moment to be alive. He checked names on the tombs. Many were from the George family. The Chief's was a small, humble marker among many, shared with another, perhaps his brother's. Renard opened the hand which held the penny he'd been given. He could think of several explanations for the visit, but nothing logical seemed to account for exactly what had happened. The date on the penny, 1899, was the same as the birth date on the stone. He left the copper there as a small tribute to the man. He walked out of the burial ground through the gate of a picket fence to where Charlie waited in an old Ford pickup truck. Renard looked up to see three crows harrying a pair of bald eagles around the crown of a fir tree. Scavengers.

34.

· ·

They followed Mary down the path to Tower Beach. The forest floor kicked up dust the colour of brown tobacco snuff in the late afternoon light. All was warm and still; burgundy and chartreuse trunks of arbutus, tall Douglas firs and red cedars surrounded their trail. Ted smelled the sharp, sweet tang of resinous sap from the trees and could just feel the cool loom of the ocean as they dropped to sea level. It was steep going as Mary led their train. Dorothy carried a litre-and-a-half bottle of half-decent red wine. Along the path, empty beer cans had been stuck on light cedar boughs, the tins swaying when they brushed by. The trio were en route to the true party beach, treading down a winding desire line. It felt to Ted as though they'd passed through a curtain into an indistinct period. *We could be in 1953, 1983, or 2183, for all the bush cares,* thought Ted. The sensation was reinforced by the stillness of the woods, broken at last by the prehistoric croaking of ravens, then a bird singing a steady, pure note higher and higher past human hearing. Lazy samaras twirled down from maples.

"Whirligigs!" cried Mary, delighted.

As the track came out onto the flat, ferny bottom before the beach, it became necessary to cross a dried-up gully, slack brown water in a shrinking puddle. A pair of merry, mellow Musqueam Indian gals a long way from the rez opposite Sea Island and the airport laughed slowly as Dorothy nearly lost her footing on a rock.

"Is it five o'clock yet?" asked one of the girls.

"I don't know."

The gal laughed. "Oh, so you're on Indian time too."

As the sun set, the bonfire came to life. People trickled down to stand around the crackling wood. A slim, shirtless youth tended the blaze, feeding it from a pile of driftwood. Another long-hair gently played Nick Drake's "Time of No Reply" on an acoustic guitar. Couples sat on logs and murmured, passing beers back and forth. The bonfire's smoke mingled with a sweet, friendly bouquet of *cannabis sativa*. The steep long path and remoteness of the promontory protected partiers from all but the most ardent cops. As darkness fell, Ted heard an unseen girl's tinkle of laughter. More slow action, a hum of people talking and bullshitting. Mary drifted off to a group of friends. Ted and Dorothy watched the sun setting over Vancouver Island. There were wildfires burning there, and the sun set red as Mars. From Tower Beach, they were at the very tip of Point Grey, the city behind them. To their left a long, rocky littoral led down to Wreck Beach. From here and all the way south, the water's edge was clothing-optional, tardy nudists still sometimes visible. A couple of adventurous, liberated girls took off their tops. Everyone was cool about it. In front of Ted and Dorothy there spread out the flat orange and blue plate of the sea.

"Cast your bread upon the waters," said Dorothy.

"*Ecclesiastes*," said Ted.

They shared a look, then turned to the west as the sun burned low.

"Do you know how it's translated in the Geneva Bible?" asked Ted.

"No."

"Lay thy bread upon wet faces."

Dorothy laughed. She handed Ted the bottle of wine. They discovered neither had brought a corkscrew or glasses. A guitarist started strumming "Wish You Were Here."

"I've got an idea," said Ted.

He borrowed someone's knife and found two long, thick whips of bull kelp in the surf, then trimmed the bulbs off the stipe and brought them back to Dorothy. Each was about the size of a baseball. When Ted cut the tops off, the chambers popped seawater onto the sand. Meanwhile, Dorothy wrapped the bottle in a towel and smacked the base and punt on a log. The cork leapt out, to a couple's applause. Dorothy smiled at Ted and poured wine into the bulbs. They touched their living green cups together and sipped. The kelp gave the red wine a clean taste of fresh salt water.

"We called these mermaid's bladders when I was little," said Dorothy.

"I never heard that before," said Ted.

The sun set and people danced. From faraway, by an acoustical freak, they heard the thump of the nine o'clock gun. Stars came out. One of them was Aldebaran.

Ted woke early from a dream, back in the small Tokyo apartment he'd shared with Minako. It was the smell of creosote from treated wood that'd burned in the beach bonfire; the odour was similar to the kerosene Japanese heaters used in wintertime. Dorothy slept next to Ted. She'd drunk too much wine the night before, becoming quieter and quieter with every swallow. Finally, Ted had sought out Mary, disengaging her from a pack of rowdies. It was tough work getting Dorothy back up the hill and onto the road. Fortunately, a lonely cab plying its trade in the darkness of Marine Drive picked them up and took them home to Mary's. Ted and Mary put Dorothy to bed and then had a nightcap together in the parlour.

Now Ted wanted more clothes and the things he'd left behind at the Victoria Rooms. When Dorothy finally got her passport he'd need his. Then they could go anywhere on earth. Buenos Aires or Bali. It'd been days since they'd got the drugs and money. Detective Johnstone and the man on the bridge must have become tired of waiting. Would they give up completely? No. Everything about the whole scenario suggested that this wasn't official police business but something very personal, connected by Irina's actions straight to Ted. And now he'd made himself the true star attraction of the story. Money, cocaine, and women to spare. *Compare yourself to Johnstone, then try to think like him. How much manpower could he have at his disposal? Can he watch the hotel's entrances all day and night? No way. Go now, and be careful.*

Far from the house on Belmont, Ted caught a taxi at the concession stand on Locarno Beach. The cab went from nacreous blue waves and dusty evergreens to the dull brown brick of the Del Mar Inn at the corner of Dunsmuir and Hamilton. It was hotter here in the heart of the city, the air like the season, exhausted. Ted took an alley to the parking lot behind the Victoria Hotel, wary of every car and rooftop. He climbed the fire escape, swung himself to a half-open window, and just like that was in the hallway on the second floor, passing through the heavy metal door to the hotel proper where he stood at the stairwell with a cocked ear. Nothing.

Mr Lee showed no surprise at seeing Ted coming down the stairs to stand by the front desk. The Chinese did nothing more than crisply unfold his newspaper. Ted raised his eyebrow and inclined his head in the direction at the back office, whence Mr Lee slowly, unblinkingly nodded once. At the door Ted raised his hand, paused a moment, then knocked.

"Come in, Mr Windsor," said Samuel Olaffson.

The Norwegian looked even more formidable than usual. In front of him was Ted's bag and half a bottle of Akvavit; the owner cupped a full glass in his hairy paw. *This is strange*, thought Ted. *How could he know I was coming?* Olaffson gestured at Ted to sit, then pushed a glass across the desk and filled it to the bleeding edge.

"So," said Olaffson. "You are coming to inform me you have taken a more promising position at the Ritz Hotel. *Concierge de les clefs d'or.* Our humble house has been a mere stepping stone to greater glory."

"Something like that," said Ted.

"Drink."

Ted looked the Viking in the eye as they drained their glasses. He saw the red spark in the giant's face.

"Mr Olaffson?"

"Yes, Mr Windsor?"

STRAIGHT TO THE HEAD

"You know what happened?"

"No, Mr Windsor. Please to inform."

"I caught my mermaid."

Later, when Ted walked a little unsteadily past the front desk in the lobby of the Victoria Hotel on his way out, he heard a voice.

"Good luck," said Mr Lee.

In Ted's re-acquired hold-all, he found an unopened letter with an American stamp, postmarked California a week ago, addressed to him c/o The Victoria Hotel, Vancouver, British Columbia, Dominion of Canada, Commonwealth of Nations, Terra Nova. Those words were written in a woman's hand. He tore open the letter and read it in a taxi as it chewed its way west through Kitsilano.

> Hollywood Roosevelt Hotel
> 7000 Hollywood Blvd.
> Hollywood, California, USA
>
> Dear Ted,
> I missed your call. Here I am down in Hollywood, *Pueblo de Nuestra Señora, la Reina de los Angeles*, or Lala-land to you and me. I had to come here before I went gaga up there with you. No, that's not true. Actually now I'm in Oceanside, just south of the city on the other side of a Marine camp. It's called Mount Ecclesia, and I'm painting pictures for the Rosicrucians. Isn't that wild?
> I can't even describe the place, it's such a trip. Maybe you could come down someday to see what I'm doing. Or I can bore you to death with a slideshow of the grounds and temple. It's a Healing Temple. Keep your toes crossed. I'll jitterbug again!
> Anyway, part of the reason I'm writing (because we never had a chance to say a proper goodbye in Scamcouver) was to tell you, you were always some other woman's man. And you know what? The universe moves in mysterious ways. You'll never guess who I bumped into down here. Your wife! If I wasn't on a holy

mountain, I could have gladly strangled the ungrateful little whore. Anyway, you'll be happy to know she's renounced all worldly things and taken the Aquarian name of Starbright Moonshine and is headed back your way. She'll be at the Rosicrucian temple in North Vancouver next week sometime. Thought you might be interested in that.

So, wherever you are in this vast cosmos, John Edward Albert Christian George Andrew Patrick David Windsor, remember me fondly as,

Your (Once) Upon a Time,
Pauline
xox

P.S. The nude I did of you came out great.

Oceanside, California. He'd forgotten that you could get into the States without a passport (or any ID) if you took a chance driving through the Peace Arch crossing to Blaine, Washington. Most of the time, US Customs would just wave your car through. That was the only way Irina could have left the country without proper papers. And she was coming back. And now he knew where to find her.

"Well, that changes that," said Ted.

"How's that, buddy?" asked the cabby.

"Nothing. Where can I get a drink around here?"

The empty bar had a special on rye and ginger ale. Ted ordered a double, and raised a glass at his reflection, proposing the toast:

"Here's to the hole that never heals. The more you rub it, the better it feels. And all the soap they make in hell, can't wash away that fishy smell. Wine, women, song, and vice, syphilis, blueballs, crabs, and lice. We've had 'em all, by Jesus Christ. Gentlemen, the Queen."

He nodded at Mary as she sunned herself by the sapphire pool. Upstairs, Dorothy lay with her eyes closed in a soapy scented bath. In the bathroom he felt the moist heat, smelled perfume and oil, saw her body glistening in the water and light, and that the water was pink. She was moving her lips.

Dorothy opened her eyes, sensing his presence.

"Who were you talking to?" asked Ted.

"Oh, I was just having an argument with someone."

She looked at the water and back at Ted. "I'm so embarrassed," she said. "So sorry."

"Did you hear what you just said? You've got nothing to apologize for. You're a woman."

"What does that mean?"

"May I offer you a drink?"

Now it was the next day. Ted couldn't remember any dreams from the night before or much of anything at all. Was he drawing danger to himself again? Through their marriage he'd been Irina's lightning rod. Did Dorothy attract the same kind of trouble? Her parents were dead in an accident, her first love had died young. Some people were damned unlucky. He lay alone in an empty bed. Ted had gotten completely smashed and he remembered little from the night but heat, oaths, vows. And something Dorothy did for him, which she'd called *bing fo*. She popped an ice cube in her mouth and alternated hot and cold.

Drown your own mind. It's a terrible thing to always know what to do. That's how I've lived my life, he thought, *fighting the vagaries of perfect chance, the chance that'd brought me here, to this woman, this corner, the farthest I've ever been in life. Chance that forced me to keep going on.*

He rubbed his hand on his face and made the fateful choice. "Fuck shaving."

Then Ted looked over at the money and cocaine.

Mary was calling from the bottom of the stairs.

"Are you ready?"

He'd showered and dressed and now wore a wrinkled linen navy-blue Hugo Boss sport coat, a YSL sport shirt in Klein blue, cream Brooks Brothers trousers, and a pair of Sperry topsiders. Ted wore sunglasses and, for the jaunty touch, a white captain's cap belonging to Mary's father. She looked up as he came down the steps; he had a pained expression on his face, an expression that changed and brightened upon seeing her stick her tongue out at him. They clasped hands a moment. Mary squeezed his and said, "Be safe and take care of her. I tried convincing her not to go with you, but her mind's made up."

"Where is she?"

"In the car. And *she's* driving."

All Ted could manage was a comic shrug. He walked out the front door to the curved drive where Mary's cherry Mustang waited. Dorothy tapped a finger on the wheel. She'd done herself proud with the best of Mary's couture. Dorothy wore dark oversized sunglasses, a filmy silk scarf over her head, long thin gloves, and a light coat over what could be a bottle-green silk dress (it was hard to tell from where Ted stood). A perfect cross between Audrey Hepburn in her driving costume from *Two for the Road* and the Dragon Lady in *Terry and the Pirates*. She looked so good that Ted hoped, hankered, longed to know if she was wearing sheer stockings and garters close to her skin. He quickened, then froze a moment, becoming a pert English Setter excited by the scent of the hunt. It was true. Last night, in the fire of wine and messy sex, Dorothy swore to go with him wherever he went. So today they were off to the hills in pursuit of that most elusive game, a rare, dangerous, endangered species. Their quarry: his soon-to-be-ex-wife, Irina.

"You look deadly," said Ted as he got in the car.

"That's the idea. I can't wait to meet your wife again. She owes me rent."

35.

"What are Rosicrucians?" shouted Dorothy as she drove them over the Lion's Gate Bridge. Traffic was light as they sliced through a bone dry Stanley Park and onto the span; two of the bridge's three lanes were open going north. Dorothy felt a shameful pleasure speeding past the line of cars jammed and stalled in the lane headed back into the city. They headed for the mountains, the snow-capped Lions themselves, which the Natives had called The Sisters. Along the north shore, between the hillside and the inlet, smoked pulp mills. Freight trains ended their haul over the Rockies from Alberta and dumped loads at the edge of the sea. High pyramids of pigment-yellow sulphur grew against the cold blue of the water, stakrakes and girders moving the powder from train to ship. The element was destined to cross and end up in a Taiwanese matchstick factory. Keep away from children, and close cover before striking.

The north end of the bridge went right over top of the Capilano Indian reserve and its proudly named roads: Raindance Crescent, Hiawatha Drive, Wardance Avenue, Tyee Drive.

"Are you hungry?" asked Ted.

"Ravenous," she responded.

"What would you like?"

"A Triple-O burger from White Spot."

"I can do better than that."

Ted knew North Vancouver. Dorothy remembered that he'd grown up on this side of the water. It was another foreign country to her, a dull drag of car dealerships and hardware stores. First they stopped at a strip mall where Ted went into an office for fifteen minutes, emerging with a long envelope under his arm. He then directed Dorothy to Philip Avenue. She parked the Mustang by a low, nondescript, cinder-block wall faced with rough stone. Under the low-slope rooftop were wooden beams extended over an entrance flanked by brightly painted totem poles. The Tomahawk Barbecue.

A young waitress led them past the cashier's till and candy rack to a small booth. The only other diners were a group of boisterous Shriners in red fezzes. One seemed to be the restaurant's owner. Around them, the interior was all dark wood, and Dorothy marvelled at the collection of objects—potlatch masks in profusion, row upon row of crudely carved human figures, small totem poles, ravens, eagles, killer whales. Strange iron implements hung from the rafters, meathooks, leg traps. The overall effect was of a crowded longhouse, and it began to oppress Dorothy with a slightly morbid quality. The sensation lifted somewhat when she spied two portraits flanking the wings of a thunderbird, the Queen and a young Edward VIII.

"Look, it's your great aunt and your grandfather."

Ted turned. "But no Phil the Greek," he said. "When they visited Canada last time, the Duke told someone he didn't come here for his health. And speaking of health, if you're hungry, I know what you're having."

"Yes, your majesty."

Ted ordered, and while waiting they looked at the novelty placemats of an outsized British Columbia, The Big Country, which took up most of North America's land mass. According to the map, Dorothy's province was home to the world's biggest sasquatch, moose and salmon runs, fattest cattle, largest Ogopogo, hydro dam and smelter, fastest ferry for northbound Yankees, deepest snow, tallest trees, and highest totem pole. There was also a tunnel to Japan starting on Vancouver Island. Follow the Sun to The Promised Land! It's BC for me!

At the very least, the Tomahawk was home to the biggest hamburger Dorothy had ever seen. Ted smiled as the waitress set it down.

"They call it the Skookum Chief Burger, which means big, or best, or really good. Isn't it amazing?"

It was. Barely contained between homemade buns was a medium rare beef patty crowded with onion, tomato, lettuce, ketchup, and cheddar, in addition to Yukon bacon, a grilled hot dog sliced lengthwise, and the whole glorious thing topped by an over-easy fried egg, dripping meat juice, mustard, and Tomahawk sauce. Dorothy could barely pick it up. She took a luscious bite and rolled her eyes with pleasure. Ted laughed and stole a sip of her Cherry Coke.

"Once you pick it up, you can't put it down. You're going to have to eat the whole thing. Lord, I love a woman who eats," he said.

With a full mouth Dorothy could only widen her eyes to communicate.

"So," said Ted. "Rosicrucians. You really want to know? It means I have to tell you about Irina and what happened."

Dorothy nodded. She wanted to know.

"Well, it's like this. She showed up during the last year of my useless Bachelor of Fuck All. Never get an art degree. Anyway, suddenly there's this incredibly beautiful, exotic, mysterious woman, from out of nowhere. She was smoking a Silk Cut before class. Picture me, your pure-blooded Canadian boy from out west. She's a dark, treacherous Russian from back in the USSR. Who was she? I had to know, and I got hooked. Which is maybe what she wanted from the start. But I'll probably never know."

Ted stared off into the vanishing point of an infinite distance, and Dorothy could tell he was seeing the past in his mind's eye.

"She was like no one else. She smoked, she drank anything, she'd been everywhere, and could curse anyone in five languages. I barely know French. How'd she get out of the Soviet Union? Well, her father was a brilliant professor who defected, and he managed to get her out too. I met him a couple times—a very deep man. And dangerous. Like daughter, like father, because Irina was as deadly as a bullet. Even now, I'm not positive it's her real name. I mean, what did she call herself to you?"

"Anna something," said Dorothy with a full mouth.

"You know most of the rest. But to the Rosicrucians! One of the things Irina was into was magic, secrets, what she called the *arcana mundi*. I saw her try it all; Divine Light Mission, Moonies, Thelemites, the Golden Dawn, followers of the Kabbala, Scientology. That was a close one; watch out for them. She went Mormon for a week, then Seventh Day Adventist, or was it Christian Science? No, Jehovah's Witness. Flakes and fakers and weirdos. Finally, she got a job at a gallery, and it got a zillion times worse. Artists. Christ, what a bunch of fucking assholes."

He sipped Dorothy's Coke one more time.

"We had a party one night and invited a bunch of people, couples. I was bored because I wasn't working and had nothing to do. This crowd came over, and the whole thing went sideways. We had a penthouse with decks. Everyone got fucked up, and I started to lose track. Bunch of us went swimming naked in the pool downstairs, and for the first time since I'd been with Irina, my eye fell on someone else. She was this cute little thing, the girlfriend of some guy who'd passed out. Anyway, next thing you know we were in a shower together, and in the morning I wake up in bed with her and a head like a fried egg. I thought the apartment was empty, but no, there was Irina with a guy, this total jerk-off.

"So, it's done. Mutual adultery, and I think I beat her to it by five minutes. Isn't that amazing? Five minutes after I commit a sin, I get paid back in my own coin. That might be a world record. They could put it on this placemat here: BC's biggest tool. I was going to try to be cool about the whole thing in the continental manner, like a Frenchman. Besides, I felt like death. Anyway, I go back to bed. Later on, I smelled coffee and heard the door slam. When I got back up again, Irina's gone. Therefore, I proceed to spend a pleasant morning in bed with fresh coffee and little Miss Robin O'Brian. She was better than a bottle of aspirins to cure my headache. I wonder where she is now."

Dorothy listened, first amazed, and then amazed that this was somehow turning her on. She felt her juices flowing as she devoured the succulent meat and remembered her period at the same time, but she was too busy eating and listening to Ted to do anything but keep going.

"It all changed when she didn't come back," said Ted.

And there he was, back from the past, opposite her again at the table, looking a little sad. "That's it. And look at you. How is it?" he asked.

It was so good, Dorothy couldn't say anything. She licked her fingers clean. Ted came up with the best idea in all of human history. "How about pie? They make a mean strawberry cream *à la mode.*"

The pie had almost made Dorothy climax, but she had to change her tampon. Back outside in the sunshine, Ted put on Ray-Bans and held open the passenger door for her. He looked rather dashing in the bright September light, *more Kennedy than Windsor*, thought Dorothy. *And that Russian had been a fool*, she thought, as Ted turned the key, backed out, and set off. The radio played "Eyes of a Stranger" again. As they climbed away from the city up Hollyburn Mountain, the station continued with "Ride Like the Wind." The forests that blanked the north shore slopes were being massacred for suburban real estate. They passed through subdivisions going up all at once in a spasm of cheap plywood and drywall. She smelled fresh lumber and concrete dust.

"Can you believe they shot *McCabe & Mrs. Miller* up here?" asked Ted.

"What's that?"

"Movie with Warren Beatty and Julie Christie. Takes place back in the Old West. Now look at it—all gone. The music was great, this Canadian singer, Leonard Cohen."

The higher they got, the older the hills became, until they were on a switchback gravel road through bush under an empty sky. At a clear viewpoint looking all the way across Vancouver to the southern horizon, Ted stopped the car. They saw a glint of Boundary Bay.

"Look," he said. "Dark clouds coming. Japan current setting in. Could be rain."

"When was the last time it rained here?" she asked.

"So long ago we must've broken a record."

"Would you like to try for a record now?" wondered Dorothy.

"I thought you'd never ask."

They managed, and it was good. For a moment it almost got complicated and a little messy, but they improvised a few things, and by the splendid end they both felt much better. A large, redheaded, pileated woodpecker tapped at a dead tree nearby. Dorothy adjusted her skirt, sunglasses, and scarf, then touched up her lipstick in a mirror. She peeled her stockings off, legs tingling with electricity.

"You know what Confucius said?" asked Ted.

"What?"

"Man who make love on hill not on level."

He drove along with one hand, elbow on a windowsill, smiling mellowly, sometimes grinning like a fool. He'd shift up and down, then run his hand up the inside of her thighs to where Dorothy wore no panties. As they came to the Rosicrucians' gate, the FM radio played Peter Gabriel's "Games Without Frontiers." Dorothy heard the song's refrain as, "She's so popular. She's so popular. She's so popular."

This is what Dorothy saw, waiting in the car: The gate blocked the way, and behind it a driveway led to a round white temple in a clearing on a rise. Dorothy noticed an empty window on the second floor. Ted rattled the chain. Eventually a thin, white-robed hippie looking like a beardless Jesus appeared. Ted said something to him, pointed at the temple, then stabbed his finger at the hippie. Dorothy saw a figure appear at the window. This person was also in white but bald. A bald *woman*, she realized. The hippie turned to the woman, and the baldie flung her hand back at him, a gesture of disdain.

Then it looked like Ted was laughing. He handed a manila envelope to Moonbeam (that was the hippie's name, Dorothy decided) and pointed at the bald woman. He shooed Moonbeam uphill like you'd urge away a dog or goose. The bald woman stood stock still and stared down. Ted held something in one hand, blew her a kiss, threw the thing, spun around, and walked back to Dorothy.

"Watch," he said.

She saw Moonbeam hand the bald woman the envelope, the bald woman open it, read a page, then instantly begin tearing a strip off of the hippie. Jesus. It was like watching Punch and Judy with the volume off. Ted laughed and got behind the wheel. He started up and peeled out, kicking up a cloud of dusty gravel at the temple. "L.A. Woman" rumbled over the Mustang's speakers as they rolled away. Ted turned to Dorothy.

"They say the first time you serve divorce papers is the sweetest. In fact, you know the very first thing I said to her, outside the church after we got married?"

"No."

"How's it feel to be my future first ex-wife?" He shook his head and smiled sadly. "Such a shame. Of course, she had all her hair back then."

"What did you throw at her?" asked Dorothy.

"A little wooden doll."

As they drove down from the mountains, the sun began to set behind a haze of pollution massing above Vancouver. No rain and more wildfires to the west. The Mustang did seventy miles an hour over the Second Narrows Bridge, the entire inlet spread out as evening lights in the city sparked to life. Ted turned up the radio volume, saying as a song started, "Perfect. The perfect tune at the perfect time. That's why I love listening to the radio. You never know. It's poetry."

Dorothy heard the swooping opening wail of an instrument like a singing saw mixed with traffic on the bridge. A hum and cry of a bird, then an electronic pulse, the guitars kicking off as Ted pounded out the opening cry, "Lunatic fringe!"

As they passed through the Hastings-Sunrise neighbourhood, the Italian grocers put away their street barrows of fruits and vegetables, and pasta and pizza joints started to turn on their bright neon. They purred along East Hasting through the pulse of the city, getting closer to the towers downtown, headed for Mary's house where the $300,000 (minus such expenses as the bill at the Tomahawk) and cocaine were hidden in a hamper of dirty laundry. The song ended and another started. Ted said, "No way. I don't believe it. Two in a row. Seger, 'Turn the Page.'"

After that, CFMI completed the trifecta with "Baker Street" by Gerry Rafferty, a saxophone wailing like a lost soul.

Ted continued to power the Mustang past Commercial Drive. Dorothy woolgathered distractedly, the song pulsing in time with the city. She thought of nothing until her peripheral vision caught the red neon of the Pink Pearl Restaurant. It took a moment to register consciously. They crossed over train tracks and went a few more blocks before it suddenly stabbed like a sharpened chopstick through her heart. The Pink Pearl restaurant. Her mother. Her father.

Her home.

"Turn left here," snapped Dorothy.

"What?" asked Ted, startled from his groove. "Are you okay?"

"Turn now."

Ted slalomed without braking onto Hawks and she urged him on with her hand.

"Oops," he said, running a stop sign

Ahead of them opened a park walkway.

"Here we go."

The Mustang swerved through the park. On the other side, Dorothy pulled Ted's elbow and pointed right up the alley behind Union Street. The Mustang bucked uphill and Dorothy commanded, "Stop."

Ted obeyed and turned off the car by the garage and fence at the back of her house. It had been just like that moment in the *Wind in the Willows* when Rat and Mole are travelling together, and Mole gets just the faintest scent of home. He had to go back. And so did she. The most powerful urge. Now here she was.

"What's that?" she asked.

They went through the gate into the yard. "Do you hear it?"

"Yes," said Ted.

They walked to the kitchen entrance. A persistent sound came through the wood. Dorothy unlocked the handle and pushed open the door. The sound was music playing; it was one of her father's favourite records. The song started again.

"What is that? Don Ho?" asked Ted.

"Tiny Bubbles," said Dorothy.

Her teeth started to chatter. She turned on the light and said, "No."

The kitchen was trashed. Cupboard doors had been torn off, glasses and plates smashed on the floor, food from the fridge crushed underfoot.

"No," said Dorothy, in a faraway voice, the cold gone, a warm flush of anger and rage stopping the chattering shivers.

Like a sleepwalker she went through the wreckage in the kitchen to even worse damage in the dining room, and then she looked through the doorway arch to see more destruction in the living room, where the hi-fi played. Everything was totalled, too much devastation to register through her shock, until something moved on the couch. She screamed. Ted rushed to her. A man stood, his hands up. He had a beard, saw Dorothy. The stranger said, "It was like this when I got here. The record wasn't broken, so I put it on. Hope you don't mind."

35.

. . . .

The Chinese girl and Ted Windsor watched the hunter. He was careful to stand still, his hands raised and palms visible. Don Ho played on. The woman was inanimate, Windsor the first to speak.

"Man, you look like hell."

That brought the woman back to the room. She turned and said, "You know him?"

Ted Windsor nodded. He put his hand at the nape of her neck.

"This guy and I had a moment. He was with Detective Johnstone after the post office."

"What's he doing here?" she asked, angrily.

"Let's ask him and find out."

Ted righted some chairs from the dining room and indicated one to Renard. They sat amid the ruin. The Chinese girl became very collected, almost to the point of rigidity. He could read nothing in the Asian mask of her face. *Like the Vietnamese*, thought Renard. *That was our problem. We could never tell how furious they were. And we thought we were helping them fight the Commies. All they wanted was for us to leave.* Ted leaned over and turned down Don Ho. The needle lifted, and "Tiny Bubbles" started to blow again.

"You came here for a reason," said Ted Windsor. "Might as well tell us."

Renard took a breath. This would have to be a convincing performance. He was in a poor position. He knew no one else in the city that he could to turn to. There was no way he could ask Mallory or Mr Peters for aid; they'd notify the San Francisco syndicate, and Renard would be finished. *I have no money, no car, no gun, and I need to take a run at two cops. This pair has smarts. They'd managed to make off with what was in in the post office box, right under our noses, and Windsor had slipped the handcuff noose.*

Renard needed their help and had to make them realize that they needed *his*. The hunter took a chance. He told the truth.

"Johnstone won't stop until he gets it," said Renard.

He looked at the Oriental woman. "What they did to your house was just a start. Now they move toward the end game. It's him and Hickey together. They're running out of options, and they're mean, and they're dumb, so it's going to get uglier. Either they get what they want, or they kill you, or both."

"What about you?" asked the Chinese.

That was good. Windsor gets it right away, I knew that the moment he walked in. It's her I need to win over. Do that, and it's done, thought Renard. *But be careful. What was her name again?*

He paused to choose his next words, then indicated the healing cuts and bruises on his face. "They did this to me, Dorothy. So I'm going to do something back. But I need your help. Together we can get rid of them."

"Kill them?" asked Dorothy.

"Better," said Renard.

"Better's good," said Ted.

Renard started to talk. He told them more of what he knew about Johnstone and the other one. They all three had the same enemy. It was simple as that. Whether they believed him or not, they were on the same side.

He made his play.

"I don't care about the money. You keep it. I can take care of my own. But I could use the drugs."

Windsor agreed immediately. He turned to a now-alert Dorothy, then shrugged his shoulders. "What're we going to do with all that coke? If he can use it, he's more than welcome. What do you think?"

"I think I've had enough 'Tiny Bubbles' for the rest of my life," she said.

Renard was exhausted. He asked, "Any chance of a drink and some fresh air?" They convened on the shielded front garden patio in twilight. Windsor created Singapore Sunsets with what remained of the ice, some salvaged cold vodka, a few slices of orange, and a drop of Rose's Lime Cordial. That rare thing happened. The three came up with a plan together.

"I might need a gun," said Renard.

"I've got one," said Dorothy.

Renard and Windsor turned to her, both amazed. She withdrew into the house and returned with a heavy piece.

"Nagant M1985," said Renard. "I haven't seen one in a while. May I?"

He took it from Dorothy. *I could easily shoot them dead right now*, he thought. The hunter weighed the heavy weapon, opened the Abadie gate, and spun the cylinder. Every chamber was empty except for one. A single round of 7.62mm. One bullet: a real Russian Roulette revolver. You could fix the fucking thing with a hammer, he remembered. Like an AK-47 that way. Good thing he hadn't squeezed the trigger. Renard handed it back to Dorothy.

"That's a real antique, but one bullet's not enough for anything but suicide. I've got a better idea. Is there a hardware store nearby?"

While shopping in the hardware store, Ted came up with a novel way to get the cops. It had the element of the ridiculous, which helped Renard to go along. He felt loose. Maybe it was all the marijuana he'd been smoking, or residual traces of kava in his system. His pituitary gland had been stimulated, Renard thought. The third eye opening.

While pushing a cart up and down the aisles, they worked the plan around. Three days from now, enough time to set it up. Ted fronted Renard $500 and arranged a meeting in two days to hand over the cocaine. Ted bought a Polaroid camera. Dorothy purchased two briefcases.

"Why two?" asked Windsor in the parking lot.

"It was buy one, get one free," said Dorothy.

"But we only need one."

"Just in case," said Dorothy.

Ted handed one to Renard. They were now three people against two cops and the whole damn world. Renard had some other business to attend to in the interim. He offered to guard Dorothy's house, and she simply nodded in agreement. As they dropped Renard and his purchases at her house, a sudden squall of hail fell down, rattling roofs and gutters. Ted pointed up to hail coursing down the boughs of a cedar tree and said to Dorothy, "Pachinko!"

"What'd you call me?"

"Not you. It's a Japanese game."

"Yeah, a hard one to win," said Renard. "Good luck."

His hosts drove off in the Mustang. The hunter would need a car of his own soon, but that was easy. In the busted-up living room, Renard assembled his purchases from the sporting goods and home improvement departments of Canadian Tire. The store had given him some company money with his change. It showed a smiling tam o'shantered Scotsman with huge sideburns and moustache. The hunter made himself secure, smoked part of one of Charlie's joints, and tried to get comfortable in the ruins of the Chinese girl's house. *Need some rest before morning*, he thought. *Demain*.

In the morning, Renard made a long-distance call from a payphone at a deli up the block. His answering service had been left a message. Renard called the number and listened, nodding. The long-distance call to San Francisco he'd made weeks ago had panned out. Renard's signals man had tracked the telephone number that Mallory had given him to contact the mysterious Mr Peters. The radio phone was registered to a traceable address. He'd go there tomorrow and wing it. Renard's healing collarbone gave out a slight twinge, but he put the pain away.

Before dawn the hunter hotwired a car from an alley near the Chinese girl's house. It was a shitbox AMC Pacer, and the radio didn't work. Renard stashed it in Dorothy's decrepit garage. Back in the wrecked kitchen, he made wieners and beans, rested, and waited some more. His shoulder felt a lot better now.

On a stack of *Provinces*, Renard read the date: Sunday, September 18th, 1983. From a different payphone the hunter went over the plan again with Ted. After a hasty breakfast of coffee and *bombolini* from Benny Foods, Renard swung by the Hummingbird Cabaret on Seymour. *There might be a way to get a jump on the* cochons, he thought. *Stay loose, stay open to possibilities.*

Nope. Something heavy had gone down. Blue and whites with flashing lights guarded a yellow police line. Morning rubberneckers strained the tape as a stretcher rolled out of the club to the black coroner's van. Renard parked and joined the edge of the crowd.

"What's up?" he asked some geek.

"Cops say someone shot the owner, old Cooch Delbianco. Put a couple in the back of his head and robbed his safe."

Johnstone and Hickey, it had to be, thought Renard. *Tying up loose ends. First they'd tried to kill me, now they've waxed Joe. Chickenshit cops. Who's next? Mallory. Have to act today. Time to move.* The hunter felt better; he hardly noticed his arm. Juice started to pump through Renard now that he was back in harness. He got into the shitbox and burned around, booting over the Burrard Bridge to Cornwall, then west into Point Grey.

A few blocks from the Royal Vancouver Yacht Club, Renard stopped and found a space. Although it was mid-afternoon on a Sunday, the club's parking lot swarmed with cars. His luck. The chaos might help. *Feel it. Will it into shape.* Carhops hustled Cadillacs and Rolls Royces around. At the hut station, Renard grabbed a valet jacket off a chair back and put it on. The club was an overturned kettle of fish. Renard held car keys shoulder high and shook them as he walked up the carpeted steps under the portico to the entryway. Some kind of reception taking place. Putting on a dumb act, he jingled the keys at an officious old soldierly gent in a half-coat who was distracted by various comings and goings. Beneath a group of helium-filled balloons a sign read, Benefit for the BC Social Credit Party and 1986 Vancouver World's Expo Committee.

"What do you want?" asked the majordomo.

"Mister Mallory Peters asked me to bring him his keys."

"Do you mean Peter Mallory?"

"That's right."

"Commodore Mallory."

"The Commodore," repeated Renard, his jaw slightly slack on purpose. "Told me bring 'em up."

"He did? Then hop to it," said the majordomo, jerking his thumb up the stairs.

Inside it was all nautical splendour: gleaming polished brass, rich waxed wood, deep money thickly carpeted throughout. He heard a politician giving a stem-winder in a dining room and looked in, scanning the room for his man. The crowd was composed of wealthy WASPs wearing blue blazers and Sebago deck loafers with tassels. A tall, orange-tanned politico with a heavy five o'clock shadow thundered out:

"The Solidarity movement is one that'll take the great province of British Columbia back to the Bronze Age! The New Democratic Party and their pals, the public sector trade unions, want what they call a level playing field. That means they want to put hands in your pockets. That's not the BC I want! In two years, the whole world's coming to Vancouver. Expo 86 is going to showcase the best of British Columbia. Let's show them that means the Social Credit Party knows how to do business, and knows how to do it right! Something's happening here!"

Applause. Renard missed his target and went back out. Nobody guarded the reception, so he drifted up a spiral staircase in the general compass-heading of the Commodore's office. Following a plush blue hallway took him to a door that the hunter nudged open with his toe. Renard saw with pleasure a note of alarm on the face of the man he'd called Mallory, who looked up. Renard smiled. The Commodore said, "I've been expecting your call."

"Saved myself a quarter," said Renard.

Renard met Windsor on the roof of a dead-empty parking lot above a failing supermarket at Alma and 4th. Both stayed in their cars. Ted handed a briefcase of cocaine from driver's side to driver's side.

"Are you a free person or a voluntary slave?" asked Ted.

"What?"

"The cry of the self-made man."

Renard remembered the missionary wearing the infinite sandwich board. "Free person," he said.

"And I'm the King of England," laughed Ted as he drove off.

That afternoon Renard staked out his spot. The shitbox Pacer sat in a parking lot in front of a silver crab sculpture at the planetarium in Kitsilano. It was fucking hot on the acre of boiling macadam. The faint rush of steady traffic on the bridge hissed just past a line of trees. By the sun and shadows it was near time. There they were. Driving a prowler for total domination. The dirty cops were in character. Renard slid low. The shitbox faced the Music Conservatory, its façade fronted by glass. From where he was, Renard could see right into the lobby as the cops parked in a handicapped loading spot. Johnstone heaved out of the passenger side and checked his watch. Still the same yellow-eyed pig, in a new hat and London Fog, Renard noted. Johnstone spat, hitched his belt, and insolently entered the lobby, where he affected boredom. But Renard noticed the way the detective started out of his skin when the payphone rang. Ted had set this up.

Windsor was the one who called Johnstone direct at the cop shop. That message had been short and imperative: be at a certain place at a certain time to get your drugs and money back. This was the place, this was the time. Even if Johnstone and Hickey looked right at Renard, the swine would never see him. He was dead, after all. They'd had Charlie the Hawaiian kill him and dump the body in the harbour. Cops go blind when they get dirty in the mud.

Detective Johnstone answered the phone and tried to get into a short argument with the person at the other end of line. Ted Windsor again, telling the detective how it was going to be. In the middle of a tirade, Johnstone took the receiver from his ear and looked at it. Windsor had hung up, Renard guessed. Johnstone came back out to talk to Hickey, who waited near the patrol car. Renard heard them raise their voices, bullies in a schoolyard fight, and then the cops got back in the prowler, arguing like a married couple all the way out of the lot.

Renard wouldn't follow them. A tail was no good in a Pacer, and he didn't want to be seen by the cops, even by accident. Besides, he didn't need to. He knew where they were going. If it all went down the way they'd planned it, Renard, Windsor, and the Chinese girl had just split the cops up. Now the odds were better: two on one, and one for the hunter.

He got out of the shitbox and went into the lobby. The phone rang again. Renard picked it up and said, "They're on their way."

37.

Across the ocean, he heard a navy band thumping out "Rule, Britannia!" from the shore. The sailboat's bow sliced through the green water of the Strait of Georgia. Ted didn't need a chart to tell him where he was on the saltchuck. He was piloting a C&C 27 that they'd rented from Granville Island. Dorothy had gone home to lock up her house and finish some business in Chinatown. They'd met at the rental place where the guy'd been so eager to see cash, since tourist season had dried up, that he let Ted have the boat for a hundred bucks a day. Ted gave him three, just in case.

He knew C&Cs well; in fact, his family owned one. *Irina'll never see that,* thought Ted. *Or anything else of mine. Including her post office money. As much as she'd kept hidden from me, I concealed even more from her. Such a good thing the wife renounced all her worldly goods. I just made the choice easier for her.* Ted allowed himself to relish, just for a moment, the memory of serving notarized divorce papers and throwing the *matryoshka* at her. He turned the helm east toward Wreck Beach. *Enjoy it while it lasts.* The memory was all he had going right now.

A slack, useless breeze came off the land against him, so Ted wasn't able to haul up sails. Too tiring, beating tack after tack opposing the wind, and it was never fun alone on the boat. Even though Dorothy was with him.

No, this was nothing like a sweet, quiet reach with the wind on your beam and your toe on the tiller, he thought. Ted had the sailboat under power. Even with its inboard Mercury, the noise and smell of fuel was slightly nauseating, combined with the engine's ugly puttering. An aromatic essence of bilgewater reached Ted's nostrils. He was fighting not only the wind but a lousy tide, and a current of crud from the Fraser River, pouring its stomach out into the sea. *Power on a sailboat, a crime against nature,* Ted thought.

And worst of all by far, Dorothy Kwan was pissed at him.

One: she was deadly seasick.

Two: they hadn't had sex last night or this morning.

Three: that could be because of her period, Ted conceded.

But, fourth: she'd been sullen and uncommunicative even before they'd got into the boat. And the puking hadn't helped her disposition one iota.

So: fifth. What to do?

He shrugged. Keep sailing smooth and hope for the best.

Ted heard the dying strains of "God Save the Queen" floating from the bandstand in the rose garden of the university on the hill. He imagined someone sitting on a folding chair on the green, listening to the music, watching in the western distance a sailboat on the whale's road. How pleasant. Grasp at any straw you can. Eat something.

In Mary Worthington's kitchen, Ted had built margarine, Marmite, mayonnaise, and cheese sandwiches on brown bread. Smelling the contents of the Marmite jar for the first time, Dorothy wrinkled her nose.

"Smells awful," she said.

"English cuisine, but the taste's what the Japanese call *umami*."

"*Umami*, my ass, *lan hoi gweilo*."

"What?"

"Never mind."

Imagine that! The Cantonese would eat anything that swam that wasn't a submarine, anything with legs that wasn't a table, and anything with wings that wasn't an airplane. Seated in the cabin, Dorothy folded her arms and looked away from him. He couldn't eat in front of her. Her face was as composed as a mask, faintly green under her yellow skin. Had Ted done something? Talked in his sleep? Was there any telling with a woman? He ransacked his conscience for any transgression she hadn't found out yet. What red-blooded man doesn't have a guilty secret to hide? *Certainly not our hero*, thought Ted.

With this, turning portside to the east and landfall, Ted began to have misgivings. It was all part of his plan, a stupid plan that he'd basically joked into existence. And the other guy, Renard or whatever he called himself, the bearded stranger now had all the cocaine and a promise to perform a part. Could Ted trust him? *Jesus, anything could go wrong.* He shook his head. He couldn't think like that. It was too late now. This was the play they'd have to make to get the cops off their backs. It was worth it, maybe. With nearly 300,000 bucks and the rest of their lives, he and Dorothy could do a lot together. At this very moment, however, Ted Windsor wouldn't trust Dorothy Kwan to throw him a life preserver if he was drowning.

He couldn't eat anyway; he was going swimming within the hour. Don't want to cramp up. Ted checked his watch. This was close enough.

Through the heat haze, Ted could just make out nude bodies on Wreck Beach baking in the sun. From this distance, it was a simple matter to swim to shore. The problem now was Dorothy. He turned to her. "How're you feeling?"

"What do you think?"

"We can still call it off. It's not too late. Only problem is, if we do, we'll be letting down our end of the bargain. While that guy Renard's taking care of his. He probably wouldn't like it. And he doesn't seem the kind of fellow you get away from twice. Either of us."

Ted looked at her meaningfully. "So?" he asked.

"I'll be fine," she said, reaching over for the tiller.

Off and on, off and on. Ted gave Dorothy her instructions and showed her the easiest way to steer the sailboat. They went back and forth a few times for practice, the engine nice and slow. She'd give him fifteen minutes on shore, and if Ted didn't make it back she was to use her best judgment, beach and abandon the boat somewhere (preferably back at Granville Island, but this point didn't really matter. Ted had rented it with one of Mary's brother's old driver's licences). What would Ted do if it all went wrong? What was Plan Zed? Run.

"Well, this is it," he said, taking off his shirt and kicking out of his deck shoes.

From the cabin, Dorothy handed up the briefcase wrapped safe from water in a green Glad garbage bag.

"Wish me luck," he said. Ted leaned down and Dorothy gave him a dry kiss. *Well then*, he thought. *Here goes everything.*

He tossed the briefcase into the ocean and followed after in a graceful, diving arc that cleaved the water cleanly.

With his left holding the bagged briefcase, Ted swam one-armed toward the beach. The water was warm. Spill from the mouth of the Fraser pulsed along the point. He bumped into floating pine cones that had washed all the way down from the heart of British Columbia. To his right ranged a long, crude breakwater of rude granite boulders that protected huge booms of sawn logs. The wood waited to be tugged away and milled. *Or turned into endless miles of telephone poles*, he thought, *to be stretched across the Dominion from here to the lighthouse at Peggy's Cove on the Atlantic.*

Closer to shore Ted's foot touched sand, and he started to walk through the diminishing surf. Now he could see the nudists more clearly. Most of them he wouldn't want to see clothed, never mind naked. Long-haired hippies and old bags with saggy tits, hairy-crotched, pale Englishmen blinking in the light. Lots of dumb-looking dudes with big dicks, the only place they could legally show off their shlongs. A bearded stoner drifted around, selling cold Kokanee beer stashed away in a cooler behind a log. Wreck Beach had a culture. It tried to avoid cops. This was technically the jurisdiction of the RCMP, one of the reasons Ted had chosen the spot. He smelled pot smoke and suntan oil. In a seagrass clearing behind prone logs where nudists sunned on towels, an enterprising fellow had set up a booth made of driftwood and twine. Colourful sarongs, Tibetan prayer flags, and Communist banners fluttered in the heat. Even further behind the vendor were secret green paths that led up the hill into strange dells where homosexuals sported. Ted suddenly got distracted.

An absolutely gorgeous blonde wearing nothing but mirrored aviator shades dashed into the sea as he sloughed along. She had perfect ripe breasts topped with delicious pink nipples and a whispered slip of blonde pubic hair. The Aphrodite looked even better slipping back out, slick with beaded seawater. Ted eyed her and kneeled down. This allowed him to do two things: untie the neck of the garbage bag and take out the dry briefcase, and hide the sudden erection in his wet khaki shorts. He heard someone call the beauty's name.

"Honeydew!"

"I'd love a fresh slice," whispered Ted.

He cooled his lower parts off in the surf, then stood more easily. In any case, what he saw next was something that'd shrink the erection of a horny bull in a bordello of cows. Constable Hickey of the Vancouver Police stood stark naked twenty yards away, sweating in the hot sun.

The cop couldn't look more self-conscious and embarrassed if he'd had an apple in his mouth, turning on a spit. His short moustache bristled with sweat, his porcine eyes darted in agony from the naked hippies over the beach until they clapped on Ted walking along the sand. *This was the plan*, thought Ted. Get the cop somewhere he can't be a cop. With no badge, belt, or gun, Hickey was just a fat white gut hanging over a small prick.

Ted walked closer and stopped a few feet off. Constable Hickey gritted his teeth in his red, strained face.

"Got it?" squealed the cop.

Ted opened the briefcase. *Wait a second. This is all wrong. This isn't the plan.*

The plan was for Ted to hand over to Hickey some of the money dusted with cocaine. While Renard took care of Johnstone, Ted would also take Polaroids of the naked pig for back-up insurance. Then, when Hickey returned to Johnstone, a group of RCMP Mounties acting on an anonymous tip would bust the dirty city cops.

All that was in the briefcase was a loose sheaf of Hell money bearing the image of the Jade Emperor. That and Dorothy's Nagant revolver. The money started to flutter away. Stunned, Ted picked up the gun. Without thinking, he pointed it at Hickey, hearing his own empty, faraway voice say the words, "I've got it right here."

33.

Renard waited in the stolen shitbox, well out of sight, backed into a corner of a parking lot underneath trees overhung with ivy growing wild. The low grey concrete bunker of UBC's Anthropology Museum squatted nearby. Because it was Sunday, the institution sat closed to the paying public. The hunter had done a survey all the way around. In a clearing on the west side of the museum, an Indian village of longhouses and totem poles had been built near the cliff side. In this somnolent hour, the hot afternoon slept, empty of tourists, students, innocent bystanders, witnesses. With the windows open, Renard smoked cheapish Captain Black tobacco in a corncob pipe bought at a gas station. In the passenger footwell, five cans of Labatt Blue sweated next to a mickey of Wild Turkey. The bourbon was for later. On the seat next to him the hunter had arranged a crossbow, a blue-metal caulking gun, its fresh silicone tube prepped and ready to go, and what were called "secateurs" up here. Renard puffed his pipe contentedly and took another swig of beer. *It's good to stay loose when you're about to commit an act of violence,* he thought.

Renard allowed himself to remember his encounter with Commodore Peter Mallory at the Yacht Club. The commodore had worn a regimental tie with a blue blazer, the RVYC's crest on the breast. In the office there was, of all things, that same framed poster of the tennis girl and her nude fanny he'd seen at the Royal Maui Import/Export.

Peter Mallory, amateur criminal, bum man.

"You used your own name?" asked Renard, shaking his head with pity.

"Far simpler to remember than a pseudonym."

"And you acted as your own middleman. You don't know what the hell you're doing, do you?"

"I'm afraid it's all been rather new to me," said the commodore.

"No kidding. You need better help."

"Better than two policemen?"

"Two corrupt policemen. They've got too much to lose. Besides, they're idiots. Cops are too institutional. It removes their initiative and intelligence."

"It's true that none of this would have happened without their staggering incompetence."

"Don't blame yourself. Every organization is filled with liabilities. Where I come from, there's over a dozen intelligence agencies—CIA, NSA, Army, Navy, Air Force, Marines. Even the Coast Guard. Then you've got the FBI, state police, city and county cops, you name it. Talk about a clusterfuck. You've got what, up here in Canada? The RCMP?"

"Ah, but the Mounties always get their man," said the commodore.

"Maybe in the movies. But in the real world you need a manhunter. *Comme moi.*"

"*Alors*, Mr Renard," said Mallory urbanely, "then we have much to discuss."

And so they had, over an excellent cognac.

"The policemen are short-sighted," confessed the commodore. "It is not about drugs, or even money, exactly. It is about control and always has been."

"Control of what?" asked Renard.

"Real estate. How would you like to get in on the ground floor?"

Now the hunter was here with a brand-new mandate, a new identity in the works, a whole alternate future ahead of him. The self-made man headed forward into the world of tomorrow.

The police prowler pulled up and stopped near the museum entrance. Again, Hickey parked in a handicap spot and both cops got out. They conversed for a minute or two, Detective Johnstone giving emphatic orders to his reluctant constable. Hickey was dressed in shorts, a bright Hawaiian shirt, and flip-flops. He said something nasty to Johnstone and slouched away down a trail through the woods, the picture of a reluctant cur told by its master to hurry up and take a shit. So far, so good, the plan was unfolding per the script. Hickey would walk the long, steep path down to Wreck Beach, far away from his partner and support. Johnstone would wait. The dirty cops had been told they'd get all the drugs and money back. Greedy for their ill-gotten loot, they'd allowed themselves to get split up. Better odds, by far. Renard liked the part where Windsor would face the naked pig. The hunter only wished he could be in both places at once. There'd be time to settle with Hickey later. In the meantime, Johnstone was the higher target. In his weakened state, still recovering from the beating, Renard's guile, rather than strength, would work to take the detective out. He finished the Blue and cracked another.

Not even ten minutes later, he saw what he wanted. Detective Johnstone, policeman down to his bone marrow, kicked the seat back in the patrol car with the window open, tilted his hat over his eyes, and caught some zees. Perfect. The heat and quiet were working. Renard tapped the smoked ashes from his pipe and slipped out of the shitbox with the crossbow and caulking gun in hand.

He catfooted it right behind the prowler. Light chatter at a low volume burbled out of the police radio. The hunter levelled his crossbow at Johnstone's neck and said, "Put your hands up, real slow."

The detective snapped out of a reverie, and his hat fell to his lap. As he turned, Renard had the satisfaction of watching the sweating detective's face go white and those yellow eyes open wide in fear.

"See this?" asked Renard.

Johnstone looked to the sharp tip of the crossbow bolt.

"Cuff your right only."

Johnstone submitted. *Is he angry or afraid? Doesn't matter now.*

"No tricks," Renard told Johnstone. "Get out, hands up."

Johnstone opened the passenger door. Hatless, he lugged himself to an upright position.

"Now walk. If this thing misses your artery, it'll still go into your windpipe. Do as I say, and I won't kill you."

Johnstone walked ahead of Renard to the Indian village. Renard scanned the terrain for hostiles. None. The fake village had been set on a rise of smashed oyster shells simulating an ancient midden. Renard looked at the concrete arches of the museum, each ascending, each faced with streaked glass. Inside he glimpsed ancient weathered totem poles. In front of the longhouses stood newer, painted copies, topped by carved frogs, beavers, and birds. With the crossbow he motioned Johnstone toward one. "Cuff yourself backward to it and sit down."

Now clumsy, Johnstone struggled. He still hadn't said anything. Maybe he hoped his partner Hickey would get cold feet at the nude beach and come back to save him. *He's hoping in vain*, thought Renard. The click of the cuffs locking sounded loud in the quiet clearing. A raven chuckled, then another. Renard circled around the pole. He put down the caulking gun and frisked Johnstone. The hunter took the *cochon*'s handcuff keys, replacement revolver, wallet, and anything else in pocket. No badge. Renard belted the gun and held on to the other effects. He tossed away the keys into an underbrush of mingled huckleberries and Scottish broom, then picked up the caulking gun and walked back to face his prisoner.

Renard said, "You're done. Mallory disowns you. Your plans are shit. No World's Fair Expo monopoly, no cocaine empire. I'm not going to kill you, I'm going to do worse. With my own hands. That's what you never got. You're a cop. On my side, *you're* the fucking tourist. You never ask someone to do something for you; you do it yourself. That's why I'm the one pointing the gun."

"Caulking gun," said Johnstone at last.

Renard laughed.

"Better this way. After I'm done, you'll wish you were dead. Know what happens to narcs in prison? Drop me a postcard when you find out. It goes like this. Apparently we're on Federal Government of Canada land here, jurisdiction of the Mounties. No friends to cover for you. You and your fucking buddy are going to have a helluva lot of explaining to do to the RCMP. Do the horsemen and the Vancouver fuzz play nice together? If I know my pigs, you don't. You should see what happens in the States when the FBI walks into some sheriff's patch. The paperwork alone'd choke you. Which I should do. But killing a cop's more heat than I want. I'm just going to ruin you."

"How?"

"Watch."

Renard put down the crossbow and from his jacket took out a Ziploc bag. It held about an ounce of cocaine. He opened the plastic neck and poured most of it over Johnstone's head, flinging the white powder into the dirty cop's face and sputtering mouth. Renard pocketed the empty bag, leaving no fingerprints behind.

"*Alors,*" he said. "*Le coup de grâce.*"

The hunter watched the cop's eyes go wide as he leaned in and put the snipped tip of the caulking gun into Johnstone's nostril. "This'll seal you up good and tight against the rain."

Renard squeezed the gun trigger and pumped white silicone into the cop's nasal cavity. Johnstone thrashed. Renard took out the gun and charged it again. He leaned down, grabbed Johnstone by his slippery, sweating hair, and put his knee on the detective's chest. Then Renard put the tip of the gun in the other nostril.

"Nice and easy."

Johnstone gagged as the caulking filled up his nasopharynx and dripped down the back of his throat. The cop jerked once more, then sat still, in some kind of chemical shock. Renard stood back to admire his handiwork. A splooge of white silicone came out of the pig's mouth. He'd emptied the whole tube of Alex-Plus Fast-Dry Latex into Johnstone's head. Amazing what one can do with products on sale at your neighbourhood Canadian Tire. He was going to enjoy living in Vancouver. What had the conductor on the Amtrak called it? Terminal City. The hunter took out the secateurs. Time for a souvenir.

39.

He couldn't do it.

He was supposed to be taking a Polaroid of the naked cop, not shooting the man dead.

Ted pointed the gun right in Hickey's face and couldn't pull the trigger. Hickey saw the hesitation in Ted's eyes instantly and swiped at Ted's head. Ted ducked with a glance of a blow off his shoulder and started to run. He couldn't kill the cop. What was going on? No time to wonder about how it had gone so wrong. With the ocean at his back and a nude beach before him, Ted darted away to the right, one hand holding the briefcase, in the other the Nagant.

Hickey gave chase. Ted jumped over slumbering nudists, scattering sand. He pelted though the square of sarongs, shouting something at the hippie selling cloth. Wrong way. Ted ran east on the estuarine flats between beach and cliff forest, into the land of cruising queers, a fat naked cop hot on his heels. His heart thundered with fear and aggression. Ted was fucked. *What had she done? Why?* Ted couldn't think. He ran.

Pelting along a winding path, naked fairies appeared from wooded coveys like startled hummingbirds. He had to get away. *Maybe it leads uphill.* Barefoot, and wearing nothing but shorts, Ted hurdled over a log and through some sticky, stinking muck to where the trail rose. He could hear the naked cop closing in. From here Ted could keep running all the way along a ragged path to Musqueam country, but didn't have the wherewithal. To his right, a steep cut branched up to Southwest Marine Drive, Ted hoped, and he took it. Alder boughs whipped across him as he sprinted. He hit the grade and started to scramble up the soft steep path, kicking dust down to the cop running behind him.

It happened quick. Ted clawed panting up to a point, Hickey coming after on hands and knees, scratching at the loose dirt and stones. To the left sprawled a riot of brambles. As Hickey lunged at Ted, Ted aimed a kick with his left foot that connected with the cop square on the chin. The naked cop pitched back downhill into a huge patch of blackberry canes. When he hit the thorns, he started to scream.

Ted's heart beat normally now. He'd circled north, away from any pursuit, back to Tower Beach. The tide was way out, and an infinity of golden sand stretched away. He kept running, shocked to his core, gun still in one hand, now-empty briefcase in the other. The sunshine fell warm upon him. He aimed his steps toward a point, a wooden navigation tower that marked the drop-off to deep water. Ted now existed on a plane beyond the world. And he was sure that Dorothy and the C&C 27 were just out there on the water. Ted's desperate eyes scanned the horizon. Suddenly a buzzing hum became the louder droning of a rotary engine, and Ted was in the shadow of a low-flying deHavilland Beaver floatplane, the friendly pilot waggling his wings, guiding the plane toward the city. Turning back, Ted spotted the sailboat's bare mast and trimmed his steps in her direction. But the tide was rushing back and curving around. Ted found himself on a swiftly created island of flat sand, and in another moment the island was gone. The closer Ted got to the sailboat the higher the flood; it went up to his waist and soon Ted waded with some difficulty through the cold sea. Far away to his right the city sprawled, indifferent to his problem. Ted spied the green roof of the Hotel Vancouver: hard, straight geometry under the looming irregular cardiograph of broken mountain peaks. He looked back over at the boat, so close now, and called out, "Man overboard!"

With the water now swelling up to his neck, Ted came near enough to witness Dorothy at the helm. He waved both briefcase and gun over his head. When a wave dunked Ted under, he came spluttering up for air and there was a flash of light, followed by Dorothy throwing a small black square his way. Reflexively, Ted dropped the gun, and it splashed into the drink. Complete clarity and enlightenment: she knew what he'd done. Dorothy had found out about him and Mary on the night of the beach party. Rising water lifted Ted off his feet into a swell. He snagged what Dorothy had tossed him with his free hand.

It was a Polaroid of Ted in way over his head.

WORLD IN MOTION

But a great sleepiness lies on Vancouver as compared with an American town: men don't fly up and down the street telling lies, and the spittoons in the delightfully comfortable hotel are unused; the baths are free and their doors are unlocked. You do not have to dig up the hotel clerk when you want to bathe, which shows the inferiority of Vancouver. An American bade me notice the absence of bustle, and was alarmed when in a loud and audible voice I thanked God for it ... Except for certain currents which are not much mentioned, but which make the entrance rather unpleasant for sailing-boats, Vancouver possesses an almost perfect harbor. The town is built all round and about the harbor, and young as it is, its streets are better than those of western America. Moreover, the old flag waves over some of the buildings, and this is cheering to the soul. The place is full of Englishmen who speak the English tongue correctly and with clearness, avoiding more blasphemy than is necessary, and taking a respectable length of time to getting outside their drinks. These advantages and others that I have heard about, such as the construction of elaborate workshops and the like by the Canadian Pacific in the near future, moved me to invest in real estate.
—Rudyard Kipling, *From Sea to Sea*, 1889

40

"Hong Kong! City of wonder! Hong Kong! City of action! Hong Kong! City of joy! A city of wonder and joy! Hongggg Konggggg!"

With the song and the music echoing within her, Dorothy Kwan stepped from humid darkness into daylight. It was pouring rain. A cloudburst flooded the atmosphere. She huddled under an awning with several other visitors to the fair: an elderly couple of New Yorkers, two bleached-blond German lads, and a family from Nanaimo. Others rushed by, soaked newspapers and souvenir programmes held up against the torrent. *Monsoon weather*, thought Dorothy. *Just like Kowloon.*

The pavilion reinforced the illusion. Its exterior was deliberately clad in an intricate exoskeleton of white bamboo scaffolding, peopled with life-sized mannequins of construction workers, referencing the Hong Kong condominium boom.

"Fragrant harbour," Dorothy whispered.

"What's that, lady?" asked one of the New Yorkers.

"Smell," said Dorothy.

The Germans looked at one another as the old man shrugged at his wife, then took a deep whiff.

"What is that?" the old man asked.

"Petrichor," said Dorothy. "The perfume of the earth after a long dry spell."

As suddenly as the rainstorm started, it was over, and soon Dorothy was swept back up into the living fair. She joined the teeming thousands streaming along wide concourses between the great pavilions. The concentrated fall of rain freshened the scene remarkably: bright Day-Glo yellows and aqua blues popped, while silver and chrome sparkled against opalescent white walls. Everything was in motion—tourists and wildly costumed entertainers, clanking motorized sculptures, a knot of street corner musicians playing a super-synthed version of Corey Hart's "Eurasian

Eyes." It was all a little too frantic for her, with too much happening, creating the anxious sensation that you were missing something wonderful happening somewhere else.

"Something's happening here! Something's happening here!"

It was the endlessly echoing refrain of the fair's official song being sung by a squat silver robot in an astronaut's helmet: Expo Ernie, mascot of the fair. A little brother and sister, he in an Ocean Pacific shirt and surfer Jams, she a curly-haired cutie wearing mirrored Oakley sunglasses, together cried out at the robot, "What? What's happening? Are you okay?"

Dorothy let herself be pulled along by shifting currents of movement. A space shuttle looped around weightlessly back and forth on a massive pendulum as people screamed; the Challenger had exploded a few months before, and the ride had been renamed. She looked up at the Observatron revolving on the Minolta Space Tower as parachute capsules dropped. Whistles and horns and voices on megaphones, jets of water, the smell of popcorn and freshly fried beaver tails (a sweet pastry), and everywhere, *everywhere*, snaking lineups of people patiently shuffling forward and gawking at the carnival. Seagulls swooped and squealed. World in motion, world in touch.

Dorothy hadn't seen much. So far she'd managed the California, Northwest Territories, and Cuban pavilions. In the General Motors Exhibit, she witnessed the mysterious "Spirit Lodge" performance, still wondering how they'd done it. So much more to see: the United States of America and Union of Soviet Socialist Republics, the Million Dollar Gold Coin, Great Hall of Ramses II, the Pavilion of Promise. She had to see the People's Republic of China and Canada pavilions too. But they'd all have to wait. It was almost teatime, and she had an appointment to meet with someone very special to her.

She showed her exclusive entry pass to an alert security guard with an earpiece. Dorothy noticed his discreet steel-toed shoes; the man was police, slightly undercover. He unhooked a velvet rope and nodded her along. She walked through automatic sliding glass doors and wondered idly if they were bulletproof. A cheerful woman at a kiosk checked her pass under black light, then sweetly called for an elevator. Dorothy got in and rode it up. Her first ride at Expo 86.

A totally different world here, a world of money. The club breathed exclusion and quiet excellence. Floor-to-ceiling windows overlooked the hoi polloi heaving below. An elegant maitre d' ushered Dorothy to a fine booth with a very good view. Waiting for her there was Inspector Brian Kwok of the RCMP. He rose, took Dorothy's hand, and to her surprise kissed her lightly on the cheek. Her skin burned pleasantly; she hadn't been touched much lately. Instead of tea, Brian Kwok ordered champagne. When it came he raised a glass and said, "We're celebrating."

"What?"

"Here's to crime."

They drank. Dorothy slyly examined her uncle over the glass. Time hadn't changed Brian Kwok. In fact, if anything, he looked younger than when she'd last seen him. The difference was in his hair. His grey was gone, and Dorothy detected artifice, perhaps a touch of Grecian Formula. Inwardly she remembered the commercial featuring Rocket Richard.

"Hey, Richard, two minutes for looking so good," quoted Uncle Brian. Her eyes widened.

"Have you become telepathic?" she asked.

"Not yet. But I noticed you noticing. That's my job."

"For the RCMP?"

"Not anymore. I have new masters."

For an early supper they ate lobster bisque, followed by squab Manhattan with wild rice and tiny green peas. Dessert was raspberries and brandy. Throughout the meal, the restaurant filled with very important people, some of whom Dorothy recognized. The Urban Peasant and Wok with Yan shared a table together. The Man from Glad clinked glasses with

Reveen. Was that the Friendly Giant and Mr Dressup laughing at some joke? Noted architect Arthur Erickson built leaky castles in the sky for his colleague Bing Thom. Pierre Berton, Dr Foth, and ex-Prime Minister John Turner guffawed and drank triple scotches on the rocks. A lounge band played muted covers of current favorites. As Uncle Brian led the conversation to Dorothy's travels, he sneezed.

"*Daaih gat leih sih.*"

"Your Cantonese has improved," replied Kwok in that language.

"I can swear like a fishwife from Aberdeen, if that's what you mean."

"That's good, very good."

"Uncle Brian, why have you asked me here?"

"To see you, of course. How was the world?"

"Bigger than I thought."

Kwok touched each finger with his thumb, saying, "Hong Kong, Macau, Bangkok, Sydney."

He started again from his pinky. "Rome, Paris, London, New York." He gave up. "Then Los Angeles. Did you enjoy the train ride to Seattle?"

"First Class on the Coast Starlight's the only way to go," smirked Dorothy.

"And your parents?"

That sobered Dorothy. She said, "I honoured them."

"Good."

"Can you tell me more?" she asked.

Uncle Brian looked out the window, but Dorothy could tell he didn't see the giant hockey stick leaning against a pole flying the world's largest Maple Leaf flag.

"I'm sorry, but I can't. Not fully. Not quite yet. That's part of the reason I asked you here."

"I'm touched you thought of me," she said.

"My eye's been on you for some time, niece. Everywhere you went."

"As part of your new job?"

"You could say that."

"What is it?" she asked.

"Dorothy, have you ever heard of CSIS?"

"I read about it in the paper."

"Would you like to come work for me?"

"It would be an honour."

"Wonderful. You're hired. Your first job: can you identify the man in the corner?"

Dorothy waited before moving her eyes in the direction Brian Kwok indicated. Sitting at a choice table was a dark, medium-sized man next to a vivacious blonde. The man had a neat goatee instead of a full beard, but Dorothy recognized him immediately. She turned her black eyes back to Uncle Brian and blinked slowly, once.

Uncle Brian smiled and ordered another bottle of Veuve Clicquot.

A change came over the genteel crowd of well-heeled diners, a subtle shift in electricity. Dorothy noted watchful men with earpieces guarding each exit. Heads turned. The band fell quiet as a small bald man like a leprechaun came fidgeting in, walking alongside the gorgeously well-tailored, instantly recognizable figure of former Prime Minister Pierre Trudeau. His haughty, inscrutable, slightly Oriental gaze scanned the room from the height of a remote mountaintop. The little man was Jimmy Pattison, richest man in British Columbia, CEO and president of Expo 86. It seemed the room held its collective breath until the two sat down together. Jimmy talked a mile for every sixty seconds, a used car salesman down to his cheap socks. Trudeau concealed the slightest superior smile.

The band resumed a low-key version of "Lookin' Out for #1." A flunky brought Jimmy Pattison his trumpet, and the little man jumped up to vamp with the combo. Trudeau spread his arms back. He turned his head and caught Dorothy watching him. She was favoured with a cultivated, close-lipped smile, and for the second time that day she felt her cheeks flush. Trudeau gave Uncle Brian a regal nod, which Brian Kwok returned.

"February 29th, 1984," murmured Kwok to Dorothy.

"Pardon me?"

"Remember that date," he said. "And when you think of your father, know that he died for his country."

"Which one?"

For the first time in her life, Dorothy took a SkyTrain from BC Place, exiting with a polite crowd deep under the Bay. She rode the escalator up and walked out onto the downtown streets. Expo had changed parts of Vancouver superficially, but three years hadn't been enough to transform its fundamental character to Dorothy's discerning eye. At Granville she turned east and looked down Georgia Street to the silver geodesic golf ball of Expo Centre. In the other direction, very far west indeed, past the Hotel Vancouver and the sentinel buildings leading to Stanley Park, the view terminated with the slice of a far-distant hill, part of a mountain slope cloaked in dark green firs.

She walked that way. The Goose Lady still passed out fortunes near the fountain behind the Vancouver Art Gallery. Its sign used only the initials: VAG. Dorothy laughed, saying aloud, "*Vaj*. Priceless. Mary'll love that."

Her goal was the Hotel Georgia. Dorothy went downstairs into the loud and smoky Press Club. A pianist tinkled out, "The only solution, is there is no solution. The only solution, is to start a revolution."

She was early, as always. At the table next to her two drunken reporters from the *Sun* and *Province* shouted over the din, "Did you get a quote, and will they run it?"

"No and no. He spoke off the record, and the paper won't print it anyway."

"What'd he say?"

The hound flipped open a notebook covered in shorthand.

"He said, and I quote: 'Vancouver was founded on three things. Real estate, immigration, and drugs.' And it is ever so."

"Fuck, that's perfect. What's your angle?"

"That Expo 86 is the biggest real estate open house in human history. All we're doing is advertising to the Hong Kong Chinese that Vancouver's for sale to the lowest bidder. All those rich chinks are going to be running for the exits before the handover in '97."

"Hey, watch it, buddy."

"What?"

They turned and looked guiltily Dorothy's way. She feigned not to hear.

"You're right," said one.

"Huh?"

"They'd never print the truth in that fucking rag for all the tea in wherever. Bad for business."

The piano player said, "This one's from a special admirer, going out to a young lady by the name of Dorothy Kwan. It's a little number by local boys Doug and the Slugs, and it's called 'Too Bad.'"

He started to play. Dorothy looked up to see Mary Worthington coming her way.

They walked together through the city.

"So you got it?" asked Mary.

"I'm here, aren't I?"

Mary was talking about a clipping cut out of the California magazine *Sunset* that she'd mailed to Dorothy in Los Angeles.

"Is it why you came back?" she asked Dorothy.

"Not entirely. Didn't you hear the news? The world is coming to Vancouver."

"The world can kiss my ass."

It was a small gallery on a little-known street. Attendance was respectable, with sleek, modern sophisticates in slim black, eating salmon sushi. They sipped whites from the Napa Valley and cheap dry Ontarian Hochtaler. *Sunset* had written up the exhibit as cultural counter-programming to the World's Fair hype. Mary made for the bar. A strikingly beautiful woman with a streak of white in her golden hair sipped wine from a bottle through a crazy straw while sitting in a wheelchair. As though by magnetism, Dorothy was drawn to a painting on the farthest wall.

It was a life-sized portrait, a nude of a man pulling blackberry cane from his bloodied, naked foot. Behind her a familiar, thrilling, nearly forgotten, treacherous voice said:

"You look like trouble."

Without turning around Dorothy replied:

"You know, I really am."